DISTURB

Michael Christopher

First published in 2025 by Blossom Spring Publishing

ISBN 978-1-917938-33-4
E: admin@blossomspringpublishing.com
W: www.blossomspringpublishing.com

I distinctly remember the smell of sand and cement, the freshness of the air and the puddles. Barely five years old and gripping my father's hand, we walked amidst the labourers to see our next home – number 9 in a long terrace of newly built houses. There is another memory from that moment that has no such defining form. It is of something I did not physically see, hear, touch or smell. Yet the remembrance of it lingers, no less clear than first it was.

The sensation – for that is the best description I can muster – is difficult if not impossible to describe. No more than a fleeting moment, it was a flash of something, somewhere, at some time – provocatively familiar yet fragile and elusive. The only certainty I have is that it was real.

As I think of that moment in the dusk of my life, I see it differently, perhaps a portent of things to come.

Michael Christopher

Chapter I
Nottingham 1965

Memories are for vanishing generations. It is the sixties, and we that are young believe we are truly special. There is a distinct and unique changing of ways, a new age evolving from the emergent rebelliousness of the previous decade. In some ways I am part of it – at least the version that's come to my city.

I like to visit the pubs, clubs and dance halls that cater for us adolescents and our eclectic mix of music. Odd times I go with the lads from work, though more often I go alone. I sip my beer and watch others – carefully, for it's not healthy to stare for long.

In truth I am in limbo, caught between yesterday and tomorrow – never quite finding today. There are newcomers and old hands in our mix of youth. The modish talk is of Beatles and Stones, the dated of Presley and Jerry Lee – smart and chisel-toed plays drape and drainpipes, leathers and biking boots. I am neither fully of this time nor of that which is passing or gone.

It seems it is my lot not to fit in.

Meeting Mr Booth in The Horse and Groom at the bottom of St Peter's Gate turned out to be a somewhat disturbing experience. He was considerably older than me and distinctly dated. He'd dashed in to escape a sudden shower, vigorously shaking his gaberdine mac as he reversed through the door. His appearance caught the amused attention of a rowdy clique enjoying drinks after work – that curious mix of opposites which inevitably melts away before the serious revellers materialise.

The bespectacled Mr Booth sported a haircut reminiscent of the wartime forties, the matted combover plastered flat to his forehead by the unexpected downpour. Ignoring the whispers and sniggers, he awkwardly eased his way to the bar, muttering apologies whilst navigating the maze of immovable bar huggers. Obliged to buy a drink in exchange for shelter, he reached into his worsted jacket and brought out a dog-eared purse.

'Erm ... half a shandy ... if you please.'

Those words drew a subdued chuckle or two – the landlord's face a picture. Discerning the reaction, Mr Booth immediately coloured to puce. Of course, I didn't know his name at that time. I was to find that out shortly after he took an exploratory sip of his drink. He'd turned to smile at me before surprisingly introducing himself, almost like a fellow guest at a garden party.

'Hello there, my name's Booth ... never set foot in here before ... not that bad, really.'

I looked around sheepishly before answering, instantly turning the same shade as he was.

'Arthur ...'

And that's how it carried on for a while, him doing most of the talking, me returning token responses. I detested small talk at the best of times, avoiding unwanted attention whenever I could. And so I was somewhat relieved when the bar crowd eventually tired of the interlude, huddling together before continuing to change the world and vilify the boss, or perhaps the other way round. Then just when I began to settle, Mr Booth looked at me and raised his eyebrows.

'Do you come here often?'

The line was cliched and dangerously open to misinterpretation. And for a fleeting moment I had to wonder. Nevertheless, we continued to converse in familiar fashion, him rambling in an overfriendly way, me struggling to look even vaguely interested. And then, mercifully, after draining his glass, it seemed he was ready to leave.

'Ah, well ... must get off home ... been a pleasure, Arthur ... might see you around sometime, you never know.'

Thankfully, he didn't offer to shake hands, choosing instead to stare rather directly into my eyes. After a moment of reflection, he leaned in close, intensely whispering as though to impart a secret.

'Never fear, Arthur, I'm certain she'll take good care of you.'

Without another word, he glanced over my shoulder and theatrically closed an eye. Of course, I immediately turned to see who it was he was winking at. When I did so, there was no one there, only a chalked-up blackboard promoting ham and cheese cobs ... with salad or without.

By the time I turned back to ask the obvious question, he'd already departed, the exit door in the automatic process of closing. A polished brogue at the end of a trailing leg was the last I saw of the curious Mr Booth ... at least, it was for a while.

***

I was born in Nottingham in 1947. My family, the Campions, rented a three-storey house a steady walk away from the city centre. Home was wedged into a row of similar properties, typifying the deprivation of the area at that time.

I shared the musty eaves with two elder sisters, separated from them by a makeshift wall nailed to the rafters. Dad was a shop worker, uncommonly for the neighbourhood, travelling to work in smart collar and tie. Mam and Grandma kept house between them, Mam assisting Grandad occasionally. Grandad claimed to be a businessman, though in reality he was a second-hand clothes dealer renting a stall on Sneinton Market.

Wartime food rationing lasted well into the fifties, and I remember queuing with Grandma to see what was available and how much it might cost. Once a week, we kids got free orange juice from the health centre to stop us getting scurvy, whatever that meant, and occasionally, we'd be allowed a comic that whiffed of fish from the bottom end of Central Market.

School was a miserable experience for me as I endured the regimented system of the time, achieving fundamental qualifications relating to reading, writing and arithmetic. I was generally known for being quiet and shy, intermittent friendships rarely coming to anything much – me more often favouring my own company over that of others. I would contentedly withdraw into my own little world, there to draw and paint for hours, sometimes reading stuff that reflected my quirkier interests.

Leaving school at fifteen in '62 without meaningful ambition, I was obliged to accept the first offer of employment that came along, subsequently spending three cheerless weeks in an uninspiring factory, picking garments from shelves and falling out with my fellow workers for refusing to pay union fees out of my three quid a week.

After various attempts to find alternative employment, Dad managed to secure me an interview for a job he thought might be better suited to my creative aptitude. In essence, my new occupation promised little more than the one before. I really had no idea what might become of me in the greater scheme of things. Work was simply a necessary means to an end. Like so many others of my kind, I was fated to tramp the tedious treadmill of working-class life. In those early days, it never entered my head that in time I would enter a distinctly uncommon circle of existence.

Chapter 2
Nottingham 1965

It is now early summer and I've officially been a man for nearly three weeks. I am still at the factory, as I call it, writing posters. On occasion, I get the opportunity to be creative – a drop of blood dripping from horror titles, a bullet whistling through wood-grained letters announcing the latest western – but most of the time I simply go through the motions. I think I've learned a lot and changed somewhat since I first came here in sixty-two. Confidence comes with age, they say, but equally, I think it born of necessity.

I moved out last week, left the old homestead and rented a flat of my own in Radford – a couple of rooms in a scruffy terrace with a shared bathroom. Still, it means I can spread out a bit, what with my books and stuff. And then there's the privacy thing. Some of my latest reading material might well be considered weird. It was Grandma's sarky asides that first drove me underground, hiding things as best I could in the cramped conditions. Now I'm free from all that and feeling much the better for it.

There were no visible tears on either side when it came to my leaving. I just said cheerio – manly handshakes from Dad and Grandad, pecks on the cheek from the women, Mam lingering a while longer than the others.

Still, I was only moving down the road, not to the other side of the world!

I often think of my first morning. Damp and

misty it was. I had spent the previous night fretting about oversleeping and missing the bus ... about finding the building again without getting lost, like I did when I attended the interview. Then there I was, bright and early, following the lad ambling along a few steps ahead of me. He had bright ginger hair combed into a quiff and was turning the same corners as me. I just knew we were journeying to the same destination and was thereby content to follow in his footsteps. It was one of those weird things I occasionally experienced. I'd never quite understood why or even given the matter much thought. I simply accepted such incidents happened from time to time.

I was therefore not in the least surprised when he entered the very building I was heading for. It was partially shrouded by thinning mist, a weathered Victorian edifice with rusted railings and a fancy arched door. Up the stairs to the third floor, they'd said. I nervously entered the tiled porch and unhurriedly climbed the stone steps, careful not to come too close to the ginger lad, who was by then rounding a bend in the staircase. After he disappeared through a door on the second floor, I carried on up to the third. When I arrived, I took in a breath before pushing through the door that faced me.

I entered a sizeable room, its floorboards worn and wavy where heavy machinery must once have stood. The flaking walls were pinned with lewd messages and glossy pictures of risqué women and racing cars. Men of various ages and stature leaned purposefully over their wooden benches, workstations strewn with lunch boxes and fag packets, cloudy jars rammed with brushes and pencils, clustered pots caked in layers of coagulated paint. That morning I did little more than discover the toilets and meet my peers, instantly forgetting their names. I inhaled the odours of paint and thinners and noticed the resonance of rustling paper, the tapping of brushes on pot, the systematic shuffling of feet and the muted chatter. Even in my uneasy state, I was drawn to the ambience of it, all of a sudden eager to fulfil my creative ambitions.

Disappointingly, I was soon reminded that it was simply another job, being tersely informed that I must serve my time as a lad, fetching and carrying, lifting and loading, and making the tea. A month or more went by before I was abruptly allocated a space at the end of an elongated bench, its surface strewn with scraps of paper, a few receding brushes and a rusting can of glutinous poster paint. That morning I first endeavoured to form letters on guillotined strips of paper and promptly made a terrible mess of it. Writing with brushes is a testing discipline, particularly when suffering the disparaging observations of crudely vocal workmates. Nevertheless, I continued to practise whenever my menial duties allowed. Eventually, after endless attempts, I came to form lines and curves with ever more confident flourishes. I had somehow acquired the knack of it. They said it was akin to riding a bicycle, similarly achieved through patience and perseverance. Once mastered, the technique is ingrained for life. Only hand speed and dexterity diminish with the passing of time.

Achieving the rudimentary standard had been challenging, and although I experienced a sense of accomplishment, I envisioned a future of endless repetition. The constant production of handwritten posters is not unlike that of a factory assembly line.

I remember thinking there surely must be more to life ...

In time I became independent, laying out my own work after tediously tracing other writer's originals. It was when preparing to transcribe the title of a particular film that my curiosity and ensuing fascination were first aroused.

At the beginning, the subject matter was of cursory interest, with me having no conception of the unsettling obsession it would later become. *Séance On A Wet Afternoon* concerns a mentally unbalanced medium who convinces her husband to kidnap a child so that she can appear to use telepathy to assist police in solving the crime, thereby achieving celebrity.

I recall the blank sheet of paper before me, the studio synopsis beside it. As I reviewed its details, I couldn't help but envision a circle of unbroken hands, a shadowy room and lurking spirits. Stimulated by such imaginings, I resolved to see the film as soon as I could, eager as I was for the thrill of its promise.

As it turned out, I came away rather disappointed. The film was well made and worth seeing, but I'd envisaged something more frightening, mistakenly expecting haunting messages from beyond the grave and ethereal wraiths skulking in the gloom. I'd wanted to experience a corporeal sense of fear, albeit cocooned in the company of others. Though pleasingly atmospheric, it wasn't quite what I'd anticipated. Even so, I was not to be discouraged. The seeds of interest had been well and truly planted.

During the following weeks and months, I became an avid collector of anything remotely supernatural, devouring as many magazines, comics and books as I could afford – fact and fiction alike. I developed a mild addiction to the subject, thrilled that my monotonous existence had unexpectedly taken a more stimulating turn. I'd discovered a new and thought-provoking activity with which to fill my time ... something I thought best kept under the radar.

***

It was a warm Saturday in the July of '65. I was working the market stall with Grandad. An extra few bob came in handy, and I was more than happy to spend time with old Fred. Grandad had worked at the market for most of his life, in due course inheriting the second-hand clothes business from his father, Sam. Fred's only extended break from the popular stall was in the service of the Royal Horse Artillery during the first war. He was knowledgeable about horses and caring for them, often bragging he could ride before he could walk. When the recruiting officers recognised his equine capabilities, army logic kept him on horseback. Private Fred became Corporal Fred, hauling cannons and wagon loads of ammunition through the muddy fields of France during the worst of it. When he arrived home, he was missing three fingers and wheezing something awful – never stopped him smoking, though. Twenty a day he smoked, even more when he could afford them. No filter tips for him – 'ladies' fags', he used to call them.

When Grandad began whistling his favourite tune, I knew it wouldn't be long before he took himself off to The Fox and Grapes – 'Pretty Windows', they called it. He was usually gone for a while, chewing the cud with his market mates before reappearing, whistling that same old tune despite having blown the best part of the day's profits.

It was sometime after Grandad departed when it came about. I was watching two women diligently sorting through a stack of knitted jumpers when I happened to glance up and notice him. He was half turned away, carefully inspecting a teapot at one of the crockery stalls. I recognised him immediately. He stood out like a sore thumb, what with that haircut and the flappy flannels. It was him and no mistake. For some perverse reason, I was almost pleased to see him. The strange encounter in the pub had played on my mind ever since. Those extraordinary parting words of his called for some kind of explanation, and I wasn't about to forego the opportunity. In the meantime, Grandad had reappeared, fussing around the two women, a mite unsteady on his feet and slurring his words.

'Won't be long, Grandad. Got to see a man about a dog!'

I shot off before he could answer, hot on the heels of Mr Booth, who was striding from the market at a pace.

'Mr Booth … Hello, there!'

The skurrying Booth stopped in his tracks, for a second motionless, before turning to display a knowing grin.

'Arthur! Dear boy … how the devil are you?'

It was uncomfortably intimate, a bit like he'd chanced on an old friend.

'I simply can't believe it, Arthur. I've been thinking about you quite a lot recently, and damn me, here you are!'

I was embarrassed by his brazen familiarity, reluctant to engage in friendly pleasantries with someone I barely knew.

'Only I've been wondering, Mr Booth … something you said in the pub … when you were leaving …'

I was faltering, my tone accusatory. All of a sudden, it felt ridiculous and blatantly petty. I was confronting a peculiar old man over nothing very much at all. I saw his eyes narrow then, his cheery grin levelling to a taut line.

'Yes, I admit to regretting my foolishness, Arthur. I thought afterwards you might dwell on what I said … silly of me, really, I shouldn't have …'

'Tell me why you said what you did, then. What did you mean by it?'

I had him on the back foot and resolutely stood my ground.

'It's not something easily spoken of here in the open, Arthur. I can only apologise for my behaviour and offer to explain myself in more comfortable surroundings … fancy a tea and some cake?'

'Did you say tea and cake? I don't believe I'm hearing right! I'm supposed to be flippin' working!'

'I'm sure your grandfather wouldn't mind. Why not make your excuses and join me for afternoon tea? It might be worth your while, Arthur, please believe me.'

To say I was dumbfounded would be an understatement. As annoyed and exasperated as I was, I was fascinated to know the meaning of those words. Then I wondered how he knew about Grandad, the thought causing something to creep up my spine – something not altogether pleasant. Uneasy as I felt about the proposition, I instinctively knew this was something of importance that needed resolving. There seemed to be no avoiding the improbable circumstance that had unexpectedly entered my life.

Chapter 3
Nottingham 1965

The beginning of October and Goose Fair has arrived, the second biggest travelling fair in the country, they reckon. I can see my breath in the chill autumn air and hear the drifting echoes of piping music, the squeals of merriment from the rides and stalls. My hands are warmed by a tub of hot peas. I soak up the atmosphere and I am content in the moment.

At last I appear to have a friend of sorts, though it's a relationship that transcends normality. And with it, my life changes beyond expectation. It will not be long before I begin my next adventure – a new and exciting chapter in my recently invigorated life.

It has been arranged, and I cannot wait.

Walking from the fair in the damp chill of late evening, my thoughts revisited that warm afternoon in July when life took a very peculiar and stimulating turn. After squaring things with Grandad, I walked with Mr Booth through Hockley to The Old Dutch on Thurland Street. The lunchtime rush was over, the popular café now all but empty. After ordering fruit cake and a pot of tea, we awkwardly settled for a table at the steamy window overlooking the street. There was no preamble, no need to prompt or question him. Uncertain of his intentions, I simply opted to listen, absently stirring my tea, allowing Mr Booth to explain himself.

'This is going to sound really strange,

Arthur, but here goes. Whether you choose to believe me or not, the reason for my parting comment at The Horse and Groom was the unexpected appearance of your personal spirit guide. She chose to materialise at your shoulder just when I began to say goodbye to you …'

He paused, screwing up his eyes at me as though expecting a reaction. I offered a frown and nothing more. The man was clearly round the bend, and I was not inclined to encourage him further. Mr Booth simply shrugged his shoulders then, seemingly undeterred by my show of indifference.

'Whilst some people prefer to call them guardian angels, I would rather think of them as spirit guides. I don't think they're angels, by any means, certainly not in the biblical sense. I believe they exist purely to protect and advise mortal beings – helping hands when we're most in need. However, I'm pretty sure your personal guide appeared to me because you and I have some unfinished business to resolve. And so, she wished to accord me her blessing … so to speak.'

I must have sipped my tea and nibbled some cake, though I don't recall doing either of those things, mesmerised as I was to hear the stream of complete mumbo jumbo that poured from the poor fellow's mouth. I'd originally thought him somewhat eccentric, but the unadulterated fantasy of his rationalisation caused me to seriously doubt his sanity. That he genuinely believed what he was saying was beyond doubt. The man was obviously living in a world of total make-believe. Nevertheless, I couldn't help but balance my conclusions with the way he'd so casually referred to Grandad. Had he been shadowing me and my family? Or had he simply overheard us talking to each other at the market? Then again, was it something else entirely? As though reading my thoughts, Mr Booth leaned in towards me, his eyes boring into mine as if to emphasise the importance of his ensuing disclosure.

'Arthur ... I have reason to believe we have known each other before, if not in this life. Firstly, however, you need to understand that all our souls repeatedly return to this earthly plane until such time as we are ready to pass into the eternal light for ever. We exist in recurring circles – family, acquaintances, friend and foe alike. Those circles are rarely broken, Arthur, and only then to accommodate our diverging longevities. We are destined to live recurrently in the company of intimate souls, though in each life we may present ourselves in differing guises.'

I stared long and hard at him, probing his expression for proof of madness or deception, or even both. This curious chat over tea and cake had taken an even more extraordinary turn, so much so that I began to wonder how I'd first allowed myself to be lured into such a bizarre situation.

Mr Booth then proceeded to devour his cake and quaff his cooling tea. It seemed he was allowing me time to digest his outrageous assertions. Then again, despite my misgivings, my instinct was telling me there might be more to the matter than I was currently extracting. Furthermore, I couldn't shake off the feeling there was something reassuringly familiar about him. I sensed myself relaxing, my anxiety curiously draining away as if someone or something was reassuring me.

'Look, to be perfectly frank, Mr Booth, this is altogether too much for me to swallow. I can't help thinking it's been planned in advance. I only met you once before, by chance or otherwise. Then earlier this afternoon, there you were at the market. When I followed you and began asking questions, you casually invited me to afternoon tea, mentioning my grandad as though you know him. On top of that, you're now talking about spirits and stuff, even claiming we've known each other before – that we've some mystifying business that needs completing! I'm sorry to be rude, but surely you can see how any normal person might think there was something not quite right going on here!'

He was methodically dabbing his lips with a napkin, staring at the ceiling as though weighing his options before responding.

'Well, you've certainly no need to apologise, Arthur. You're quite right in what you say. I admit to being impulsive – Mrs Booth did warn me. I honestly meant no harm. You see, I often neglect the fact that others are not as intuitive as me. They simply do not see what I see ...'

His voice trailed away then, a wistful look

crossing his face. In that moment, I couldn't help but feel sorry for him. If the poor man was truly deluded, he urgently needed some professional help. Then in the next moment, I thought I recognised a fellow lost soul. If only for that, I simply couldn't bring myself to leave it there and walk away.

'Tell you what, Mr Booth, I'll fetch us another pot of tea and we'll try to make better sense of it, shall we?'

I tried not to think about leaving Grandad on his own. In any event, he wouldn't be overly worried. I was known for my strange behaviour and unpredictability. He'd be more annoyed than anything else – either he'd forego another session in The Grapes or he'd close the stall early. Most likely he'd choose the latter and clear off to the pub for the rest of the day. In which case, he'd be thinking less about me and more about Grandma stoking her temper for when he got home.

'What do you really want from me, Mr Booth?'

I knew it was a question he wouldn't answer in a single sentence. He was holding a steaming cup of fresh tea to his puckered lips, blowing cooling ripples across its surface before taking a hesitant sip.

'You suggested our meeting was in some way premeditated, Arthur. And in a sense, you're most probably right, though please believe me, there was never any malicious intent on my part. Truth is, I've been looking for you for some while. I didn't actually know your name or where you lived … not exactly. I knew I was likely to find you somewhere in the city or its suburbs. You're not one for straying too far from home, Arthur – you never have been.'

I decided not to respond to that last remark. One way or another, I needed to understand what was really going on in that head of his, imaginary or otherwise. So I chose to say nothing and waited for him to continue.

'Have you heard of regression, Arthur?'

I thought about that for moment before shaking my head – now where were we going?

'Regression is generally carried out by means of hypnosis. The practitioner puts you under and takes you back to a time before the birth of your existing life. I deemed the concept interesting enough to arrange a regression of my own. I thought it might make a refreshing change from my usual occupation and hoped to learn enough to verify or disprove the authenticity of the theory.'

I was completely at a loss. The man was really stretching the limits … spirit guides … past lives …

'I don't need to be a mind-reader to sense your scepticism, Arthur, but please allow me to explain why I think there's something here that concerns the both of us. My experiences proved more fruitful than I could ever have imagined. I won't labour the finer details for now. Suffice to say that what came to light caused me to believe your spiritual being is in some way related to my own. So there we have it: that was my primary motive for finding you, perhaps even if I wasn't supposed to. I don't exactly know why just yet, but I'm convinced there's good reason for my seeking you out.'

Chapter 4
Nottingham 1965

It is very cold; frost forms in the night as winter sets in. It is early on Friday and I am in Clumber Street. I gaze longingly at The Lion and The Crystal Palace. Later, when evening comes, I will visit one or both of these hostelries, later to slouch against a wall at The Palais to watch the dancing and listen to the music.

I am on holiday today. I am walking to Huntingdon Street to catch a 62 to Newstead Abbey. I am excited by the prospect. The expectancy of the venture has awakened a hundred butterflies in my belly.

Newstead Abbey lies between Nottingham and Mansfield. It has associations with the poet Lord Byron and boasts tales of ghostly happenings within its scenic ruins.

After getting off the bus, I walked from the abbey gates as directed. When I came to the row of houses, they were screened by walls and hedges set back from the highway. As I wandered along the footpath, I became conscious of the leafy location and compared it to the dour streets of the city.

Apart from a whole week in faraway Devon, my travels thus far were limited to a few days on the bracing east coast. Now, merely a few miles from the concrete of my own city, I felt conspicuous, as though an interloper in some far-off country.

When I found the house I was looking for, it

was virtually obscured by overgrown trees and tangled shrubbery. I imagined it would disappear entirely during the abundance of summer, save perhaps for the red-tiled roof and ornate chimney stacks.

***

It was when I visited their home for the first time that Mr Booth offered me a session with his hypnotist. Mr Booth had invited me to his modest house to meet his wife and for the three of us to have dinner together. The evening turned out to be reassuringly normal. Mrs Booth was a pleasant lady, petite and cheery in chintzy apron and shocking-pink lipstick.

After observing the conventionality of his homelife, I came to feel more at ease in his company. Even so, his credibility remained very much on trial. We ended by agreeing to meet on The Embankment the following Saturday for a walk and a chin-wag by the Trent. It was a typical autumnal day. I remember we waded through a covering of fallen leaves, chatting as we watched a crew rowing smoothly over the river's reflective surface towards the bridge.

'You see, Arthur, at the risk of you thinking me stranger still, I have to tell you that my association with unearthly matters is even more complicated than I've led you to believe. You've had to deal with me professing to have seen your spirit guide when we first met in the pub. Then there's the assertion I made regarding my previous life and your potential involvement in it. And if that were not enough, I must tell you there is something more for you to come to terms with.'

I was beginning to understand the benefit of silence when faced with such situations. That was quite easy for me, as it was in my nature to avoid unnecessary confrontation. Whatever greater mystery Mr Booth was about to reveal would not be affected by any comment I might make, so I politely waited for him to carry on.

'You might have wondered how I make a living, Arthur. Well, I can tell you that Mrs Booth and I live off the contributions clients pay for my services.'

Once again I had to wonder what was coming next. I was getting used to hearing some pretty strange things from him, though I was not yet completely immune.

'I'm clairvoyant by nature and profession, Arthur, a spiritualist, a psychic – whatever designation people are comfortable with. In essence, I foresee things, or sometimes … just see things. Clients pay me what they think I'm worth. However, I want you to appreciate exactly why I'm so interested in pursuing the premise of past life experience … not to mention the journey that beckons the both of us. There must be some reason for that, Arthur.'

He adopted that wistful look again, as though edging close to something teasingly out of reach. I was reminded of when my interest in spiritual matters first gripped me – that blank sheet of paper, the brush in my hand poised to write *Séance on a Wet Afternoon.* Was this what I'd been wishing for in those early moments of attraction? Deep down, I think it was.

I knew I'd little choice but to embrace the opportunity. Here was a chance to delve into the 'other side'. Whether it was real or not was of little consequence. I was beginning to notice the intensifying twists and turns of fate, sensing that the course of my future was in some way preordained.

***

The paving meandered through dense shrubbery to an entrance porch with a slate roof. The door boasted a brass knocker in the form of a grinning pixie. I gave it three raps and waited. The oncoming sound of heavy feet was almost instantaneous. When the door opened, it revealed a red-faced man clutching a mean-looking claw hammer. He noticed me staring quizzically at it and grinned reassuringly, revealing a generous gap in his protruding teeth.

'Don't worry, I'm fixing some loose beading on the staircase. You must be Arthur, Edgar's acquaintance.'

I nodded, recognising I was yet to address Mr Booth by his first name – it had never seemed quite right somehow.

'Yes, that's me. Mr Langham, is it?'

'Bob's the name. Get yourself inside, for God's sake, man. It's bloody freezing out there!'

He casually kicked aside the scattering of tools that littered the gloomy hallway, leading me to a shabby room with dark panels and a parquet floor. There was a bay window, and a fireplace laid with fresh logs which caught the flames licking between the pile.

'Take a seat, Arthur. Tea or coffee, is it?'

There were two saggy armchairs and a leather couch with a large tapestry cushion. I chose one of the chairs.

'Tea, please. Thanks very much.'

The only coffee we ever had at home was gooey black syrup in a tall square bottle that Grandad tolerated with three heaped sugars.

Bob Langham was a hypnotherapist and an acquaintance of Mr Booth. He straightaway made a point of telling me he'd regressed Mr Booth and therefore understood the reasons behind my visit – or consultation, as he called it. He said we weren't to dwell too much on that, though, as he thought it better to start afresh and see where it led us.

We sat opposite each other, watching the fire and passing the time of day until we finished our tea. Bob said it was good practice to relax before a session and that he was in no particular rush if I wasn't.

'Do you know much about regression, Arthur?'

'Very little, to be honest, Bob. Mr Booth told me a few things ... thinking about it, he mentioned a bloke called ... Bloxton, or something.'

'Bloxham, actually – Arnell Bloxham. He was

a noted hypnotherapist who developed an interest in reincarnation. By all accounts, not only did he consider past life regression an avenue for proving his theories, he was thought to use it to treat selected patients. Bloxham's wife, Dulcie, wrote a book in 1958 called *Who Was Ann Ockenden*, describing the seven different lives recalled by one of her husband's subjects. The Bloxhams were trailblazers, though sometimes criticised by sceptics. However, what really engendered public awareness was the Bridey Murphy Case, when a hypnotist called Morey Bernstein regressed a housewife from Colorado named Virginia Tighe. Bernstein wrote a book about the woman's memories of life as a 19th century Irish immigrant. Apparently, that was similarly criticised and subject to allegations of inconsistency.'

Hearing that resurrected my own uncertainties, but I said nothing, finding it better to listen when you didn't know what you were talking about. Mr Booth had suggested we had known each other in a different time. He'd made a point of saying that discovering an eternal soulmate was virtually impossible for most people, but because he was clairvoyant, he'd acquired a sense of me – a perception of my spiritual being, as he'd described it. He reckoned he recognised me, not by my looks or the sound of my voice, but by my aura. He said an aura was a nonphysical uniqueness we all possess: his elaborate words, not mine. Whatever the actuality, I'd become increasingly eager to experience my own regression.

Bob was asking me how I was, me thinking I felt strangely relaxed ... what with the warmth and the crackle of the fire ... the subtle variation in his tone, still affable but with a more formal edge.

'Slacken your shoulders, Arthur, and place your hands in your lap. Close your eyes, if you would, and concentrate on the rhythm of your breathing, nothing else. All you need do is simply breath – in through the nose and out through the mouth – nice and regular ... in through the nose ... out through the mouth ... counting back now ... ninety-nine ... ninety-eight ... nice and regular.'

I remember thinking it was actually working, his calmative words matching the tempo of my breathing.

Chapter 5
Nottingham 1965

Christmas is almost upon us. Fog blankets the city. It is bitterly cold regardless of the hour. Writing posters with numbed fingers is challenging. The archaic boiler in the cellar slowly sends heat to the higher floors. It warms us a little. Even so, we shiver and complain.

I have changed. Things once of import now trivial and meaningless, disregarded for the interest that has come to absorb me. We are to meet tonight – the three of us – to listen to the recording.

Meanwhile, I look at my writing list – my workload for the day – Zulu, Mary Poppins *and* The Ipcress File *amongst the titles that await me. I load my brush and dab away the excess paint before offering bristle to paper. My hand aches with the cold, and the brushstrokes are not as clean and sharp as they should be.*

Mr and Mrs Booth lived in Arnold, an urban bus ride from the city centre. Newstead Abbey was a few miles further on, a practicality Mr Booth most likely considered when choosing Bob Langham as his past-life intermediary. Having eaten meagrely during the day – a buttered cob and crisps – I stopped for chips on Front Street, eating them from newspaper soggy with vinegar. It was entirely satisfying, the searing morsels warming me as I made my way along Calverton Road.

The Booths' house had mossy steps leading

steeply to the front door. I thought of them gathered round the fire awaiting my arrival, the butterflies fluttering in my stomach in anticipation of what might be revealed.

My new acquaintances were people of superior education and experience. There was little doubt that spending even limited time in their company had quickly increased my knowledge and improved my social development. My natural shyness was slowly receding, my confidence soaring by the day.

Mrs Booth encouraged me to read the works of Dickens and Wells, Mr Booth advocating the darker works of Lovecraft and Poe – authors I'd never thought to attempt before. A door of enlightenment was gradually opening, a portal hitherto closed to an ignorant oddball like me.

'Arthur, here you are at last. Get yourself by the fire, my boy.'

I'd come in out of the cold in more ways than one. Seeing them again was as warming as the blazing coals that warmed their modest sitting room. Mrs Booth fussed like a mother hen, serving mugs of tea with a drop of whisky, and a tray of buttered muffins, giggling for no particular reason before taking her leave.

'Something on the wireless I'd like to listen to. See you later ... shout if you need anything.'

Mr Booth had earlier confirmed his wife would not be joining us for the recording. He said she thought it might unsettle her too much. Apparently, she rarely accompanied him to séances either. I thought that sounded contrived for some reason. In the short time I'd known her, Mrs Booth had never struck me as being the nervous type.

The Booths were financing my regressions, partly because they'd suggested my involvement in the first place, but mostly because I couldn't afford Bob's fees anyway. Sometimes money really does speak louder than words. I took their willingness to pay as an indication of their good intentions. Although at first I'd wondered at their generosity – were the childless couple looking for a surrogate son? – on reflection, I thought it more likely they considered me integral to the objectives they were pursuing. After Mrs Booth had left the room, we began to consume our tea and muffins. I thought Bob looked vaguely uncomfortable. Observing his demeanour immediately took me back to the moment when I awoke from the hypnosis. I remembered opening my eyes to find him looking at me in a rather detached way.

***

'How d'you feel Arthur?' He was staring at me in a funny sort of way, as though preoccupied with something else.

'Yes, okay, Bob, not feeling much different, to be honest.'

He continued to stare with that same distracted expression until the crackle of a displaced ember came to break whatever spell it was that held him.

'Good ... er ... would you like some water? Hot

drink, perhaps?'

He'd certainly been disturbed by something. His tone seemed distant and detached.

'Do you remember anything at all, Arthur?'

The question surprised me. For one confused moment, I thought I was still waiting to be hypnotised and wondered what he was talking about. When I came to realise it'd already taken place, I experienced a pang of disappointment. I'd expected to remember everything – imagined or otherwise – but try as I might, I couldn't remember a single thing.

'No … nothing whatsoever!'

The resentment in my voice was unmistakeable. I was certain Bob must have noticed. If he did, he seemed unruffled by it.

'That's usually the way of it, Arthur. It's one of the reasons we record the sessions – so clients can be assured there's no deception involved.'

Bob's professional bearing had returned. Whatever had been distracting him was summarily expelled.

'Surely I must have said something of interest, Bob …'

Quite purposely, I allowed my voice to trail away, hoping for a positive response.

'I really think we should leave it there for now, Arthur … one step at a time, old chap. Better to wait until we meet with Edgar … okay?'

I recall feeling irritated, thinking I'd been dismissed like a disgruntled schoolboy, but what more could I have said? After all, Mr Booth was paying for the session. He was Bob's client, not me. I would hear the recording eventually, though how long it would take would mostly rely on Bob's workload. Having not cared for his attitude, I elected to leave with an air of petulance. Later, with the benefit of hindsight, I came to regret my immature conduct. I thought meeting Bob next time might not be so easy. I need not have worried.

***

My earlier concerns were dispelled the moment Bob purposely reached out to warmly shake my hand.

'I realise you were upset with me for not answering your questions, Arthur. I really am sorry about that. I must admit I could've handled it better. Please accept there was no disrespect intended. Truth be told, I wasn't feeling entirely myself at the time.'

That was good enough for me. I knew I could be temperamental, often taking things the wrong way. Grandma said much the same to me on occasion – and to anyone else who bothered to listen.

The muffins were very welcome, as was the drop of whisky in my tea. I felt involved again, comfortable in their company and excited at the prospect of hearing the recording.

It was the first time I had heard my voice as others might do, and I squirmed as the words echoed out from the recorder. Like most others, the Nottinghamshire accent has its distinct peculiarities. Nevertheless, I was shocked to hear the familiar brogue crudely delivered from my very own mouth.

Once the tape played on, however, such trivial thoughts retreated in the face of more significant matters.

Bob had finished counting down. There was an interim silence before his voice resumed.

Where are you, Arthur?

Silence save for the whirring of the recorder, a suggestion of breathing, the more distant crackle of the fire, and the sound of Bob's pencil scratching on paper.

It is dark.

I cringe anew as I hear my voice again. It is tinny and distant now.

Look about you, Arthur. What do you see?

Another pause, briefer this time.

Light ... I see a dim light.

Move towards it.

Mr Booth coughs nervously and clears his throat as we wait.

Where are you now?

Inside ... home.

The words falter. The latter voice is not entirely mine.

What is your name?

Mind yer business!

It is of another now – me but not me. This voice is harsh and quarrelsome. There is muttering and vague obscenities.

Where is home?

A better place than some has!

And where would that be?

More muttering and snuffling.

Where is home?

St Mary, if yer must know.

Mr Booth cannot help but nod at that. The gesture is slight but I do not miss it.

Is there anyone with you?

There is a sighing, heavy with impatience, then ...

No, there in't!

Whereabouts in St Mary's?

More sighing. Then, with a resonance so harsh it unsettles me ...

Always!

Mr Booth glances at me as the echo of the outburst reverberates in my ears.

What d'you mean by always?

It is dark, I am lost ...

It is my voice – no longer that of the other. I have returned.

Mr Booth looked fit to burst, as though he'd a million things to say but was refraining from doing so. It was Bob who splintered the silence. Smiling thinly, he turned to me with an almost consoling expression.

'Thing is, Arthur, that was not a typical regression. If anything, I'd say it was closer to being a séance. That might go some way to explaining why I was a bit cagey at the time. To my mind, it wasn't an entirely normal experience. The content was disquieting if only for the depiction of the contact. The response to my questions came from you. The voice was yours, but its transformation was more profound than many I've previously experienced. Of course, there's more we could say. But, in my professional capacity, I don't think we should risk inducing something that might unwittingly influence future regressions. There's much to learn, and your opening session was disappointingly brief. I propose we do the sensible thing and arrange another consultation as soon as we can. We can only hope you experience the same life again. And with a bit of luck, we might get more definable detail next time ... assuming everyone's in agreement, of course.'

***

I met with Bob a few days later – just the two of us. He said he'd been meaning to visit the Co-op store on Upper Parliament Street, so we arranged to meet in The Three Crowns just down the road. It was partly Mr Booth's suggestion that we meet. He reckoned Bob and me should get to know each other better before the next regression came round. We both agreed it might be an idea, given the awkwardness between us at the end of the first session.

It took a couple of pints to loosen us up. And then out of the blue, Bob began to talk about his personal circumstances, revealing more and more as he went along. It felt like he was offloading for his own sake more than anything else – using me to wash out his troubles, so to speak. It seemed odd, a man of his age pouring his heart out to someone as young as me. I was slightly uneasy with that at first. Then the more he unburdened, the more I took it as a compliment, thinking maybe he was beginning to treat me as an equal.

In some respects, Bob's circumstances were not that different from my own. Like me, he lived by himself, having split from his wife four years into a shaky marriage – Lou, he called her. He said she liked to dance and have a good time, saying he'd grown-up but she hadn't. I thought he was convincing himself more than he was me. From what I could make out, it sounded like they were natural opposites – looked it, too, if the picture on Bob's sideboard was anywhere near a likeness of her.

Bob was a professional hypnotherapist with a string of letters after his name. He ran a small practice in nearby Mansfield where he treated people for phobias and anxieties – smoking, spiders, or whatever they needed help with. Apparently, he'd drifted into regression after attending a seminar in Manchester. He said he preferred to keep that side of the business separate from his daytime job, as it might give him a reputation for being a quack.

It was interesting to encounter someone as outwardly confident as Bob so openly exhibiting signs of insecurity, particularly given his line of work. It caused me to regard him in a different light, one I was more comfortable with.

After a while, the conversation inevitably turned to Mr Booth. Initially, I found it difficult to talk about someone who'd become something of a friend and mentor to me. Bob mistakenly assumed I knew all about the Booths and their eccentricities. Equally, I thought he'd known them both for years. I'd imagined they were old friends. In fact, that was not the case at all. Mr Booth had contacted Bob only the previous year to enquire about regression, and it was only after the first session that their relationship began to deepen.

'I don't mind telling you, Arthur, it took me aback. I'd never before experienced an outcome like it.'

I think Bob assumed I was familiar with what he was talking about, so I simply shrugged and waited for him to continue.

'To the best of my knowledge, it doesn't happen very often. Regression, by its nature, is somewhat unpredictable. The subject – that is, the person being regressed – more often reveals a past life entirely dissimilar to that of their current existence. This might include factors such as gender, physical characteristics, location, et cetera. Less often, it involves non-human entities. It's not that unusual for someone to recall a previous life spent as a dog or a cat or ...'

Bob stiffened when I chuckled. I found it difficult to hide my amusement. My outburst probably reminded him just how naïve I was about life in general, let alone a specialist subject like reincarnation. I imagined Bob to be the wrong side of forty, Mr Booth at least ten or fifteen years beyond that, maybe. Whereas I was only in my late teens. I thought there were times when the others needed to remember that.

'I'm really sorry, Bob ... don't forget it's all very strange and new to me. I don't have anywhere near the experience and learning you and the Booths have. Even so, I'm very interested in what we're doing, even if I'm not exactly sure what that might be just yet. I really want to understand and be part of everything – it means something to me, so please forgive me and carry on.'

Bob flashed that gap-toothed grin of his to reassure me. He reminded me of a breezy fighter pilot, the rogue quiff he continually swept back doing little to spoil the impression.

'You know, I forget what it's like to be your age, Arthur, and just how daft some of this must sound to someone who's never been involved before. Nevertheless, don't underestimate yourself too much. I'm convinced you understand more than you think you do, if only instinctively. You simply haven't processed it entirely, not yet at any rate. You're aware enough to know where this is going, though. And I know for a fact Edgar thinks much the same. I shouldn't say, but he firmly believes you've been around a few times yourself, maybe even more than he has ... or Mrs Booth for that matter.'

He suddenly appeared like a man who'd said

too much, so I looked away as though his comments had passed over my head. However, it caused me to think about the three of us listening to the recording: the quizzical looks on their faces as they watched mine so intently.

'Can I ask you a direct question, Bob?'

'Of course you can.'

'Is Mr Booth genuinely psychic, or just a trickster like most of the others are?'

He hesitated before answering, frowning as though he wasn't sure of his footing.

'I had similar thoughts at first, Arthur. Strictly between you and me, I did some digging on Edgar to see if anything dodgy turned up. I also tested him to see if he was as perceptive as he claimed to be. I fed him some erroneous information about my ancestry. It sounds underhanded, but like you, I wanted to be sure he was genuine. As it happened, he barely faltered, revealing more than enough to prove his legitimacy. What he told me concerned extremely private matters, details he could never have found out, even were he able access my personal records. And don't forget, Arthur, I have the advantage of being trained to detect falsehoods – those little tell-tale signs that intimate when someone is looking to deceive.'

The intensity of Bob's reassurance was quite telling – if nothing else, he certainly believed Mr Booth was genuine.

'I think you were leading up to saying something about Mr Booth's regression before I interrupted you – about it being unusual or different in some way?'

'Yeah, that's right, Arthur ... it was certainly uncommon. At least for me it was. To start with, I'd never previously regressed anybody claiming to have second sight. Never mind anyone whose past life was located in the same geographical vicinity as their current one. Then all at once, both of those variables popped up during Edgar's sessions. If that were not enough, you subsequently appear on the scene. That's when things began to take an entirely more interesting turn.'

There were moments when I thought I might be making sense of it, but it was like a complex jigsaw. On opening the box, the only directly identifiable pieces were the easy ones that fit the edges.

Once again, I thought Bob had revealed more than he should have done. I didn't press him further. I was learning to bide my time, sensing there were more twists and turns to be exposed.

Hopefully, the results of my second regression would reveal something of more substance.

Chapter 6
Nottingham 1966

It was Christmas when we met – under the glittering ball at The Palais. Her name is Ann. She has long black hair and is very pretty. Though the sparkle of festivity has dulled, the latent mood of it endures within us.

Hand in hand, we walk to the top of Friar Lane, immediately grounded by the crazed destruction that has visited our city. We both agree we do not enjoy seeing buildings demolished in the name of modernity. We are young, so do we not represent modernity? Do we not lean in favour of it? We do, but those treasured structures are part of our history – our lives and those of our kin before us. Old Nottingham is changing. It will be relentless. It will be regretted.

This girl makes me feel normal. The other world fades for a while. Whilst not entirely gone, that shadowy place is no longer quite as significant.

What with the weather and Bob falling ill, it began to feel as if the second regression might never happen. From Christmas through January, his chest worsened by the day. The prolonged bouts of ferocious hacking were worrying, to say the least, even more so when seeing him anxiously inspecting his handkerchief after a particularly violent attack.

It was therefore not until February that we dared elect a date for my next regression. Due to Bob's lingering incapacity, we decided to meet at his house to be certain he was up to it. That evening, my sporadic inattentiveness made me realise my fascination was declining. That the timing of this coincided with meeting Ann became immediately obvious to me. She had entered my life at Christmas, and there had barely been two days together when we had not seen each other of an evening. Though I was hopelessly infatuated, I was determined not to completely abandon my interest in what I had come to think of as 'the project'.

I looked forward to being regressed for a second time, certain something more would come of it. However, the lengthening period of inaction had tested my commitment to the limit. Coupled with that was the recurring notion that something was missing from my relationship with Bob and the Booths. I had thought for a while there were things they shared that they kept to themselves.

I left Bob's house with a date confirmed for my next regression. Though he had recovered a little, he was still fighting off whatever it was that ailed him. Nevertheless, he insisted we press on regardless. Bob's fortitude was admirable, and thinking of my casual indifference made me squirm with guilt. The comparison served to deliver me a deserved kick up the backside.

Perhaps that was part of the reason for my thinking it might be an idea to introduce Ann to the Booths. Apart from the stranger aspects of my relationship with them, I liked to think they'd become good friends, and that my interest might be revived if Ann became acquainted with them. With that in mind, I contacted the Booths to tell them I had found a girlfriend, and would they like to meet her. I remember being bemused by the silence that met my suggestion. I should have sensed even then that the idea might not have been such a good one after all.

It was Mrs Booth who'd answered the phone. Though she'd placed her hand over the mouthpiece, I could hear her muffled whispers resonating in the callbox. It was a few seconds later before she answered.

'Yes ... that's okay, Arthur, of course it is. We can do Friday evening if ...'

I met Ann outside Player's factory, where she worked as a clerk, then we walked into town and caught a bus to Arnold. I had already told her a few things about the Booths and their curious way of life, though not enough to concern her. Likewise, I'd told the Booths about Ann, asking if they wouldn't mind not revealing too much about our psychic endeavours.

They made us welcome enough, but neither of us were entirely at ease during the time we were there. There was nothing we could put our fingers on, but we both sensed an underlying resentment in the couple's demeanour. Mrs Booth cooked us egg on toast, and we chatted about everything and nothing until we noticed them glance at the clock a few times. We took the hint, and after we had said our goodbyes and were walking to the bus stop, Ann said it felt like she'd intruded on a secret society. We both laughed at that, Ann more casually than me.

***

I could hear Bob coughing as I walked up the paving to his door, thinking to myself that it sounded slightly better. Then the actual sight of him only served to rekindle my concern. He was pale and drawn, and he looked completely exhausted.

'Hello there, Bob, you sure it's all right for me to bother you like this?'

He nodded unconvincingly and ushered me through, mumbling something about tea. I followed him into the same room as before, thinking it looked like he'd slept in his clothes. The heap of smouldering ash under the fresh logs in the hearth suggested a night spent by the fire.

I opened the bag I carried and brought out a half-bottle of cheap brandy, the best I could afford at the time.

'Thought this might help to ease the old chest a bit, Bob.'

He welled up at that, and I was lost for something more to say. The token kindness might have been the proverbial straw that broke the camel's back. Somebody once said, 'you may suffer a thousand cruelties with not so much as a tear, though one kind word might make you weep.' Bob didn't weep exactly, though he disappeared into the kitchen quite rapidly.

When he returned with two steaming mugs of tea, we laced them with brandy. It warmed us both and brought some much needed colour to Bob's sunken cheeks. Not long after that, his mood began to lighten, and so we made ready for the second regression.

I'd not been overly concerned by the contents of the first recording. When all was said and done, they were only words. There was no denying it was a peculiar experience, and the thought of what else might come to light distracted me for a while. Then, when things were overly delayed because of Bob's illness, my thoughts about the first time faded into little more than hazy recollections.

One thing that did continue to intrigue me was the fact that after we'd listened to the recording, Mr Booth hadn't said very much at all. His unresponsiveness seemed purposeful, as though he'd decided beforehand to hold back on something. Having become accustomed to his annoying ambiguity, I decided my best option was to play the waiting game rather than demand immediate answers. I knew he'd tell me when he was good and ready – it was all about timing with Edgar Booth.

On this occasion, I decided to recline on the couch, making myself comfortable whilst Bob shot off to the kitchen again, this time for a lengthy bout of coughing. Again, I thought it sounded looser than previously, and was pleased that he was showing signs of recovery.

Bob had turned out to be a nice bloke. I had come to look on him as something of an ally, if not a friend.

When he returned, he went to stand with his back to the fire, enjoying the warmth and a generous measure of neat brandy before beginning formalities. I stretched out and relaxed, only for the butterflies to flutter their wings the second I heard the menacing click of the tape recorder. My earlier bravado immediately deserted me, my mood tensing at the prospect of once again drifting into the mists of time. And so it took a while longer for my thoughts to wander ... Bob's soothing tones becoming ever more remote ...

Unlike the first time, there were no awkward moments at the end of the second session. I had prepared myself and knew what to expect on this occasion. We'd agreed beforehand not to discuss the results until we met the following evening at the Booths' house. I didn't say anything, but I couldn't help but notice a couple of things at the end of the session. The clock on the wall told me I'd been 'away' a while longer this time.

And then again, there was the small matter of Bob's expression.

***

'I thought you'd seen a ghost!

I chuckled and Bob chuckled along with me,

but I thought his amusement forced and unconvincing. The good news was that his cough had loosened even more. I demanded an accolade for that, claiming it must have been the brandy I'd treated him to. Whatever it was, he was looking much better than he had been. We were relieved to see him recovering. Mrs Booth made a proper fuss of him, the poor chap flushing with embarrassment when she unexpectedly squashed him to her considerable bosom.

There was an unanticipated conviviality about the atmosphere that evening. It sometimes happens like that – everyone in a good mood at the same time. I'd imagined it might be a miserable affair, what with Bob's health and the recent coolness between me and the Booths.

Then seemingly out of the blue, there we were, pretty much back together again.

The three of us sat listening to the pad of Mrs Booth's feet climbing the stairs to her ironing room, or the guest bedroom, as she preferred to describe it. Bob croaked and cleared his throat.

'We'll get on then, shall we?'

There they were again, those flimsy creatures that slumbered within me, the whir of the recorder eerily emulating the flutter of their stirring wings.

Where are you, Arthur?
It is dark … there are others here.
Bob pauses before responding.

What ... where are you?

Singing ... there is smoke.

What sort of singing, Arthur? What kind of smoke?

Hardly see a bleddy thing in 'ere!

That voice again – my own at once lost in its coarse substance. Bob readjusts.

Who is that? What is your name?

You again!

I mean no harm.

There is a cackle; it is dry and harsh, like grit scouring a bone.

It's me as does the 'arm, Mester ...

That cackle again – it chills me even as it fades.

What is your name? Please ... tell me your ...

Mind yer business!

Where are you?

There is a throaty sigh, almost one of resignation.

Gate ...

The word is breathed more than spoken.

What gate d'you refer to?

Hey?

The gate ...what is the gate you speak of?

Christ!

It is a curse, not a reference, and is followed by the resonance of laboured breathing.

Postern ... understand?

Postern ... Gate?

Ah, that's it ... good brew an' all.

You're in a tavern?

O' course it's a bleddy tavern!

Tell me what day it is.

There are muttered curses, then a long silence

before ...

Friday o' course ...

The tone is less aggressive, now more conversational.

Are you with friends?

So called, ah ...

What town are you in?

The tone slightly changes again, a hint of returning annoyance.

Stupid bleddy questions!

Please, I'm a complete stranger here ... where is this place?

This time the delay is extended, though there is a faint sound of breathing. Is it him, or have I returned?

Why ... Nottingham ... o' course.

Mr Booth smiles bleakly, as does Bob. It is, in its way, collaborative. I feel excluded again.

What year?

The question is important. We wait patiently. A stifled cough – it is Bob. Time passes and there is nothing more. I wonder if it is over. My companions wait with expectant certainty. They have the advantage of me. They know there is more. A rasping cough. This time it is not Bob, but it is Bob's voice that follows, sharp and demanding.

Who rules England? Who is on the throne?

Yet another sigh, one of resignation again.

Tired ...

Please, before you leave, tell me who is on the throne.

I hear the escalating desperation in Bob's voice – the fish is slipping the hook – a further sigh, then ...

Vic ... toria.

It is partly his voice, partly mine, and I shudder. Insects are crawling along my spine.

Mr Booth looked pleased with himself, Bob not so much. More often than not, and for reasons I was yet to understand, Bob seemed increasingly uncomfortable with what we were doing. From our recent conversations, I knew his views didn't entirely concur with Mr Booth's perception of regression. Bob was of the opinion that past life experiences were fundamentally inherited memories, genetic recollections passed down through our ancestors. Whereas Mr Booth preferred to believe regression to be merely an alternative form of clairvoyance.

I was unsure as to who was right – perhaps either or neither of them. One view I continued to entertain was that Mr Booth was keeping something of significance from me. I'd come to realise he was inherently manipulative. Even so, I couldn't help but like him enough to believe his intentions were in no way sinister. That notwithstanding, I was increasingly irritated by his evasiveness. That knowing smile suggested he knew more than he was letting on. I think Bob did too, though perhaps not for the same reasons. Bob was proving a man of his word. If he'd agreed with Mr Booth to keep a confidence, then he would do so to the best of his ability.

'I think it's only right to share a few things with you, Arthur.'

'And about flippin' time too, Edgar!'

Mrs Booth had returned from her ironing, affording her husband a critical smirk as she settled into her chair.

'Like a number of things in life, Arthur, the impartation of critical knowledge is all about timing. Please consider that if I'd revealed absolutely everything when we first met, you might have thought me entirely insane!'

Mrs Booth shot me a warning glance, clearly directing me not to make fun of his last remark. When I'd first listened to him in the café after seeing him in the market, I'd thought him raving mad anyway.

'You may recall me saying that I believe our paths have crossed before ... in a previous life, I mean.'

I was hoping for a more startling revelation of some sort, but rather than interrupt his flow, I simply nodded and instinctively glanced at Bob. He was perched on the edge of his seat, nervously contemplating his navel.

'Well, Arthur, even though finding you was gratifying, I confess I needed to understand just how receptive you were. I didn't want to go off half-cocked without knowing the strength of your ... capabilities.'

Was there something meaningful about that pause? Or was it simply another evasive manoeuvre? I looked at Bob again, and then at Mrs Booth, though there was nothing in their expressions that gave much away.

'The good news is ... I needn't have been concerned, Arthur. You've exceeded my expectations. It's no secret that Bob and I differ about the mechanics of past life experience, but we both acknowledge the authenticity of your results, sparse as they are. Nor can we deny the growing number of coincidences that have come to aid our speculation.'

It felt like they were waiting for me to contribute. Mr Booth was one of those exasperating people who more often than not went round the houses to reach his destination, assuming everyone else understood the direction he was taking. He frequently talked in riddles, inevitably raising more questions than answers. After pausing for thought, and against my natural inclination, I decided it was time to take a more direct route for once.

'Mr Booth, I really don't know what you're talking about! Maybe I'm not clever enough to understand, or it might be the fact that you rarely get to the point!'

It came out snappier than intended, but clearly it hit the mark. Mr Booth looked halfway between hurt and quizzical, at the same time disappointed and surprised. I turned to the others, but there was no support forthcoming. Bob gazed even more intently at his navel whilst Mrs Booth appeared disturbed by my unfamiliar outburst.

'Arthur! There's really no need for ...'

'It's okay, dear ... Arthur's quite right. I tend to think everyone's on the same wavelength as me. Forgive me, I understand why you think I'm playing games, Arthur, but please be assured I'm not. I've nothing but your best interests at heart.'

There, he was doing it again! He simply couldn't help leaving something in the air to be guessed at. I resisted the temptation to say as much, instead letting it rest with a sigh of frustration.

And then, as though nothing of any note had occurred, he continued as before. And I stood for it, almost ashamed that I'd dared to challenge him.

'Regardless of what you choose to believe, Arthur, I stand by my affirmation that we shared a past life together – perhaps one of many. Do you not agree, Bob?'

Bob squirmed and blushed, clearly not wishing to deal with the implication of what Mr Booth was saying, though at the same time recognising the futility of refusing to do so.

'I can agree ... in a sense. When I regressed Edgar, he did have a comparable experience, Arthur. I can't in all honesty deny that some of your respective details appear to intersect ... limited though those details are at this point.'

Bob glanced at the Booths in turn, raising his eyebrows as if to ask a question. It was telling that Mrs Booth was the one to nod her approval.

'Take "always" for instance ... "always"'.

I remembered the word from the first recording. Taken in isolation, the utterance had confused me at the time, though I'd dismissed it as unimportant. And I had thought little of it since. Thinking back, I remembered the question as being 'whereabouts in St Mary's?' The answer had simply been 'always'.

'Always,' exclaimed Mr Booth, interrupting Bob's elucidation and looking at me much as a teacher would a student.

'Always is an adverb, in the same vein as "constantly" or "continually". However, if we make the lowercase "a" into an uppercase "A", the word becomes a proper noun. We can therefore deduce with a modicum of certainty that in this instance, it refers to a defunct location once known as Always Yard – late of the parish of St Mary in the Lace Market area. Regrettably, it no longer exists, nor can we be precise about its exact whereabouts. It's generally thought to have been somewhere off Pilcher Gate, perhaps near the junction with Halifax Place.'

I was momentarily lost for words. Listening to Mr Booth speak of familiar places in that context caused the back of my neck to prickle. The coincidences were indeed adding up, and I was immediately back into the swing of it.

'I can tell you, Arthur, that some of the details recovered from your brief regressive experiences dovetail nicely with those of my own – the locality and timeline, for instance. Even so, there are variances I don't care to reveal at this juncture. You must appreciate how counterproductive it would be for me to influence your thoughts in advance of your third session.'

I feared he was yet again ending on an ambiguous note. I was about to challenge him on that very point when he sensed my frustration and resumed before I had the chance to interrupt his flow.

'I think it's safe to say that we can proceed with more confidence. We have a defined location – a datum point from which to centre our ongoing investigations. What we desperately need to know, though, is the name of the very person whose voice speaks through you, Arthur. The one, perhaps, whose life you lived before this one.'

Cynics might argue regression is but a scrambled hallucination – discordant episodes staged in distinguishable locations. At one time, I would, more than likely, have accepted that hypothesis. However, dreaming up a past life was one thing; Edgar Booth claiming an association with me in a previous century was quite another!

I reasoned his purpose was to verify and make sense of his own past-life existence, and that my own recollections might help him to achieve his objectives. Whatever the case was, if his speculation came to be substantiated, I needed to understand exactly who I used to be.

'Think again about the coincidences, Arthur. The inferred location of Always Yard near Pilcher Gate, the very area where you work today. Then there's mention of the inn at the gate that came up in your second regression, the location where your other self claimed to be …'

'The Postern, you mean.'

That name had stuck with me. Bob then chipped in with some enthusiasm, interested now things were being shared more openly.

'Actually, I've done a bit of digging on that. As the name would imply, the Postern was an original gateway at the intersection of Middle Pavement and ...'

'Drury Hill.'

That prickle again – yet another coincidence.

'Exactly, Arthur. Then you'll know the building is now a post office, or at least part of it is. It hasn't been a pub for donkey's years. Apparently, before it came to be The Postern Gate, it was known as the Bull's Head. That's before parts of the original gate were uncovered during renovations. That's how the name changed to The Postern Gate Inn.'

Even before Bob said what he did, I intuitively knew it would be that very building: the post office to which I had carried armfuls of cardboard tubes containing cinema posters, there to be stamped every evening of the working week, when I was serving my time as a lad.

Chapter 7
Nottingham 1966

The mad March winds are upon us. Arm in arm, we brace against the sleet-laden squall that gusts along Stoney Street. Ann is warm and snug in her fur collar. We are just minutes from the edifice where I labour each day, yet in her company, I am in Shangri-la.

The church is ahead of us; the trees that dapple its form are animated and leafless – St Mary's, the epicentre of my life. I see now why I am drawn to this place. I think it has always been so. It is an enduring magnet.

Ann and me are in love. It is very real. It is what keeps me steady amidst the strange happenings. Is it possible we might marry at St Mary's? It seems right that we should, if only in our dreams.

Nottingham has long been renowned for its production of fine lace. The escalating progression of industrial revolution encouraged legions of workers to abandon farm and field to labour instead in the multiple factories and businesses emerging in nearby towns and cities. Those not familiar with Nottingham's Lace Market might imagine an alfresco haberdashery: a mélange of canvassed stalls displaying elaborate cloths and fancy garments. The reality, however, is the austere assemblage of factories and warehouses constructed over Nottingham's erstwhile garden parish. Many employees coming to work in the vicinity of St Mary's also took rooms in the dwellings that cluttered the nearby alleyways and cobbled yards.

I know the area well. Not only did I write posters in one of the old manufacturing works, many of my ancestors were involved in the lace industry. Little had I known how far my association would advance beyond those conventional boundaries.

***

Some time had passed since we had gathered to discuss my second regression. Looking back on it, I see that particular meeting as a watershed – the defining moment when my interest was reawakened.

As the evening had worn on, I underwent a resuming sense of inclusion. Perhaps for varying reasons, each of us was equally keen to disentangle the mystery that in some elusive way implicated us all. Settling comfortably into the fold, I realised I'd subconsciously separated the two infatuations of my existence – as my affair with Ann flourished, my fascination with the paranormal had decreased. Looking back with fresh eyes, I was obliged to question why the two entities should conflict at all. My relationship with Ann was entirely separate. When I first rather tentatively explained the pursuits I shared with the Booths, she appeared genuinely interested and even pleased for me, although I did notice her eyes widening from time to time. It must have sounded weird to her, but in any event, there didn't appear to be any problems from her perspective. Ann wanted to be with me as much as I did with her. Regardless of what else was occurring in our lives, we were both convinced that nothing would affect our relationship – we simply wanted to be happy ... together.

The brief hiccup with the Booths appeared to be a passing squall and best forgotten. On reflection, I thought they might have associated my attachment to Ann with my growing disinterest in the project. In which case, their concern was completely understandable.

I was under the impression that the purpose of our next get-together was to elect a date for my third regression, as well as to discuss anything that had come to light since we'd last met. I'd certainly not expected the schedule to expand quite so extensively as it did. Engrossed as we were in the subject matter, we only became aware of the changing weather conditions when we noticed the wind moaning in the eaves and the animated branches rapping at the window. All that was missing was the rumble of thunder.

Mr Booth, tumbler of ginger wine to hand, took centre stage and requested our attention. With glasses liberally charged, we settled into our seats to hear what he had to say. It may have been the atmospheric conditions, the comforting alcohol, or perhaps a combination of the two, but when he came to speak that night, it brought to mind a wandering poet orating from under a canopy of stars – a circle of credulous listeners lost in the moment his story took form.

'In the interests of completeness, I feel obliged to mention my earliest experience – nothing more than a fleeting sense of another place at another time – yet I had been nowhere. I was barely five years old but, even at my tender age, I had a sense of something otherworldly. Whatever its meaning was, it was somewhat tame compared to what happened during my first day at primary school. I was just one of a number of equally bewildered children sitting cross-legged on the floor of the assembly hall. The headmistress was tiresomely explaining too many things for far too long, and I recall drifting into my own little world, something I'm prone to do. Then something urged me to look up, and when I did, I became immediately aware of an old gentleman standing by the headmistress. As far as I could tell, no one else there exhibited any sign of noticing his arrival. There had been no opening of doors to disturb the assembly, no footsteps or words of introduction. It was almost as if he'd materialised on the spot. Then as I leaned forward to look more closely, I was certain he was staring directly at me. I don't recall reacting in any particular way, though I sensed he wanted something from me, but I was at a loss as to what that might be.'

It seemed Mr Booth was reliving the moment – perhaps something he'd done many times before. We waited patiently, allowing him his reflection. I noticed that when he raised his head to carry on, there was a pitiable sadness about him.

'I didn't think of him as a ghost ... at least not until much later. He was not, as you might expect, of ethereal form. He was at first as material as anyone in that room. But the look on his face as he faded away will live with me forever. I was far too young to make logical sense of it, although I genuinely recall feeling the depth of his grief and exasperation. Only later did I realise he'd desperately wanted to convey a message to the headmistress. He'd sought to use me as an intermediary for that singular purpose. Sadly, though, I had yet to discern my own spiritual empowerment.

'They say you always remember your first time, and psychic experiences are by no means an exception. The memory of that encounter stays with me to this very day. I've experienced innumerable manifestations since – some more noteworthy than others – but there was a distinct enchantment to that moment. I don't think I've ever experienced anything quite so memorable since.'

In recalling his experience, Mr Booth displayed a level of emotion I'd not appreciated before. His passion moved me, and judging by her expression, Mrs Booth shared his sentiment. The two of them were especially close, and I had to wonder if their deep attachment went beyond the life they currently shared. At the same time, in more practical terms, I couldn't help questioning exactly what conversing with the dead might possibly bring to a marriage – and I hoped I never would.

When I turned to speak to Bob, I found him already staring in my direction, as though he'd been studying me. I put it down to professional observation: the therapist looking for signs of a personality disorder. Realising he'd been caught out, he smiled affectedly and casually returned his attention to Mr Booth, who'd obviously not finished his discourse.

'Arthur, I thought it might be advantageous if you were to understand more about the singularities that bind the four of us together. Bob and I have discussed these matters on more than one occasion. He's already familiar with my objectives, as is Mrs Booth, of course. Nevertheless, I wish to emphasise how the practice of clairvoyance has influenced my existence since the incident I related only moments ago.

'I see things, Arthur, and I journey to places others can only imagine. Though it might sound far-fetched, I can honestly claim to have travelled beyond the astral plane to the realm of celestial spheres. Words cannot begin to explain the sheer expanse of what endures beyond our physical existence. My familiarity with such phenomena gives me considerable advantage in the affairs the four of us are currently concerned with. Please ... excuse me for a second.'

Mr Booth stopped to take a gulp of water, as would a public speaker, or even a wandering poet, perhaps. He loved an audience and was very convincing. Even so, in the last few minutes, he'd stretched belief considerably beyond his theatrical capabilities. I had to wonder what on earth – or anywhere else for that matter – he was going to regale us with next.

'I think I always sensed that I had lived a life before this one, if not more than one. That may be the reason for me accepting the essence of re-embodiment. When I began to research the matter in more depth, I was amazed how many faiths embrace the spectrum of reincarnation. We often equate recurring life with more Eastern religions. It might surprise you to learn, therefore, that many early Christians believed in various forms of rebirth, as did Egyptians, Romans and Greeks, not to mention Norse and Native American mythologies. This makes our own involvement all the more notable. Like me, Bob has consulted numerous records, but so far we've discovered very few instances to compare with the circumstances we're researching on behalf of the four of us. To the very best of our knowledge, the percentage of regressions that even broadly cross-reference by type with our own is negligible – specific examples where two or more past lives have been found to intersect in time, circumstance and location!'

That I now reacted to such sweeping statements so casually was perhaps evidence of my growing acceptance. I was beginning to think there was more to regression than a few sessions of induced subconsciousness. Within a short space of time, I had come to acknowledge notions I would once have dismissed as pure fantasy.

That was not the end of it, though, not by any means. Mr Booth was preparing himself again.

'To some extent, my regressions are different from your own, Arthur. With great respect, you attended your first session without the benefit of even a cursory understanding of reincarnation. Whereas I have the advantage of spending a considerable part of my life studying the obscure and extreme vagaries of existence. That's not to suggest I'm any more or less intelligent than you, or anyone else, for that matter. It's important to me that you believe that.'

I smiled and shrugged my acceptance.

'Thank you, Arthur.'

The growing tension in the room was exacerbated by a strong gust of wind and the demanding rap of branches against the window momentarily taking our attention, though Mr Booth himself smoothly moved on without pause.

'Arthur, we all of us think you've already deduced something of the truth: that you have within you the capacity to understand more than you currently believe you do. For now, though, you need only accept the belief that the four of us have known each other before – that we existed in this very city, in another time, though perhaps in differing circumstances.'

Mr Booth was staring at me intently, measuring my reaction, as in their own ways were the others. Bob was shifting in his seat, looking ill at ease, whilst Mrs Booth did nothing more than smile benevolently. She rarely gave much away.

'I don't know what you want me to say, Mr

Booth. In simple terms, it's no more than you've been saying all along.'

'Arthur, before you say anything else, there's something more you should hear.'

I detected a hint of annoyance in his tone. Maybe they thought me even more naïve than I actually was. That the three of them were obviously disappointed with the casualness of my response was totally understandable, but I was rarely one to display my emotions. I preferred to think things through before jumping in with both feet; it was just the way I was.

Not wishing to sour the atmosphere further, I eased back into my seat and waited to see what else they were about to come up with.

I had to admit to being secretly fascinated by the idea that all four of us might have known each other in previous lives, and particularly in what circumstances. Even so, I wasn't quite ready to say so. He gave me one of his looks then, and sniffed expressively – a bit like Grandma would do on occasion.

'Quite deliberately, I chose not to tell Bob about my psychic capabilities before my first regression with him. I didn't want to influence his thinking or methodology in any way. At that stage, I was simply looking for evidence of a past life experience – anything that might offer a degree of validity. It was a casual interest for me at the time, nothing more or less than that, really. I'd considered pursuing the idea for some while. It was intended to be a temporary distraction, though not completely detached from my customary undertakings ... so, let's hear what happened.'

Mr Booth nodded at Bob, who obligingly reached for his haversack. After extracting his tape recorder, he carefully positioned it on the table before connecting its cable to the mains. At the same time, Mrs Booth quietly left her seat by the window and padded to the kitchen. The impromptu sequence of activity looked to have been choreographed beforehand: Mr Booth's contrived exposé obviously intended to pave the way for an airing of his own regression. I mentally rubbed my hands together in genuine anticipation. In spite of my adopted composure, I was more than eager to hear how Mr Booth's experience correlated with my own.

While Bob twiddled with the spools, Mr Booth excused himself and disappeared to the bathroom. Shortly after that, the tinkling of glass heralded the return of his wife. She carried a silver tray laden with four upturned tumblers and a bottle of something. It looked like she intended to remain with us on this occasion. By the time Mr Booth returned, his wife had filled the tumblers and was passing them round.

'Splash of Armagnac. Bottoms up, everybody!'

We acknowledged the toast and sampled our drinks. The liquor was strong but pleasantly smooth. After smacking his lips to signify his appreciation, Bob leaned over the recorder and pressed the play button. The resultant click immediately claimed our concentration, the ensuing quiet disturbed only by the wind outside and the whirring tape within.

There came the now familiar whisper of rhythmic numeration – the cadence of formal invocation.

Where are you, Edgar?

The tape whirrs.

Where are you?

I'm here!

The voice is unmistakeable – it is Mr Booth. There is an irritability about it.

Where are you?

The tape whirrs on ... and on ...

Where ...

Catchin' me breath! I'm busy!

Much like mine did, the voice transitions – at first a subtle fluctuation.

What are you doing?

Sittin' on a bucket, catchin' me bleddy breath!

Harsher now, not dissimilar to that of my own other-self, though it is not mine.

Why are you out of breath?

The tape whirrs on ... there is a rootling cough. It is not Bob. The offender is hawking and spitting.

Why are you out of breath? Are you ill?

It's the dust, yer see! Nuff ter mek me hoss cough!

Is it your horse? Is it with you now?

Ah ... course ... when's it not?!

Bob is encouraged. There is an emergent rhythm to the exchange.

What is your job?

The tape whirrs ... there is more coughing, then ...

Black dust ... stains me spit ... coal as what does it.

You're delivering coal?

Ah ...

The mood is more conversational.

Where are you delivering to next?

The tape whirrs, but not for long.

Square.

Market Square? Sorry, the ... The Exchange, I mean.

Bob is flustered, his rhythm disturbed.

What yo on abart?

Tell me what you mean by square – what square? I'm a stranger. Please help me understand.

The tape whirrs on ... the voice is more distant. He is talking, but not to us. He is laughing now, but not with us. It causes him to cough and spit again.

Please tell me where you are.

The tape whirrs ... there is a loud sigh. He is back with us.

Milk Square.

Where is Milk Square?

Bleddy 'ell! Nosy bogger! I'm busy ... I've got wok ter do!

Sorry ... please ... please tell me where it is.

He is tutting ... he is becoming exasperated.

St Mary ... St Mary ...

It is a fading echo. Has he gone? Where is Mr Booth?

Are you still there?

Ah, I'm here .... but not for long.

I am surprised to hear him. I thought him gone for good.

He's come back wi' me ...

Who has? Who is that with you?

George ... sez yer know 'im well enough? So why ask, 'ey, mester?

The tape whirrs .... Bob is silent. He does not answer the question. For some reason, he does not speak at all.

George ... George Davy, sez 'e knows yer, mester!

The tape whirrs and Bob responds ... there is a catch in his throat ...

Edgar ... Edgar ...

The snap of clicking fingers ...

It's alright, Bob. I'm back.

It is Mr Booth's voice. It is perfectly calm and normal. He appears unperturbed. He asks for tea with two sugars – and a biscuit.

Chapter 8
Nottingham 1966

May has arrived. Sunshine is warming the pavements at last. It might be 'Miserable Monday' but I walk to work with a definite spring in my step.

The weekend turned out better than expected. Ann and me went to Earnest Jones to look at rings on Saturday. Her eyes lit up when she saw the one she liked. Eternity ring, it's called. I'd never heard of one before – said I'd save up and see what I could do about it.

Then on Sunday I took Ann to meet the family and they loved her. Even Grandma was impressed. We had our tea together in the front room – polished and hoovered it was – tinned salmon with the bits taken out and fresh salad off the market. Grandad let us down as he often does, demanding bread and butter with the peaches and Co-op cream we had for afters.

Mr Booth has asked me to accompany him to a séance in Sherwood this evening. It'll be my first one and I'm really looking forward to it.

It was a séance, but not on a wet afternoon. From my perspective, it turned out much like the film: in my view, frustratingly lacking in psychic activity. I found the experience overly dramatic, what with the stagey incantations, the clumsy table knockings and the contrived draughts that fanned the circle of hands at well-timed junctures.

The medium – worryingly, an old

acquaintance of Mr Booth's – was overtly Shakespearian. His name was William Webb, a portly chap with a hare lip and halitosis. The only thing he convincingly invoked was a flood of tears from a hawk-faced old lady in a black felt hat – said her dead husband had arrived to see her, that he still loved her and sent his best to her brother.

Not much else of interest emerged that evening. At least we'd been handed a large sherry to put us in the mood, though the effects of the cheap wine disappeared at least as quickly as William Webb's legitimacy.

'What did you think, Arthur?'

We were walking towards Mansfield Road to wait for our respective buses. It was a pleasant evening, and despite my disillusionment, I didn't want it to end on a disparaging note. Mr Booth had been kind enough to invite me along, so I thought it might be rude to complain.

'It was okay – bit old hat, perhaps, but an interesting experience all the same.'

'You're being polite, Arthur. It was worse than awful and you know it! Before you protest, I knew it would be a complete sham, and a badly enacted one at that.'

'Then why did you invite me, Mr Booth?'

'Because I wanted you to see the other side of the other side – if you'll pardon the pun – and indeed it was just about as bad as it gets. Now, though, I want you to encounter an authentic experience. I want to prove to you that there is such a thing as a genuine séance.

Hopefully, it might demonstrate just how deeply I've journeyed into the limitless domains of spirituality. I need you to understand the difference between the shady world of popular clairvoyance and the genuine article.'

I thought, here we go again: yet another occasion morphing into a supernatural extravaganza.

'Exactly where are we going next time, then, Mr Booth?'

'Well, Arthur, ambience and mood are critical to a productive sitting. So why don't you come along for tea on Wednesday evening after work?'

I thought about it for a moment and decided I'd like to see if Mr Booth was as psychic as he claimed to be. And Wednesday would be convenient, as Ann was meeting a friend that evening who was soon to be married. Ann had been asked to be her bridesmaid, and I'd been invited to attend the wedding with her.

'Yeah, okay then, Mr Booth. Sometime after six if that's alright?'

'Perfect, Arthur. There's just one more thing, though. Would you mind calling me Edgar from here on in? Mr Booth sounds terribly formal. It makes me feel old and rather dated.'

Strangely, I was a bit put out by that. I'd always thought he appreciated the respect I gave him and his wife.

'Of course ... why not? Might take some getting used to, though. And what about Mrs Booth when I see her?'

'Oh, you must call her Kate. She'd love it if

you did! And by the way, while I think about it, Kate said how nice it would be to see Ann again. The pair of you should come for Sunday lunch sometime – we could ask Bob if he'd like to join us.'

I saw a bus coming, with *City* on the front, and waived it down. I thanked Edgar for the evening out and hopped on. Perching myself on the side seat next to where the conductor stood, I looked through the opposite window as we moved away, noticing Edgar Booth standing exactly where I'd left him. I thought he should have crossed the road to wait at the bus stop opposite by then, but there he stood, following the movement of my bus. He wasn't actually looking at me, more so staring by me. I shook my head and had to wonder.

When the bus neared Slab Square, I deliberately dismissed any further thoughts of séances and associated happenings, deciding instead to sink a quick pint in the Bell and get a hot dog from the cart over the road.

Later, when I put my head on the pillow, my mind went into overdrive. I couldn't resist speculating about what might await me at the coming séance. Then there was that unexpected display of overfamiliarity, him suddenly insisting we should be on first-name terms, followed by an equally surprising invitation to Sunday lunch. What with that and him stood transfixed at the bus stop with that vacant look on his face, it took a while for me to nod off that night.

***

Mrs Booth answered the door and greeted me as she might a long-lost son.

'Hello, Arthur, come on in!'

Her smile couldn't have been any wider, those imperfect teeth smeared pink with lipstick. I was a little taken aback by the exaggerated generosity of her welcome, not to mention the physical closeness of her. She'd always been quite friendly, but her behaviour was bordering on the extreme.

'Hello, Mrs ... sorry, Kate. How are you?'

'Oh, how wonderful, Arthur, you remembered! Edgar said he'd mentioned it to you. It's lovely you should call me Kate. Feels so much more ... comfortable ... personal, even!'

With that, she grabbed and hugged me like a crazed wrestler – not the kind of conduct I was used to, not even from my own mother.

'You're part of the family now, you know, perhaps more than you think!'

'That'll do, dear! Put him down, you don't know where he's been!' Mr Booth's one-liner was probably older than he was.

'Alright, Arthur?'

'Yes, thanks, Edgar. Yourself?'

'Better for being less formal ... thanks for that, Arthur; it's nice to be taken notice of once in a while.'

He look accusingly at his wife. They giggled in perfect unison and I smiled along politely, wondering if they'd been at the bottle already. It was certainly unusual behaviour for the couple I'd come to know.

It was quite light for the time of day, so I knew what was coming when Mrs Booth prematurely closed the curtains. The table had been cleared, one of the four chairs purposely put to one side. Edgar Booth disappeared into the kitchen and returned moments later, looking like Scrooge at Christmas with a lit candle on a copper tray. He carefully nudged it to the centre of the table, its presence immediately bringing an eerie glow to set the scene.

'Do take a seat, Arthur, and we'll begin.'

At Kate's request, the three of us extended our arms and self-consciously reached for each other's hands. It was a classic arrangement, a touch of theatre to engender the mood. The couple's faces were transformed by the soft glow of the candle, their expressions stark and detached in its dancing light. I sensed I was experiencing the business end of the Booths' existence.

I was a little surprised when Kate came to the table. Then I thought of those coy little glances and innuendos, each barely distinguishable in isolation. She was slowly, perhaps even deliberately, revealing herself to be an active participant, as if choosing her time by design. It's sometimes said that those who observe are often best placed to judge. Had she been watching and assessing me? Was she more than the dutiful wife and perfect hostess she'd so far portrayed? As there had been no mention beforehand of her inclusion, I couldn't help thinking I was being manipulated in some way.

As if to dispel my uncertainty, Kate flashed me a feeble smile, waxen as it was in the candlelight. I smiled in return but purposely narrowed my eyes, a juvenile gesture to let her know I thought something wasn't quite right. There was no reaction whatsoever, her eyes remaining unwaveringly fixed upon me.

'Shall we?'

Edgar broke the spell and I became aware of their hands gripping mine all the tighter. He did not call out or utter any archaic invocations. He did not invite spirits to make themselves known. There were no mysterious raps on wood or whispers from the shadows. This was no William Webb – this was Edgar Booth, the consummate professional. I then became aware of the volume of his breathing. It was slowly increasing, not only louder but faster too. The seconds turned to minutes, then ...

The strangled resonance that emerged from Kate Booth's weirdly distorted mouth did not remotely belong to her. It had an aged timbre and was unmistakeably male in origin.

Who are you?

It is Edgar. His voice echoes as though from the depths of a tunnel. There is an extended silence before we hear the response, and when it comes, it is more than congested keening ... then ...

S... Sam!

The utterance is wheezy and strained.

Welcome, Sam, who do you seek?

The sound of fractured breathing is prolonged; it is reminiscent of the recordings.

Who is it that you seek, Sam?

Arthur!

The answer is swift and urgent. The abrupt utterance of my name causes me to flinch and shudder, but it does not completely take me by surprise.

Arthur is here. He is with us, Sam. What do you want of him?

The anticipation becomes insufferable.

Tell Fred … Mam here … not there … we are … together …

The words are disjointed. I hastily attempt to make sense of them. And when I do, my head grows taut. The hairs on my neck begin to prickle and I am shuddering more than I have ever shuddered.

Edgar turns his head towards me with silent purpose. There is a question in his expression. I understand what he is asking and I answer with a nod. He turns away and addresses his wife.

Sam, what more do you wish to say?

I observe Kate intently, fearful of what more is about to be revealed. I gape in horror as her mouth unlocks and her lips quiver uncontrollably. No words are forthcoming, only an appalling screech that comes from deep within her. Her head rocks and twists to a ghastly rhythm, her crooked mouth opens and shuts mechanically. It seems an eternity passes before she is calmed.

'Hold steady, Arthur, I sense we're not done yet.'

Mr Booth casts a warning glance in my direction. I've never before seen him as serious as he is at this moment. He looks worriedly at his wife. She is slumped forward, head bowed an inch from the tabletop. She appears lost in sleep, her breathing deep and regular.

Who is there?

There is nothing – silence save for the flicker of the candle.

Who is there ... I know there is someone ...

She is suddenly bolt upright. I catch the movement out of the corner of my eye and immediately turn my attention back to her. She is staring ahead as though petrified. It is barely her.

Who is there? Who is it that comes to us?

A friend ...

The voice is hard and guttural – the vernacular familiar. There is menace in the delivery.

Whose friend? Someone here, you mean?

Ah ... 'ere alright, all onyer!

The sneering cackle that follows is coarse and fearsome.

Please tell me your name ... friend.

More cackling, longer this time. I am once again reminded of the recordings.

Why, it's George, o' course

George?

The question is inordinately tentative.

Ah, George ... George Davy. Surely yer recognise me!

A feral howl instantly follows the harshly whispered words. The table is violently toppled and the candle's light cuts an arc in the gloom as it gutters and sails to the floor. The circle of hands is broken and infernal chaos comes to the darkened parlour.

With fists clenched, Kate maniacally thrashes at the indiscernible threat that besieges her. It is shocking and terrifying to witness her vehement distress.

I gasp with relief when Mr Booth goes to hold her, though she continues to flail and snarl even as he hugs her to him.

I stand shocked and immobile as she is calmed. And when she is once more of this world, I am deeply distressed by her pathetic sobbing and can only reflect on what I have witnessed. I remember my excitement at the beginning: the enticing desire to experience the weird and wonderful world I'd barely imagined existed beyond this one. A world of which I had no real concept.

No wonder they say be careful what you wish for.

Chapter 9
Nottingham 1966

It is my first wedding, and I meet more people than I have ever met in one place before. Ann introduces me as her boyfriend and shows off her eternity ring. We are in Heanor, only a few miles west of Nottingham, and I cannot believe how much their accent differs from my own. Ann's friend is nice and so is her smart new husband. There is talk of meeting up again, but I doubt we'll see much of them after today – I don't mix well. Still, Ann says she loves me for what I am, and not to worry.

The music is okay, beaty pop to get things moving. We dance and posture in the strobes, after a fashion. The flashing lights remind me of the candle – I imagine Kate's face iridescent in the throbbing glow of the orbs. I wince at the memory of her contortions.

I dance on amidst the jollity and wonder at the course of my other life.

The relief I felt at seeing Mrs Booth return to her prosaic self was somewhat short-lived. The ease and rapidity of her recovery served to highlight the enduring effect the disturbing experiences were having on me. If nothing else, my curiosity had been well and truly satiated, any doubts I had previously nurtured now summarily dismissed.

Normality was quickly resumed: the curtains hurriedly drawn back, the light snapped on and the candle retrieved from where it had landed, its solidifying residue earnestly scraped from the linoleum with determined enthusiasm.

Mr Booth set about pouring us a stiff whisky whilst his wife tutted and fussed as she righted the upturned furniture. Once everything was returned to its usual place, the three of us retired to the more comfortable front room, where we sat quietly together in the pink light of a table lamp, allowing the whisky to warm and calm us. Apart from us avoiding each other's eyes, it was as though little of note had occurred at all. It led me to wonder how many times the Booths might have endured such moments before.

'I know who Sam is.'

It was not like me to initiate a conversation, but I was impatient to clear my head of the worrisome thoughts that continued to torment my mind.

'Yes, I thought you might.'

Though Edgar had acknowledged me, he remained distant and reflective, as if not quite with us.

'Sam was my great-grandad. Grandad Fred sometimes talks about him. Apparently, Sam died of something called … emphysema. Chuffed cheap baccy on his pipe for too many years, according to Fred.'

Edgar gazed at the ceiling before commenting.

'Sam's wife's name – your great-grandmother – was Violet, I think, Arthur. And if my sense of him is correct, Sam sometimes joked that when he and Violet died, they would be separated for ever. He thought he'd be sent below whilst Violet floated up to heaven.'

I could only stare back in astonishment. How would he know Violet's name, never mind the quips Sam often teased her with? Just like Bob himself said, Edgar Booth really was psychic; there was no possible way he could have known such details.

'Anyway, Arthur, be assured they're together and at peace with their fate, though there seemed to be some concern for you that I couldn't quite fathom.'

Kate quietly sipped her whisky and continued to stare at the floor, nodding vacuously as she listened to her husband pragmatically revealing my late family members' personal particulars.

***

When I said goodbye to the Booths that night, I left pondering questions frustratingly unanswered. They'd been comfortable enough talking about Sam Campion's contribution to the séance, but not quite so keen to address the materialisation of George Davy. That it was the same George Davy that commandeered my voice during the regressions was a highly probable assumption, but did that necessarily mean he had been me in a previous existence?

I could only hope not! The man's incarnation, whether or not he really existed, came over as positively bestial. To my mind, his character bore absolutely no resemblance whatsoever to my current self. Even when I arrived home, my concerns refused to fade away, and so I thought to contact Bob the following morning to talk things over.

That night my sleep was troubled, ethereal visions of George Davy and Sam Campion violently competing for my attention, and I dreamt myself cringing in the darkness as they fought it out, dancing shadows and writhing shapes cast on the walls of The Postern Gate Inn.

'I've already been briefed about what happened last night, Arthur.'

Bob had been good enough to drive into town at short notice, agreeing to meet me in The Salutation for a drink after work. Even before we took our seats, I couldn't wait to tackle the Booths' reluctance to discuss the more worrying aspects of the previous night's séance. Bob was ready for me, though, stopping me in my tracks before I got into my stride.

'Arthur, hang on a minute. I can understand you being upset by last night's events. However, like it or not, you must appreciate that it was mainly for your sake the Booths chose not to discuss what happened without first thinking it over themselves. Edgar rang me late last night, sometime after you'd left for home. Evidently, he'd given matters some thought, and on the back of that, we decided that before we go any further, we need to track down this George Davy character, research his history, and see if anything matches our assumptions – if any such records exist, of course. If not, then we'll need to think again.'

'That's fair enough, Bob, but surely they could have said something to reassure me. I was in a bit of a state. You didn't see what I saw last night. Kate's condition was ...'

'How do you think they felt, Arthur? They were both completely and utterly worn out, by all accounts. Apparently, conducting these things can be physically as well as mentally exhausting. The stress levels must be off the scale on occasion. Quite apart from that, Edgar reckons they encountered something neither of them had directly experienced before.'

I stared at him expectantly, impatient to hear what I thought might be something of significance. He screwed his eyes and grimaced. It was a look he adopted when carefully choosing his words.

'I can tell you, Arthur, that during the séance, they both had an overwhelming feeling of being ... hunted down.'

'Hunted down?'

'Yes, those were the words Edgar used when we talked last night, although I must say he gave the impression of being quite calm. After all, he does have a lot of experience. He worries more so for others, understandably for Kate in particular. You may or may not know, but now and again she permits the spirits to exploit her mind and body much as they would their own. Of course, Edgar claims to summon them, mostly by conventional means, but occasionally, he employs Kate as a conduit, mainly for some of the more ... interesting manifestations. He says most of the sessions are fairly low key, even mundane at times. With respect, perhaps a little like the appearance of your ...'

'Great-grandfather, Sam.'

'Yes, Arthur, sorry, that came out a bit ruder than I intended. But then, occasionally, a spirit emerges that is more dominant ... malignant even.'

'George Davy.'

'Correct. Though they might have anticipated his appearance, they hadn't accounted for the forcefulness of his characteristics. The words Edgar used suggested the manifestation exuded an essence of pure evil – that it appeared with singular purpose. Hence their feelings of being hunted down.'

'That being said, Bob, they readjusted very quickly once it was over.'

'Yes, I take your point, but I think that's how they generally cope with such visitations. I also think, well, I know for a fact, they needed to stabilise the atmosphere because your welfare was at risk ...'

'At risk? What do you mean by that?'

I needed to understand what he was getting at. Even so, I feared the answer. I could see Bob was nervous about it too. He often played the sceptic, perhaps only because he thought he should, considering his day job. And sometimes he liked to think he was above it all – not as deeply involved as the rest of us.

'You see, Arthur, Edgar was not just concerned for his wife; he was concerned for you too, perhaps even for me, come to that, even though I was nowhere near the place at the time.'

'Why should he be concerned for us, Bob? After all, it's not like somebody physical is tracking us down.'

'Arthur, listening to what you and Edgar both said about last night's events, Kate's experience was physical enough to make a lasting impression on all three of you. So much so that, in my view, we should give some thought to leaving well alone for a while. Perhaps we've unwittingly disturbed something dreadful that's taken the chance to manifest itself with intent. By delving into the past, we might have aroused an entity that's only too keen to respond to our regressions and séances. I know you all think I'm overly cynical, but things have moved on a bit. And so maybe I'm seeing more in it than I expected at the outset. In this instance, it's belt and braces for me. I don't want any of us to take any unnecessary risks, no matter how unbelievable things might first appear. That makes me inclined to agree with Edgar when he said there's a chance we're being hunted by the very one we're looking to find.'

Chapter 10
Nottingham 1966

I am out of place here. People stare and make whispered comments. I am wearing precipitous Chelsea boots and the navy suit with a bum-freezer jacket I bought for the wedding – from Burton's on the corner of Friar Lane.

Removing my tie makes me feel a little more comfortable, but still, I am absurdly overdressed for The Railway Working Men's Club.

I catch sight of myself in the smoky mirror and regret combing my hair forward à la Beatles. Ann said she wanted to go to a club for a drink with friends from work. It was dress-up Saturday night, so I thought I would.

I'm just as uncomfortable in the company of this crowd as I am in the suit. I know Ann shares my embarrassment. So I fidget and fret and can't wait to leave.

Some tipsy lads in the corner are drinking poor man's Black Velvet and staring at me in a threatening manner. They are greasy bikers. They act tough and are eager to show off in front of the girls.

It seems everyone is after me – not just George Davy!

Totally out of character, it was me that instigated the showdown. I demanded a head-to-head. A get-together to make sense of what was happening and where we were going next. I was completely confused and not a little concerned by the recent lack of positive action.

My sleep was all over the place, my dreams dark and feverish. I woke each morning with feelings of anxiety. I began smoking again after a long lay-off and was drinking too heavily – very much to Ann's concerned disapproval. The reason for my changing state was obvious, and so I decided it was high time to force the issue and demand some facts – especially the ones I imagined were purposely being hidden from me.

I was somewhat surprised by my own assertiveness, but it appeared to do the trick as far as the others were concerned. I'd suggested we meet on neutral ground, not the Booths' house or Bob's place on this occasion. I said it needed to be somewhere new to freshen things up. In any case, while it might have sounded ridiculous, I thought when spirits were summoned in a certain place, they might well hang around for a while. Therefore, the Booths' house was not my first choice.

In the end, after a bit of chuntering, we agreed to meet at a church hall in West Bridgford, as Mrs Booth thought a pub or hotel bar might be a bit limiting if we wanted to talk freely. Clive, one of the lads at work, was in a band that used the hall for practice. His dad was caretaker there, so I asked if I might hire it for a couple of hours on the cheap. Clive came back and said if we bought his dad a drink, we could have the place as long as we wanted, as long as it was a Tuesday or a Thursday night.

Armed with the keys, I arrived early that Thursday evening to open up before the others arrived. The summer heat had taken a turn for the better – or for the worse, depending on who you talked to. The hall was cool enough, though. It boasted a fly-spotted ceiling with fluorescent lighting, a patchy lino floor and a little boxed stage with a tangle of loose wires to one side. Some old chairs and tables were stacked against a wall, so I unfolded four of the chairs and a long trestle and sat down to wait for the others.

They turned up together, Bob having picked up the Booths on the way. They entered somewhat warily, as though half expecting someone else might be there. It was interesting to see how their confidence was so easily dented once they were taken out of their respective comfort zones. I saw that as being some kind of justification for suggesting neutral ground, although I couldn't in all honesty claim to have thought of it in that way. I'd simply wanted to take charge of my own destiny for once, rather than sitting in a corner, only speaking when spoken to. However, once I saw them submissively bowing to my wishes, I felt a bit discomfited by my earlier insistence.

'Sorry to drag you all the way here, but I thought it might help to see things in a fresh light, so to speak.'

It was Kate Booth who broke the ice, immediately dispelling any negative thoughts my idea might have provoked.

'Oh, don't worry, Arthur. I think it's a good idea. It's about time we had a change of scene.

That last episode took a lot out of us in one way or another. And if you don't mind my saying, you need to assert yourself a bit more. Now then, let's hear what you've got to say.'

True to form, she followed her little speech by uncovering the goodies in her cane basket: a flask of tea, some small sausage rolls, unseasonable mince pies, paper plates and plastic cutlery. Mrs Booth had brought her parlour to the hall and seemed content with the normality it immediately created. Not for the first time, I thought the woman was quite extraordinary – and in so many different ways.

'Okay, then ... well, I don't really know where to start. So maybe I'll begin by telling you how I feel at this minute.'

It all came out in a rush – anxiety, lack of sleep, nightmares, smoking and drinking – how I'd gone from being an ordinary lad with a casual interest in the supernatural to witnessing something resembling the set of a horror film – how I thought the rest of the group were keeping things from me, knew things they thought I was too young or naïve to share – me not truly understanding the difference between regression and séance – me still unsure exactly why I'd become involved in the first place.

I rambled on about the Booths' coolness towards my new relationship, then the recent and unexpected reversal of their attitude to Ann's presence in my life. Most of all, though, I wanted to fit a few pieces into the jigsaw – not just the easy ones, but the pieces I imagined they were keeping behind their backs.

If I expected an immediate response – most likely from Edgar Booth – I was mistaken and completely taken by surprise by the uncomfortable silence that followed my outburst. They were intermittently contemplating their feet, the ceiling or the dozy fly that lazily circled the winking fluorescent. Somewhat unpredictably, it was Bob who finally took the initiative.

'Yes, you're right, Arthur. In our different ways, we've made a bit of a pig's ear of it, I think!'

Was that a wry look of accusation he briefly flashed in Edgar Booth's direction?

'We should have been clearer with you from the start; you've made that painfully obvious. But the fact of the matter is, we are where we are, and we can only start again ... perhaps from the beginning, hey, Edgar?'

I looked to Edgar for a response, as did the other two. He was squarely in the frame and knew it. I guessed he'd been playing a mischievous game of chess, manipulating the board – the grand master of the spirit world, perhaps the only one to truly comprehended the actuality of what we'd become involved with. The tide had turned, though, and in some way the game had begun to manipulate him – the rest of us too, come to that. Even with his psychic know-how, he hadn't completely foreseen the startling turn events had taken.

Edgar suddenly looked his age, his dour countenance giving form to the weight of his unpredicted dilemma. All of a sudden, the hearty good-fellow façade was crumbling in the face of some worrisome activity.

'It had to happen someday, I suppose. Deep down, I always knew it would. To summon spirits, to enter the hazardous realm that remains an intricate and disordered labyrinth, is to risk attracting darker souls: those lurking presences. I should have been more wary of their intrusion. In my arrogance, I became neglectful.'

Ever loving and unreservedly loyal, Kate Booth moved closer to her husband, put her hand on his arm, and patted it gently. As much as I admired her inner strength and kind-heartedness, I couldn't help thinking she was complicit in his trickeries, as innocently intended as they may once have been. I wanted to believe that neither of them meant any harm, that they had become so used to living part of their lives in another world that their perception of everyday life had become unintentionally distorted. Nevertheless, the consequences of their actions needed to be addressed and put to rights for all our sakes.

'There's no mileage in pointing fingers, Edgar. What's happened has happened. We need to apply some hard reality to the situation. I think that should start with you and Kate explaining to Arthur how all this first came about: in particular, the reasons for implicating him.'

I sensed a shift in the order of things. Bob had grabbed his moment. Had he also tired of their mischievous games? Had he himself been cleverly lured into their little project, much the same as I had? The Booths looked at each other somewhat sheepishly, like guileless children, remorseful at being found out. It was difficult not to find their current demeanour emotive, seeing the two of them locked so tightly together as though to comfort and protect one another. The ordinarily effervescent Kate was welling up and struggling to hold back her tears.

'Please ... there's good reason for Kate's emotion, and it has little bearing on the matter in hand. Though, telling the tale of it would not change much at this particular time.'

Edgar's tone wavered as his own sentiment caught in his throat. Were it not for the poignancy of his words, I feel sure I would have berated him for yet another display of untimely ambiguity – yet another red herring – but there was something about his disposition telling me it was more than verbal trickery on this occasion. I glanced at Bob and caught the slightest shake of his head. He clearly thought much the same.

'Okay then, Edgar, if it's personal, let's leave it there. Tell you what, why don't I have a walk to the off-licence down the road and get a bottle before we go any further?'

Bob's softly spoken words said a lot about him. He'd recognised something was deeply affecting the Booths and was allowing them time to compose themselves. I'd grown to know Bob quite well, and not for the first time, I thought there was a lot more to his nature than first met the eye.

After he left, the mood, though amenable enough, was distinctly uncomfortable. So I walked outside for a smoke rather than enter into strained conversation. For whatever reason, the Booths were momentarily at a low ebb. I thought to give them some time alone together, hoping it might ease their anxiety – my own too, for that matter.

The air outside was humid, clouds of gnats swarming erratically in the retreating light of evening. We were in suburbia. All along the street, windows had been unfastened to ease the heat of the coming night, the muted resonance of domesticity drifting from their openings.

I heard the creak of a protesting door hinge and flinched at the touch on my shoulder.

'Sorry, Arthur, didn't mean to make you jump.'

'It's okay, Edgar, just nervy I suppose, what with everything that's happening,'

'Didn't realise you smoked.'

'It's on and off with me ... more on than off at the minute.'

'Whilst we're alone, there's something I wanted to say to you, Arthur.'

I took a deep drag and forcibly expelled a stream of noxious smoke into the cluster of swarming gnats, watching them briefly disperse before gathering again in obstinate defiance.

'I just wanted to say that we ... Kate and me

… have come to think quite a lot of you, Arthur. I want you to understand how disappointed we are – saddened that matters have not followed the course we thought they would. We openly admit it was rude and churlish of us to greet Ann as coldly as we did. You see we were rather resentful of the fact that your attention was being taken from something so dear to us. After recognising how unreasonable and selfish we had been, we thought to make amends. Well, we tried a bit too hard, didn't we? We practically overpowered you with our show of excessive affection.'

He was blurting it out quickly, as though desperate to be over and done with it. I sensed his agitation and embarrassment and couldn't help but feel sorry for him.

'It's okay, Edgar. All of us get things wrong at times. You've made the effort to put it right and thanks for that. Ann's a lot tougher than you might think, so to some extent, it was water off a duck's back. She's not one to bear grudges either. I'm sure we can draw a line under it and start over again.'

'Thanks, Arthur, that's very …'

Before he could say any more, the clink of glass on glass heralded Bob's return. He appeared from behind a row of parked cars gripping a carrier bag, grinning when he saw us together.

Those few words had cleared the air a little, but not enough to completely cool the coming night.

A little over two hours later, I looked at my watch – just after ten when we called it a day. It had been good to see the cloud over the Booths drifting away, only the slightest residue of negativity persisting in the nervous glances they shared from time to time. We had thrashed a few things out by the end of the evening, but the jigsaw remained incomplete, though at least we had a semblance of a picture. It had taken a glass or two of wine and some gentle persuasion before the complexity of what I'd become involved in slowly began to unravel.

Edgar Booth reaffirmed that his regressions had placed him in the parish of St Mary, though his name in that past life had yet to be revealed. George Davy hadn't been so reticent to break cover. In fact, he'd not only forced his way into our regressions, he'd alarmingly intruded on our contemporary lives – as vividly demonstrated during the séance at the Booths' house.

For some time, I'd suspected this George Davy character was believed by the others to be me, although I found it somewhat harder to believe they thought I'd not yet fully caught on to that particular idea. I stated that whilst it might be a convenient theory, it was not necessarily the case, suggesting there might have been a crossover somewhere along the way. All three of them looked baffled by that proposition, obviously adamant no one but me could possibly be the embodiment of the ghastly villain.

Edgar went on to reveal that he had completed a total of three sessions, during which he became familiar with the nature of the various souls he came across whilst under hypnosis. However, the only actual name extracted from our combined sessions was that of George Davy. Having listened to the resultant tapes, he thought some of the other incarnations appeared distressed when in Davy's company, quickly ceding ground to his presence on those occasions.

He went on to say he sensed that in his previous existence, he was close to George Davy in some way, even though he distinguished the evil that dwelt within him. He said it was something he was desperately trying to understand and one of his reasons for seeking Davy's current embodiment – namely me, Arthur Campion, or so he thought.

Obviously, Edgar was totally obsessed with his investigations and had thought that if he could find me and persuade me to be regressed, it might answer some, if not all, of his questions. He'd searched the length and breadth of Nottingham, totally convinced he was fated to find me sooner or later – ambiguously maintaining there were other energies he'd employed in his quest.

Edgar believed Kate to be his eternal soulmate, and that they were, together, in some way immortally involved with Bob and myself, though perhaps in differing manifestations. That led him to restate his conviction that there were not many examples of interrelated souls recurring within the same parameters of time and location. He told us he'd asked himself over and over again if the four of us were fated to gather at predetermined points in time, until we each, in our due turns, crossed into everlasting oblivion.

As a final point, Edgar addressed the ongoing question concerning George Davy, wondering why he'd chosen to intrude on our collective lives. It was something we'd yet to answer: a continuing mystery that further research might one day uncover.

What Edgar Booth revealed that evening went some way towards satisfying my curiosity, if not completely my peace of mind. And from the faltering tone of his last few words, I suspected he had little more of note to say for the time being. So I thought I would change course by referring to my so-called spirit guide, if indeed she actually existed. If she did, was she in some way involved in our activities?

I could see he was slightly irritated by my cynicism, and just for a moment, I was reminded of the pleasantly devious character I had first come to know. In typical fashion, he went on to say that she most certainly did exist and that I should be extremely grateful she did. He said he'd noticed her a couple of times since that first occasion, once through the window of the bus that night in Sherwood. He said he saw her sitting next to me as the bus moved away. And then, of course, the moment during the last knockings of the séance. He said when he'd glanced in my direction, she was stood there in front of me, as though to shield me from those terrible occurrences. He mentioned her expression had been one of intense condemnation, adding that he'd been disturbed by her chilling disapproval. He then hurried to close the matter, evasively stating he thought there was more going on behind the scenes that he'd yet to fathom.

The unanticipated talk of spirit guides had drawn anxious and bewildered glances from Bob's direction, though as ever, Kate chose to maintain a dignified and knowing silence.

Then, once the conversation had died away, we came to say our goodbyes, and I thought the atmosphere had lightened. I was thankful for that at least. No doubt the wine had soothed our tensions. Even so, I think there were those who felt better for clearing the air.

Afterwards, I felt encouraged and more inclined to carry on with the project. There was a deal of serious research to be done, and the thought of involving myself began to appeal. The more detail we could find out about the era we were supposed to have lived through, the clearer the overall picture might become. Most of all, we needed to pin down George Davy. An understanding of the life he had lived might help us figure out his intentions, be they real or figments of our shared delusion.

Chapter 11
Nottingham 1966

The streets are slick with unceasing rain, layers of sorry leaves pasted flat to the slabs. The warmth of late summer turns – memories of endless days fading in the quickening of autumn.

I leave the atmosphere of The County Tavern and stand to regard the grim façade that stands opposite me. There is an irony to my endeavour – working mere yards from the dour edifice I study, never before pausing to consider that place of justice, imprisonment and adjudicated death. Only now do I consider my other life to be in some way connected to the building and its corrective consequences.

I have grown fond of The County Tavern: its ale, its dart board and not least its characterful landlord. Ann and me occasionally snuggle in a quiet corner of an evening, eating salty ham cobs. We sip our drinks sparingly to make them last.

I was beginning to wish I'd never asked. I was out of pocket by the price of three pints of best bitter – two for him and one for me. And all for a bundle of generalisation monotonously recited in histrionic fashion by the dog-eared eccentric contentedly drinking on my money.

I'd met Aubrey earlier. He'd been half-heartedly sweeping away autumn's clutter when I walked up and casually asked if he knew of anybody I could speak to regarding court records. He said, 'You'll be effing lucky, as them snooty boggers in there's no time for idle gossip with Joe Public.'

'In there' was the Shire Hall, and maybe the answers to some of my questions. I quickly got the gist of his working-class attitude and began to make the right noises. All of a sudden we were Nottingham lads together and united, definitely not the sort who went to work 'ponced up an' knowin' nowt abart 'ote woth knowin'!'

Aubrey said he'd tell me everything about the place if I'd stand him a pint over the road later on – about six-ish, he said. And so there we were, Aubrey holding court much like an erudite professor might. His deafening stridency had drawn the attention of a few drinkers in the public bar, including two larger-than-life American tourists eagerly hitching onto his reverberating oratory. The occasional 'Gee, ya don't say!' only served to encourage Aubrey even more. It began to feel like I was funding a public lecture rather than learning anything about what I really wanted to know. However, anything involving the parish of St Mary was of particular interest to me of late. And despite my reservations, I couldn't help but admire Aubrey's cache of knowledge regarding the ancient place of justice, which had its roots in the fifteenth century.

I learned that the Shire Hall in its present incarnation had been built around 1770, since then serving as a courtroom, gaol and police station, where offenders were arrested, sentenced and executed as the law demanded. My ears pricked up at that, and a shudder ran through me when Aubrey began to recount the dreadful happenings that had occurred only strides away from where we were standing.

'Ah'm tellin yer ... used to 'ang 'em in public ... hover the road ... ah ... right hover there it wore!'

'Gee, ya don't say!'

He went on to explain that the last public hanging in Nottingham had taken place behind a makeshift wooden barrier, just across the way – saying a raucous crowd began to gather the night before, stretching from the church gates down to the police station, so popular were such events.

'1864 ... chap named Parker ... the Fiskerton murderer ...' Aubrey went on to tell terrible tales of life within the prison walls – of two, four and six legged vermin – the lingering stink of urine and excreta – the lethal whippings and the torturous treadmill. I listened with growing disquiet, certain that Aubrey would mention the one name I feared to hear. In the meantime, there were other names from the era, names that slipped off his tongue as easily as well-remembered verse – the murderous John Brooks and Joseph Tucker, the patricidal Henry Westby and many others – yet still no mention of the one that had come to haunt my thoughts.

I really needed to be certain, so when Aubrey was done and looking expectantly at his empty glass, I asked the question I most needed an answer to.

'You seem to know all the villains' names, Aubrey – how come?'

'It's me hobby, me duck. Ah like reading the records, see ... when I'm fettling the storerooms an' that ... loads a bleddy names an' pictures hover there if yer know where to look. I've gorra a good memory, allus have had.'

'What about George Davy ... know that name, by any chance?'

He took it as a challenge, eyeing me suspiciously as he scanned the annals of his memory.

'No, can't say ah do, me duck. Looking for an owd relative or summat, are yer?

'Sort of, yeah.'

I didn't really know if I was relieved or disappointed. It had seemed a good idea to investigate the Shire Hall, given the kind of man George Davy was beginning to resemble. Quizzing Aubrey outside its entrance had seemed a bright idea at the time, but I was not convinced he knew as much about the history of his employer as I had first thought he did. As I left the County Tavern, with Aubrey looking dejectedly at an empty glass, I knew I'd not quite done with that place of justice just yet.

***

I was even walking differently, striding with purpose, head held high instead of self-consciously studying my shoes as was previously my wont. At least this crazy business was having a positive effect on my personality. My confidence was growing by the day and it was being noticed, if the remarks at work and backhanded comments from my family were anything to go by.

Ann noticed it too, perhaps more than any other. She reckoned I was quite different from the shy lad she'd met at The Palais, even saying I was proper mannish now. I wasn't altogether sure about her meaning and had to wonder if she thought my new sophistication a good thing or not.

Those notions were in my head for a few days, but then the next time we met, it was like it had always been. Then again, I took it as a warning not to take her for granted – she was everything to me, was Ann, and I was determined not to get too big for my boots.

I entered the municipal building and followed the painted signs to the section dealing with city archives. Bob Langham knew how the system worked. In principle, only bona fide academics or students were allowed to access census records. Bob reckoned he qualified as both, him being an ex-student and a registered psychologist.

The dainty woman attending the archives that day was deep in whispered conversation with a horn-rimmed student type, his pimply features emerging from a sloppy rollneck jumper two sizes too big for him. The archivist was doing most of the talking. She was draped in a baggy cardigan, her sparrow legs wrapped in laddered stockings. The mesmeric pecking motion that accompanied her speech only served to accentuate her bird-like appearance.

I waited patiently until the student briefly waved his thanks and sauntered towards a door marked *Reading Room.* Meanwhile, the archivist pecked her way towards me, presenting a questioning look and a hitched lip.

'Can I help you?'

Her expression clearly implied the opposite, and that in her estimation I could not have looked less like a student, never mind an academic of any recognisable classification.

'Hello there, my name's Arthur Campion. You should have my name written down somewhere? Dr Langham rang only yesterday to say I was coming to research some records on his behalf.'

I was proud of myself. I hadn't faltered once. My tone had remained seamlessly polite yet assertive throughout – not a performance the old Arthur might have carried off so easily. There was a momentary flicker of doubt and she stood her ground, continuing to assess me whilst mentally processing my claim. Looking me up and down for a second time, she hitched her lip a tad higher as if to further signify her distaste.

Ann said I looked handsome and dapper in my new grey suit with its black velvet collar, though Grandma reckoned I looked like 'one a them teddy-boy types'. I failed to understand her thinking because I'd recently abandoned my outmoded fifties regalia. With Ann's assistance, I was more or less up to date, what with the bum-freezer jacket and the chisel toes. Still, I suppose I must have looked a bit out of place in the academic environment.

'One moment.'

Her words were strained and barely audible, and I simply nodded in return, watching her make a meal out of sifting through the pile of papers and files that lay on the desk before her. In due course, she extricated a black leather diary stained with multiple cup rings. After leafing through the pages with dampened fingers, she sighed disapprovingly when she located the entry she was hoping not to find, her thin lips moving slightly as she whispered the words to herself.

'Your name again?'

'Campion – on behalf of Dr Langham!'

I couldn't resist incorporating a trace of irritation, and it served its purpose.

'Yes ... of course ... you said.'

After more unnecessary fussing, 'Mrs Bird' led me to the reading room, grudgingly inviting me to sit at one of the vacant desks, just across from the pimply student in the rollneck.

'1841 census records for the parish of St Mary ... was it not?

'Yes, thank you ... to start with ...'

She shot me a look more vulture than sparrow before disdainfully pecking away to look for what I had asked for.

Two eye-straining hours later, my mind was a melting pot of people and locations, some vaguely familiar, some definitely not. I had kept one eye open for Always Yard, Milk Square and The Postern Gate – specific locations mentioned in the regressions, though I queried why we needed the records of The Postern Gate, thinking the only ones listed would be the landlord or landlady and their residents. However, to answer that question, Bob insisted the census records were collected differently in the early days; individuals present at a premises at the time of the census would be recorded regardless of their actual abode, even drinkers, visiting tradesmen and the like.

Of course, the principal detail I was looking for was *his* name ... and then there it was, another hour or so later – deep in the printed volume for 1891 – George Davy, no less.

Quite why my hand began to tremble when I came to record his particulars, I couldn't be sure. It felt for all the world that the temperature in the reading room had dropped from what it had been. And there was that ephemeral sensation again, as though someone or something were at my shoulder, observing my activities.

Chapter 12
Nottingham 1966

Now there are two rings on Ann's finger and one on mine. Her second ring comes with a presentiment of finality. We have not set a date yet, but sooner or later we are to be wed. It feels good – there is a future to my existence.

The party is going well; Ann's mother is the life and soul. I have come to know her and her history – the absent husband and the hard life. She is a good woman, though – a cheery woman for all that. It seems Grandma is not so sure – no words as such – glances and telling sniffs.

The sandwiches and fairy cakes are crumbs, the teapot has cooled – so comes the beer and the liquor. A mismatch of cloudy glasses are raised to Ann and me.

I am happy and content in the moment, for once enjoying the attention.

Tomorrow, when I meet the others, I hope to bask in the glow of a different light when I take centre stage in that other business.

I'd purposely asked for the meeting to be at the Booths' house, thinking it might help dispel the lingering apprehension whenever I thought of the last time I'd been there. We had not seen each other for a while – Bob being really busy, the Booths keeping a low profile and taking themselves to Torquay for an unseasonal break by the sea. It was as though they were giving me the opportunity to shine on my own – perhaps recognising my evolving maturity and attendant sophistication – asking me to research the clues arising from the regressions.

The pink-faced Booths looked well, though pale-faced Bob looked haggard and twitchy, as though impatient to return to his work: perhaps the very thing that was wearing him out. I attempted to engage him in conversation whilst Kate laid out snacks and poured the tea. However, Bob was distant and unresponsive to the point of rudeness, so I gave it up and left him to himself. I caught Edgar observing the brief exchange with furrowed brow and a questioning look. I'd arrived sometime after Bob and wondered if he'd been similarly frosty with the couple. Undeterred, I leafed through the file I'd diligently compiled and waited until I had their full attention.

'Well, you gave me the responsibility of researching the limited information we had to hand, and I'm pleased to report that some interesting facts have surfaced as a result.'

I glanced up to see the Booths were all ears – Bob looking predictably vacant and disinterested. I was beginning to get fed up with his attitude. It was so unlike him and somewhat distracting. Having had a break from each other, I had expected us to resume our activity with renewed enthusiasm.

'Is there something wrong, Bob?'

My abruptness grabbed everyone's attention. Addressing the elephant in the room was clearly unexpected. Bob's mouth dropped open, his expression wavering between surprise and desperation.

'I'm really sorry ...'

He looked to be in a highly emotional state, close to breaking down, perhaps. Kate sensed it too, and went over to him.

'Whatever's the matter, Bob? What's wrong, dear? Edgar, fetch some brandy.'

Bob gave every indication he was about to cry, but the tears never came. It took a few moments and a stiff drink before he was able to speak. When he did, his lips quivered and his words were fractured.

'It's a combination of things. I've had an unusually heavy workload, it's always busy this time of year – winter, you see – dark nights sometimes auger depression. I must admit I've had some particularly difficult patients of late, difficult and time-consuming.'

He took another gulp of brandy before continuing, and I began to wonder about him driving home.

'That's not all of it, though ... in isolation, those things don't usually get me down so much. It's more those ... bloody awful nightmares!'

'What sort of nightmares, Bob?'

Edgar leaned forward in his seat, head to one side – the disposition of a man who knew the answer before he asked the question.

'Apparitions, Edgar, half-awake imaginings, if you like. That's the only way I can describe them, or indeed, come to terms with them. They're certainly not nightmares as I understand them, they're...'

'Go on.'

'I generally nod off in the early hours – usually takes me a while to settle. Then, just as often, I wake thinking it's morning, even though there's no light from the window. When I look at the time, only an hour or so has passed. I can never be sure if I've been to sleep or if I've experienced that moment I just mentioned.'

Bob sighed to himself; it was almost a sob. We waited for him to continue, and I was fidgeting terribly, thinking the Booths infinitely more patient than I could ever be.

'It's then it tends to happen ... somewhere in a corner of my bedroom ... a rough outline. It's definitely a male form ... like a faded drawing blending into the shadows ...'

We heard his voice cracking again. Kate rubbed his shoulder, uttering expressions of reassurance.

'It doesn't happen every night, thank God, maybe once or twice a week, but the expectation of it is just as awful!'

'Just how real does it seem, Bob? You mentioned the sketchy nature of its appearance. Maybe that suggests it might be your imagination, and not ...'

It was the closest I ever saw Bob surrender to unadulterated anger, and there was a keen edge to his response.

'It's bloody well real enough to me, Arthur!'

As soon as he said that, he reddened, throwing me a look of anguished apology. It was typical of him, and I regretted questioning the authenticity of his claims.

‘Sorry, Arthur … I didn’t mean to …’

‘It’s okay, Bob. Sometimes I experience peculiar things. Maybe not as bad as what you’re experiencing, but occasionally, I get a sense of someone … somewhere … it’s really difficult to explain.’

‘I think we should leave it there and take a break. I need to think this through before it gets out of hand.’ Edgar stunned us with his sudden assertiveness. It had been some while since he’d taken the lead.

‘Would you mind topping up the glasses, Kate? Make sure they’re generous measures. Bob, dear chap, I insist on you staying the night, so forget about driving home. I suggest you have another drink or two and relax instead. You can travel back in the morning after breakfast.’

Bob gratefully nodded his thanks, but with some bemusement. Edgar turned to me then, his expression softening into a smile.

‘Sorry, Arthur, we’ve rather stolen your thunder. I promise we’ll hear from you in due course. First, though, in light of what Bob’s just revealed, I think it a good time for me to say something I should have said a lot earlier.’

I looked to see how Bob was reacting and thought he looked slightly more at peace. Perhaps Edgar’s timely intervention had alleviated his tension. Like most people under extreme pressure, Bob was benefitting from someone else accepting the burden of responsibility, if only in the short term. And so with our glasses replenished, we settled in the glow of the fire and allowed the brandy to calm our mood.

'The fact is, my friends, I believe we're being targeted.'

Kate Booth sat by her husband's side, adopting that knowing expression she employed at such times.

'What I'm about to say doesn't allow for the worrying encounters Bob just told us about, though we can't dismiss the possibility. I had not expected your experiences, Bob ... coincidence strikes yet again. You see, I believe we've inadvertently summoned a malignant spirit, and so I think we should expect to suffer its intrusion again. I must admit, the most likely cause of its appearance might well have stemmed from the night of the séance. We might have unintentionally opened a door to something already waiting to enter. There's also a chance we've encouraged its incursion through our hypnotic regressions. Then again, the occurrences could be attributed to a combination of both exploratory avenues, indeed supporting my personal belief that regressions and séances are of a similar culture.'

He couldn't resist scoring a point, playfully raising his eyebrows at Bob, who had frequently argued against that particular contention.

'Anyway, we simply can't have this malicious soul running amok without attempting to check its mischief. This sort of spirit feeds on fear and negativity, and indeed, in our belief in them. They can inhabit our minds. They don't always take solid form, though they're more likely to appear to someone like me. That's a fact I can assure you of ... because I've actually seen him.'

Edgar's disclosure came like a hammer blow, causing me to recoil from the consequences of what he was saying. It was obvious Kate Booth was already privy to her husband's disconcerting revelation. The calmness of her demeanour made me question the possibility that she too might have caught sight of her attacker during that fateful séance.

I could only wonder what Bob was thinking. Suspicion is one thing, confirmation quite another. The look of unadulterated shock on his face more than reflected his feelings. If I'd experienced what he'd experienced, I'd be even more concerned for my safety, perhaps even my sanity.

I began to think I wanted to be out of there and done with it. A normal and uncomplicated existence with Ann suddenly looked extremely enticing.

'Let's not get carried away, chaps; we can nullify the influence of this impish nuisance. You might think a séance entirely the wrong thing to undertake at this particular juncture, but trust me, I'm confident I can find the means to banish this spirit from our earthly sphere!'

Edgar's informal suggestion that we should arrange another séance left Bob and me open-mouthed. Could he be serious?

'Are you actually suggesting we purposely invite this thing into our lives, Edgar?'

Bob nodded vigorously in support of me, clearly horrified by the thought of deliberately facing the very thing that might well be haunting him.

Edgar was not to be deterred. 'It's more likely you wouldn't see a physical presence. I might see it again, but I'd be surprised if anyone else did. When all's said and done, we can't be entirely sure Bob's experiences are anything more than waking nightmares – awful dreams activated by the subject matter he's exposed to on a professional basis.'

'Then you might like to hark back to Kate's recent encounter, Edgar!'

I was aware of the sarcasm in my response, but he'd anticipated me.

'Kate didn't physically see the spirit, Arthur. In fact, she rarely does. On most occasions, she adopts the role of intermediary. More often than not, Kate experiences visitations without anything untoward occurring, though two bad incidents in a row is of some concern. Even so, given how many séances Kate has been involved in over the years, such extremes are a rarity.'

I shook my head and wondered what on earth I'd got into. I simply couldn't believe we were having that conversation. Only a few feet away was the very room where a malignant apparition had entered our world to aggressively violate an innocent woman. I felt sorry for Kate, even more so for Bob. He'd not even been present at the séance. Yet something – possibly the same unwanted intruder – had incomprehensibly found a way to attach itself to him. How that made him feel about purposely summoning the likely source of his torment could only be guessed at.

The argument persisted – opinions and views served and returned as though contesting a tournament – Edgar Booth reaching match point on a number of occasions before finally winning the day.

'It's the only way, I tell you. Otherwise there's a chance this spirit might haunt one or more of us forever. Is that really what any of us wants?'

'It's got to be George Davy, hasn't it?'

My question hung in the air for a moment, causing Kate Booth to surface from her inertia.

'Yes, I reckon it has, Arthur, and the sooner we deal with him, the better. As Edgar quite rightly says, if we don't face up to him now, he'll literately come back to haunt us again and again ... maybe somewhat stronger than before.'

The best we could do at that juncture was to agree to think about it. I simply said I'd let them know, Bob saying he'd sleep on it, though I had the feeling he'd already made up his mind. He was so agitated about his nocturnal experiences, he might just clutch the tenuous straw Edgar was extending. In comparison with what we had discussed earlier that evening, the information I had recently researched now seemed of lesser consequence, and so I made ready to leave, returning the file of papers to my knapsack before reaching for my coat.

'Hold on, Arthur, the night's still young. Providing Bob's okay with it, we should hear what you've found out.'

There was that part of me that felt like telling Edgar where to go and what to do with himself. Instead, I tamely retrieved my folder and made ready to tell them about my research.

1891 found a certain George Davy, aged 48, lodging in rented property on Woolpack Lane in the parish of St Mary. The census recorded a mix of inhabitants at the same address, including a theatrical contortionist and a bird preserver. The record stated that George Davy was a hawker by trade – hawkers generally being street merchants often of questionable repute, including, amongst others, tinkers, pedlars and rag-and-bone merchants.

National Census records were first compiled in 1841 and every ten years since then. However, I'd failed to find any mention whatsoever of George Davy before the entry of 1891. Assuming Always Yard was in the vicinity of Pilcher Gate – somewhere near the heart of the Lace Market – it would have been a short walk from Woolpack Lane, the very lodgings where George Davy was recorded as living in 1891.

It turned out that Milk Square was further

afield. I sensed that location was of little importance in the scheme of things – perhaps, for some convoluted reason, a location where Edgar Booth's regressive journey simply intersected with that of his previous self. Nevertheless, for completeness, I scanned the records from 1841 to '91 and noted names associated with the places mentioned in the regressions. From the information to hand, I produced a compilation of names and locations, hoping something might eventually fit into the puzzle we were piecing together.

'So, unless there was more than one George Davy – given that Arthur has found no other to date – we can reasonably place him in the area our regressions are common to. And the remaining information Arthur has turned up might be useful in terms of further research ...'

Edgar paused, allowing his words to trail away, studying each of us in turn without saying anything more. Bob appeared to be distracted by other matters, and with me having nothing more to say, my attention was drifting. For her part, Kate sat with her head down, looking completely ill at ease with the demoralised mood of our company.

'Hmm, it seems we might well have reached a crossroads ...'

He paused again, as though waiting for someone to respond to his despondency.

Bob momentarily escaped his stupor to feign an expression of interest, causing me to react in similar vein. Then, thinking he'd regained our attention, Edgar inevitably continued.

'It strikes me our collaboration is becoming frayed around the edges. With that in mind, I'm thinking we should consider something infinitely more important than holding a séance. Given everyone's mood, I propose we seriously contemplate the continuance of our activities. In short, I think each of us should here and now declare our interests. Sad to say, it's pointless carrying on without cooperative purpose – more importantly, without good heart!'

Edgar Booth had drawn a line in the sand, and the time had come to stay or go.

Chapter 13
Nottingham 1966

Halloween. The white of frost glitters off rooftops and dustbin lids. Through a thin mist, children emerge in tricksy outfits. For a moment they portray the evil elements I feel I am edging ever closer to. They are unknowing, though. To them it is a game, a charade – what then is it to me?

November looms. The outfits will be discarded. Soon they will scream their delight at soaring rockets and spinning wheels, bangs and bursts of coloured sparks.

Where will this have taken me by then?

They are stacking a bonfire in the park. Ann is making sticky toffee and there will be hot potatoes. The solstice steals ever closer. And then soon it will be Christmas again.

How we treasure our ancient rituals.

Our replies weren't emphatic. In fact, they were rather weak and pathetic, both carrying more than a hint of 'maybe' in their delivery. The Booths were far too perceptive to miss the fainthearted intimation, and they pounced like twin tigers upon us.

'So, exactly what are you saying, then?'

'We don't want the association to end, but neither of us are overly keen to attend a séance … at least not just yet.'

It was difficult to gauge the fusion of triumph and relief in Edgar Booth's eyes. He'd risked a game of brinkmanship, and it had sort of paid off.

Bob slept at their house as suggested and, by his own admission, benefitted from a night of uninterrupted sleep. The following day being Saturday, he and I arranged to meet in town for coffee. I'd lately become a selective coffee drinker, affectedly thinking it might augment my growing sophistication. We arrived at The Kardomah on King Street within minutes of each other, ordering our drinks before grabbing stools by the window.

'What d'you think, Arthur?'

He looked better for the rest and seemed more like his usual self.

'Well, I don't think I'm up for another séance. I don't know about you, but I'm still having bloody nightmares about the last one.'

Me and my big mouth – mentioning nightmares after what Bob had revealed to us was a bit thoughtless, to say the least. He looked up swiftly but casually shrugged the comment away.

'Sorry, Bob, didn't think ...'

'That's alright, Arthur, I know you mean well. Let it pass; it's only something for me to deal with ... problems within problems.'

He was a complex man, was Bob. Having got to know him, I thought that under that academic certitude lived an insecure being, yet another lost soul craving the security of close relationships, rather more than his professional façade would suggest.

'Having said that, I don't think either of us

really wants to break the circle ... do we, Bob?'

He smiled at that, nodding in agreement at what he'd wanted to hear.

'Not much gets past you, does it, Arthur? You're right; quite apart from the time and energy we've invested, I think I'd miss the company ... and the friendship.'

'Thing is, Bob, despite everything, I reckon we all have each other's wellbeing in mind – even Edgar's!'

Bob sniggered, giving me an old-fashioned look.

'I know you're joking. Neither of us would've taken matters this far without acknowledging his authenticity. I also believe he's genuinely concerned for our welfare. Edgar's what I'd call a likeable rogue, not dishonest exactly, but somewhat of a ...'

'Slippery bogger!'

We both laughed at that and sipped our coffees out of designer glasses, very Bohemian and cultured. In those moments, we talked ourselves into it, admitting we'd like to continue with the project. After all, it was our lives – past and present – that we were investing in. At the end of the day, we each shared a common and powerful enticement, and, if nothing else, unadulterated curiosity.

***

Bob was looking more at ease than he had been and was speaking with a good deal more assurance.

'Edgar, as far as the supernatural's concerned, I'll eternally be a Doubting Thomas, even considering my nocturnal experiences, disturbing as they might be. Anyway, to reiterate, I'm inclined to hedge my bets and oppose the idea of holding a séance. I believe Arthur has a proposal that offers some middle ground.'

Bob turned and looked at me with contrived expectancy.

We'd each given up our Sunday afternoon to hopefully put matters to bed. After a delicious roast complete with trimmings, followed by generous portions of apple crumble, we each slumped into more comfortable seats, apart from Ann, who diplomatically announced her intention to take a walk around the local park. The Booths had been keen to invite her along for lunch – perhaps a shrewd move to gain my favour. Nevertheless, the overall mood had been lifted by her presence, Ann being at her agreeable best and mixing well with everyone, especially Kate, who seemed to appreciate the female company. By that time, the autumn light was fading, and knowing Ann would return before dark, we decided to quickly move on.

'In answer to your recent ultimatum, Edgar, well meant as it was, there's no mistaking my intentions. I personally want to continue with the project, and I desperately want to know more about George Davy. Therefore, after talking to Bob, I propose that instead of a séance, we should think about conducting another regression – one that might reveal more names and locations. Given that you suggest regression and séance are bedfellows, surely a regression would be a reasonable compromise?'

He jumped at the idea. I think he'd feared the worst – that me and Bob might give up on the whole thing. That being the case, any concession that kept the pot simmering was better than nothing at all. As it was, he didn't hesitate to take up the suggestion.

'Oh, that's excellent news! Thanks so much, Arthur ... and you too, of course, Bob. That reminds me, Bob, I've thought a lot about your predicament, and I'd like to suggest something that might relieve the torment you've been suffering.'

'Please feel free, Edgar, I'm all ears.'

'Well, I hope you don't mind, but I discussed your plight with an old acquaintance of mine, strictly in confidence, of course. He, too, is a medium, though he specialises in "cleaning" habitations suffering from adverse activity ... poltergeists, et cetera. So I simply thought it might be worth consulting him ...'

Bob went quiet for a moment, probably concerned how ridiculous he thought he'd made himself appear, likely wishing he'd never said anything in the first place.

'There's no harm in giving it a try, is there, Bob?'

He looked at me and grinned, indicating his appreciation for my concern.

'Thanks for the offer, Edgar. It's a tricky one for me, though – an admission that something really exists. I'll need to give it some thought. Though as Arthur rightly says, no harm in trying. All the same, I'd like to think it over before making a decision ... if you wouldn't mind.'

The knock at the door returned the ambience to one of domestic conviviality. Ann had returned and came to sit beside me. We then discussed more normal things: the worsening weather and the glorious summer gone, and most of all, that memorable day at Wembley in late July.

Chapter 14
Nottingham 1966

Early evening in Slab Square. There are buskers and coloured lights. A wonky-bearded Santa rings a handbell and laughs ridiculously loudly.

We walk up Queen Street to The County Hotel near the theatre. We are out of place but tough it out. I suggest a Pimm's. Ann nods and smiles nervously. When it comes, it is spectacular, drawing envious attention from the lager and lime brigade. I order a fancy beer, pass a crumpled note over the bar, and hope it's enough.

Later we sit in the cheap stalls of the nearby Gaumont. We watch Julie Andrews in Torn Curtain with a choc ice, afterwards getting fish and mixed up the road. A bus home from the square – Saturday night.

Bob couldn't bring himself to conduct the regression at his house – me having neither the space nor refinement at mine. The Booths offered, but we weren't keen on that idea, not wishing to provoke anything lingering in the spiritual residue of the séance. And so it was back to West Bridgford again. This time, the only date available for the church hall was Thursday – three days before Christmas. It was that or wait for the New Year to settle in.

We decided to take the earliest availability and arrived in darkness. The lamp over the door had been thoughtfully left on, its feeble glow shrouded in grime and rotting insect matter. When finally the key grudgingly turned in the half-frozen lock, we entered the familiar surroundings of the room we'd occupied in the stifling heat of summer past – the same flickering fluorescent, stacked furniture and worn linoleum. The only difference was the opposite extreme of temperature.

The ancient once-white radiator was trying its best and failing miserably. Another hour might just see it function near to normal. And so we raised our collars and clasped the warm plastic cups Kate Booth was passing around. I had an idea and set off for the storeroom at the back. After clattering and poking around for a while, I returned with a doubtful-looking electric fire complete with frayed cable and yellowing three-pin plug. After cautiously plugging it in, we stood back and watched the twin tubes begin to redden. To our collective delight, it eventually emitted an acceptable and welcome heat. We placed our chairs around it, sitting more comfortably together to finish our lukewarm tea.

Bob said we should start as soon as we were ready. It was strange having the Booths with us – my previous regressions only involving Bob and me. Even when we had gathered afterwards to listen to the tapes, Kate usually found an excuse not to join us. I never quite understood why that was, or indeed why the custom had unexpectedly changed. Whatever it was, I decided to keep the peace by not raising the matter.

I recalled Edgar saying that getting to know

each other might not be altogether plain sailing, and that we should embrace our differences for the sake of our communal welfare, especially during the more difficult times. He suggested we also think about freshening our routine from time to time – hence, perhaps, Kate's unprecedented attendance.

We had previously discussed how difficult it might be for me to relax in the spartan environment of the church hall, but the ever resourceful Kate Booth had come to the rescue yet again. When Bob had collected the Booths, they'd loaded one of their garden chairs into the boot of his car along with a large cardboard box. The chair was curved, its canvas seat designed to recline for maximum comfort. I settled into it and made myself comfortable whilst Kate produced a squat candle and a fleecy blanket from the box. She placed the candle on a table and unfolded the blanket, proceeding to tuck me in as she might a baby. I squirmed at that, totally embarrassed by her motherly attentiveness, well-intentioned though it was.

As Bob stood by to switch off the fluorescent, Edgar struck a match, cupped his hands, and carefully ignited the candle. When the spiralling smoke began to drift over me, I breathed its scent and observed the cavorting shadows on the ceiling overhead. The miserable space was at once transformed. With a yawn, I snuggled into the comfort of the fleecy blanket, becoming unconcerned by the hovering presence of the others. I blinked tiredly at them, watching their faces whitening and darkening in the erratic candlelight.

My journey was beginning, the soothing poetry of numerical incantation gently encouraging my departure on waves of warming air.

Where are you?

Arthur, where are you?

I can hear myself, but I am not speaking. I know it is me, even though the sound is only that of my breathing – leaden and anxious.

Is that you, Arthur?

Dark place ... stones ... wet.

It is my voice, purely mine and that of no other.

There they are!

The voice is still mine, though the tone of it is harsher.

Is there someone with you, Arthur?

Not wi' me ... hover there ... waitin' ... wi' 'em now ...

I will never know how I coped with what I woke to. Emerging from the fog of induced sleep was akin to being disgorged from the dark depths of a distorted tube. Frantically, I grappled with the blanket that entangled my legs, desperately forcing the chair upright to escape its confinement. The room was dancing, the cast of the candle's unstable light revealing a prospect I shall never forget. I had been conducted into peaceful oblivion, only to wake to a nightmare of diabolic confusion.

They were doing their best to subdue her, though her mood was maniacal. Her flaring eyes were threatening to burst, so hysterically she thrashed at the unseen force she was seeking to escape. The two men fought to prevent her from tearing their flesh with fingers curled to lethal claws, even as she spat and swore in their faces.

The snarling wretch bore sparse resemblance to the woman I had come to know. Though often she chose to present an unfathomable façade, the depths to which she plunged that evening descended beyond the limits of normality. The fire glowed, the radiator bubbled, yet the room was intensely cold, chilling the bones, vapours of breath in its sharpness. And then, as the furious struggle continued, an eerie howl came from who knew where to break the ghastly impasse. I finally managed to extricate myself from the chair, intending to add my weight to the worsening melee. Though desperately wanting to help, my movements were not my own, each step nightmarishly sluggish as if something or someone was physically holding me back. Nevertheless, I continued to struggle, wincing at the deafening shrieks that pierced my ears. There were moments when I thought demons from the depths of hell itself had entered her consciousness, such was the concentration of her suffering.

Then, much like the flicking of a switch, it was over; whatever unearthly materialisation had come to invade the room had departed with equal immediacy, only the sound of laboured breathing remaining to disturb the ensuing silence.

Edgar and Bob were gasping for breath as they tended to her, both men in a state of complete exhaustion. Kate Booth, prostrate and unresponsive, was seemingly oblivious to their anxious attention. I rushed towards them, suddenly released by whatever had seized me. I saw spots of blood then, the scratches and welts, the phlegm and spittle that stained their clothes, the two dishevelled men flushed and clammy from their exertions. Despite their best endeavours, Kate remained worryingly motionless, her skin white beyond paleness. For one horrible moment, I feared she was dead. Then when I looked again, I noticed the slightest tremor passing through her body. With a startled blink, she stirred and smoothed her dress. At the same time, Edgar Booth released a pitiful cry and wept unashamedly.

Chapter 15
Nottingham 1966

I insert a coin and push through the turnstile. Walking the path by dripping winter foliage, I glance at the effigy of Captain Ball. Generations of pigeons have done what pigeons do. Yet their mess will never diminish his gallantry.

The castle grounds are a good place to think and reflect – a locale surveying the misty panorama of industry and urban sprawl beyond its precipitous walls. I think of the long-dead sentinels that once stood there – helmeted watchmen gazing over ancient pastures to the distant Trent.

I light a cigarette and think of Kate and the terrible ghost that I think once was me. I am strangely remorseful, but what can I do? What can any of us do? We surely cannot leave it now. We are invested in it. I take a last drag and leave the grounds without entering its halls, as I often do.

'I don't think I'll ever allow myself to be regressed again!'

In that moment I really believed what I was saying. It seemed the troubles occurred only when my particular past life was examined, although so far, the only other one of us to undertake regression was Edgar Booth, at least as far as I knew.

We huddled in the bar of The Test Match in Bridgford, a pub I knew quite well, having relatives that lived nearby. They were better off than us, nice family all the same and never condescending. Sometimes we'd meet them at weekends, the family fishing together at the nearby canal. Grandad whistling his tune was the signal for us to walk to The Test Match, us young ones left to guard the fishing tackle whilst the adults went inside for an hour or two. Later on, one of them would reappear, carrying a tray of pop and bags of crisps with tiny packets of salt inside. The tinkle of a piano would drift from the open windows, and soon after, the singing, familiar voices leading the way.

The time-worn piano standing neglected by the wall might well have been the very instrument of yesteryear – no singing anymore, though. The bar was quiet before the weekend, our voices blending into the restrained chatter of a few local drinkers.

'I can't disagree with you, Arthur. It's unlikely to be a coincidence.'

Edgar Booth sat on a stool next to his wife. Kate was making short work of a large port and brandy, a drink that must have cost more than the rest of ours put together. I considered the woman who only a short while ago had been a quivering wretch close to breakdown. Not for the first time, I marvelled at her capacity to bounce back, almost as though nothing significant had occurred. Kate Booth was a remarkable woman, seemingly unmoved by the horrific episode that continued to shock me to the core.

'So, where do we go from here? Is that the

end of it? Are we really done this time?'

'Certainly not!'

Kate answered her husband's question before Bob and me even had time to think about it.

'Edgar, you've said yourself many times that we four share something unique. Then all of a sudden, you're suggesting we allow tonight's incident to prevent us moving any further forward! Despite the best efforts of that brute, I'm as good as new and raring to go. You might not think it, but I've been just as engrossed as any of you have ... even if I did prefer to stay in the background at first. If you want to know, I needed to be sure we had the right mix of people before I ...'

'The psychologist in me reckons you're leading up to something, Kate.' Bob took a swallow of his stout, looking as bewildered as I was by the speed of her recovery.

'Well then, if you really want to know ... I think it's time for you and me to be regressed, Bob, don't you think?'

Her husband suffered a violent fit of coughing as a drop of liquor trickled into his lungs. Everyone in the bar went quiet, clearly concerned for the man who appeared to be choking. It took a while for him to settle and longer for the hum of conversation to return to normal. Ever the gentleman, Edgar Booth half rose from his stool and muttered his apologies to anyone who cared to listen. Once he was seated again, he glared over his spectacles at the woman who'd just fussed over him as if he were taking his last dying breath.

'Kate, really, what on earth are you thinking of? Whatever it was that took hold of you did so without being summoned. If indeed it was the same one who intruded on the séance, there's a good chance it may have lain dormant within you since then – waiting for another chance to resurface! I simply can't risk that happening again. I won't allow you to suffer such an intrusion for a third time ... not likely!'

His voice had risen in sync with his anger and he was drawing attention again, this time for a different reason.

'Shush, Edgar. You'll be getting us thrown out at this rate.'

For me and Bob, this was a new experience. We hadn't witnessed them airing their differences so vocally before, let alone in public. Edgar Booth folded his hands and obediently lowered his voice to a forced whisper.

'Sorry, dear, but you've had quite an upset, you know. Indeed, with respect, you seem to have got over it rather more quickly than the rest of us!'

'That's because I'm not treating the matter as seriously as you are. I'm surprised at you, Edgar Booth. You above all people should know that manifestations like that can be compared to menacing dogs – more bark than bite. Of course it was uncomfortable at the time. I might ache a bit right now, but my mind was somewhere else whilst it was going on. It was much like having a tooth pulled after being sedated. You know what I mean; when they ram that awful clamp in your mouth to hold your jaw open before they gas you. Weird and uncomfortable, but eventually you don't feel the pain anymore. Then once it's over, you escape the chair and get on with your life.'

It was a lesson to us all. In her own simple way, Kate Booth put the nightmare into perspective, dismissing the episode as an insignificant cog in the greater wheel of our pursuits.

'Thinking about it, I suppose we ought to expect that sort of episode now and then. After all, we have been dabbling in the occult – and even I know you can't do that without taking a few risks.'

Bob looked aghast, clearly not wanting to acknowledge the fact that supernatural forces alone were entirely responsible for the latest incident.

'Oh, come on, Arthur. That might or might not be the case with séances, but I was conducting a straightforward regression – something I've done dozens of times without any such problems.'

'I can't argue with your knowledge, Bob, but on more than one occasion, Edgar suggested that the two practices might share common ground. At this minute, that claim sounds quite reasonable to me, given what we witnessed earlier on.'

'Edgar's entitled to his opinions as much as I am mine. Yes, alright, I understand your reasoning, but I think we're veering from the point – we're not addressing Kate's proposal. In that regard, I have to say being regressed is not something I've considered. With what's going on at home, I'd be extremely nervous about getting that involved, to be honest. Quite apart from anything else, we'd need to find someone suitably qualified to regress me.'

I could understand his caution, what with his nightmares – or whatever they were. Hopefully, that particular problem would be resolved by Edgar's acquaintance – all the more reason for Bob not wanting to encourage any further visitations in the meantime.

'Before we go any further, let's not forget the irrefutable.' Edgar had been quietly listening to our exchanges, and when he took his chance to speak, his words had that scheming quality about them, suggesting he was about to steal the upper hand again.

'This troublesome spirit we've rightly or wrongly attributed to Arthur's past life seemingly appears when he himself is regressed. So then, here's a plan we should consider: why don't I undergo another regression? Let's see if this monster claiming to be George Davy is strong enough to encroach into my session as it did his. If it does, there are measures I can take to chase it away – alternative avenues none of you need involve yourselves in. On the other hand, if it doesn't appear, we should risk conducting Kate's first regression. Allow me to remind you of the premise that's intrigued us from the beginning: that the four of us were once together in a previous life. If we're serious about proving that theory, we need to push the limits.'

To his way of thinking, our eternal friendship was the common glue that held us together. Even Doubting Thomas Bob was nodding his head with a degree of cautious acceptance. It was true; we'd come too far to walk away, and whatever his ultimate purpose, we couldn't allow George Davy to stand in our way. We were a diverse mix of personalities – two that truly believed, one that wanted to believe and one that stubbornly resisted anything but concrete evidence. Nevertheless, we were as one in seeking the truth – in our different ways, we simply had to know.

Chapter 16
Nottingham 1967

♫ *Should auld acquaintance be forgot* ♫

We sing alongside the moulting tree, its baubles absent of ornate light – we do not find the faltering bulb.

♫ *Should auld acquaintance be forgot and never brought to mind* ♫

I sing in dutiful tradition, and as the final verse raises the roof, I consider the lyrics profoundly.

They come with meaning now, as does the celebratory circle of clasped hands.

The vinous dregs of last year are emptied – now popping bubbles to see in the new.

Those that mean much are with me there, fused in festivity.

Will it be so the next time round?

♫ *Should auld acquaintance be forgot* ♫

'Did you see him again, Edgar?'

'Yes, Arthur, though only briefly – she was there too, almost all the while; at least when I had time to glance, she was.'

'She? Oh, yes, of course ... was it her who was holding me back?'

'It looked like it was, yes. She certainly wasn't happy; even when I was in the thick of it, I had a very strong sense of that.'

'What does she look like?'

'That's not for me to say ... she's your guide, Arthur. You must continue to see her as you do in your mind's eye.'

Being chauffeured into Bob's driveway by a complete stranger had felt peculiar. We had pulled up behind Bob's parked car, the squeaky wipers that wafted away the driving sleet finally put to rest. I pushed open the weighty door of the ancient Humber, reluctantly exiting its warmth and fading opulence. Edgar Booth, having been quick enough to claim the front passenger seat, climbed out of its depths with considerably more effort. I had shared the cavernous rear bench with Kate on our journey from their home. We'd sat together on cushioned leather and chatted for most of the way.

Bob was already at the door, a warm and welcoming smile crossing his face when he saw how many had arrived to support him. After shedding our coats in the hall, we made our way into his cosy parlour. Bob had stoked the fire and was preparing hot beverages to order. I noticed a complete lack of festive decoration. It was in stark contrast to the expanse of weary trimmings Mam and Grandma insisted on festooning the house with at the beginning of November. We had stayed over on New Year's eve, Ann and me. I was instructed to bed down on the sofa, of course, whereas Ann was billeted in the loft with my two sisters, there to sleep on my old mattress behind the makeshift wall.

Grandma reckoned it looked like my spinster siblings would remain at home forever, even though they had boyfriends –

twin lads, as it happens. The twins reasoned it might be better to wait a while – build a worthwhile nest-egg before rushing into marriage. Grandma reckoned they were tight-arsed little boggers, same as their mingy dad – said she remembered him running around the streets as a lad, arse hanging out of his raggedy trousers with more darning than wool in his socks. Ann gave me one of her looks on hearing that. I took it to mean she'd no intention of waiting as long as my sisters had.

'Good to see such a nice car on my drive, Mr Keates.'

'Thanks, Bob, I've had it long enough. Can't really bring myself to swap it ... please call me Bertie.'

Albert Keates was a dapper man standing about five feet seven, wiry and tough looking. He and Edgar went back years, apparently. It came as no surprise to learn he was ex-army. Edgar revealed that Bertie had served in the Long Range Desert Group in North Africa during the war. I immediately pictured a camouflaged jeep – elongated gun angling skywards – deep-tanned squaddies bouncing in their seats, careering over endless dunes looking for German targets to destroy. Grandad said they were commandos, forerunners of something called the Special Air Service. It didn't take much imagination to envision Bertie in that kind of company.

Bertie Keates was the man Edgar had recommended to Bob. I had imagined him to be something of a weird sort: a type of exorcist, though not the kind the church provided. In reality, he seemed quite down-to-earth, not so much as a whiff of bell, book or candle about him.

Keates was standing alongside Edgar. Though of similar height, the two men could not have been more physically different. The rotund, bespectacled Edgar Booth with his inflamed jowls and carefully Brylcreemed comb-over stood in sharp contrast to the lean, steely-eyed veteran beside him. Then when Bob walked over to talk to them, I was surprised to see how much taller he was in comparison. I noticed Keates looking him up and down as though evaluating him before engaging in conversation.

'Obviously, Edgar's told me about your unfortunate circumstances, Bob. Nevertheless, I'd like to hear a bit more from you before we get down to tackling the business in hand – if indeed that's what we decide to do. We can talk privately if you'd prefer.'

I noticed the subtle change in Bob's demeanour. There was no doubting his intellect, but he was emotionally vulnerable and rather delicate of late.

'There's really no need for us to talk privately. These people are good friends of mine and have been only too willing to share the problem with me – in the broadest sense, of course. Please ask away, Bertie, but before you do, can I ask why you think we might not be taking things any further this evening?'

'Oh, don't read too much into that, Bob. You

need to understand that I am, by nature, a cautious man. I just don't want to wander too far down the wrong road. What you're experiencing is something I've yet to fully understand. It might sound harsh, but I have to consider the possibility of it turning out to be nothing much out of the ordinary.'

I could see Bob getting flustered. It was not entirely going the way he'd hoped it would. His claims were already being questioned, and in a somewhat blunt and dispassionate manner. More than anything, I had the feeling he might have suddenly grasped the reality of the situation, perhaps beginning to doubt his own sanity.

'Yes, I see your line of reasoning. You're right, of course. Okay then, Bertie, why don't we sit down and talk it through. As you say, it might be nothing at all – in which case, I'd rather suffer the embarrassment of looking a fool than to carry on enduring the other option.'

Kate Booth was quick to recognise Bob's discomfort and beckoned him to join her on the sofa, smiling warmly when he came to sit with her. The rest of us settled down and waited for our host to explain his circumstances to Bertie Keates in greater detail.

When Bob came to speak about what he called the 'visions', it was obvious his mental state had worsened since the first time he had openly talked about his predicament.

'I decided to spend the festive break on my

own ... but unless I'm completely losing my marbles, I don't think I actually did. You may think me unstable, but when I went to bed on Boxing Day, I found the bloody thing waiting for me in my bedroom ... yet again. For some reason, it only inhabits that particular room, though this time I thought its image more distinct than on earlier occasions. I also sensed more purpose in its presence. Previously it tended to skulk in the dimmest part of the room. Last time, however, I thought it stepped out of the deeper shadows. At first I thought my eyes were playing tricks on me, knowing that can happen when focusing on something inanimate for too long – you become convinced it's moving. As you can imagine, my instinct was to dash from the room, or even from the house. In the event, though, I couldn't move. I admit to being petrified – thoroughly convinced it was approaching me with deadly purpose ...'

Bob's voice wavered, eyes widening with the telling. Hearing him so emotionally relating the unsettling episode made it difficult to see how the occurrence could be anything other than factual. Clearly, Bob was at the end of his tether; could anything other than a genuine encounter generate such alarming consequences?

'How many times have you experienced these happenings since we were last together, Bob?' Kate gently rubbed his arm as she asked the question, and I thought I sensed Keates's irritation at her intrusion.

'Three times, although the anticipation of it

making an appearance is almost as disturbing as when it actually does. When I climb the stairs to my bedroom, the thought of what might be waiting fills me with an awful sense of foreboding. There was no sign of it whatsoever on Christmas Eve, or even on the day itself. Having said that, I have to say I was well-oiled for most of that time. The peace didn't last, though, Boxing Day proving the worst experience by far ... creeping up on me like that ...'

Keates purposely coughed at that juncture, obviously keen to regain control.

'Do you ever smell anything unpleasant, Bob, or hear anything untoward?'

'Not that I can be certain of, no.'

'Describe what it looks like ... how it's dressed.'

'It's usually quite grainy and indistinct. However, though it might sound contrived, the overriding picture in my head reminds me of someone from the last century. You might think how convenient that is when considering our current interests ... but that's a literal description of the image I perceived.'

Edgar was nodding to himself. To him, what Bob was saying simply confirmed what he himself had previously claimed. Keates continued his cross-examination in an ever more resolute tone.

'You must have switched the light on straightaway? It's a common response from those not used to that kind of thing.'

'I certainly did, and true to form, it vanished

the second the light flooded the room.'

'In truth, they don't always do that, do they, Edgar?'

'Nothing's ever certain with these things, Bertie, I remember the time ...'

'I assume you've more than one bedroom, Bob ... big house like this? You must have thought about relocating to a different one, or sleeping downstairs, perhaps?'

'Yes, I did try sleeping in another bedroom for a few hours, downstairs too on more than one occasion, though sometimes for entirely different reasons ... more personal reasons. Anyway, regardless of where I've tried to sleep, I spend most of the time awake, expecting it to come looking for me! That's why I thought to tough it out – my personal sanctuary, you understand, not his. In any case, it makes little difference where I settle; I end up twisting and turning – dreading the slightest bump or creak. Quite apart from anything else, I don't want the damn thing infecting every room in the bloody house, one room being more than enough!'

'How long do these experiences usually last, Bob?'

'Hard to say ... seems longer than it actually is ... a few minutes, maybe.'

'Have you challenged it in any way? You would if it was a burglar, wouldn't you? Have you asked what it wants - tried shouting at it – told it to bugger off?'

'I chucked the bloody clock at it when I thought it was creeping up on me!'

'And how did it react to that?'

Bob had grown wide-eyed and breathless under Keates's unrelenting examination, gulping mouthfuls of air as he struggled to form the words.

'I swear it bloody well grinned at me!'

I was uncomfortable with Albert Keates's interrogative style, thinking he was taking Bob to the limit. However, when he'd finished, he appeared satisfied with the results of his questioning, even giving Bob's shoulder a manly squeeze of encouragement.

'I've decided I'd like to take myself upstairs in due course – nothing beats attending the scene of the crime, I always say. During that time, I'd ask each and every one of you to stay where you are – say and do nothing. I need to concentrate my thoughts ... more so, my senses, all six of them. Extraneous noise will only distract me from my purpose. Also, the more mischievous ones usually react like frightened children when confronted by someone who knows what they're about. That's a good reason for treading carefully. The last thing we want to do is frighten the bugger away before we learn what manner of entity we're dealing with.'

As he continued to lecture us, I wondered about Albert Keates's time in the army. He certainly had that soldierly detachment about him. He was also well spoken and articulate, leading me to think he might have been an officer of some rank.

'Edgar, earlier you said you'd observed the

image of a spirit relating to the one we're dealing with here. In which case, it might be an idea if you and Bob were to jot down your respective descriptions as you remember them. I'd be interested to see if they match sufficiently well enough to suggest they're one and the same, wouldn't you?'

Kate rummaged in her handbag and produced a small notebook and two stubby pencils. After some deliberation, the two men jotted their notes on the torn-out leaves. Only minutes later, first one, then the other looked up to Bertie Keates, their manner not dissimilar to that of anxious schoolchildren about to hand their homework to a teacher.

Keates preserved the scholastic analogy by squinting through a pair of narrow reading glasses, as would a critical tutor.

'Okay then, let's evaluate what we've got here.'

His lips moved silently, extended fingers tracing the two descriptions. Once he'd finished, he removed his glasses with a flourish and fanned the two notes in our general direction.

'Hmm, there are similarities here, though they're open to interpretation. In the broadest sense, I think there's enough to suggest a reasonable comparison. But let's not assume too much at this stage. You should be reminded that you're currently investigating people who might match these depictions, or at least in part. Furthermore, I think an informed sceptic might view the descriptions and insinuate that anybody with a modicum of historical knowledge could conjure similar depictions if asked to do so. That aside, should I encounter a figure resembling anything remotely similar to what you've defined, I think you might be on to something extraordinary.'

Without another word, Bertie Keates departed the room, leaving the rest of us to contemplate our navels in submissive silence. We cocked our ears when he climbed the stairs, the sound of his ascent soon replaced by the complaining creak of loosened floorboards overhead.

We waited with nervous expectancy – the minutes dragging on – and still we heard nothing to suggest Keates had encountered anything untoward. I had half-expected to hear some form of invocation or liturgical prayer. In the event, however, nothing of the sort occurred. There were no irregular movements, no phantom knockings or banging doors: all the more reason to wonder why the man who returned to us was ashen and somewhat subdued in his demeanour. Later, Albert Keates would say he'd neither seen nor heard a thing. That notwithstanding, he quietly confirmed that there had definitely been something up there with him.

Slumping heavily into an armchair by the fire, Keates nervously massaged his forehead and requested a glass of water. After fidgeting for a while, Edgar Booth's patience snapped, breaking the onerous silence by asking the question we all craved the answer to.

‘Are you going to tell us what happened at some point, Bertie?’

Keates sat upright with something of a start, almost as if he’d forgotten we were there.

‘Yes, of course … sorry … I just needed a minute.’

‘You sure you’re okay, Bertie? You look a bit shaken up, old chap … peaky as well, if I might say. What did you encounter up there, my friend?’

Keates shuddered involuntarily and shook his head, fumbling in his pocket for a handkerchief before vigorously clearing his nose.

‘Do please excuse me … the straight answer to your question is that I didn’t actually see or hear a damn thing.’

‘Well, you’re obviously distressed about something, Bertie. What the devil’s wrong, man? Are you holding something back? Do we have an actual problem?’

I glanced to see how Bob was reacting, and sure enough, the colour had drained from his face. After taking a deep breath, Albert Keates straightened himself. He must have realised he’d allowed his emotions to get the better of him and was clearly embarrassed by his loss of control.

‘An actual problem, you say? No, Edgar, not anymore. The thing turned out to be incredibly feisty, though. Even so, after a lengthy tussle, it departed with its tail between its legs. I have to say the bloody thing was remarkably durable. As I said, I didn’t actually see or hear anything, but I was soon aware of its presence and I believe it knew my purpose. Likewise, I grasped a feeling for its intentions – a sense of retribution, unless I'm mistaken.'

'Thankfully, there were no physical consequences, Bertie. It seems to have been lingering without immediate intent.'

'It could have been trapped in limbo, Edgar; that's one theory anyway. Whatever the reason for its presence, thank God I was practised enough to deal with it. It was a close call, I can tell you – it very nearly had me at one point. A less experienced person might well have succumbed to its obstinacy.'

'That's incredible, Bertie ... and certainly not typical. You sure you didn't see anything?'

'Yes, I'm sure ... as I keep saying. I heard nothing either. Even so, I instinctively knew it was evil in nature, and I admit to being startled by the strength of that. As I think you know, Edgar, it takes rather a lot to disturb me. I've experienced spiritual intimidation a few times, but never anything quite as strong and determined.'

Bob coughed to attract attention, staring at Keates with a degree of apprehension before nervously asking his question.

'Do you think it's gone altogether?'

He'd sat through the exchange with growing unease, and so Bob's question came out as more of an entreaty, like an anxious child desperately seeking assurance that nothing more than nightmares lurked under his bed.

'Don't worry, Bob, it has definitely gone. It

knew when it was beaten, right from the moment I said the words that sent it scurrying to whatever vile place it crawled in from. You'll quickly realise it's gone for good – these types of entity pollute their victims with their evil filth. Only when properly exorcised does the sufferer notice the absence of its foulness; think of it like opening a window to let in some fresh air.'

Bob hung his head before exhaling with relief at the thought of his liberation. 'I can only thank you, Bertie. It must have been very testing for you.'

Keates casually waved Bob's gratitude aside before slumping into his chair in evident exhaustion. Wearily, he studied us in turn, blinking as he glanced from one to the other, eyes narrowing as they came to settle on the countenance of Kate Booth.

'Assuming it was the same thing that entered your own body, Kate, you ought to give thanks to God for your deliverance, and to Edgar for protecting you from the worst of it. You should also be proud of yourself for having the strength to withstand its wickedness.'

We waited patiently whilst Keates swallowed the remainder of his water, watching him watching us. After placing his empty glass on a nearby table, he turned to look sombrely at us.

'You people need to be on your guard – each and every one of you. This entity might be hunting for a living body to occupy – an exclusive host to satisfy whatever its purpose might be. If what I'm led to believe is correct, it's already broken your circle on more than one occasion. If that's the case, it's reasonable to assume it's one or more of you that it's after. On this occasion, though, it might have simply been probing your defences. That might explain the purpose behind Bob's experiences. Thankfully, that particular portal has been closed off to it. Nevertheless, you might consider the possibility that Bob was not its ultimate quarry – a mischievous distraction maybe, whilst selecting the one it's really after. It might even now be festering in whatever hellhole it's returned to, awaiting another chance. Make no mistake, it's a vengeful and destructive spirit, even more so for the beating it's taken. I had a sense of it searching over a long period of time – in real life, maybe, as much as in spiritual essence.'

I thought Keates's discourse was overtly theatrical. Nonetheless, there was no doubting the sincerity of his cautionary advice. We'd seen and heard nothing of actual note. That notwithstanding, it had turned out to be quite a night.

Chapter 17
Nottingham 1967

With the wind at my back, I'm propelled the length of Long Row towards the square. Folk shiver and shelter from the gusts as they wait for buses under Pearson's porticoed entrance. I pass the timeless columns and vaguely think of Dad. He's somewhere beyond those window displays, professional in collar and tie. He's a manager now with fancy ambitions – ideas above his station, some might say.

Ann waits outside Griffin's with a glowing nose. We peck each other on the lips, much like the pigeons that scrat by our feet and peck at nothing we humans can see.

We are coldly blown to Wheeler Gate, where we take welcome refuge in Sisson's, idly leafing through glossy books we can't afford.

We're saving like mad, Ann and me – just one more year before our bells ring, or so we intend. I dearly hope we make it.

The man that answered the phone didn't sound much like the man of late – the voice altogether too jovial. Yet Bob it was, for sure, projecting an entirely different aura from the one he'd miserably exhibited only weeks before.

'Hope you're not in the middle of anything, Bob.'

'No, Arthur, nothing at all.'

'Only, I thought I'd check to see if everything's alright.'

'Yeah, absolutely fine. Thanks for ringing, though, really appreciate it.'

The Booths had telephoned Bob every couple of days, asking if he was okay. I called when I could as I was the only one without a home phone. The nearest phone box to me was three streets away. Repeatedly vandalised, it stank of urine and was sticky with discarded gum.

'I thought about bussing over to see you sometime, if that's alright?'

'Course, Arthur. Why not bring Ann along? One Sunday for tea? She's not been here as yet. Be nice to have somebody normal visit ... no offence. Clients, I mean, not you.'

'None taken. Thanks for the invitation. Sounds like a good idea.'

'Tell you what, Arthur, get yourselves into town and I'll collect you from outside Victoria Station, then you can catch the bus back. That way we can have a drink or two together.'

'Sounds great, Bob, thanks for that!'

***

The wind was definitely warmer, a weak sun playing peek-a-boo with the passing clouds. As we walked along, Ann pointed to a drift of spears poking through some rotting vegetation, a clump of yellow-tinged tips impatient to flower. She mentioned something about them being late for the time of year. I didn't know what to say to that. It appeared she knew a lot about that sort of thing, saying they were fleeting splendours to be treasured in the moment. To me they simply looked nice, assuming I would notice them in the first place – another lesson in life and another reason to love her.

We carried on nattering as Bob led us along the winding pathway to his door, causing me to think of treading the same paving with entirely different purpose. Once inside, I showed Ann into the back room whilst Bob pottered in the kitchen. I knew him well enough to think he wouldn't mind me stoking the fire without first asking him. After I had fed the embers with a couple of logs, the two of us sat and relaxed, content to gaze through the window at the rambling greenery and blossoming trees. I hadn't been raised in such surroundings, only stark pavements and backyards: somewhere to put the bins and kick a ball about. Not many folk bothered planting anything much where we lived – a few prickly sticks bearing the odd flower, maybe, wiry climbing things creeping into crevices.

'There we go, cuppa to start with. Help yourselves to milk and sugar. I have to say it's nice having social company for a change. Glad you decided to visit!'

It took a while for Bob to ease up on the talking. I think he was happy with the ordinariness of having people over for tea. He'd been through an upsetting time of late, and it was good to see him in a brighter mood. Later on we had sandwiches: neatly cut triangles of thick bread with the crusts cut off, with marzipan fancies and jam tarts to follow, together with a fresh brew of tea.

Afterwards we did the washing up, leaving Bob to read through the scandals in the Sunday paper while we clattered in his kitchen. When we returned, he was out for the count and snorting like a tethered bull. And so we decided to leave him to his slumbers and take a spin round the garden.

We stepped on flat stones leading to a distant confusion of vegetation at the end of an uncut lawn. Startled birds fluttered as we entered their domain, whistling frantically to warn others of our passage. Heeding their counsel, a pair of nervy squirrels scurried up the bark of a nearby tree. After a few minutes of aimless wandering, we came to the edge of the undergrowth. Seeing little point in wading through knee-high foliage, we turned instead to view the rambling house, pausing to admire its ornate gables and chimney stacks. I wondered if Ann was having similar thoughts to me, imagining we owned the place, or something like it. Her wistful look answered my unspoken question.

Retracing our steps, our eyes were drawn towards the parlour window, where Bob was waving cheerfully in our direction. We returned the gesture and continued to walk to the house. In that same moment, I was distracted by a similar movement and my heart began to beat faster. Instinctively glancing at Ann, I found her staring at me, brow furrowed with concern. Had she seen what I had seen, or had she sensed the sudden tension within me?

I was conscious of blinking excessively, purposely not looking at the house, whilst all the while knowing I had to. With mounting trepidation, I grudgingly looked up to the bedroom window, relieved to observe only gloomy space behind the glass. Had it been a trick of the light – a bird's reflection or a passing cloud? Whatever it might have been, I found it difficult to dismiss the impression that Bob was not the only one who waved to me that afternoon.

Though I chose to say nothing, my worsening mood was difficult to hide, and when Bob disappeared to fetch more beer, Ann duly whispered her concerns. Reluctant to spoil the afternoon, I feigned a troublesome headache. Then, after one more drink, we said our goodbyes, leaving Bob on his doorstep, frowning as he waved us away. I thought better him puzzled than knowing the worrying truth.

Consequently, the return journey was awkward, to say the least. Ann persisted in asking me what was really wrong, and though tempted to tell her the truth, I doggedly stuck to my lame excuse.

To an extent, Bob must have accepted my explanation, if only because he insisted on bringing me a couple of seltzers before we left. Even so, I didn't think either of them entirely believed my story. I had been determined not to say anything to Bob at the time. He'd been more like his old self since Albert Keates supposedly banished whatever was tormenting him. And true to what Keates claimed, Bob reckoned he sensed the absence of the presence, believing both he and the house were at peace again.

And so for me to reveal I'd seen something waving from the window of the very bedroom where the spectre appeared to him was not exactly the best thing for Bob in the circumstances. I also refrained from telling Ann the truth of what had happened, having long ago decided I didn't want her involved in the funny business, as I sometimes thought of it – not at any cost. All the same, I needed to tell someone.

***

The following evening found me dashing across town to catch a bus to Arnold. After saying goodbye to Ann the previous night and watching her bus turn towards Alfreton Road, I decided to find the nearest phone box. Kate Booth had answered, and when I asked to speak to Edgar, she said he was away attending some event in London – something about psychic phenomena. I immediately remembered him telling me about it, Bertie Keates inviting him to something off the back of dealing with Bob's intruder. It had completely slipped my mind, what with everything that had happened.

It felt quite strange talking things over with Kate, and I was surprised when she invited me over. She said she thought it might be better for me to talk to her, rather than let whatever was worrying me fester until Edgar returned the following Wednesday. And so I agreed to visit the very next evening.

'Spring's just around the corner, but it's suddenly got colder again, don't you think, Arthur?'

The two of us were sat in front of the banked-up fire, nursing tumblers of whisky. Kate enjoyed a drink – never one to miss an opportunity to have a few. Edgar was much the same. He enjoyed a tipple or two almost as much as his wife did.

'I expect Edgar's propping the bar up in some pub or other near the society – him and Bertie chewing the cud over old times. Worse than a pair of gossipy fishwives, those two!'

'Society?'

'Yes ... Society of Psychical Research – easy for me to say – in London, somewhere near Kensington, if I've got it right. They're lodging close-by, somewhere Bertie's stayed before, apparently. Bet the old bugger knows all the boozers within staggering distance!'

I'd never heard her laugh like that before – a cackle Grandma called a 'chuckin' out laugh'.

'What event are they attending, then, Kate?'

'Oh, I don't know ... never sure what Edgar's up to most of the time. Anyway, never mind about that, what's all this malarky about something happening at Bob's house, hey?'

She was slurring her words enough for me to wonder how long she'd been at the bottle before I arrived. Maybe she drank more when Edgar was away. That notion caused me to question if I had done the right thing by seeing her on her own, especially as she'd obviously had one too many.

I had long thought Kate Booth to be deep and unpredictable, and for that reason, I sensed the need to tread more carefully. Even so, having brooded over Sunday's disturbing incident for a couple of days, I desperately wanted to get it out of my system. I'd barely slept a wink on Sunday night, and when I did manage to snatch an hour or so, every time I woke, I felt extremely anxious.

Incapable of containing myself any longer, I simply let it pour out. And when I got to the part about seeing somebody or something waving at me from Bob's bedroom window, Kate visibly paled and promptly drained her glass.

'I really don't know what to say. Arthur … you're sure Bob's okay, aren't you? It's not started bothering him again … has it?'

'No, I didn't notice anything untoward in that respect. Quite the opposite – he's as happy as I've seen him for a while. That's why I chose not to say anything to him – "What you don't know won't hurt you" – thought that was for the best at the time. Promise not to say anything to him, Kate, won't you? We don't want him slipping back into that awful state again, do we?'

She nodded and clumsily topped up my tumbler, having already poured herself yet another stiff one. 'Thinking about it, Arthur, I remember Edgar saying sometimes it's the place that's haunted and not the people that live there. Bertie was confident he'd seen it off, but then ... maybe he only made it disappear from Bob's consciousness. If that's the case, the rotten bogger might still be in there ... just that Bob can't see it anymore.'

Kate looked up from her glass, a trace of contrition in her expression, almost as though she'd said something out of place – something she hadn't thought about until it was too late.

'I think I know what you're getting at, Kate, but if that's the case, why should it appear to me when I don't even live there?'

She mumbled something incoherent. The drink was having its wicked way with her, her eyelids drooping and blinking as she resisted the urge to sleep. Then I thought some more about what she'd said and tried to engage her again.

'There's another way of looking at it, Kate. Could it be the other way round, do you think? Might it be that people are haunted and not the location?'

After slurring something that sounded like a response, her head slumped against a plumped-up cushion, her eyes slowly closing. It was clearly time for me to leave. There was little point in staying any longer. In the end, I realised it'd turned out to be a rather fruitless exercise. She must have heard me rummaging for my coat. Her head flopped in my general direction, and she began to mutter something, her voice alternately rising and fading, words slurred and barely audible.

'You off already, darlin'?'

'Yeah, thought I would. Tell Edgar I'll contact him when he gets back, if you wouldn't mind. Thanks for listening, Kate ... and for the whisky, of course.'

Her eyes briefly fluttered, a wan smile creasing her cheeks, one arm raised in a token attempt to wave me goodbye.

'See yer later, then, Alfie... mind the road ...'

Alfie?

Chapter 18
Nottingham 1967

I fashion the concluding letter of the final poster of the day – The Night of the Big Heat, *main feature, cast and full supporting programme, duly committed to crisp white paper.*

It is accordingly approved and chalked, tightly rolled, inserted in a tube, stamped and ready for the post office that in another life was The Postern Gate.

I clean my brushes and neatly lay them to rest. I rinse my revolting mug, tidy my bench, and don my precious corduroy jacket. Talk of the night and coming weekend is lively – pubs, clubs and dances, the Forest match, a bike ride to Gunthorpe, Wollaton Park with the kids … and then there's me. The Arthur they think they know won't be doing over much – nothing special – after all, he's saving for the big day.

Could they even guess at what the other Arthur might really be doing? I dearly hope not. Explaining that would be …

I walk the narrow streets and alleys of the Lace Market, departing the sombre maze of industrial edifices that inescapably backcloth my life – out into the light of Slab Square to encounter the buzz of that Friday feeling.

If only my life were that simple.

We sat like hardened gamblers surrounding a poker table, each playing a hand from an incomplete deck. My experience at Bob's house was known to everyone who sat there, except to Bob himself. We – the Booths and me – had resolved not to tell him about the apparition that had supposedly appeared at his window that Sunday. The influencing factor was that Bob had not experienced a single issue since the day Albert Keates mysteriously expelled his tormentor. According to Bob, it was quite the reverse. Not only had he not experienced anything since then, it looked like he'd lost his fear of it into the bargain. Moreover, he was rejuvenated and willing to continue his involvement in our endeavours. This came as some surprise. I would've put money on Bob being the first of us to opt out.

The second Sunday in May and we were back at the Booths as though nothing had happened since the episode with Albert Keates. Spring had stealthily stolen a march on us, and we were sat on canvas camping chairs at a weather-bleached table in the blossoming garden. The cups and plates had been cleared away and we were ready to resume the finale of our deliberations.

I continued to resist the idea of Kate Booth being the next one to be regressed. That her husband continued to champion the idea was a source of irritation. He was well aware of the anxiety I'd been enduring since my disturbing encounter at Bob's house, and for Kate's sake as much as anything else, how nervous I was about risking another mystical intrusion into our circle. The fact I couldn't mention the incident at Bob's house was one of the reasons why part of me didn't want another regression, or indeed, a séance, for that matter.

'We simply can't allow this spirit to dominate us, Arthur. It'll torment us even more if it senses a weakness. Now, look here ... we've already decided to press ahead, regardless of our individual concerns. We agreed, despite the risks involved, that each of us was eager to discover the truth about our past associations. There are many outstanding questions to answer, and I doubt any of us will settle until completely satisfied that we've gleaned every last bit of information. Let's not forget how we were at the beginning: the four of us, each in our own way motivated by the incredible possibilities presented.'

He was in full flow again, and at his most convincing – but I wasn't yet ready to succumb to his influence.

'That's all very well and good, Edgar, but with respect to Kate's experiences, it looks very much like I'm the one in the firing line here! That George Davy is actually me in another life is what you're all assuming, whether you openly admit it or not. If that proves to be the case, then me in a previous life turns out to be exactly what you warned us about: a very dangerous and incontrollable spirit. It's also been said that it's hunting one of us down – looking for a body to live in. Well, it looks like I'm in the frame for that, so thanks very much!'

The silence that followed my outburst might best be described as moderately disapproving. On such occasions, I inevitably regretted speaking my mind, an outcome that exasperated me even more after promising myself that next time, I'd try harder to control my emotions.

'Better it's me that takes the risk, hey, Arthur?' Kate had jumped in, and I could only wonder at the strength of her resolve. I hadn't suffered the extraordinary ferocity she experienced that night, though I'd witnessed its terrifying intensity. My body hadn't been wracked with pain, nor had my mind been tormented by malicious intent. The only comparable occurrence I'd endured was thinking I'd seen a vague figure waving at me from behind the glass of a misted window. I'd questioned the authenticity of that experience myself on a number of occasions, and I remembered Edgar's comment when we discussed the occurrence on his return from London.

'Not wishing to cast doubt on the veracity of your claim, old boy, but can you be absolutely certain about what you saw? After all, the intensity of the events you witnessed during the séance may have played with your thinking; when the mind is occupied with such underlying thoughts, it's capable of the most astonishing deceptions.'

'Aren't you worried it might take another sinister turn, Kate?'

She just smiled and gave me one of her looks, leaving her husband to address my reservations.

'I thought someone might raise that question, so I made provision for countering any such consequences, however likely or unlikely they may prove. Assuming everyone is amenable, I've asked Bertie Keates to join us. We witnessed his remarkable talent to some good effect, so should the same manifestation favour us with an appearance, it would be discouraged to find Bertie Keates waiting for it. Moreover, knowing what we're up against, I'd like to think I might offer some assistance in dealing with the damn thing. Admittedly, I'm a medium, not an exorciser, but I have my uses all the same.'

I shook my head and glanced at Bob, seeing there was no support coming from that direction. I'd talked to him a couple of times since we visited his house that Sunday, somewhat inconsiderately hoping the haunting might have resumed. If that had proved to be the case, then it might be reasonable to assume it was something to do with the house and not anything directly personal to him or anyone else – me in particular.

In the event, part of me was thankful to hear the manifestation had not returned. Bob had become a good friend, and I didn't want him hurt in any way. What should I do, then? Should I walk away and leave them forever? Edgar Booth had made a decent point when he suggested we were searching for a shared truth. I had to concede the project had become more than simply the exciting interest it was at the beginning. I felt there was something common to the four of us – something that was urging us on. Elusive as it was, it had become deep and meaningful. I think we each sensed we were, in our different ways, in it together – drawn to each other.

When all was said and done, despite my doubts and moods, they already knew what my answer would be, and I think they always had. It seemed there was no escaping the destiny of our endeavour.

Chapter 19
Nottingham 1967

I gaze across the sand through gritty eyes. Ann is a distant shadow against the grey of the cold North Sea. A few precious days away from the drudge of life – just the two of us. I watch her wandering the shore, looking for shells, while I dream of our future – of little people grasping bright buckets and red handled spades, screaming and scampering from the incoming tide. The sky is darkening and the wind sharpens, so shall we too scamper away? Back to the cosy nest that is ours for a while. There to love each other, play cards and draw daft pictures that make us laugh until we cry.

Ann cooks. We eat at the little table by the window and talk of our destiny. Later we stroll illuminated streets and seedy arcades, feeding ravenous slots with copper pennies. After that, a drink to wet our whistles. A bag of chips to take us home. Arm in arm, we skip along and warble 'Waterloo Sunset', snorting when we sing the wrong words.

Each precious day is short and sweet. Too soon, we board the bus for home, my pockets, her purse exhausted. Sleepy hours to Huntingdon Street. A wistful kiss goodbye.

Work on Monday …

Good holiday, Arthur?

'Good holiday, Arthur?'

'Yeah, not bad, Bob, thanks.'

'Not got much of a tan, Arthur.'

'You don't get much of a tan in Mablethorpe,

Kate – more likely rust!'

'Mablethorpe? "Aunty Mabel" we used to call it – there's lots more to do in Skeggy.'

'Yeah, at a cost – don't forget, we're on a limited budget, what with saving up and that.'

'Set a date yet?'

'Don't you start! Already got another five other women asking me the same question!'

'Five?'

'Yeah ... Ann for one. Then there's Mam and me two sisters, of course, and last but not least, dear old Grandma – how could I possibly forget her?'

I commandeered the front seat this time, aiming to observe Bob's driving technique – coordinated gear changes and clutch control, mostly. I couldn't afford it yet, but I was keen on taking lessons. I often dreamed of owning a car, but when I mentioned it to Grandad, he said that during the war he'd dreamed of soft paper to wipe his arse with but never saw any. I suppose his generation looked at things differently – the 'war to end all wars' and all that.

The Booths lounged in the back seat, aimlessly chatting whilst Bob negotiated the twisting lanes that led to Southwell. It had been Albert Keates's idea to meet at his place: neutral territory, he reckoned. I think Bob and the Booths were more than happy to agree to his suggestion. It made little difference to me, though I had to admit to being somewhat relieved. I don't think any of us considered

Bob's house the best location for Kate Booth's forthcoming regression

Edgar said that Albert Keates lived in a big house not far from Southwell's celebrated minster and the nearby garden where Bramley apples were first grown. He was full of interesting information, was Edgar Booth. For a born city boy like me, it simply made a pleasant change to experience the rolling pastures and treelined hedgerows. Nevertheless, much as I enjoyed cruising through gentle vales in evening sunshine, it was hard to equate the pastoral splendour with the anomalous purpose we were travelling for.

When we eventually reached the ancient town, it wasn't long before the medieval architecture of the towering minster came into view and, of course, the very garden we'd been informed about. Only minutes later, we swung through a pair of ivy-swathed gateposts crowned with sculptured eagles, a leafy canopy darkening our approach as we coasted on crunching gravel towards the grand residence at the end of the drive. He'd heard us coming and was stood with his back to the open entrance door. Albert Keates casually waved his arm but gave no other indication of a friendly greeting. It seemed he was a man who didn't smile easily.

The house was impressive, entirely in keeping with the neighbourhood. The surrounding area positively shrieked of wealth, causing me to wonder just how profitable the spirituality business really was. I remarked on the style of the leaded windows and Bob said they were mullions – same as the doorway – and I said they reminded me of The County Tavern opposite the Shire Hall, the place where Aubrey worked.

After shaking hands with Keates, we entered a gloomy hallway dominated by a tarnished chandelier. The wainscoted panels and sweeping staircase reminded me of playing Cluedo at Uncle Barry's house on Boxing Days. Apart from the threadbare rug, lonely side table and outmoded phone, the hall was bereft of any decoration, suggesting a home not loved as much as it might have been.

The reception room did nothing to lighten the ambience: faded settee, bulbous-legged table, eight matching chairs and an oak sideboard shamefully decked with a huge bowl of plastic fruit. The once-splendid fireplace was solemnly empty, bearing little evidence of recent use – only a forsaken poker and the soot-grimed chimney bearing witness to its former glory.

Outdoors, the evening air had been pleasantly warm, yet the temperature within stirred memories of more wintry days. Kate Booth shivered, unconsciously stating the obvious, a performance not entirely lost on our host.

'Bit chilly in here for you, is it, Kate? Hang on a minute, dear ... I'll sort something out.'

She looked suitably sheepish at that but flashed a grateful smile all the same. The expression on Keates's face when he left the room failed to equal the willingness his words suggested. After watching him disappear, Edgar Booth glanced sideways at his wife, shaking his head with silent disapproval.

We shuffled and muttered as we waited for our host to return. The somewhat brighter mood of our journey had clouded a little since we entered the dreariness of Albert Keates's house.

When at last we heard the patter of returning footsteps, it was obvious Keates wasn't alone. I glanced at Edgar and noticed his puzzled expression. He'd clearly not expected anyone else that evening.

'Before we go any further, I'd like to introduce Violet Manners; Violet's assisting me with my business for a while.'

Albert Keates coloured with embarrassment, stumbling over his words and pointlessly fiddling with the cord of the heater he carried with him.

''Lo, everyone!'

Violet Manners grinned nervously and waved limply at us. Her shrill, childlike voice was in harmony with her flawless complexion, immediately reminding me of an old-fashioned porcelain doll.

'Very pleased to meet you, Violet.'

Kate Booth, ever one to break the ice, smiled warmly and proffered her hand. The young girl timidly responded, acknowledging the rest of us in similar fashion. When she weakly shook my hand, I found her touch cold and formal. And yet the look she gave me insinuated something more than indifference.

'Now we've been suitably introduced, I suggest we sort ourselves out.'

Having connected the heater, Keates attempted to lift the atmosphere with a display of cheery assertiveness, clapping his hands as though to bring us to order.

'Take your seats then, folks ... there you go, Kate ... settee's for you, dear. Violet's volunteered to organise the drinks, so place your orders if you would. There's tea, coffee, squash, even something stronger if you want, though it might be best to resist the strong stuff for now – that other kind of spirit might be about!'

It was a weak attempt at a poor joke. Nevertheless, Bob took the statement seriously and was quick to make a point.

'We certainly don't intend to summon any spirits, thank you, Bertie. We're here to conduct Kate's regression. And with the greatest respect, we shouldn't, consciously or otherwise, encourage any unwanted visitors. Not on this occasion, if you don't mind.'

Everyone chuckled, though Albert Keates reddened, perhaps more in irritation than embarrassment. Violet took an age to note our orders, afterwards trotting off like a waif from a Dickens workhouse. For some reason, I couldn't help feeling sorry for her, and that caused me to study Keates more closely, questioning his relationship with the young girl – assistant didn't sound right to me. If anything sordid was going on, it would at least give me a tangible reason to dislike him. There was something about the man that disturbed me from the moment I met him, though I couldn't put my finger on exactly what it was.

As if to answer my question, as soon as Violet left the room, Keates immediately began to explain her presence. He must have sensed the pall of suspicion. More than anything else, he'd obviously noticed the questioning looks when he'd unexpectedly reappeared with Violet at his side.

'I don't know why I should, but I feel the need to explain who Violet actually is: something I should have mentioned earlier perhaps … especially to you, Edgar. Sorry about that. I realise I should have told you beforehand, but then things came to a head rather quickly. You see, Violet is in fact my niece – my sister Betty's daughter. Betty recently contacted me in a bit of a state. I already knew about Violet's paranormal gifts; she's much like me and my mother before me in that respect. Betty's not the least bit psychic, though, and has always been distressed by the thought of such practices being conducted by those dear to her. My father held similar views, but with liberal help from the drinks cabinet, he chose to ignore that his wife and son were dabbling in what he annoyingly referred to as the black arts.'

All of a sudden, Albert Keates looked like a troubled man, perhaps worn by the negative reactions he'd experienced since childhood. It didn't seem right to interrupt him, and I was keen to hear the rest of his tale.

'Things weren't too bad to start with.

However, when Violet reached her teens, she began to openly talk about seeing ghosts. That revelation frightened her mother half to death, hearing her young daughter talking so casually about her experiences. Without going into detail, it played on Betty's mind so much that she genuinely feared a mental breakdown. That's when she asked me to take Violet under my wing and guide her along the right path, so to speak. So there it is, pure and simple. I can see how it must have looked, and in truth, I'd rather not have become involved, but I admit to finding it difficult to say no.'

That Keates was genuinely troubled by the situation he'd been obliged to concern himself with was unmistakeable. The realisation of his unwanted predicament caused me to feel guilty about my earlier misgivings. Why I instinctively jump to the wrong conclusions, I really don't know.

'Oh dear, Bertie, I'm sorry to hear you've been landed with such an unwelcome situation. Why on earth didn't you speak to me about it when we were in London together?'

'As I just said, it only came about very recently, and I was in a proper muddle, wondering how Violet might benefit from being with me. I did think to mention it to you, Edgar, but decided it was too complex and somewhat of a personal matter ...'

The sound of approaching footsteps and rattling crockery from the corridor brought the subject to an abrupt close. And in the awkward silence that followed, I think we each came to see Albert Keates and his young niece in a considerably different light.

***

On social occasions, the impression Bob Langham generally conveyed was that of an inveterate follower – a man seeking the comfort of another's direction, whereas in his professional capacity, he invariably morphed into the most assertive of leaders.

That is why our host found himself reluctantly acceding to Bob's unexpected authority. And once the pecking order was recognised, everything quickly fell into place. Violet was diplomatically steered towards the sanctuary of her quarters, and only after she left the room did we began to agree the ground rules for the regression: we were to refrain from promoting anything of a spiritual nature, and we must preserve Kate Booth's wellbeing at all times – agreeing to abandon proceedings if anything of a dangerous or threatening nature were to transpire. I think most of us were thinking of George Davy at that moment, knowing the rules were purely a consequence of his previous disruption.

With the guidelines agreed, Kate made herself comfortable on the settee and began to relax. Given her previous experiences, I couldn't believe how willingly she'd agreed to subject herself to the regression – even more so when recalling those early days when she preferred not to involve herself at all, content to play the accommodating hostess and confidante. Had her ongoing participation been in some way premeditated? Was she too in fact more leader than follower? With Kate, it was hard to be sure. Then there was that other question, the one that persisted in needling me: just who on earth had Kate Booth been referring to when she called me Alfie?!

I nervously waited for Bob to begin his countdown, dreading what consequences might arise. Would the ghastly spectre once again intrude on the regression? If so, would he once more assault the woman who now reclined contentedly on the settee? My heart pounded at the thought of yet another manifestation – could it really have been him at Bob's window? Would he attempt to approach me this time? I squirmed at my cravenness, sighing with relief at the unwavering presence of the veteran combatants who sat by my side.

Where are you, Kate?

Kate?

Ay-up, what yo after then, mester … hey?

There is no preamble this time – not the slightest intimation to suggest the presence of Kate Booth.

Who is it speaking to me? What is your name?

Don't really matter does it, sweetheart?

Yes, it matters to me. Please, tell me what your name is.

Takes all sorts. Why, it's Ethel, sweetheart … Eth, they call me.

Where are you, Eth? Please tell me where you are at the moment.

This is a strange do, if yer like!

The tone of her voice brusquely alters – enticement turning to outrage in a single breath.

Bob tactfully pauses before answering, then …

Forgive me, Eth, I'm really lost, you see. Please help me. Tell me where this place is.

She curses under her breath, but there is a manner of acceptance in her whispered tone.

Up along Parliament Street!

Thank you, Eth. That's very kind of you. If you don't mind me saying as much, you do sound very young …

Oh, 'ere we bleddy go … ah'm old enough, sweetheart! But …

She sniggers knowingly.

Try Bell Yard if it's a proper young un' yer wantin'.

Bell Yard?

There's a club there …

There is growing indifference in her tone.

Eth? Eth?

Too late, duck … no time fer your kind … got to goo now …

Eth, believe me, I'm only interested in you.

There is a ripple of warm laughter, not so much a snigger this time.

Yer seem familiar somehow, sweetheart … reminds me … got ter get home soon.

Is your home somewhere nice?

She snorts derisively.

Bogger all nice about Narra Marsh, me duck!

Narrow Marsh, you say? Eth, please, tell me your surname before you go.

Edgar shifts in his seat; he shares my anticipation. If the answer arrives, it will be a revelation.

Surname?

Yes, your full name. I know it's Eth for Ethel, but Ethel who?

Another pause, briefer this time.

Ah reckon ah do know yer now, sweetheart ... yer must know me an' all, then?!

The words are profound and suggestive, yet there is an edge of fear.

Yer do, don't yer? It's me, yer daft bogger ... Eth ... Ethel Bentley!

Bob shakes his head and stares into space before responding. When he does, he exhibits an emergent unease.

Ethel Bentley ... and you live in Narrow Marsh?

She exhales meaningfully, as though resigned to something that saddens her.

Got to goo now, sweetheart ... best ter get supper ready afore ...

Bob leans forward, eyes widening as he asks the question.

Is there something more you want to say, Eth?

His head tilts to one side as though straining for an answer. There is a touch of desperation about him.

Always, remember?

What's that, Eth?

Oh, for the love of ... Oh my good God ...

You're here!

A dreadful keening comes from Kate's twisted lips, and her body is at once enlivened.

I fear the worst is about to happen again.

Chapter 20
Nottingham 1967

Morning in the city. The early strength of the sun augurs the oppressive heat to come. The square is empty save for last-minute workers hastening across its slabs. As 'Little John' peals the last chime of nine, I vacate my bench and abandon my Daily Sketch.

I ignore the muttering tramp elatedly retrieving my discarded paper and head for Cheapside and Bridlesmith Gate. It is a route to work, but not today. This day is reserved for other purposes. A day off – a day to myself. A morning of strolling the familiar streets before savouring the beery delights of the Tavern.

I think of last weekend spent with Ann – Saturday in Jessops looking at white dresses. Sunday in Gedling, giggling with her mam at dusty old albums. Come the autumn, we plan for spring in earnest. Rings and dresses, cake and music. Who do we invite, and who do we not?

Try as I might, I cannot turn my mind to those things at this time. My love and intentions are as one with Ann's, but I cannot completely enter her world. Part of me is snagged in that other place – a foot this side, a foot that. They are grave matters that divert me. Matters to be settled before we follow our dream.

Those few days in Mablethorpe had dented our savings, therefore it was heads down till the wedding. The only problem was the holidays we had to take before the end of the year, otherwise we'd forfeit them and not be paid for their loss. After discussing it at some length, we agreed it might be nice to take a few winter days together – do something inexpensive like sitting by the fire reading our books or playing games. Then Ann said she needed to visit an aunt in Grimsby who was poorly. And then there was the old schoolfriend who'd moved to Doncaster that she'd promised to share a weekend with. This was good news for me in a way, because I too wanted a day or so on my own to attend to things I might have found awkward to explain. And so I took the opportunity to ask Ann if she minded me taking a day now and then – just a few things I needed to sort out. Being a good sort, she agreed without any fuss, and no difficult questions either.

***

I thought to walk to places we'd identified from the regressions and subsequent research. With that in mind, I decided to spend the morning in the Lace Market area, trusting I wouldn't meet anyone from work and be obliged to explain why I was spending a precious day off only yards from my workbench.

Reaching the end of Bridlesmith Gate, I paused to study the post office that stood on the opposite corner, the one identified from my regressions as originally being The Postern Gate, the very inn my other self had allegedly frequented over a century before. In a fanciful moment, it seemed the chimes of Little John not only foretold the passing of time, but also the intensifying heat of the coming afternoon. Yet despite the growing temperature, a cooling breeze came from nowhere to gust at my back, chilling me slightly as I contemplated the building opposite – its doorway and windows.

I stared more attentively, desperately squinting through flashes of sunlight reflecting from nearby shop windows, my heartbeat increasing with anxious expectation. Thankfully, though, I didn't see what I rather absurdly expected to see – no staring eyes or waving hands. Then, as quickly as it had arrived, the breeze died away, the intensifying heat returning to sweat me. For some obscure reason, it crossed my mind to thank the Lord for coincidences and to wonder how much deeper my imagination might take me.

I turned away and wandered through Weekday Cross to Pilcher Gate, drawing perilously close to the building where I worked. Keeping a sharp eye open for skiving colleagues, I analysed the surrounding buildings at length, vainly looking for breaks in the patterns of the brickwork, anything to suggest the outline of a former alley or extended wall. Despite my best efforts, I could find no evidence of Aways Yard. I knew it had to be somewhere thereabouts, most likely a cobbled courtyard enclosed by tenements, maybe accessed by a narrow entrance from Pilcher Gate, itself a constricted carriageway.

These were streets I walked on workdays,

sometimes in the company of fellow workers, with little chance of finding what I was looking for whilst in their presence. Then I realised that discovering the exact location of Always Yard wasn't that important, but as Edgar had once said, 'One always learns more by paying attention to detail.'

My next location was eminently easier to find, and with clearer purpose. And so I set off for the city archives with the intention of re-examining the census of 1891, hoping to find something else of interest relating to that particular year. I had already found George Davy, but now I wanted to search again, this time armed with details arising from later regressions, scant as they were.

With the help of a more receptive assistant, I searched by trade for coal merchants, or coalmen, as they were often described, hoping the one from Mr Booth's regression might materialise as someone associated by age and location with George Davy. I found a few potential candidates and was narrowing the search even further when the young assistant came over and asked if I'd found what I was looking for. When I shook my head, she put a finger up to her eye and asked me to stay where I was. She'd obviously had an idea.

When she returned, she was carrying a weighty tome, which she placed on the desk before me. She introduced herself as Alice and, being polite, I told her I was Arthur. With that, she almost jumped into the seat next to me. Alice seemed nice, and we got on with each other right away – as you do sometimes. She was sitting awfully close, though, and I couldn't help thinking what Ann might say if she saw us now, cosily sat together as we were.

'It's a copy of an old Wright's Directory relating to Nottinghamshire, Arthur. This one covers the 1890s and lists all the trade names and addresses registered at that time. You'll probably find a lot of references to coal ... so make sure you've got plenty of lead in your pencil!'

She giggled suggestively and gave me one of those looks. Alice was quite pretty in a studious sort of way, and it looked like she'd taken a shine to me. I smiled noncommittedly, more out of courtesy than anything else. When I glanced at her, I couldn't help imagining Ann sitting beside me and thinking nobody could ever take her place.

Alice looked a bit miffed when I returned the directory to her desk. I simply thanked her for her help, smiled, and nodded goodbye. I felt a bit awkward, though, belatedly saying I'd be back sometime and hoped to see her again. I think that managed to take the edge off her injured feelings; Ann reckons I'm too sensitive about what people think about me.

It was one of those moments when things turned out better than I could have hoped for. That evening, after visiting the archives for the second time, I sat at my kitchen table and sifted through the pile of notes I'd earlier scribbled down. Barely ten minutes later, I discovered a coal dealer on Carrington Street trading under the title of Watts & Robertson. When I cross-referenced those names against the ones I'd recorded from the census, I could hardly believe what had fallen into my lap.

There it was, an entry for one William Watts, aged thirty-nine, widowed, working as a coalman, and residing on Woolpack Lane. The fact I'd stumbled upon a plausible link filled me with great excitement. Those words first written in 1891 glowed like beacons on the darkest night – surely it was too much of a coincidence: George Davy living on Woolpack Lane at the same time as William Watts. I didn't think it overly whimsical to imagine Watts delivering coal to Milk Square with a better than equal chance of having some kind of association with George Davy.

He's come back wi' me ...

Who has? Who is that with you?

George ... yer know him, don't yer? So why ask, hey, mester?

***

Early afternoon, and the temperature in the glare of the sun was bordering on ridiculous. Those lucky enough to have been there reckon that during August you only have to walk a few paces in a place like southern Italy before complete exhaustion sets in. If that was indeed the case, I certainly wouldn't be booking a Roman holiday anytime soon, more easily and cheaply achieving the same effect in Nottingham and with a better chance of knowing what people were talking about. Well, most of the time anyway.

The doors of the City Tavern were propped wide open, the temperature within offering meagre respite from the brutal heat. It was busier than usual – a few more legal types from across the road hogging the bar. I waved to the landlord and he waved back, mouthing, 'usual?' I answered with a thumbs up and looked around for Aubrey. And there he was, sitting near the dartboard, waving an empty glass at me. Noting the dregs of foam popping at its rim, I guessed he'd drained his pint as soon as he'd seen me walk in. The landlord picked up on it and raised his eyebrows. I duly nodded and pushed through the moneyed bunch to get to the bar. Waiting for the drinks, I wondered how many more pints would eat into my fiver before I got the information Aubrey had promised.

'Yo din't gimme a lot o' time, me duck!'

'It *was* last week, Aubrey.'

'Yeah, Thursday, though. Any road, ah might o' got what yer wanted – woth another pint or two, mind yer!'

During the previous week, I had spent one or two of my valuable lunch breaks outside Shire Hall, waiting for a sweeping brush with Aubrey on the end of it. When I eventually caught up with him, I said it might be worth a drink or two if he'd double check to see if there were any references to George Davy hidden away. When I'd mentioned that name to him the first time, he'd said he'd never heard of him. However, I thought it worth another try, being convinced a character like Davy would have had some sort of relationship with the local constabulary.

'Go on then, spill the beans.'

'Well, matter o' fact, George Davy's on record after all. Not for owt serious as far as ah can see – a bit o' drink an' rough stuff mostly, and a few warnin's. Ah also found aht he worra witness one time. Ah've gorra friend in the archives, yer see. I gerrim them mucky magazines sometimes ... so ah've sorta gorrim in me pocket, if yer get me drift. He's one o' them posh boggers, so he wun't want folk in the office thinkin' he were a bleddy pervert!'

I leafed through my notepad to find a clean page and started to write down some notes.

'Yo don't wok for the newspapers, da yer? What wi' yer writing it dahn an' doin'?'

'No, I've just got a bad memory, Aubrey.'

'Only ah don't want me name on the bleddy front page!'

'Be assured, Aubrey, I'm not a bleddy journalist. Everything you say is strictly in confidence.'

'That's all right then, me duck. Thosty weather today, in't it?'

He'd emptied his glass already and was suggestively tapping the base of it on the table. I told him I'd get him another one just as soon as he'd finished what he was saying.

'Like ah were sayin', he weren't exactly a well-known villain. But he worra character witness one time. Spoke up for a bloke called … nah then, what worris name agen?'

Aubrey scratched his head and resumed tapping his glass. I ignored his unashamed gestures and firmly told him there'd be no more free drinks until he gave me everything he'd found out.

'Alright then, have it yer own road, me duck. But don't goo boggering off wi 'aht treating me ter a couple more!'

I resisted the impulse to respond in kind, choosing to play the waiting game instead.

'Funny enough, it were another fella wi' the same name – another George, ah mean. George Boyd it wor, well-known house-breaker, in an aht o' clink since he worra kid. He spent hover 'arf 'is life inside – got ten years, one time. Never made no difference, though. He were still thievin' in 'is owd age.'

Aubrey went quiet then and gave me a sly grin, leaning in close to me, as though ready to share a secret.

'Ah've gorra picture on him in me pocket.'

Hot as the day was, his words sent a shiver through me.

'A picture of George Davy?'

'Nah … t'other bogger … George Boyd!'

'Oh.'

'Well it's gorra be woth summat, an't it?'

'Yeah, okay. I'll get you another pint, Aubrey.'

'Owd on, me duck … it's woth more than

that!

That was when the idea occurred to me. It had to be worth a try. I grabbed hold of Aubrey's glass and made ready to go to the bar.

'Tell you what, Aubrey ... why don't you lean a bit harder on your posh friend and ask him to spare me half an hour or so. Maybe I could meet him here one night. Tell him you'll sort him out with a few more of those dirty magazines for his trouble. It could put a fiver in your pocket ...'

Aubrey's eyes lit up at the magic words. There was no need to wait for a response; I already knew what the answer would be.

Chapter 21
Nottingham 1967

Down in the basement, saws buzz and hammers beat a steady rhythm – hardboard cut and nailed to frames. One floor up, the painter paints. Another flight, and writers write. Unrelenting regeneration – boards and banners in jolly hues – our future reliant on this faddish craze.

Cinemas close and production declines. It is slow but we notice the steady loss. The writing is on the wall, but we are not employed to inscribe its putative message. I am fortunate – time-served men are at risk. Luck comes at great cost, though. No more cosy benches and predictable days for me. Early starts and random hours assigned to ageing auditoria, erstwhile theatres once transformed to cinemas now of a sudden to bingo halls. Endless nailing and screwing, painting and writing till the job is done.

This week Leicester, next week Hull. Overnight stays and convenience living – chips and pop, fags and chocolate.

Time away from Ann. Tender exchanges in stinky phone boxes, handfuls of pennies pressed into slots. Kisses blown across the miles – see you Saturday ... Still, it's a living.

It was the height of summer when my life changed in the twinkling of an eye. One morning I was summoned by the boss and told redundancies were looking likely. I wondered why he was making a point of telling me, concluding I was in line for the high jump. As it happened, he said some nice things about how hard-working and honest I was. Then he said if I liked the idea, he'd see about transferring me to the installation team. I spluttered and said it was a bit sudden and would like some time to think about it. The disapproving frown that creased his forehead made me think it was then or never – and so I said okay.

After clearing my bench on Friday afternoon, the following Monday morning saw me crammed into a lorry laden with boards, tools and ladders, crawling its way to somewhere in Yorkshire. We knew the poster trade was dying on its feet, but we'd chosen to ignore the fact and hope for the best. Much against working-class principles, we praised the boss for winning a contract to convert a bunch of old cinemas into bingo halls, agreeing that at best, it would be a stay of execution. The work would only last until the venues ran out – either that or the advent of plastic signs would hammer the final nails into the coffin of handwritten expertise.

Quite apart from the underlying worry of redundancy, my new role impacted badly on my personal life. The hours were unpredictable and I was never sure where I'd be beyond the next few days. To make matters even more difficult, I was warned that Fridays occasionally encroached into weekends. The upshot was that spending time with Ann and arranging meetings with Bob and the Booths suddenly became quite the task. Luckily, Ann was adaptable, there being very little that fazed her too much.

'Going up in the world, then, are we, Arthur?'

'Not really, Kate ... bit more on my basic and some overtime pay.'

'More for the wedding fund then, hey, Arthur?'

'I'm pretty sure Ann will see it that way, yeah!'

There we were, chit-chatting and relaxing in the evening breeze that relieved the dog days of late summer. There were a few ominous rumbles of thunder in the air too, each roll more distant than the previous. We were in the Booths' garden again, quaffing fruit punch and munching on crisps and salted nuts. I had better things to tell them than mundane matters relating to work. They'd straightaway understood my time was more limited, and so we decided to restrict our meetings to Mondays whenever possible. A day or two here or there made little difference to the Booths, with Bob saying Mondays were fine with him.

'We appreciate you've been busy on our behalf, Arthur, so please do tell.'

Edgar was obviously keen to get on, and I understood the reason for his impatience. To an extent, we'd dallied the summer away, each of us spending our time in different ways since the last time we'd been together at Albert Keates's house in Southwell.

***

I recall fearing the worst when that awful

clamour emerged without warning from Kate Booth's gaping mouth – arms instantly flailing at some unseen assailant. I still picture her husband leaping from his seat, his toppled chair clattering to the floor behind him, Bob instinctively recoiling, an open palm clasped to his mouth, Albert Keates seated throughout, calmly enunciating a whispered prayer.

It was with equal suddenness that the disturbing interlude mercifully concluded. As if waking from a redundant nightmare, Kate blinked and yawned, her eyes widening as she slowly regained her senses. With normality returning, Edgar emitted an audible sigh, wiped his brow, and casually righted his chair. Bob raised his hands skywards in a gesture of bewilderment, and Albert Keates swivelled at the sound of an opening door.

'Sorry ... but I thought I heard something.'

Violet Manners was stood in the doorway, saucer eyes conveying an innocence not quite as convincingly as she might have thought. Not for the first time, I thought there was something more to her than met the eye.

Once we'd calmed ourselves, we sat together to discuss the outcome of the session, the details that had arisen encouraging our conviction that the four of us shared a previous existence. The plausible references to real locations and the actual name of the subject offered at least an opportunity to extend our investigations. It was, however, one particular comment that really tweaked our curiosity.

The woman called Ethel had given the impression of knowing the person she was speaking to – Bob Langham? It was an interesting supposition. Albert Keates implied the reference might acknowledge the involvement of anyone present ... or even someone else entirely. He went on to explain that the spiritual sphere didn't work in the same way as the physical world. He maintained spirits were transient souls that sometimes attached themselves to living beings in dissimilar ways. The point he made inevitably led to good-natured but intense banter between him and Edgar, serving only to distract us from our prime objective. Inevitably, it fell to Kate to interrupt the two men's opposing speculations.

'Gentlemen, please! Interesting as it is to hear your observations, we're not here to debate the finer points of spirituality. As Bob earlier pointed out, it's a regression, not a séance. Just because I rolled my eyes and made funny noises doesn't necessarily mean I experienced a ghostly visitation; after all, I know well enough what it's like to be harassed by mischievous spirits.'

She glanced at me before looking at the others. Quite what she meant by that, I wasn't sure.

As usual, I said nothing and waited for her to continue.

'There's something else we ought to bear in mind as well: this kind of thing has happened before. Just think about when Edgar was regressed – the contact in that session revealed he was delivering coal. And that "someone" who was with him recognised Bob. If I remember rightly, he said something like, "He's with me and he knows you".'

What Kate Booth was saying was correct. The same message had emerged from two separate sessions involving two separate subjects; it was too much of a coincidence. Regression or séance? The dividing line was becoming thinner.

***

I made a show of producing my notes from an old satchel I'd recently found in the family loft when visiting there with Ann. It had been in poor condition, so I'd detached the shoulder-straps and burnished the leather with boot polish. I was quite proud of it and thought it made me look professional.

'If you're ready, I'll tell you where I've got to. The summer's been quite fruitful as far as research is concerned. Before I get carried away, though, let's see what the rest of you think.'

I found it satisfying to see they were paying attention, thinking it an indication of my newfound sophistication. Everyone at home had certainly been surprised by the refinement of my words and expressions. Ann had been amongst the first to notice. She'd responded by encouraging me even more, suggesting one day I might even write a book about my mysterious escapades. I thought that might be a bit of a stretch, though maybe an idea for later. Hopefully, by then, everything would be resolved.

I began by talking about my investigations regarding the two locations referred to in the regressions, telling them about locating the approximate whereabouts of Always Yard before confirming that Milk Square had been somewhere off Glasshouse Street. I added that neither location was of value in the greater scheme of things, and by the time I moved on to the census records, their expressions had transformed from expectancy to something close to disappointment.

Admittedly, it was one dreary detail after another, there being little of revelatory value to stir their interest. However, I had purposely saved the best till last, one of the ploys I'd learned from Edgar Booth: the art of delayed delivery.

And so, after suitably pausing for effect, I reminded them of Woolpack Lane and the lodging house where George Davy was recorded as living in 1891. They nodded at the dated material – old news we'd discussed on previous occasions. Then I told them I thought I had found the very building where he lived, or at least where the building once stood. It was a minor revelation, but they seemed mildly roused by the disclosure.

'More interestingly, though, there was someone else who lived on Woolpack Lane at the same time as George Davy. The name I unearthed was William Watts ... and William Watts was a coalman by trade.'

'A coalman! Are you saying it's the very same man who appeared in my own regression, Arthur?'

Edgar Booth was suddenly all ears, his face purple with excitement. He wasn't the only one, either. Bob Langham was agape and scratching his head with some intent.

'You mean the one who said he was sitting on a bucket? The one talking about delivering coal to Milk Square? Yes ... yes, of course it is.'

'He also said he knew you, Bob ...'

Kate Booth had a fondness for reacting differently to the rest of us. After making that comment, she leaned back in her chair, staring ahead as if at some distant horizon. A shadow crossed Bob's face when he realised the implications of her mischievous observation. Was he concerned about how much seemed to be revolving around him? Given the recent hauntings at his house, he could be forgiven for thinking in that direction.

'And that's not all ...'

They turned to me with renewed interest as I told them about Aubrey and his knowledge concerning the Shire Hall. I then went on to describe Aubrey's presentation at The County Tavern, revealing George Davy's minor criminal history. Shortly after that, I brandished the picture of George Boyd, the villain Davy had vouched for in the Shire Hall courtroom. Much like me when I first viewed the image, they were surprised by the sharpness of the nineteenth century mugshot. The black and white print might have been developed that very morning, given how fresh it appeared.

The image of a morose George Boyd personified a Dickensian villain; unlike many lawbreakers of the day, Boyd preferred to sport a bowler hat and tailored jacket. The overriding feature of the felon, however, was the unrestrained anger radiating from his likeness. If the image had been of George Davy himself, not one of us would have been surprised.

'There's a date stamped on the back, Edgar.'

He turned the photo over and smirked meaningfully, tapping the print against his knee before making a comment.

'1888 ... Now let me see, what date was the census recording George Davy's residence?'

'1891, Edgar.'

'Yes ... that fits well enough, doesn't it? What about the chap who's supposed to be me? What date did you discover for him?'

I looked him square in the eye and observed the tension in his expression. He put me in mind of a Christmas scene – of a child anxiously staring at the last gift in the pile, hoping against hope that it might be what he'd wished for.

'I'm sure you've already guessed the answer to that question ... or maybe you've had one of your visions, hey, Edgar?'

His lip curled slightly when the barb found its mark. I had selfishly indulged myself in a moment of modest power, regretting the comment almost before it slipped out. I continued with barely a pause, hoping the moment might pass and be forgotten – least said, soonest mended.

'1891 census, Edgar ... how does that suit you?'

He closed his eyes for a moment, as though offering thanks to some invisible deity. I sensed the corroboration meant an awful lot to him.

'In answer to your previous remark, Arthur, I rarely experience psychic insights relating to myself. Still, regardless of your cheek, I have to thank you for the energy and diligence you've expended on our behalf. It's genuinely appreciated.'

I had been put in my place, everyone in the room recognising the moment for what it was. I smiled awkwardly and chose to say nothing. Obviously, growing out of my adolescence remained a work in progress.

'So they lived on the same street at the same time, did they? George Davy and Billy Watts.'

It was as though Kate spoke those words to herself.

'Kate ... can I ask why you just called him Billy and not William? It's almost like you already know him.'

'Dunno really, Bob ... I suppose it just came out like that.'

Bob eyed her with a degree of scepticism, and he wasn't the only one. Edgar, deliberately or otherwise, ignored the exchange, as though lost in his own world and oblivious to the conversation around him. It seemed everyone but me thought we'd finished for the day. Even so, I bided my time and waited for the right moment.

'Well done indeed, Arthur. Like Edgar said, you've come up with some very encouraging information.'

'Thanks for that, Bob, much appreciated.'

Kate languidly rose from her chair, stretching before sharing the dregs of the fruit punch between us. Though it was the onset of evening, the light from the dipping sun and the gentle breeze caused us to linger a while longer.

'Sorry, folks, but I haven't quite finished yet. I've got even more to tell you about ...'

The three of them looked over with more than passing interest, Edgar blinking forcefully as though waking from a heavy sleep, suddenly eager to hear me out.

'You may be interested to know that I spoke to someone else from the Shire Hall – an office type who Aubrey knows. You might recall me saying that Aubrey's a cleaner there. Quite how he came to be associated with a senior member of staff is probably best left for another time. Suffice to say, the chap agreed to search for some additional information. Let's call him Herbert: suits him well enough, I'd say. Anyway, Aubrey arranged for Herbert to meet with me one evening last week. Though it cost me a few bob, I think it was worth the expense. He seemed nervous at first, so I treated him to a whisky or two before he eventually agreed to examine some records for me. We met again a couple of nights later, when he produced a bit more than I expected.'

I paused for a moment to clear my throat, swallowing the last drop of cloudy punch, chewing away the excess peel rather than picking it from my teeth.

'Sorry about that … I'd asked him to look for anything concerning George Davy, William Watts and Ethel Bentley from roundabout the 1890s. He reckoned he'd not been able to unearth much more concerning George Davy other than one or two recorded warnings and the same witness entry Aubrey had found. The really good news, however, was that he'd found a few mentions of Ethel Bentley. You might not be surprised to hear that her records mostly related to some form of prostitution. It suggested she was well known to the authorities for incidents referencing hotel visits and common street walking. To be crude, it looks like she was putting it about a bit.'

'You can never tell what causes people to degrade themselves in that way, Arthur, specially in those days. Times were really hard then, and some women made their way as best they could, many of them so desperate they'd do just about anything to put food on the table.'

I silently accepted what appeared to be yet another gentle scolding, this time from Kate rather than her husband. I reminded myself to watch what I said in their presence. They were from a different era, one that lived by more traditional values, many of their generation finding the impudence of the '60s difficult to tolerate.

'There's something else about Ethel Bentley you might be interested to hear ...'

I deliberately hesitated before delivering the punchline, once again thinking I'd spent too much time listening to Edgar Booth.

'One of Ethel Bentley's records mentions a common-law husband who pleaded clemency on her behalf. The husband's name was recorded as being ... William Watts.'

My moment in the spotlight was over. In spite of the modest reprimands and disapproving glances, they made it obvious how pleased they were with what I'd unearthed without their supervision. It's funny how people suddenly view you in a different light. It's the look in their eyes that gives them away: that, and the manner in which they address you. For the first time in my short life, I experienced that particular glow in the dusk of a summer's evening.

Chapter 22
Nottingham 1967

Ann's in Doncaster, so I visit the family – gossip and cackle from the other room.

Men don't do that, not in this family. Spending time with Dad and Grandad was something I did when I was a kid … not anymore, though.

Dad and Fred – chalk and cheese – me the one in the middle. With Fred, it's listen and laugh in all the right places. With Dad, it's mostly talking to a vacant space. He's ever dreaming his big ideas – not much time for us, it seems, not these days anyway.

Bottles of stout, black and creamy, conversation hit and miss … awkward silences … fishing … football and the price of fags. Dad's playing a game, I think – doing his duty for peace and quiet – husband, father and son. I wonder what he's really doing … wonder where he's really going … something and somewhere for sure … just a matter of time, maybe.

How they natter on and on, Grandma, Mam and sisters too …

'Young Arthur thinks he's summat now. Fancy words, airs and graces. Gets more like his dad. Young Arthur's changed … thinks he's grown … getting married to prove the point. Strange boy, Arthur … always has been. Nice girl, she is … will she last, though? Proper loner, in't he … always been a funny bogger. That poor girl's got no idea …'

If only they knew … what would they say? How different their nattering might be.

We stampeded into the Co-op along with others of similar mind. The deluge came without warning, soaking pavements and people alike. Bonding in our common calamity, we chuckled together as we patted our clothes and brushed out the rain that sopped our hair. It was the price we paid for trusting the blue of the sky and the white of the clouds and not thinking to take our macs.

Ann and me were in town to look for some wedding stationery, as I was told to call it. Our wedding plans had expanded from the modest proposals we'd first scribbled down. There was no blame or fault apportioned to either of us for that. Things had simply developed the way things sometimes do. A few instances of 'wouldn't it be nice', and costs had suddenly shot through the roof. We were both in work and I was earning good money from overtime, so we had some decent savings between us. It wasn't so much a question of money, more how it might look to our families. Neither of us were from privileged backgrounds – quite the reverse – and we didn't want anyone thinking we were showing off.

I loved the place we used to call 'Big Co-op', its sprawling floors accessed by contemporary staircases, modern lifts, and, wonder of wonders, an escalator – not many of those about when I was a lad. We used to play on the magic stairs, shouting and laughing until chased away. I matured with that building, every occasion and season accommodated for:

childhood, adolescence and all points beyond. And there was that special place deep in the basement, the wonderland that enticed the teens of the day. There we'd huddle in acoustic booths, listening to records for free, eyeing the girls in their weekend finery, rocking and posing to the tunes of the day. Oh, those teenage dreams.

I was patiently waiting, indolently staring into space, when I became aware of someone watching me. Ann was only steps away, elbows perched on a glass-topped counter, examining a variety of cheap necklaces – she really loved cheap necklaces. It was quite early, not many people about, the floodtide of Saturday shoppers yet to materialise.

The man appeared to be looking in my direction, craning out from behind a supporting column, one hand on its marbled surface as if to support his exaggerated posture. Just to make sure I wasn't mistaken, I turned to see I was the only one in his line of sight. Ann and the assistant were the nearest, though not near enough to be the subject of the man's attention.

When I looked back, for some elusive reason I expected him to be gone. Yet there he stood in exactly the same position. Annoyed by his perceived rudeness, I returned his stare with similar intensity. My response made no difference. Completely undeterred, he maintained his ridiculous gaping without turning as much as a hair.

And so with a surge of cavalier fortitude, I decided to approach him and question his motives. Not being the quarrelsome type, I admit I found that proposition somewhat unsettling. Though having no recollection of knowing him, I was left with little alternative but to challenge him head-on.

Having glanced to see Ann still immersed in the necklaces, I turned with the intention of walking to where the man was standing … or rather … where he had been standing. This time he really wasn't there. Although relieved at not having to confront the fellow, in my aggravated state I really wanted to know the reason for his disconcerting behaviour.

On arriving at the column where he'd been standing, I thought to catch sight of him scurrying away. But when I scanned the stairs and the footways between the various displays, I saw no sign of him. To all intents and purposes, he'd completely disappeared.

Thinking it over, I thought he might have worked there – simply looking to see if I needed any assistance. After all, he was dressed appropriately … if a little outmoded, his age perhaps … and that moustache …

***

Meeting Edgar without his wife was a reasonably rare occurrence, though not as rare as the other way round.

'What can I do for you that's so urgent, Arthur?'

'A couple of things are bothering me, but I wouldn't say they were particularly urgent.'

'It's not what you say, Arthur, it's more the anxiety you're projecting. You clearly want to unburden yourself of something; I detected as much when you rang me. There's an anxiety inside you bursting to come out.'

I couldn't say much to that. Thinking about it, he was more than likely right.

'There's something of a personal nature I'd like to ask you first, Edgar. I don't think it's anything much. You might even tell me to mind my own business. It was something Kate said when ... then again, perhaps it's not for now ...'

'Of course, Arthur. Stop putting yourself under pressure. You're as tense as I've ever known you. Whatever's the matter, old chap?'

With anyone else, I might not have said anything about it, but out of everyone in my small circle of family and friends, Edgar Booth was the only one I thought might understand me.

'Idiotic as it might sound coming from me, Edgar, I think I might have seen a ghost!'

'Yes, we all know about that, apart from Bob, of course. You reckon something was waving at you from his window.'

'Well, yes ... but that's not what I wanted to talk to you about. Maybe I was imagining things then, what with everything that was going on at the time. No, this is entirely different.'

'Oh, I see. Go on then, Arthur, get it out of

your system.'

'It was the strangest thing, Edgar – in the Co-op of all places – broad daylight on a Saturday morning, can you believe? It couldn't have occurred in a more conventional place.'

'You might be surprised how many things thought to be commonplace aren't necessarily so, Arthur. Anyway, please tell me exactly what you saw.'

He was taking me seriously and I knew I was doing the right thing by seeking his advice. I went on to reveal my experience, recalling as much detail as I could remember. He didn't interrupt me once, preferring instead to fix his gaze on me with much the same intensity as had the manifestation I was telling him about.

'At first I was annoyed, Edgar; maybe that clouded my thinking. I should have noticed he didn't entirely belong there – the way he was dressed and that funny moustache I think they call a handlebar. He had bushy sideburns as well, not so unusual on younger people these days, but he was more your age, Edgar and ...'

'Men my age don't usually sport those sort of whiskers, do they, Arthur?'

'Sorry, Edgar, didn't mean to be rude or anything.'

He chuckled and slapped my shoulder to take the edge off his remark.

'You know, I could see something like this coming, Arthur ... said as much to Kate only the other day. It's almost like explaining the birds and bees to an adolescent – not that you're adolescent anymore, of course.'

'Sorry, I'm not following. What d'you mean exactly?'

'Well ... sticking with the birds and bees analogy, some believe the best way of dealing with the eternal "coming of age" dilemma is to tackle it when an incident occurs to suggest sexual awakening – an episode that conveniently triggers a conversation.'

I recognised where he was coming from and guessed what was coming next.

'Please don't be perturbed by what I'm about to say, Arthur. You see, I believe you also have the gift.'

'The gift, Edgar?'

Though I thought I understood what he was saying, I desperately needed clarification of what I feared he meant.

'You should be in no doubt that you have the innate ability to see things others do not see.'

'You really think I saw a ghost, then, Edgar?'

'Yes, I believe by some vague circumstance, you unwittingly permitted a bewildered soul to enter your psychic sphere. Indeed you may have observed other such souls without realising their lifeless nature. You are by no means alone in that. While there are many that teeter on the edge of the unknown, others like me embrace the endowment with forbearance. Those who hesitate at the threshold and never cross are legion. In your case, for instance, although you have strong embryonic ability, you naively deny its presence. At the same time, you welcome the thrill of the chase but fear the reality of the darkness beyond. I suppose that's quite understandable.'

I had no idea what to say in response to those claims, though I thought perhaps he might be right. It was a notion I'd flirted with for some time – teetering on the edge, as he put it. The worst thing was the creeping apprehension that muddled my thinking. I had no desire whatsoever to see apparitions of the dead; the very thought of experiencing what Bob had been suffering scared me witless.

'I hope I don't experience anything again, Edgar. It might sound cowardly, but I don't think I'm built for that sort of malarky.'

'Oh, I think you are, Arthur. You simply don't understand it well enough yet. In the meantime, try to understand that as long as you resist your talent, you're unlikely to have too many similar experiences. Enough for now, though, I need to get home. We're going dancing ... at least Kate is. I can only clomp about and make a complete fool of myself. Did you say there was something else?'

'Yeah, a couple of things, actually, but one of them can wait.'

'Go on then, no disrespect, but I need to make haste or I'll be late.'

'Well, I was thinking, Edgar, if we're working on the assumption that our four past lives are in some way connected, why have only three of us been regressed?'

'Except for Bob, you mean?'

'Yeah, so ...'

'I've been thinking along the same lines,

Arthur. It's something we need to address sooner rather than later, and I really must remember to raise the matter when we meet next Monday. Are you certain that's it for now?'

'Yes, I'm happy to leave it there. You get on your way and give my best to Kate. See you next Monday, and thanks for the advice.'

He tapped his head as though remembering something. Then, finding his purse, he extracted a neatly folded ten pound note, which he discreetly placed on the table in front of me.

'Pay for our teas out of that, Arthur, and please keep the change. Hopefully, it'll cover some of your recent expenses ... County Tavern, et cetera.'

He grinned and was off before I could thank him properly. Once again, I thought a true gentleman lurked under that irritating flannel of his. In light of his generosity, I was glad I'd not asked the other question, then wondered why it continued to nag at me so much. At first I'd thought Kate calling me Alfie was simply a boozy clanger, but for some reason, I thought there was a lot more to it than that. Perhaps Edgar was right about me having the gift.

Meeting him in the café in Arnold had given me more to think about than I had anticipated. Sipping the tepid dregs from the bottom of my cup, I watched him crossing the road, making his way home to his wife. What he said about me having the gift had immediately filled me with dread – surprising, then, how quickly that feeling was fading.

It seemed I was adapting to the weird occurrences, more lately seeing them as an inevitable part of my life. Even so, the incident in the Co-op wasn't something I'd rush to share with anyone else, though I was certain Kate Booth was mere minutes away from knowing all about it. I hadn't mentioned anything about my ghostly experience to Ann as I didn't want to spoil the memory of what had turned out to be an otherwise pleasant day. Even if I did decide to tell her at some stage, or even someone else, what was I supposed to say? 'Oh, by the way, did I tell you about that ghost I met in the Co-op last Saturday?'

Chapter 23
Nottingham 1967

We're in South London – have been since Tuesday – never travelled this far before. Job's gone well – Thursday and we're done – inspection passed and signed away. Chris says okay then, tomorrow we'll see the sights – but not a word to anyone.

Tomorrow's here. We park the lorry. Chris knows his way from demob days – 'Off this road somewhere, I think.' We turn a corner and there it is, only a statue, but it's England to me.

Zipping tubes to here and there, abbey, cathedral, parliament and square. Bacon cobs over the winding river, back to the lorry for the long trip home.

Oh, what tales to tell, though not a mention to anyone. The boss knows nothing and never will. Oh, what a day for us working lads.

Home at last at late o'clock. I sit and muse – my two lives are turning in different ways – one life takes me far... the other farther still.

'Yes, okay, then, it's a reasonable request and I guess it makes sense.'

'As long as you're absolutely certain, Bob.'

'I don't think I'll ever be that, Edgar. Even so, it's only fair for me to take a turn. Though God only knows what might happen come the time.'

'In that case, I'll ring him – Albert I mean, not God – see if he can do next Monday. Failing that, we'll go for the first available Monday after that.'

I couldn't help feeling we'd pushed Bob into it. Had we not made the suggestion, I was convinced he'd never have offered to undergo his own regression. That would have appeared hypocritical, seeing as how he'd been happy enough to regress the rest of us. I could understand his reticence, though, given what he'd experienced at home. Then there were those characters who appeared to recognise him during the regressions – moments I thought especially chilling.

We agreed that one of us was most likely the incarnation of George Davy, but we couldn't be certain as to which of us it actually was. In the early days, it looked like being me. But then the game had moved on, and it could have been any of us – even someone outside the circle, according to Bertie Keates.

The conversation died away when Edgar dialled the number. Except for Edgar himself, the intended venue was not an especially popular choice. However, given that the hypnotherapist Bob recommended lived somewhere near Grantham, Keates's house in Southwell made practical sense.

'Bertie? Hello ... Yes, it's me ... How the devil are you, old chap? Well, you and me both. We're getting on a bit, you know. Listen, I've got yet another favour to ask of you, and I promise not to be offended if you refuse. Is there any possibility we might convene at your place again? Another regression, actually ...

Next Monday would be perfect for us, but if that's difficult, don't worry ... Oh, really? Thanks so much, Bertie, that's extremely kind of you. Needless to say, we'll bring the goodies, so don't get anything in ... Yes, same crowd but with one extra ... nice young lady, I hear ... Now then, Bertie, we'll have none of that ... Oh, that's wonderful of you, thanks. See you somewhere around seven? Tremendous, looking forward to it. Thanks again, Bertie ... bye ... bye.'

Edgar gave us a thumbs up, as if we hadn't already got the drift.

'All set for next Monday then, folks. Bob, I assume you'll be informing ... er ...?'

'Julie. Yes, of course, I'll ring her in the morning to confirm. She's already agreed in principle.'

'Wonderful! We'll drink to that, then, shall we?'

***

The number was growing, though not by design. Four had turned into seven, the once cheerless room gently reverberating to the resonance of something approaching sociability. Normally to be found in the kitchen at parties, I extracted myself from what I thought was becoming an overshadowing crowd and took psychological refuge in a tempting nook.

The superficial pleasure of conversation continued to confound me. I couldn't deny that my confidence was improving, regular discourse with the Booths and Bob Langham helping me a lot in that respect. Even so, my emergent maturity tended to desert me when faced with larger gatherings. Inevitably, I reverted to type, faltering like the awkward and inarticulate teenager I thought I'd left behind. Then Violet Manners spotted me, coyly treating me to one of her infantile waves before sashaying in my direction.

''Lo, Arthur.'

'Hello, Violet.'

'Nice party, in't it?'

'Not exactly a party, Violet.'

''Tis for a bit, though, in't it?'

'If you'd like to think so.'

'I know what I would like, Arthur – to watch the regression, but Uncle Bertie said no.'

'Does he think you might be frightened?'

'Frightened! Me?'

She threw back her head and laughed, if the shriek that came from her could possibly be described as such. It more resembled the squawk of an outraged rooster, having the effect of muting the chatter of the startled assembly now staring in our direction.

'Weird stuff like that don't worry me one bit, Arthur. I think it's more that Uncle Albert don't want me involved in things that might start me off.'

Raising my eyebrows was sufficient for her to explain her last comment.

'I see things, Arthur ... sometimes not very nice things ... just like last time you were here.'

I couldn't immediately remember the name of the film. It was the one about a ventriloquist's dummy developing an evil mind of its own. Funny that Violet reminded me of that.

'What did you see, then, Violet?'

'Big, nasty looking bloke in a funny hat standing next to your tall mate over there.'

After glancing in Bob's direction, she noticed me shiver, smirking at my reaction.

'That's the reason I'm not allowed to stay, Arthur. You see, every so often, they speak to me ... and sometimes they're not nice ... not nice at all. Know what I mean?'

This time her eyes widened when she smirked. It was one of the things I remembered from last time – the blatant impudence in those saucer eyes.

'But you weren't even in the room last time, were you, Violet?'

'Well, he was still here when I came in.'

I couldn't help adversely reacting to her sharp riposte, my heart beating quicker still when her words trailed away. She winked to acknowledge my response, rolling her tongue over her bottom lip, purposely leering at me. Whatever her shady purpose was, it seemed designed to unsettle me.

'Violet, sweetheart, we need more drinks over here, if you wouldn't mind helping?'

Keates was glowering in our direction, obviously displeased at seeing us chatting so closely together. Violet treated me to another meaningful smirk before teetering away on impossibly high heels, collecting a tray of glasses on the way.

The imagined image of George Davy swam into mind, as did those of William Watts, George Boyd and Ethel Bentley, leading me to wonder if one or more of those long-dead people might grace us with their presence that evening. If it happened to be George Boyd, then at least one of the psychics might recognise him from the mug shot we now possessed. That in turn begged another question – if anything were to appear, just how many of us would actually see it? It seemed more people were witnessing those sorts of things of late.

***

Julie Sommers generated a breath of fresh air in the musty environs of the Keates household. Chic and attractive, bright and breezy, she was the complete opposite of what I had imagined. I had assumed that being a professional hypnotherapist, she'd resemble a female version of Bob Langham, whereas nothing could have been further from the truth.

Watching Bob drawn to her, like a moth to a flame, told me much about his motivation in recommending her services; the man was helplessly infatuated. Nonetheless, even if I'd had the confidence, let alone the looks, she wasn't a woman I might chase after. Attractive as she was, she simply wasn't my type. That was no reason to stop me from liking her, though. In fact, my mood improved from the moment she said hello. After experiencing the dubious attentions of Violet Manners, the charm and sophistication of Julie Sommers came as something of a welcome relief.

'You must be Arthur, hello. Bob talks about you quite a lot.'

'Does he, now?'

'Yes, he does. My name's Julie. Very pleased to meet you, Arthur.'

'Nice to meet you too, Julie.'

Her melodic tone was light and encouraging, and I thought how being hypnotised would be effortless under her supervision. The more she talked, the more positively I responded, my usual self-consciousness easily evaporating under her relaxed magnetism.

'Ladies and gentlemen, nice as it is to converse with each other, I think we should get down to business, if you don't mind.'

Edgar was politely calling the tune, stepping in smartly before Albert Keates had the chance to assert his own authority. It looked to be a timely manoeuvre, that idea reinforced by Kate conveniently cornering Keates in conversation.

Much like the last time, the furniture was carefully positioned: an exact number of chairs facing the settee Kate Booth had occupied during her own regression. Bob prepared himself by removing his jacket and loosening his tie before nervously assuming the required position. Julie Sommers flicked at her fringe, smiling benignly as we took our seats. She adopted the attitude of a teacher waiting for her class to settle, hands clasped against her tummy, one leg forward in classic pose.

'Before we begin, I'd like to request your cooperation concerning a couple of things. Firstly, I would be grateful if you'd maintain complete silence during the session. I know you've experienced regression before, so you'll understand how important it is for both me and Bob to maintain concentration. The next point I'd like to raise is a little more ambiguous. I understand there've been some unexpected occurrences during previous sessions. I can only say that personally, I'm very sceptical about such things. Therefore, I should reiterate that I'm here specifically to attempt a regression and that I have no intention of becoming involved in anything else. I'm sorry if my insistence appears unwarranted, but I must ask you to refrain from bringing anything else into play. If, however, any improbable circumstances do arise, I'll have no choice but to terminate the session immediately. Thank you for your cooperation. I'm sure you will understand my position.'

She turned away with no intention of waiting for a response. Though she'd been pleasant and courteous, there was no mistaking the steel that lay beneath the effervescent facade.

Bob Langham closed his eyes, allowing himself to sink into the cushion that had been placed under his head. Julie Sommers' opening directives were softly spoken, barely audible to those of us watching. I suspect I wasn't alone in wanting to ask her to speak up, fearful of missing any details of significance. I need not have been concerned; Julie was exercising much the same method of suggestion that Bob himself employed, her voice taking on a more strident tone once she began to enumerate. I thought how Bob might struggle to resist assessing a fellow professional's technique. That might have explained why it took longer for him to succumb. None of us reached the stage of tapping our fingers with impatience, but I for one was beginning to think we might have had a wasted journey. Then, almost at the point of exasperation, he went out like a light, eyelids fluttering as he descended into the deepest of slumbers.

Can you hear me, Bob?

Bob, listen to my voice. Can you hear me?

Her tone borders on demanding, and it produces a response, though the meaning is unintelligible.

Answer me, Bob ... please!

The plea is terse. It is an interesting approach.

What ...

It is definitely Bob's voice; the resonance is unmistakeable.

Whereabouts are you, Bob?

Who ... Whereabouts ... under the lamp ... trying to see ...

At first it is of him, then ... something of

him.

Raining hard, drenched to the bloody skin.

Now his voice is completely that of another. It has a mature intonation, conveying a more cultured drawl.

Who is that speaking to me?

What?

I said ...

Thurgood.

No awkward hesitation – little left hanging for us to guess at. This one appears different.

Thurgood? Would that be Mr Thurgood? Lord Thurgood ... perhaps?

It is teasingly phrased to elicit a response and it works. It brings laughter.

Lord - ha! Not likely, madam. Just plain old Victor, that's me.

How d'you do, Victor Thurgood. Very pleased to make your acquaintance.

Really, well, aren't you the one?

Do you mind me calling you Victor?

No ... not at all, madam.

Why are you standing under a lamp, Victor?

Here to meet someone, of course.

What street is the lamp on?

For the first time, there is no response, though we hear his laboured breathing. Bob's chest is erratically rising and falling. Julie feels his wrist for the beat of his pulse. She stares from painted lashes and nods her satisfaction. All is well.

Did you hear me, Victor? What is the name of the street where you are?

Bob is clearing his throat. His breathing is

less arduous.

Pilcher Gate.

Both the Booths look sharply in my direction, and I nod in recognition of their meaning.

Pilcher Gate, you say. Is that far from your home, Victor?

Why do you question me so precisely, madam?

Because I'm interested in you, Victor. I want to be your friend.

Really ... well, then ... if you promise not to tell ...

His words are playfully conspiratorial. He is responding to her flirtatious asides.

It'll be our little secret, Victor ... promise.

Hmm, well now. It's a good walk across town. Might be worth the slog, though ... Derby Road ... d'you you happen to know it?

Oh yes, Victor, I most certainly do.

Might I escort you there? Should you've a mind, that is. Business first, though ... and don't ask me about that!

I might enjoy a nice walk, Victor. It's nearly my birthday, after all ... not near your birthday, is it, by any chance?

Birthday? Oh no, madam. It's not mine for a while.

Go on, then, tell me what year you were born ... you sound quite young to me.

It was becoming quite the conversation. Was I the only one to wonder if we were simply listening to Bob in disguise? Was he dreaming about Julie Sommers? It seemed likely he was.

You're a cheeky madam and no mistake. I'm

a good bit older than you might think, young lady ... born in 1839, would you believe?

That's interesting, Victor ... you sound much younger. Derby Road, you say. Do you own a house up that way, then?

There is a pause, Bob's sucking in deep breaths, chest expanding with the effort.

No, a drapery ... oh, I have to go now ... another time perhaps ... he's almost here ...

In my ignorance, I thought it was some sort of muscle convulsion, almost like epilepsy. Only later did I come to understand Bob's excessive spasms to be the result of unequivocal terror. That the infernal spirit of George Davy was abroad once more was a continuing consequence of our exploratory activities, serving only to further accentuate the tenacity with which he pursued his intentions.

Unlike Kate Booth, Bob found it difficult to cast off his fearfulness once he'd fitfully returned to reality. Though he remembered nothing of what had occurred, he suffered the intense anxiety that came from the experience. Only later, when we sat together talking, did we address the cause of his waking condition. The compassion and words of support that accompanied the tea and brandy did much to improve his state of mind. Nevertheless, it was evident that Bob Langham was the weakest of us when it came to dealing with the disturbances that increasingly infiltrated our sessions.

At first, Julie Sommers listened without

comment, though she was clearly perturbed by what she'd observed. When she did speak, she disparaged the suggestion that something otherworldly was the cause of Bob's waking condition, steadfastly contending that he'd suffered nothing more than the intervention of a nightmare – unpleasant imaginings intruding upon his experience.

Though we said nothing, we knew better than that. We didn't know if Bob had given Julie all the facts: the history and coincidences of our investigations. Julie was believing what she preferred to believe, perhaps without the chance to evaluate the evidence we had accumulated. Julie Sommers was clearly a doubter when it came to the supernatural. She was obviously close to Bob, and I had to wonder how much she might influence his further involvement. Like me, Bob's resolve had weakened on more than one occasion – were four soon to become three? On a more positive note, another piece had appeared from the box, and I was determined to understand where to place Victor Thurgood in the developing picture. Would the revelation bring me closer to accepting my own past life associations? I knew in my heart the project had come to mean more than the thrill of the ride. Edgar Booth had provocatively implied I was one of those nascent voyagers that teetered on the edge of the void, fearing to step into its darkness. I thought ... *we shall see.*

Chapter 24
Nottingham 1967

The year turns again and the days are briefer. I laze abed to the rhythm of rain on dustbins and the pitter-pats at my window. I turn and search for things not there, things that hide in shadows I have no wish to see. I have the gift, they say – more of a curse, I think. All the same, I search and wonder ... is that something moving there? Something standing by the door? Something crouching by my bed?

Just arcing lights from passing traffic – nothing more than that, it seems.

Do I really see them? Faces at windows and figures at large – real or abstract, I cannot be sure. Sometimes I fear the answers more than I do the questions.

The incarnation of Victor Thurgood that surfaced from Bob Langham's regression encouraged me somewhat. For no definable reason, I thought him uncluttered and something of a character. I held onto that view when I came to search the archives for his records. In quick time, he proved the most obliging of those that had emerged from our regressions. For that reason, I wasn't surprised at the ease with which I traced his extended history. There he was, his name recorded every ten years from the very first census of 1841 through to and including 1891. From that point, it became a simple task to chronicle the relevant data.

Hairdresser Rowley Thurgood married vaudeville dancer Nancy Rice in 1838, Victor subsequently being born in the Nottingham suburb of Carrington in December of 1839. The census documents covering the next twenty years recorded him as living with his parents and three siblings at the very same address. His occupations were accordingly listed as errand boy in 1851, to shop assistant ten years later.

It was at that juncture that I looked up from the records pertaining to a man whose long-dead voice I had listened to only a few days previously. In a moment of melancholy reflection, I thought how desensitised I was becoming, thinking it due to the constancy of my exposure to otherworldly matters. Prior to embroiling myself in the weird world of the Booths, I never could have imagined myself being so inured to the peculiar happenings I was now involved in.

The records for 1871 and '91 showed Thurgood residing at Derby Road: the very road mentioned in Bob's regression. The entries also mentioned the site being a drapery store, leading me to wonder if he might have lived above or behind the business. The dates suggested our man continued in his chosen profession, two census records showing Victor Thurgood rising from assistant to retail manager in ten years: a progression most likely explaining his cultured persona, whether natural or assumed. I glanced at my watch, at once resolving to search for the location on

Derby Road.

Seeing the sharp-eyed Mrs Bird attending the archive desk came as something of a relief. I had no real desire to suffer the more pressing attentions of the amorous Alice again. On balance, I was therefore marginally more at ease with the fragrant Mrs Bird.

After I had stood waiting at the desk for an excruciating number of seconds, she glanced up from sealing an envelope and immediately feigned not to recognise me. Then, after listening restively to my request, she sighed and inexorably hitched up the corner of her mouth before leading me into the reading room.

Once I'd finished with the census records, I really pushed my luck and asked for a business directory encompassing the years I was concerned with. After treating me to a prolonged look of unreserved distaste, the puce-faced Mrs Bird reluctantly stormed away to comply with my request. Having previously searched the directory, I quickly found listings for Nottingham drapers. The only one I discovered relevant to Derby Road was a draper's emporium trading under the name of Renshaw. I thought it likely to be the one I was looking for and made a note of the details. Returning the directory to the desk, I gave Mrs Bird a smile of thanks and, much to her annoyance, waved a hearty goodbye. Grinning disgracefully at my own impudence, I exited the building and headed for Derby Road, one of the city's major arteries. It wasn't far away and

I walked at pace, motivated by the ridiculously faint hope of Renshaw's drapery still being in existence.

When I came to climb the hill, I noted the numbering of the establishments, reasoning the building I was looking for would be somewhere on the right and near the top. When the numbers appeared, my naïve optimism rapidly evaporated. The double-fronted shop was nothing at all like a drapery. The picture windows to either side of the entrance were plastered with posters pronouncing *SALE ON*, *CASH DISCOUNTS* and *HIRE PURCHASE AVAILABLE*. Edging closer to the misted glass, I detected a cavernous showroom randomly strewn with furniture – wardrobes, drawers, cabinets and the like – everything screaming cheap as chips. There was movement within: a slender youth with hands clasped behind his back authoritatively pacing the floor. I thought no harm in asking and pushed through one of the doors.

'Hello, there.'

The gangling youth crossed the floor at some speed, eyeing me like a starving cheetah. He looked the type whose idea of selling was to talk you out of the shop when you'd barely crossed the threshold. That sort rarely listened, overly occupied as they were with regurgitating their practised patter.

'Sorry to trouble you, I don't really want to buy anything, but ...'

The fixed smile vanished, his mood plummeting before I'd even finished speaking.

Judging by his noticeable dejection, I must have represented the first and last potential of the day.

'I know it's a bit of a cheek, but I wanted to ask if you know how long this place's been a furniture shop for.'

He surveyed me with abject indifference, his erstwhile aspirations totally in tatters.

'How would I know? Only worked here a couple o' months or so!'

His attitude was aggressive, bordering on threatening, and I thought he might be better looking for work that didn't necessitate human discourse.

'Smoke?'

I held out a packet of Player's, and his eyes immediately blinked like beacons.

'Oh, ah, classy fags, hey ... thanks a lot, pal, don't mind if ah do.'

We duly lit up, subsequently blowing plumes of white smoke over the furniture. Then, after a few drags, we were virtually mates.

'Only I'm doing some research, see ... erm ...'

'Steve.'

'Ay-up, Steve, mine's Arthur.'

We nodded our formal greetings – shaking hands being more for old geezers.

'Like I were saying, I'm doing a bit o' research. Trying to find out if this place used to be a drapery business at one time.'

'Now yer say it, I think I might've heard the gaffer talking about that a time or two.'

'There's a few fags in it if you can find me any more information.'

He was hooked and more than ready to help now we'd got to know each other. Just like it was with Aubrey – never took long if you said the right things. Working folk were like that, us against them and bogger the others.

'He were sayin' as when he took hover a few years back, there was heaps o' rubbish needed clearin', bags stuffed wi' crabby ode cloths and the like ... so it must a' been a what-yer-call-it.'

'Draper's shop.'

'Yeah, that's it. Tell you what, the ode boy's in the back cooking the books – I can ask him if yer want me to. He's norra bad bloke, ode Benny.'

'Okay then, if you think he wouldn't mind. Thanks a lot, Steve. Here, have the rest o' these for your trouble.'

His eyes flared all the more when I passed him the rest of the packet. Edgar Booth's tenner had turned out quite handy over the last few days. Steve couldn't have been more pleased. I watched him pocket the fags as he dodged between the furniture, heading for the back wall, whistling cheerfully before disappearing through a squeaky door.

It wasn't long before it squeaked again, this time revealing a balding man with shoulders practically as wide as he was tall. Steve followed behind like a faithful puppy.

Benny reminded me of a lantern-jawed movie mobster as he swayed towards me, shoulders rolling like breaking waves.

'Hullo, young fella. What's the game, then, eh?'

Benny was clearly from other parts. I put money on him being a cockney, the edge of his accent dulled by years of residence in the East Midlands. Sensing his character, I decided to get as close to the truth as possible without implying anything unearthly.

'Well, I'm trying to trace somebody who might have worked in this building a long time ago … when it was a drapery, I mean.'

'And why would you want to do that, old son?'

I was ready for that one and answered without a hint of hesitation.

'It's for a friend of mine who doesn't live round these parts anymore. He's looking for some information about past relatives – you know – tracing dead family, so to speak.'

They both gave me a funny look. To them it was just a furniture showroom, and I'd have laid odds that they'd never in a million years expect anybody to enquire about stuff like that.

'It's Arthur, ain't it?'

'Yeah, that's right … and you're Benny, so Steve tells me. From London if I'm not mistaken.'

He liked that – funny how people enjoyed having their origins recognised.

'Yeah, spot-on, old son … East Ender as a matter o' fact. I've been up here for donkey's years, though I nip down the Smoke now and then, and …'

I smiled and nodded patiently, tolerating his reminiscences and straining not to yawn like Steve was doing behind his back.

‘Never mind about that old guff, eh, Arthur? How d’you come to know about this place, then?’

‘Easy, it’s listed in an old business directory. Apparently, this place used to be called Renshaw’s at one time.’

‘So it did, old son, so it did. They were here for many a year, all the way back to the last century as a matter o’ fact. I bought the lease just after the war, though it’d been well run down by then, nothing like the business it used to be, according to the grapevine anyway. Well respected at one time, apparently. I heard the governor was a bloke called Critchlow back in eighteen-whenever it was, and then there was somebody called Caborn, I think, as well as that other bugger, o’ course.’

‘Was he called Thurgood, by any chance – Victor Thurgood?’

He shot me a penetrating look then, and I sensed it was part surprise, part suspicion.

‘You ain’t telling me he’s the one you’re looking for, are yer? From what I heard, he was a bit dodgy, robbed ’em blind, ’e did, or so they reckon. Apparently, Thurgood and his mates had it away with a stash and pasted one of the owners into the bargain! It was a scandal that ended badly, by all accounts. Can’t remember the exact details, but they reckon it headlined in the local papers for a while.’

I waited for him to finish, hoping to hear more of the sordid details, but that seemed to be all he had to say.

‘No offence, Benny, but where did you hear

this from? After all, it did happen an awful long time ago.'

'This old boy popped in to see me when I first took over ... must have been in his eighties even then. He reckoned he worked here before signing up for the first war – cleaning and handyman stuff, he said. I wasn't surprised to hear that as he didn't look the sharpest knife in the drawer. It was him as told me all about it – said it upset him to that day, and that it wasn't right to speak ill of the dead, though ...'

Benny looked me up and down for a moment, as though making a decision.

'Do you want to see where 'e lived?'

'Who, the handyman?'

'Naw ... That Thurgood bloke, I mean.'

It was getting better and better, and already, I couldn't wait to tell the others.

Chapter 25
Nottingham 1967

I nearly told him, but never did. If ever I told anyone, it'd be him. I trust Grandad more than any other – apart from Ann. And she already knows ... well, some of it.

Grandad round to mine for a fag and cuppa – has a bad back and would I help him Saturday. What could I say? Once we started talking, it was – you sure you're okay, Arthur? ... not yourself these days ... Grandma's noticed, and your mam ... looking tired and full o' worry ... you sure you're okay, Arthur?

I nearly told him about my gift ... how the thought of it was draining. Be nice to tell old Fred. Not much he hadn't experienced ... 'cept for hearing the voice of his own dead father. I have ... I've heard it.

Market's filling despite the drizzle. I view the coursing of passing faces with fresh fascination – sleep-walking punters and pasty kids – dead or alive, who can tell? If I did have the gift, surely I'd know ... wouldn't I?

How I wished he'd not said that ... sometimes that we'd never met. Yet there I'd be on Monday night.

We were at Bob's house, and I thought I would need to be really desperate before I used the upstairs toilet next to the haunted bedroom that overlooked the garden. That was one risk too far in my present state. Since Edgar Booth had suggested I possessed psychic abilities, my emotions had taken a turn for the worse. At first I shrugged it off, thinking it was another ploy to lure me deeper into his tangled web. Then the more I thought about what he'd said, the more those sinister imaginings began to dominate my thinking. I was sure he hadn't meant any harm. Even so, if he thought I could accept such assertions without worrying about the implications, he was sorely mistaken. It seemed everyone around me noticed that something about me had changed: Ann, of course, Bob Langham, and even the blokes at work. Kate Booth occasionally hugged me without explaining why, whilst Edgar chose to stare into space, avoiding my eyes as much as politely achievable.

My old satchel lay on the table, its contents disregarded. Clearly, they were waiting for an explanation, and I thought to seize the moment. Taking a deep breath, I gritted my teeth and began to share my demons.

'Have you stopped to think how much worry you've caused me by saying what you did, Edgar?'

The dryness in my throat brought a hoarseness to my tone.

'I thought you were ready to hear the truth, Arthur. I naively meant it as a compliment. With hindsight, I should have let things lie where they were, perhaps never to be truly discovered.'

I think he'd anticipated my question and made sure to have an answer prepared in order to defend himself. I was determined to keep my emotions under control, there being a considerable part of me no longer wanting to be the old Arthur. Rightly or wrongly, I thought I'd moved on since meeting them, and I desperately wanted to rid myself of any adolescent baggage that might prevent me from completely entering their circle.

'Trouble is, Edgar, since that day, people have been asking me what's wrong. I know well enough what the answer is, but not how to reply without being ridiculed! I thought I was managing to cope with issues arising from the regressions ... even with the goings-on at the séance and what happened at Bob's ... and I'm really enjoying the research, but when you suggested I was psychic, it all became a bit too much for me.'

I glanced at the Booths, noting the nervous shift in their posture. As far as I was aware, Bob was still in ignorance regarding my claim of seeing something at his bedroom window. And there was me almost upsetting the applecart by unwittingly referring to it. I had solemnly agreed with the Booths to keep that particular incident between the three of us, at least for the immediate future.

'What I'm trying to say is, you claiming I'm psychic has given me the heebie-jeebies. What with everything that's going on, I'm finding it hard to cope with. I've had sleepless nights, imagining things, thinking I might actually see something awful.'

'Oh dear, I'm really sorry, Arthur. I admit it was wrong and completely selfish of me not to consider how much it might concern you. I see now that I could have broached the matter more diplomatically. Nevertheless, at risk of upsetting you further, I must stand by some of what I said ... if only to prepare you for future eventualities. I repeat that as long as you deny your capabilities, you're unlikely to experience anything of consequence. In any event, now you're aware of your potential, anything you do by chance encounter might not upset you as much.'

The implication was clear – recent happenings supported what he was saying, and who knew how many similar incidents had occurred over the years without me knowing? I began to appreciate what he was saying, and for some obscure reason, I felt a wave of relief. At least any such experiences had come and gone without causing any lasting damage, and the fact that Edgar was genuinely sorry for what he'd said served to soften my resentment.

'I can accept your motives, Edgar, but at the end of the day, it's simply your opinion.'

'It isn't just Edgar who thinks that way, Arthur.'

Kate was sitting beside me, gently stroking my hand.

'Oh, not you as well, Kate? Don't tell me you think I'm psychic too.'

I chuckled dismissively, looking over to Bob, expecting his customary denial. But there was no support coming from that direction. If anything, his expression was one of reluctant acknowledgment. Kate took my face in her hands and gazed meaningfully into my eyes.

'Try not to completely deny it, Arthur. It's somewhere deep inside you, dormant for most of your young life. The older you become, the more you'll understand and accept it. There's really nothing to worry about. It's totally under your control. There's nothing to say you'll be seeing ghosties everywhere; relax and stop looking for them. Your talent is waiting to be developed, but only if you really want it to. In the meantime, move on with your life, Arthur. You've many years ahead of you, and you don't know what's waiting round the corner.'

The catch in her throat was barely audible, and I suspected I knew the reason why.

***

After dropping the Booths at their house, Bob kindly drove me to my digs in Radford, with me thinking it was good of him to ferry me home at that hour. The clock had ticked on to something past eleven before we realised how long we'd been talking. I was learning that it sometimes takes a problem to bring people closer together. I think that's what must have happened that night. Our common belief and endeavour held us as one. And from a personal viewpoint, that closeness allowed me to express my anxieties, even if one of our company was in part accountable.

Edgar Booth had been right about my earlier motivations. I had willingly taken the opportunity to add excitement to my life without appreciating the consequences. Though the resultant journey inured me to the weird and wonderful, it was only at the eleventh hour that I began to understand what I had become involved with. I was at last acknowledging the existence of alternative dimensions, places where everything and anything is possible: the interacting spheres that coexist with the earthly domain.

***

The results of my research proved of great interest. The more we immersed ourselves, the more my earlier anxieties diminished. Once the subject of my personal issues was exhausted, attention finally turned to the leather satchel that lay on the table. The content within represented the principal reason for our meeting that evening, and there was an air of expectancy when I came to withdraw the notes.

I began by outlining my research from the archives before moving on to the intriguing revelations arising from my visit to Derby Road. It was of no surprise to anyone when Victor Thurgood – the contact from Bob's regression – proved to be an actual person who had lived within the same timeframe as the characters previously uncovered. On reflection, we agreed we ought to be ashamed by our casual response to such revelations.

In the early days, we might have greeted such news with significantly more enthusiasm. However, when I confirmed I had visited the very premises where Thurgood was employed in the nineteenth century and had viewed the actual rooms where he lived, there was an outpouring of genuine excitement.

I went on to tell them about Steve and his boss, Benny – how we climbed the stairs to cross the floor that mirrored the one below – how we came to a corner with a secret door leading to a room cloaked in the dust of time – how we stood before a wormy cabinet by a flaking wall.

What I delivered next, however, exceeded anything they'd ever anticipated. With the panache of a vaudeville magician, I produced a flat piece of card and dramatically placed it on the table. Over the years, the once vibrant image had bleached to a sallow sepia.

'There he is in all his finery – you do know who that is, don't you?

The eyes shifted as one to the photograph, settling on the image of the man who smiled back at them. Edging closer, they studied the well-dressed figure posing for the flash of an antiquated camera over a century before. The fading likeness portrayed a man of indefinite age, dressed in a dogtooth-check suit with a matching waistcoat and harmonising cravat. The rascally face that beamed through the ages suggested a man of some vanity – the impression emphasised by the waxed moustache and the rakish angle of his fashionable homburg.

'Victor Thurgood!'

'Right first time – Benny found it behind a cupboard some years ago and kept it in an old set of drawers because he didn't like to throw it away. Yeah, that's Thurgood, right enough, Bob. Or, of course, it could be you in that other life, hey?'

'We can't know that for certain, Arthur.'

Edgar Booth tutted and raised his eyes to the ceiling.

'For goodness sake, Bob, stop hedging your bets, man. Anyway, given this wealth of information, I'm thinking we should pen some kind of ...'

'Documentation, perhaps, Edgar?'

'Yes, that's it. That'd be just the ticket, Arthur.'

'Already done, Edgar; it took my mind off those other thoughts for a while.'

With that, I opened the folder again, this time retrieving the remaining sheet of paper.

'There you have it – a basic timeline. I've listed names and locations, together with a few particulars.'

The evening progressed better than any of us could have hoped for. Thanks to me and my funny moods, we'd got off to an awkward start. In the end, though, it seemed we were as one again. Much like family, we underwent our differences occasionally, and, after all was said and done, we were an eclectic mix of uncommon people, each one of us prone to reacting differently. We'd finally arrived at an interesting juncture on our journey to yesteryear. From somewhat questionable beginnings, we had accumulated some thought-provoking data concerning the suggestion of our interrelated existences. That there were caveats attached to that accomplishment was only to be expected – how could we justifiably ascribe ownership of those long-dead souls with irrefutable certainty?

Whilst it might have been reasonable to congratulate ourselves, there remained some serious tidying to be done: further collaborative evidence to be uncovered before we could admissibly claim proof of multiple past life existences. I studied my scribblings for the umpteenth time whilst the others made copies for their own records. Then, finally and harmoniously, we agreed to a temporary parting of ways, an extended break to allow us to live our respective lives in comparative normality for a while.

The names had become familiar, as had the timelines and associated locations, the connecting date being the census of **1891**:

George Davy*, born 1843, a boarder lodging at Woolpack Lane in the parish of St Mary, age 48, occupation described as hawker.*

William Watts*, born 1852, a boarder lodging at Woolpack Lane in the parish of St Mary, age 39, occupation described as coalman.*

Ethel Bentley*, born 1850, a boarder lodging at Woolpack Lane in the parish of St Mary, age 41, occupation described as lace mender. (1881 census has Ethel living at Red Lion Street,*

Narrow Marsh, occupation described as domestic maid.)

***Victor Thurgood**, born 1839, a resident lodging at Derby Road, age 51, occupation described as retail manager.*

We had a photograph of Victor Thurgood and a mug shot of George Davy's villainous associate, George Boyd, aged 52 in 1888, when the image was captured. We knew that William Watts and Ethel Bentley were cohabiting by 1891 and that one of the drinking establishments favoured at least by George Davy and William Watts was The Postern Gate Inn. We were also aware that Victor Thurgood had in some capacity been involved in unlawful activity of a violent nature.

There is more to understand of this multifaceted array of circumstances. No doubt we could chart the history more productively, but would that in itself prove the theory? History is but one component of a wider and more complex mystery. In simple terms, we are attempting to interrogate the dead in order to ascertain a heritable link to the living – namely ourselves.

The waters are further muddied by two component parts – hypnotic regression and psychic communication – one teasingly working against the other, often inadvertently.

The substance is complicated – are our motives compromised? Are our objectives of equal purpose? In different ways, we have barely scratched the surface of this perplexing journey. Therefore, it is not beyond possibility that more detailed and perhaps more sinister consequences are yet to unfold.

Chapter 26
Nottingham 1881

It was still early, and she was uncomfortable with the sound of her heels clacking on the paving as she hurried to work. She might just make it on time, although she knew she could get away with being late. The household rarely roused itself for at least another hour or more. All the same, she hated to think she was letting Miss Polly down. It wouldn't seem right somehow. Miss Polly had been good enough to give her work when she really needed it. The very last thing she wanted was to take advantage of the uncommon trust she'd recently been awarded.

Ethel Bentley briskly made her way along Wollaton Street, eating up the last few yards to her destination. The air was dry and distinctly chilly, with no sign of the warming April showers someone said were on the way. That optimistic forecast had been drunkenly slurred in the pub late the previous evening, that mellow time when revellers turned to chatting about all and nothing.

Ethel loved the convivial atmosphere of the local tavern, even more so the familiar company that gathered there of an evening. Landlord Charlie was popular in those parts, often chalking up credit for locals he knew were sure to settle on payday. Charlie was a proper 'marsh boy', one of their own, a man who understood the meaning of genuine hardship.

She pushed at the terrace gate to enter the

small yard that fronted the house, the narrow strip of earth beneath its bay window sprouting swathes of forget-me-nots and a few early tulips. After extracting a key from the pocket of her shabby overcoat, she unlocked the door and quickly escaped the biting wind that had chased her all the way from home.

It was an impressive residence and she was proud of having her own key, and within just a month of working there. After hanging up her coat and bonnet, Ethel swapped her ankle boots for a pair of soft slippers and hurried along the entrance hall to the kitchen.

Gently closing the door behind her, she set about her morning routine. The year was moving on, and early light filtered through the cloudy kitchen window, allowing her the luxury of not having to light the tallows. Instead she stoked and fired the oven range before putting a glowing taper to the single gas lamp. The kitchen needed to be warm and bright for the girls when they decided to vacate their beds.

Ethel methodically worked her way through her chores – a pan of porridge on the stove to simmer – the last of yesterday's loaves, sliced and ready for toasting – cups and saucers neatly placed – kettle boiling and teapot readied for brewing.

Then it was into the parlour and then the 'death room': ironically, the best in the house, traditionally the place where you laid out the dead. There was always a lot to clear and tidy in those particular rooms, and that morning was no exception. There was the leather to wipe and cushions to plump and a sweep and a polish to make it smell nice. That was after she'd cleared the ashes, laid the fire, emptied the ashtrays, cleared the empties into a box for the yard and taken the glasses to the sink for washing. Much to Ethel's regular distaste, some of the other stuff was lying about as well. She didn't ponder on those sorts of things – just a wipe and a tidy and call it a day. Then in no time at all, the rooms had come to life again, clean, aired and ready for the goings-on. The sound of pattering feet from the stairs took her back into the kitchen, just in time to see one of the girls yawning her way towards the chair nearest the fire.

'Alright, Eth?'

'Yeah, not bad, Miss Mary. How about you?'

'Ready for bed, matter o' fact!'

Ethel laughed obligingly; the conversation was rarely much different. Mary was one of the nicer ones. At least she acknowledged Ethel's presence, unlike some of the others. As if on cue, Helen appeared, face as sour as a jug of vinegar.

'Tea brewed yet?'

Ethel said nothing and poured the tea into two of the everyday cups, finishing them off with a splash of milk and a spoon of sugar for Helen. *Might sweeten her up a bit* was what she thought, pushing the steaming brew under the noses of the two women.

'Ta, duck.'

Rolling her eyes in Helen's direction, Mary looked up and winked at Ethel as she said it. Next down were the twins, as Ethel liked to think of them. Though Sophie and Charlie were not related, they might as well have been – one rarely seen without the other in tow. Sophie was what some called an albino: hair as white as snow and eyes that flared when she stared at you, whereas Charlie was dark, sultry and hardly broke into a walk, inclined instead to sashay like a laden donkey. Charlie was the other one Ethel didn't think much of, only called her 'oy', or 'you' if she was lucky.

With tea poured and porridge ladled, Ethel left them to it and retreated from the kitchen. She'd heard little Amy coming into the hall and wanted to say hello.

'Alright, Amy, me duck?'

'Suppose ...'

'Want some tea, darlin'? Plenty left.'

'Naw, thanks, Eth – best get started on the upstairs afore Miss Polly starts creatin'.'

'She ain't up yet – Mary and Helen are though, and the twins.'

'Right-oh, then, I'll get me stuff and mek a start in their rooms ... God help me.'

Miss Polly employed two housekeepers – Ethel and Amy – as well as evening staff to look after clients' drinks and other domestic requirements. There was a cook called Gemma who arrived at noon to see to dinners and suppers, then of course, there was Big Cyril. He frightened everybody, especially Ethel, who he openly courted without so much as a bye-your-leave. She'd often catch sight of his bulky frame prowling the dim-lit corridors, but she'd evaded his clumsy advances thus far – him with his massive hands and bloated lips. Ethel knew he wouldn't stop until he'd well and truly 'nailed her', as he crudely put it. She had held off complaining to Miss Polly, not wanting to rock the boat or be thought a trouble causer. Nevertheless, the day would have to come, and sooner rather than later by the looks of it.

Big Cyril rarely arrived before four-thirty in the afternoon, just in time for when business started. The girls needed to rest during the day and have some time to themselves.

However unpopular with the staff he was, Cyril was a useful man to have around. The very look of him was enough to put most men on the back foot, what with his bulging arms and barrel chest bursting from his fancy waistcoat. Ethel witnessed him punching a cocky young rake on one occasion. It was just before she was due to leave for the day, and in the death room, aptly enough. The poor chap hit the floor like a poleaxed bull – the price he paid for having the audacity to proposition Miss Polly herself. Ethel remembered picking up three of his scattered teeth the following morning.

When the day wore on without a sign of her mistress, Ethel became somewhat concerned. Miss Polly generally appeared around eleven of the clock, looking for all the world like she was dressed for the opera, powdered and lip-sticked as she inevitably was. And where was Eadie? Funnily enough, Eadie's roommate,

Angie, had come down later than usual that morning, looking even more bleary-eyed than she normally did. Angie had doggedly refused to answer the other girls' probing questions, preferring to sulk and nurse her stewed tea with barely a word spoken. It looked like something untoward had happened, and likely only Angie knew what it was.

Ethel carried on helping cook to prepare the vegetables, slicing carrots the French way as Gemma said they'd to be done. When the kitchen door creaked, Ethel automatically turned at the sound, fully expecting to see Eadie or even Miss Polly herself. It was little Amy, though, eyes flitting nervously across the girls' faces, obviously discomfited by the quizzical attention she was receiving. The diminutive teenager nervously padded across the kitchen, tipped her head in the direction of the door, and meaningfully pulled at Ethel's apron. Shrugging her shoulders at the equally bemused Gemma, Ethel submissively followed Amy out to the hall without a word spoken until the door shut behind them.

'Whatever's the matter, me duck?'

'Summat's happened, Eth. Miss wants yer upstairs ... and this minute, she said.'

***

'Come in.'

Ethel pushed at the door, the heady mix of pungent perfume and fresh polish immediately assailing her nostrils.

'Ah, Ethel ... come over here, dear, where I can see you properly.'

True to character, Miss Polly was coiffured to perfection. She was sitting at her leather-topped desk, peering at Ethel through pince-nez spectacles neatly perched on the bridge of her elfish nose.

'Sit yourself down over there, Ethel. I've something serious to say to you, dear.'

Ethel duly obliged, perching on the edge of the gilded chair opposite the desk. She wondered what on earth was coming – had she done something wrong?

'Now then, Ethel ... you must keep this to yourself for now, but you need to know that Eadie's gone for good and won't be allowed back under any circumstances. I sent her away in the early hours after ... well ... you don't need to know the sordid details. Suffice to say, there was a bit of a commotion involving people who shouldn't have been in the house at the time. Thankfully, it wasn't noisy enough to wake anybody. Even so, Angie was so disturbed by it, she thought to come and tell me, despite the hour. And I'm glad she did; I can't be doing with untrustworthy employees at any cost.'

Ethel could only wonder what Miss Polly was alluding to – had Cyril been involved? There were rumours ...

'Her going has created an extra problem, though. Tonight should be about as busy it gets, so ... I'm wondering what to do about it, Ethel dear. It's what educated folk refer to as an interesting conundrum.'

Ethel was wondering too – why Miss Polly thought it necessary to tell her of all people.

Miss Polly purposefully removed her spectacles, smiling a tad too winsomely for Ethel's liking.

'You've been getting on extraordinarily well since you came to work here, Ethel ... in fact, you've impressed me so much I was thinking about promoting you. I've been looking for a capable personal maid for a while. What with you being able to read and write into the bargain, I'm thinking you might be very useful to me. And it would be a step-up for you dear – accord you respect in the household.'

Ethel thought the sugary words hadn't come out of the blue. All the same, she couldn't believe what she was hearing. She was already doing well enough, but this latest opportunity was an entirely different kettle of fish.

'Of course, it'd mean extra money for you, Ethel, starting next week if you've a mind.'

Ethel's thoughts were all over the place. It sounded too good to be true. But when she reflected on it, the mention of extra money was the only thing that really stuck in her mind.

***

Someone said there was a good and bad side to everything. In the event, the good side was that Ethel Bentley quite unexpectedly had the means to pay her debts and buy her friends a round of drinks. She'd tapped her nose when they asked how come she was so flush of a sudden, the gesture accompanied by a wink and a sly smile to keep them wondering. Then she remembered the bad side and winced at the memory of it, all the while managing not to show her discomfort in front of friends.

True enough, she'd gone up in the world – a proper lady's maid now, not just a common skivvy. It was a decent progression for someone like her. Then again, her new position came at a cost, and not an insubstantial one. In words alone, the deal had been simple enough, no more than a favour for a favour. Just the once, and never again, of course. That being as may be, the fateful arrangement was to foreshadow a great deal more to come.

Ethel Bentley permitted herself to be painted and adorned accordingly. The image she came to view in the boudoir mirror astounded the once dreary girl from Narrow Marsh – garish lipstick and rouged cheeks – pinned hair and feathered hat at a cheeky tilt – figure-hugging dress and powdered breasts – was that really Ethel Bentley from Red Lion Street?

When it actually came down to it, the literal functions were of little note – a slavering boy only seconds in performing his duty and a bullish butcher stinking of his trade and lingering a bit too long. Neither were difficult or overly demanding, both paying a generous gratuity – done and dusted before the clock struck ten.

Even after Miss Polly had taken her share, the short night's work left Ethel more than enough to square her debts. The worst of it was thinking her dignity lay in tatters. Though it was not by any means her first time, they were, however, the first ones to pay her for services rendered. She swore it would be her one and only venture into the netherworld of dubious engagement. And so it proved to be – at least until times became inexorably challenging once again.

Chapter 27
Nottingham 1891

It was unusually hectic at the corner of Carrington Street, the tram from the station caught in the diverging traffic travelling from Canal Street, the constable on duty all but lost in the conflicting throng of horse-drawn carts and carriages of diverse occupation.

William Watts was sat aboard his stationary cart, well and truly stuck in the middle of the mayhem, idling his time away by staring at an obstructed tram stuffed with railway travellers heading for town, those on top perched precariously, hats and bonnets gripped tightly against the freshening wind. One or two of the horses in the tangle of heaving traffic were growing skittish, thereby adding to the dangerous confusion of uncommon congestion.

Watts knew enough about horses to know it would only take one of them to rear up in its nervousness to cause a dangerous disturbance of thrashing hooves and overturned vehicles. That made him all the more grateful that his own horse was placid enough to stand completely still and unconcerned amidst the growing chaos. The irony of his predicament was not lost on William Watts – his destination being barely minutes away. However, the path to the yard's entrance lay in the same direction as the nearby railway Station, its approach jammed solid with opposing vehicles.

Watts speculated where his partner might be, wondering if he'd finished his round early and was at that very moment contentedly swilling a mug of steaming tea. Then again, maybe he was similarly stuck in the middle of the worsening obstruction. If he was, Watts knew his partner, Dave Robertson, would be shouting the odds, telling the boggers faffing about to sort themselves out – and in no uncertain terms.

Dave was a bit of a lad and always up for a squabble. William Watts grinned to himself. He and Dave had known each other for a good few years. They'd chipped in to rent the coal yard only months previously and were doing well enough as partners. As ever, though, it was the cough that spoilt things for William Watts, the penetrating dust that clagged his throat. He took it to bed with him at night and woke the worse for it in the morning. Whenever he hawked and spat – something he did on a worryingly frequent basis – the phlegm he expelled was as black as the coal he hauled, awful thick and gluey as it was. Thinking about it only bothered him the more, causing him to ponder his fate and longevity. Even worse, he knew it bothered his girl more than it did him.

His life had changed for the better when he'd met Ethel. Admittedly, she was no spring chicken, but then neither of them was, come to that. Eth, as she preferred to be called, was a year or two older than he was. Even so, she was still a good-looking woman, turning men's heads, particularly when she dolled herself up for a night on the town. Ethel Bentley had lived in Narrow Marsh for most of her life. Watts knew the Marsh was considered by some to be just about the worst area in all of Nottingham after the Rookeries had been demolished. The Marsh was a dilapidated warren of cobbled backstreets and earthen yards, a forsaken slum rife with rats, roaches and open sewers. Still, folk couldn't help where they were born, and it was the devil's own job to escape such situations without having the means to do so. Although there'd been some loose talk about clearing the Marsh and building it up from new, ordinary folk thought it unlikely – just as they considered rumours about the town becoming a city to be nothing but council pipedreams.

He remembered Ethel being in two minds when he'd asked her if she'd like to move in with him. Woolpack Lane wasn't that far from Narrow Marsh, but it was a step-up in terms of residence. Woolpack was in St Mary and popular with the lace workers. Watts's neighbours were mostly labouring types, factory hands, tradesmen and the like – folk similar to himself – though there were ever blackguards and tricksters in the jumble of humanity.

He'd met Ethel in The Postern Gate Inn one Saturday night, knowing immediately what she was getting up to. Even if he hadn't noticed, it wouldn't have been long before someone tipped him the wink. Watts had been taken with her straightaway – pretty, she was, and with no outward signs of the ravages of her trade.

It was the way he and Ethel got on with each other that warmed him the most, right away finding her pleasant and easy to talk to, seemingly more interested in him than she was herself. They often talked long into the evening at The Postern. The childish sniggers and whispered asides soon fizzled out, nobody taking notice after a while and caring even less, come to that. Not once had she mentioned doing some business, and Watts had liked that about her, though he might have taken the bait had she fished deep enough.

One particular evening, they left The Postern together at closing time. It was getting late and Watts offered to walk her home. Ethel agreed without hesitation, and so they walked arm in arm down Drury Hill towards the Marsh, chatting like they'd known each other forever. When they came to Red Lion Street, Ethel offered to buy him a drink in her local. Though it was gone closing time, it was still open for business, and the constables rarely patrolled those streets after dark. Sounds of merriment and disorderly behaviour were drifting from within, and Watts had heard that strangers weren't always welcome in the Marsh. Hence he politely declined, adding he'd like to see her again, though, and might she fancy a walk along the river the following Sunday?

Ethel had said she wouldn't mind in the least, and so they named a time and agreed to meet by the bridge. After ending the night with a peck on the cheek and a wave goodbye, her eyes followed his progress until he disappeared into the night. Only much later in their relationship did they admit to thinking their meeting each other was meant to be.

***

His thoughts of Ethel were interrupted by the sardonic cheers suddenly rising from the crowd. The constable had somehow solved the problem and spaces were beginning to appear, allowing a degree of positive movement to slowly commence. William Watts clicked his tongue and shook the reins, his horse flicking its ears as if to signal its understanding. A few minutes later, Watts negotiated his way through the narrow entrance, bringing the cart to a halt behind a similar vehicle to his own. After watering the horse and throwing down some hay to keep it occupied, he turned to the tumbledown shack that stood in the corner of the coal yard. Announcing his arrival with a familiar cough, Watts pushed through the worm-ridden door into what the partners liked to refer to as their office.

'Did yo get caught up in that mess an' all, Dave?'

'Naw, avoided it. Seen it building up, though – it's them bleddy navvies digging up Arkwright Street what's causin' it – traffic's bin diverted, an't it.'

They chatted like that for a while. It was Friday, and Fridays were for early starts and early finishes. Then Dave said he had to go as he was off fishing with his lad. And so they divided the day's takings after setting some aside for the 'business tin'.

William Watts watched his partner onto Carrington Street before hiding the tin and turning his cart around. It wouldn't be long before he was settling the horse and walking the short distance from the rented stable to his lodgings on Woolpack Lane.

Ethel was waiting in the kitchen, looking extremely attractive and a bit too alluring for William Watts's liking. As always, his heart sank at the thought of it. Even so, he didn't allow his disappointment to show. He reasoned it was almost necessary to her: craving the security of knowing she could pay her own way and be thought of as someone of worth. Nonetheless, it cut him deeply just the same. He appreciated the extras her earnings brought in as well: nice rugs and curtains to brighten their home, flowers on the table and a decent larder. All that said, he couldn't bear to think where the money came from.

He'd met Miss Polly once or twice and was still in two minds about her. Ethel didn't skivvy for her anymore, yet in another way, she was still in her employ. At least Ethel wasn't one of the girls plying her trade in Miss Polly's house. Ethel was independent in that respect and very fussy about who she entertained. They needed to be clean and tidy for a start, and at least looking trustworthy.

'You off out then, Eth?

'Yeah, Friday, in't it? Yer know I have ter

work Fridays, Billy.'

'Bit early though, in't it? I thought as how we might have a bit o' tea together afore yer go.'

'By the time you've scraped the muck off, it'll be too late. I expected yer back some time ago.'

'Got stuck coming off Canal Street – I were there a good while waitin' to get to the yard for a count up wi' Dave.'

'No fault o' mine then, is it, me duck?'

William Watts left it that – all he was doing was annoying her, and that was the last thing he wanted to do. After all, she was only doing what she thought was necessary to keep them afloat. The coal money only went so far: enough for basics and little else. As much as he hated what she did, he loved her all the same. And despite everything, he knew Ethel's heart was in the right place, and that she loved him as much as he did her. Watts thought life was funny like that – it gave you something and then it took something away.

Chapter 28
Nottingham 1891

She felt really terrible about it, but needs must. Ethel was building a nice little nest-egg for her and Billy's old age. The way his health was going, they'd most likely need a stash to see them through before he got much worse. There was barely a day went by without him suffering at least two or three serious bouts of coughing. That was quite apart from him clearing his throat and chest every few minutes. When the worst attacks came, he even struggled to breathe, his face coming over all red and twisted.

Billy was a lovely bloke, unlike some of his so-called mates. One or two of them had tried their luck, but she was having none of that. Never muck on your own doorstep, Miss Polly reckoned. No matter how much they offered, work was work and home was home.

Ethel Bentley came to Lower Parliament Street and took a turn to the left. Upper Parliament Street was where she normally plied her trade, not the unsavoury denizens of the lower township. She preferred to hang around the theatre and music hall, and the more productive taverns at the top of town. She had a few contacts thereabouts, business types mostly. They'd tip her the wink and set her up with a nice gentleman on occasion. But today was different – she didn't need to linger round her usual haunts. Instead she hastened to quite a different destination.

Victor was a regular and a proper gent. She'd grown quite fond of him in a funny sort of way. He treated her like a lady and boasted the means to do it in style. He always bought her flowers or a box of those divine truffles. The only trouble was, she needed to eat them before she got home. Billy knew full well what her business was. Even if he did, though, she didn't like rubbing it in. Another good thing about Victor was that he paid over the odds. She knew he had a decent job at the drapery, but she couldn't believe it was anywhere near enough to fund his lifestyle. Anyway, that was his affair and not hers.

Most times they would see to business in Victor's rooms, Ethel knowing to knock at the back door so as not to embarrass him by using the main entrance on Derby Road. He'd usually take her out on the town afterwards. There was a little restaurant up near Canning Street where they'd sit and eat like doe-eyed lovers by candlelight. Proper posh it was, and the food was to die for. She'd never had fine wine before Victor treated her, not to mention a nip or two of expensive brandy to finish the evening in style.

It was an experience being out with Victor Thurgood in his top hat, folk often tipping their own brims and passing the time of day. He was a strapping fellow, was Victor, strong and big-limbed. She felt safe with him and proud to be promenading with such a well turned-out gentleman, though for all his charm and finery, he'd never take Billy's place in her heart. Her attachment to the humble William Watts was deep and unwavering; in fact, they were so close, it was like she'd known him forever.

***

Victor Thurgood couldn't wait. He'd finished work early, telling the boss he'd be sure to make up the time during the following week. Jimmy Caborn had been good about it. Caborn was one of the partners, a man who liked to show his importance by regularly wearing two-tone spats and a stylish top hat, not to mention his elaborate cane. For all his flamboyancy, Caborn was a decent enough sort and always treated Victor well. In return, Victor worked hard, more importantly proving himself a natural salesman as well as being very popular with the lady customers.

The job came with rooms upstairs, a nominal rent deducted from his weekly wages. The arrangement suited Victor perfectly. He didn't have to worry about missing a tram and arriving late – he could be at his desk within minutes of washing and dressing. But the real bonus was that the rooms were convenient to town ... handy for lots of things.

Smiling on hearing their secret knock, he opened the door to find Ethel waiting at the top of the staircase, a cheeky grin greeting him as he surreptitiously ushered her inside.

'We staying in today, then, Victor?'

'Only for a while, Eth ... only for as long as it takes, you might say.'

'It won't be long before we're away, then!'

They laughed together at that, both completely comfortable in their relationship. A long hour later and they were leaving for town. Victor had promised Ethel a special dinner, adding that after that, they'd spend some time at the Cross, assuming the entertainments that night were worth seeing.

Nicely tipsy and with their bellies full of steak pudding and all the trimmings, Victor Thurgood and Ethel Bentley giggled and chatted their way through the crowds gathering around St James Street. Nottingham on a Friday night was a bustling melange of pleasure-seeking revellers. Apart from for a few, there'd be no work till Monday – two precious days to spend as they chose.

The atmosphere around St James was particularly vibrant, the ancient thoroughfare a magnet attracting an eclectic mix of desirous clienteles. The music hall was bursting at the seams, jostling visitors vainly crowding its entrance, futilely attempting to enter its tempting portal.

Ethel smiled sheepishly and shook her head when Victor waved to catch the doorman's attention. Less than a minute later, they were shepherded through the chattering crowd and led up the stairs to the gallery. She noticed the silver coin changing hands and was not at all surprised when a space miraculously opened for them to occupy.

What a night it turned out to be, and how she wished her Billy could be there to enjoy it as much as she was. Ethel had long ago learned to hide her remorse on such occasions – what point was there in both of them being miserable? She'd be sure to make it up to him with a few treats, like a bottle of that French stuff he liked to slowly sip by the fire. At least to see him enjoying his modest pleasures made her feel slightly better about what she was doing.

Ethel Bentley and Victor Thurgood sang along to the chorus of popular songs and laughed at the common jokes of a jaunty comedian. Their arms entwined, they swayed along with the bibulous throng that crushed together in elated moments of bonded revelry. It was certainly a night to remember, though not just for its merriment.

After they departed the boisterous atmosphere, they crossed over The Market Place and were walking up by The Exchange when they noticed a lone figure approaching them. Victor had insisted on accompanying Ethel to the corner of Woolpack Lane to ensure she got home without being bothered. They'd been quietly singing to themselves as they affably walked arm in arm. Then, suddenly, Victor stopped dead in his tracks. The figure approaching was big and threatening, Ethel recognising him the second he swayed into the pale light of a nearby street lamp.

She knew him well enough; he lived just doors down from their lodgings. Occasionally, she'd seen him drinking in The Postern, a couple of times with Billy. She'd felt his beady eyes on her a time or two. Ethel had nodded and exchanged a few words with him now and then, though avoiding the man's attentions whenever she was able – as did most others in those parts, truth be told.

'Victor ... well ah never.'

'George.'

'How yer doin', matey?

'Tolerably well, thanks, George ... yourself?'

'Yeah ... not as well as you, though, hey?'

The man called George chuckled, throat rasping in protest at the pungent tobacco he drew deep into his lungs. He'd tilted his head at Ethel when he uttered those words, and there was little humour in his subsequent laughter.

'Ah know you an', all, don't ah, me duck? You're Billy Watts's tart, aren't yer?'

An even rougher chuckle accompanied the question. At the same time, he was looking her up and down, blatantly leering as he did so.

'I heard as how yer let a bit out on the side.'

Victor let go her arm and took a threatening step forward, fists clenched in sudden anger, the vein in his forehead pulsing fit to burst.

'Don't be bleddy daft, Victor – we both know how that'd end up. You're a big bloke but yer ain't in my class, me duck!'

There was a moment when Ethel thought they'd get to it, but then the moment passed. Both men relaxed, though George was not done.

'Don't either on yer worry, ah'll not be tellin' tales on yer. Any road, don't forget yo an' me's got some talkin' ter do, Victor. I'll see yer Sunday like we said. Be sure ter be there!'

With that, George casually sidled past them, tipping Ethel a cheeky wink as he did so. It soured what had been a wonderful evening, Victor saying no more than a formal goodbye when they parted, both of them feeling the loss of their earlier mood.

Her Billy was asleep by the dying fire, a half-eaten slice of bread and dripping on a plate beside him. The dripping greased his chest and eased his condition, or so he reckoned. She thought to leave him where he was. After all, he'd only start coughing if she woke him up.

Chapter 29
Nottingham 1891

The Postern Gate was crowded and loud, the drifting fug swirling all the more after the latch clicked and the door swung open. Heads that turned to complain about the draught turned back at least as quickly once the offenders were revealed.

They were sometimes known as the two Georges, and occasionally, the terrible twins, though not a man there would say as much to their faces. It was difficult to say which George was the one more feared – Davy the villainous hawker or Boyd the notorious felon. But then, the latter description might equally apply to both of them, a more heinous pair being hard to find in the town of Nottingham.

Gaps in the crowd unsurprisingly appeared as they made their way across the room, one or two drinkers nodding cautious salutations when the two men came to lean at the bar.

George Davy returned the landlord's murmured greeting and ordered strong ale without a please or thank you. Turning from the bar with foaming tankards, the two men proceeded to occupy a suddenly vacant table closest to the fire and furthest from the stink of the privy.

'Ah seen Thurgood last night, Georgie. He were wi' that tart as lives wi' Billy Watts.'

'She's on the game, in't she?'

'Oh ah, she is an' all – thinks she's better than most on 'em, mind yer.'

‘Looks alright to me. Any road, ah wun’t mind a goo wi’ ’er ...’

‘Yo stand abart as much chance as ah do, Georgie ... she don’t let it out ter rough boggers like me an’ thee, me duck, not for nowt, she dun’t!’

‘Lives a few doors down from yer, don’t she? What wor ’er name again?’

‘Ethel ... bin roundabouts fer a while, she has, up from Narra Marsh afore she bedded down wi’ Billy Watts. Moved to Woolpack not long after I flitted from Always.’

‘Ah might hang abart and catch her unawares one night ... it’s not like Billy Watts could do much ter stop me.’

‘Ah don’t know abart that, Georgie, strong fella is Watts, what wi’ hauling coal and that. Then there’s his partner, that Robertson bloke. They reckon he’s a bit of ‘andful an’ all.’

‘He in’t no match for us, though, George, specially when together, hey?’

With that, George Boyd returned to the bar for refills, rhythmically tapping a coin on its wooden surface as he waited. He smiled at the averted eyes. Billy Watts and Dave Robertson; they wouldn’t stand a chance in hell. Boyd liked to rate himself number one, apart from George Davy, maybe, thinking it might be too close to call, though ... one way or another.

With glasses replenished, the two villains resumed their conversation, glancing occasionally to see if any of those nearby were listening to what they shouldn’t be.

‘So what’s to do wi’ Thurgood, then, George?’

'He's summat on the go, matey.'

'Oh ah, like what?'

George Davy tapped his lips, his voice lowering to a grating whisper.

'Enough cash for a good share-out. Thurgood reckons one of his gaffers is hidin' money he should be tekkin' ter the bank – likely summat ter do wi' taxes, he reckoned.'

'How much we talkin abart?'

'He's not sure ... reckons it must be a good amount 'cause he's bin doin' it for a while.'

'Ain't Thurgood bothered abart thievin' from his own boss?'

'He's struggling for money, George. Reckons he owes a bundle to some market lads, gambling debts by the sounds on it. Thurgood thought he were smart enough to delay payin' 'em, but they're vicious bleeders, that lot. Threatened to slash his pipe if he don't settle up sooner rather than later.'

'He must be shittin' his sen'.'

'Naw, not Victor. Like ah said, ah seen him only last night, him and his fancy bit, laughin' and singin' ... till they saw me comin'! He's full o' his own importance, is our Victor. He don't give a bogger, so long as he's got money to fritter.'

'Must a' filched some cash already if he can afford regular nights on the town.'

'Either that or he's 'ad 'is 'ands in the till. That's a common do in shops, they reckon.'

They drank more beer and talked some more, and the more they talked, the more they drank and the easier it became. Thoughts of filling their pockets without turning a hand was almost as pleasurable as sinking the fifth pint of The Postern's strongest.

'So when's it on for, then, George?'

'Ah'm seein' him tomorra' up the road, only he dun't want ter be seen out drinkin' and doin' wi' me ... not havin' summat like this planned, he dun't.'

Another pint and the landlord called time. They'd had a good session and no bother. Davy waved Boyd off and stumbled out into the dark to Woolpack Lane, passing Billy Watts's lodgings along the way. Seeing no light from the windows, Davy wondered if they were canoodling in bed and felt a stirring at the thought. Maybe Georgie Boyd was right; catching Ethel whatshername unawares might be just the thing for a passing thrill.

Chapter 30
Nottingham 1891

There weren't many municipal lamps alight in the darkened streets of the Lace Market of a Sunday night. No one about much either, apart from himself. The solitary lamp he stood under reflected the heavy raindrops that bounced off the cobbles to chase down the slope of Pilcher Gate, then away to who knew where. It seemed he was the only one foolish enough to be out in the deluge. It had tumbled down all day and was presently drumming on his canvas umbrella like an inundation of falling bullets.

Victor Thurgood was thoroughly fed up and still in two minds – agonisingly puzzled as to what to do next. He really liked his boss. Jimmy Caborn had been good to him over the years, and Thurgood was suffering an attack of remorse just thinking about what he was planning to do. At the same time, the option of calling it off caused him to physically shudder. Victor swore George Davy would stop at nothing to avenge himself if anyone was foolish enough to cross him. And then there was the other George to consider; he wouldn't need much of an excuse either.

The trouble was, a gang of market boys were after him like a pack of fevered sewer rats. Each and every one of them carried knives, one such blade recently resting threateningly on his windpipe. Victor quivered at the memory. The prospect of the razor edge slicing through his neck was becoming increasingly more of a probability. All things considered, there was nothing to be done but to carry on with the plan. If it proved successful, his debts would be cleared and he could rest easy. All that was required of him was to behave normally. Davy and Boyd would see to the nasty business. They knew what they were doing in that respect ... at least he hoped they did.

Victor intended to be in town on the night in question, making certain to be seen by people who knew him. He thought to take Ethel along, to err on the side of caution. He and Ethel were a regular sight of an evening. Being seen together would conveniently reinforce his alibi should any corroboration be required. He thought of her husband then ... well ... common-law husband. Billy, she called him. Victor knew she'd never leave him, poor chap, and in a way, he was thankful for that. He liked Ethel a lot. She was never any trouble and there were no strings attached; he paid and she performed. It was an understanding that suited them both equally well. Nevertheless, he sometimes thought their relationship might too easily veer into something more than an expedient arrangement. Ethel had turned out to be a friend as well as a convenience. He genuinely enjoyed her company ... just as long as it didn't get awkwardly serious between them. He often felt there was more to Ethel than met the eye. Sometimes he got the feeling she knew what he was thinking. Strange, it was, the peculiar way she looked at him now and then.

Victor heard footsteps approaching from Always Yard – heavy and purposeful. He'd no need to turn to see who was coming towards him. He imagined the swaying gait and the sheer bulk of the man, his enormous thrusting head emphasising the squareness of his grizzled chin. George Davy was alone and, much like Victor, completely saturated.

'Fine bleddy night we picked to meet!'

'Evening, George.'

'Let's not mess abart, Thurgood – what's the plan?'

'It's on for Tuesday. My boss visits a club near Goldsmith Street on Tuesday nights, plays a few hands of cards and gets pissed with his well-heeled mates. He won't be anywhere near the shop from six in the evening till he walks back by Derby Road. He likes to try the shop door around ten-thirty – a pointless habit – before carrying on to his home in the park.'

'Ah've bin thinkin', how d'yer know he won't suspect yer of bein' involved, what with yer livin' hover the shop an' all?'

'Because I'll be watching and waiting for him to leave his club. After that, I intend to follow him at a distance until he reaches Derby Road, then we'll meet as if by chance. I'll keep him company and we'll stroll up the hill together. Then I'll say goodbye and make as though to walk round to the back entrance. By that time, you should be well away, leaving only a busted lock for him to conveniently discover. No doubt he'll shout me back, at which point, we'll enter together to find a burglary's been committed. You'll need to make it look good – create a mess before finding the safe.'

'Gorrit all worked out an't yer, hey, Victor?'

'Just as long as you have too, George.'

'Don't goo worryin' on my part, me duck. Ah know wor ah'm doin'. Tuesday it is, then, unless ah 'ear different.'

'Right-oh, then, George. All being well, we'll divvy up on Thursday in the manner we agreed on. We need to be careful though ... not a word to a living soul!'

Chapter 31
Nottingham 1891

She'd totalled and checked the amount meticulously, her spirits lifted by the outcome. Ethel made a habit of adding Victor's money to her own private stash, the one she was saving for a rainy day. Well, the rainiest day she could ever remember had been the previous Sunday. And that became a good excuse for treating herself ... and for treating Billy as well, of course.

It was Tuesday before the sun finally broke through, the heavy rain having eased to a light drizzle the night before. Ethel spent most of Tuesday morning with Miss Polly, taking tea and fancies together. It was little Amy who brought in the tray, purposely ignoring Ethel and bobbing to Miss Polly before leaving in a conspicuous mood. Ethel wondered why old friends like Amy were treating her differently these days. It made her feel like a traitor for some reason. Billy said it was because working folk only wanted the company of other working folk, and that when you stepped up in the world, they thought you were no longer one of their kind.

Ethel dismissed that idea, thinking if anything, she'd stepped down rather than up. But then perhaps the way she conducted herself suggested otherwise. She liked to think that those who didn't know her would never guess her true vocation. Ethel had taken care not to dress and act like a common tart, reasoning that if she didn't look decent enough, men like Victor Thurgood wouldn't want to be seen out on the town with her.

Miss Polly said there were many different kinds of professional ladies, from the rough and desperate types that entertained lowlife to the so-called escorts that served the cream of society – adding that she thought Ethel was operating somewhere at the upper end of the market, even if she did happen to be of humble stock. Ethel thought to take that for what some might call a backhanded compliment.

Arranged business was certainly better than loitering on street corners, and she'd never entertained the idea of working in Miss Polly's establishment. For one thing, she didn't like the atmosphere. Then there were those inevitable looks of disapproval from the girls she'd once skivvied for.

Regardless of her preferred independence, Ethel made sure to keep in touch with Miss Polly. For a share of the proceeds, her former employer would recommend her to gentlemen of a certain manner, as had happened with Victor Thurgood. And if any of the selected clients played rough or attempted to avoid paying, Miss Polly would ask Big Cyril to 'have a word' with the offending gentleman – for a nominal fee, of course. The arrangement suited everyone and was mutually profitable: the classier the client, the more beneficial the financial return for both parties.

Ethel Bentley stepped out that Tuesday

morning, determined to have the day to herself. She decided to take the route through Hockley, browsing the modest shops there at a leisurely pace whilst making her way towards the centre. Once she arrived in the heart of town, she thought to buy some fresh meat for tea. Entering the chill domain of The Shambles, she ignored the stench that pervaded the ancient market beneath the municipal Exchange building. Deep in its dank environs, Ethel swapped pleasantries with the ageing butcher she tended to favour, choosing and paying for two pork chops, saying she'd collect them on her way home.

After emerging from the murk of the chambers into dazzling sunlight, Ethel strolled along Cheapside, smiling and nodding to the flower sellers informally pitched outside the shoe and boot shop. Shortly after that, she proceeded to make her way across the panoramic square that fronted The Exchange building, negotiating the tented stalls and the blankets spread on open ground that displayed copious quantities of miscellaneous pottery. The aproned marketeers in their pork-pie hats were boisterously calling to prospective customers, whilst hansom cabs and horse-drawn trams disgorged ever more workers and shoppers onto the cobbled expanse locally known as 'The Stones'.

Ethel was content to melt into the seething confusion of humanity that gathered there of a weekday morning – easing her way through huddles of loafing men and callow youths in tattered threads and flattened caps, and the weathered tradesmen who pulled their barrows and drove their carts.

She dared to promenade with the corseted ladies with their flowing dresses brushing the ground, who cast teasing glances at admiring gentry sporting bowlers and black frockcoats. How she loved the vibrant diversity of the old town square. Nearby stood the classical emporium that was Griffin & Spalding: Ethel's selected destination. It was her favourite shop and well worthy of the time she'd taken to dress appropriately. Ironically, the prestigious store was situated near to where the Rookeries once stood – that infamous chaos of tumbling slums cleared some years earlier, its very ground fumigated and purged of its manifold infestations.

Approaching the elegant entrance, Ethel intuitively adjusted her comportment, easing into the graceful stroll she observed in ladies of superior standing. The entrance door was immediately held open by a smiling young man, resplendent in his smart suit. To Ethel's delight, he nodded and smoothly tipped his hat, as indeed he had for the vogueish lady who preceded her. She thought how satisfying it was to be treated in such a manner, particularly when visiting what was said by some to be the most sophisticated store in town.

The intermingling fragrances of soaps and perfumes saturated her senses as she rather affectedly made her way through the purposeful confusion of attended counters. Proceeding to the far corner, Ethel found the silk scarf irresistibly hanging from the very same rail, as though waiting for her alone to buy it. She thought it far too expensive for what it was, but more than worth what it might later do for her.

Little by little, Ethel was building a secret wardrobe. Billy wasn't one for rummaging through cupboards to see what she'd been spending. And so neither he nor anyone else knew what she planned for the future. The way business was going, she'd be able to leave the profession behind; a couple of years, perhaps, and she might well claim to be a proper lady.

Chapter 32
Nottingham 1891

By the time Ethel Bentley arrived back at Woolpack Lane, her feet were aching something awful. The day had become markedly warmer, causing Ethel to regret the extra layer she'd slipped on that morning. Never mind, a few more yards and she'd be home. Once inside, she'd stow her shopping, have a wash and change into something cooler.

It was then she saw him slouched against a wall, only a few doors down from where she lived. There was never any mistaking George Davy. How could anybody not recognise that brute of a man? He was just about the roughest bloke she'd ever come across, then she thought of his equally vulgar mate; George Boyd wasn't far behind in that respect. Regardless of the man's reputation, he had every right to lounge against the wall of his own lodgings. She thought, *Fancy living on the same street as somebody like that.* Even the house where he resided had earned a bad reputation, local folk commenting what a funny lot they were that lived there. Whispers of strange goings-on in that house did the rounds quite regularly.

Ethel purposely lowered her head and made to hurry past as quickly as she could without making it obvious. Then just when she thought she'd made it, his hand snaked out and grabbed her arm. The pain of his digging fingers made her cry out loud, causing her temper to flare. 'It's the Irish in her,' her mother would say, 'what with those green eyes and red hair, 'twas ever going to be so!'

'Gerroff, yer lousy bogger!'

The unexpected show of temper took George Davy by complete surprise. So much so, he reflexively released his grip before looking her up and down with a frown.

'Sorry, me duck, ah din't mean ter 'ot yer.'

'No, it dun't bleddy feel like it!'

She realised that despite her ladylike pretensions, the blood of the back streets still surged through her veins.

'Ah were only trying to catch yer attention, Eth.'

'What for?'

'Ah've bin noticin' yer just lately ... can't blame me fer that, can yer? You're a bit of a looker, yer know.'

'Ah, and look is all you'll ever do, matey!'

He didn't like that. George Davy wasn't used to anybody answering back, particularly in that tone of voice.

'Tek care what yer say, me duck. Ah could pull yer in 'ere and gi' yer one afore yer could blink them long lashes o' yorn!'

'Ah can believe that an' all! Yo look like the quick in-and-out type to me.'

'Yo should know abart them things in your game, an' that's a fact!'

They'd got to shouting louder. Net curtains were twitching, doors opening a crack to see and hear the better. Ethel stormed away then, muttering in temper. She'd not be cowering to an animal like him. Not like the so-called men thereabouts did!

George Davy swung around, his glowering eyes scarching for anybody foolish enough to be looking in his direction – desperate for anybody he could vent his anger on. Most likely it wouldn't be long before he found some poor soul or other.

Chapter 33
Nottingham 1891

The nights were drawing in and the leaves were falling, yet summer lingered on. Victor Thurgood was dressed for a night on the town, wearing his good suit and attendant trappings. After tweaking his cravat, he adjusted his hat to the angle he thought suited him best. Then, after inspecting his image in the long mirror for the umpteenth time, he gave a final twist to the points of his waxed moustache and made for the door.

Setting a brisk pace, he soon arrived at the top of Parliament Street. It was there that he'd first met Ethel one balmy summer's evening two years before. And there she was now, in the very same spot, pretty as a picture and well turned out as usual. Victor rebuked himself for thinking that when Ethel opened her mouth to speak, only then did the gentle illusion of her ladylike image swiftly evaporate. Despite her best endeavours, Ethel had never quite mastered the nuances of sophisticated conversation. Even so, he admitted she was improving, at least when she thought about it.

''Lo, Victor. You look smart tonight.'

'And you look lovely as usual, Ethel, my dear.'

'Seems strange us meeting on a Tuesday, Victor. I don't think we've ever done that before – glad we are, though. I've been looking forward to it all day.'

'I thought we'd stroll down to The Bell for a

couple first, then perhaps a quick bite to eat across the road afterwards. What d'you think, Eth?'

'That's fine by me, Victor. Back ter your place after that, is it?

She saw he was uncomfortable with the brazen suggestion and thought to say no more, thinking his reaction a bit on the curious side. She sometimes had a sense of things, second sight her mother called it, though Ethel wasn't so sure about that.

'Truth be told, Eth, I need to be up really early in the morning – urgent business matters, that's why. Otherwise, you know I'd be more than pleased to retire to our little nest.'

'Oh, don't worry yourself, Victor. I'm sure we'll make up for it soon enough.'

She liked to hear him laugh, uncomfortably loud as it was sometimes. On this occasion, though, she thought it didn't sound quite right.

The town was almost devoid of activity, unlike Fridays and Saturdays, when it seemed the whole of Nottingham turned out. Even so, the resonance of music and merriment occasionally drifted from the pubs and clubs to fashion a muted but convivial enough atmosphere. The Bell was usually busy no matter what the day or time, and after seating Ethel at one of only a few vacant tables, Victor marched to the bar to order drinks. She noticed him making a proper fuss of people on the way, clapping some on their shoulders and loudly greeting others from across the room, slightly bewildered folk raising their glasses in recognition. Not for the first time that evening, Ethel thought something wasn't right with Victor's behaviour. Her forehead creased even deeper when he performed the same routine on his return from the bar, acknowledging anyone and everyone he thought he even vaguely knew.

Ethel was aware of how well known Victor was about town. He'd frequented the same establishments ever since he'd been old enough to get away with it. Even so, it was the first time she'd seen him making such a spectacle of himself. After Victor had settled in his seat, they made the usual small talk, though Ethel thought his mind was somewhere else – distant somehow. She caught him gnawing his bottom lip on occasion too, thinking that was something he did when things were niggling at him. It was much the same when they left The Bell, Victor making a show of saying his goodbyes, his conviviality disappearing like magic as soon as they got outside.

They ate at the Oyster Bar over the road, Victor picking at a plate of food he'd normally swallow in half the time it took Ethel to clear her own. Then she noticed him yanking his watch out of his waistcoat now and then, as though nervously checking the time. They parted as soon as they left the restaurant – on the pavement immediately outside, with scarcely a peck on the cheek – Victor leaving her standing there, walking away without so much as a backward glance. She had to wonder if he was tiring of her. If he was, she questioned why he'd been so keen to ask her out in the first place.

Ethel had intended to tell Victor about George Davy accosting her earlier that day, but given Victor's mood, she thought to save it for a better time. What made it worse was that Ethel had been thinking a lot about Victor of late. Then she reminded herself that he was simply a casual acquaintance and paying client, not her lover and protector. Regardless of that, big and strong as he was, Victor would be no match for the likes of George Davy. She'd considered having a word with Miss Polly, wondering if big Cyril might intervene on her behalf – what a contest that might have been! – but then she thought that taking that route might only make matters worse. In the end, Ethel concluded that she'd deal with George Davy in her own way should he try it on again, all the while hoping to God he wouldn't.

***

Had he overplayed his part and made it too obvious? Had he upset Ethel with his unintentional insensitivity? Victor Thurgood scraped his teeth over his bottom lip. The anxiety was getting a bit too much for him. He began to wish he'd never thought of the idea in the first place, wishing even more he'd not involved Davy and Boyd. And then when he thought about Parry and his gang of cutthroats, he wished he'd never been talked into that hand of cards either.

Victor had become acquainted with 'Skipper' Parry when playing billiards in a backstreet hall near Sneinton Market. He enjoyed the leisurely ambience of the game and came to play the amiable Parry a few times, the two men getting on well together and proving of equal proficiency. Then after one particular session, Parry, who had previously introduced himself as a market trader, asked Victor if he fancied a hand of cards and a drink or two. Always up for a lark, Victor said he might, whereupon Parry promptly invited him to what he called a private club somewhere off Carrington Road.

Not wishing to appear discourteous, Victor hesitantly agreed, quickly regretting his decision when they came to a neglected building and entered its questionable entrance. The place looked to be nothing more than someone's ramshackle accommodation, the ambience of it somewhat stale, a hint of human excretion tainting its atmosphere.

There were others already in the room he was led into – two rough-looking types slouched at a table and one of similar character sprawled on a grubby armchair by the wall – Parry's men, market porters, he called them – just to make up the numbers. Two untidy piles of well-thumbed cards had been placed on the table. Then just as one of the porters began to shuffle the decks, a curvaceous young woman wearing little more than a diaphanous nightdress appeared from nowhere with a bottle and some cloudy tumblers.

Feeling obliged to at least show willing, Victor played a hand or two for a stake of small change, surprising himself by winning three out of four, much to the garrulous admiration of players and onlookers alike. The woman stood beside him throughout, ensuring Victor's glass was frequently replenished, suggestively brushing his shoulder each time she poured a generous measure.

All was lost once his head began to swim, and in that timely moment, Parry suggested upping the stakes. After Victor declared he'd not much money with him, his host said not to concern himself, especially now they were mates. Parry offered to write it down, saying Victor could settle later in the week ... in the unlikely event of him losing, of course.

Only when Victor eventually sobered up did he recognise he'd been set up from the very beginning. During the early stages of their relationship, Victor had innocuously bragged to Parry about where he lived and worked. Victor being Victor, he embellished his status to appear more affluent than he actually was. From thereon in, his fate was truly sealed.

The cards began to run against him, his earlier good fortune strangely petering out as the evening wore on. In the end, the amount he owed was equal to over a month's wages. Even so, they said little more of the significant debt, allowing him to stagger home without a copper penny to his name. Just two days later, Victor became aware of someone tapping at the shop window and was shocked to see Parry beckoning him outside. Once on the pavement, he noticed two of Parry's men loitering close by. The grinning Parry duly reminded Victor of how much he owed, explaining in gruesome detail exactly what would happen if he didn't settle his debt within seven days. Much as Victor pleaded his case, it was to no avail. With his men by his side, Parry grinned slyly before sauntering away, drawing a finger across his own throat as he turned to glance back at his credulous victim.

Later that week, after pulling together barely half the amount he owed, Victor nervously arrived at the market. Parry snatched the bag from him and counted the notes, shaking his head and sneering before nodding meaningfully at two of his men. The pair of bruisers forced him into the bowels of a darkened warehouse, with Parry at their heels. After hurling Victor to the ground, one of the men – an evil-looking character with rotting teeth – drew a blade and pressed it to Victor's throat, a thin trickle of blood proving its sharpness.

Praying silently to his maker, Victor thought the end had come. Then, without a single word, they silently beckoned him to his feet. With legs wobbling and head spinning, he eventually forced himself upright, cowering before them in abject shame, his humiliation intensified when he felt the patch of dampness that spread from between his legs.

In his desperation, Victor thought to seek out George Boyd. He'd had various dealings with the villain since casually meeting him in The Postern one night. They'd got on well enough, and when Boyd found out what Victor did for a living, the conversation straightaway turned to business of a certain kind. Boyd claimed to know someone who might be interested in the occasional bolt of cloth – strictly on the quiet and no questions asked. Victor, a man up for any deal that might advance his lifestyle, agreed without hesitation. Ever since then, a bolt or two of cloth would find its way to the loading bay of a Thursday afternoon, Thursday being the day Victor oversaw the business unaccompanied. Boyd would duly turn up with a cart, load the cloth and be away with nobody the wiser.

This mutually lucrative arrangement became a weekly regularity, proceeds changing hands in The Postern on subsequent Friday evenings. On one such occasion, whilst enjoying a tankard or two together, Boyd got to telling Victor about one of his associates – a certain George Davy – expressing how tough and crafty Davy was, how he had his uses and was not a man to cross. With Skipper Parry and his boys after him, Victor's survival instinct prompted him to recall that particular conversation.

After turning it over in his mind, the germ of an idea began to take shape – a simple solution to get Parry off his back, and sooner rather than later. There'd be a nice little earner in it for Boyd and Davy and hopefully enough to pay his debts. It was a plan born out of desperation, and once he'd thought it through, Victor wasted no time in putting it together.

Trawling the felon's usual haunts, Victor chanced on George Boyd ambling towards The Reindeer Inn on Wheeler Gate. They met and entered the hostelry together, Victor buying the ales before relating the rudiments of his predicament. Boyd listened intently, immediately sensing an opportunity. He said he'd best leave the arrangements to George Davy, as Davy was a sight better at planning those kind of things. The next time they met, Boyd brought Davy with him. Victor then saw for himself what a brute of a man he was. After a cursory introduction, Boyd immediately backed off, allowing George Davy to do the talking. With George Boyd's reputation for being habitually arrested, Victor could understand why Davy insisted on taking the lead. Time was pressing, though, and Parry wanted his money by the end of the week – and with added interest. After Victor outlined his proposition, George Davy went ominously quiet, eyes narrowing as he weighed the odds.

'A course, yer know what yer riskin', don't yer, fella? Could well be yer job gone and a trip ter the magistrates.'

'I can't see any other way out, George. Parry's after me and he means business.'

'Skipper Parry! He might be dangerous with

his boys by his side, but ah know him well enough and he knows me an' all. Why, he'd run a bleddy mile if he knew ah were after 'im!'

Victor breathed a sigh of relief at hearing that. Maybe there was another way; maybe he'd simply pay Davy and Boyd to scare Parry away. But then how would he pay them? He'd had his hand in the till a few times for beer money, never mind the risk of pinching larger amounts.

'Tell yer what ah'll do, Thurgood, ah'll think on it, and you do the same. We'll meet again on Sunday – me and thee. Norr'in in town, though. It wun't do for us to be seen together too often. Thinkin' abart it, there's a lamp on Pilcher Gate where we could meet. It's not far from where ah live. No bogger's usually thereabouts on a Sunday night. Mek it eight sharp under the lamp, and be sure yer want ter carry on wi' this lark. If yer don't, it'll cost yer a few drinks ... so don't bogger me abart wharever yer do, me duck!'

***

It had started spitting with rain. Victor had forgotten his brolly, and it was a mite too warm to think about overcoats. His earlier regrets about Ethel and just about everything else apart from immediate business had temporarily receded to the back of his mind. Breathing harder than usual, he reached the top of Market Street, crossing by the theatre before walking on to Goldsmith Street. James Caborn's club was near Goldsmith Place, and

Victor thought of a number of spots nearby where he could wait in the dry to keep watch.

Knowing it would be some while before Caborn exited the club, Victor lit yet another cigarette and settled into the recess of a doorway, the position allowing him a clear view of the building he was monitoring. Approximately thirty minutes later, four well-dressed men appeared from inside the club, huddling together under the light of a portico lamp. Spiralling tobacco smoke was billowing from the quartet of tipsy gentlemen, the echoes of cheery farewells resonating over to where Victor waited. He immediately recognised the figure of James Caborn breaking from the group, soon after hearing the rhythmic beat of his cane on the paving slabs across from where stood. Easing even further into the shadows, Victor waited for his employer to pass him by. Then, after a suitable interval, Victor set off to follow the distinctive sound of his employer's tapping cane.

He knew Caborn was a creature of habit: that he would cross to Wollaton Street and pass by the light works before cutting through Shepperson Street onto Derby Road. He'd walk up the hill to his treasured premises, try the door three times, take a step back, and gaze at the building to ensure everything was as it should be. Then, and only then, would James Caborn continue his journey home.

Victor carefully shadowed his quarry until Caborn passed the buildings that housed the town's electric light works. Precisely at that point, Victor ran over to Toll Street and along Globe Street to bring him to Derby Road, only a few steps down the hill from where he knew his director would emerge. He had timed it perfectly – the very moment James Caborn appeared from Shepperson Street, Victor all but collided with him.

'Evening, Mr Caborn!'

'Victor! Well met, young man. Been out on the town have we?'

'Oh, just taking a lady friend out for a bite to eat.'

'Really? Well, it's good to see you're keeping decent hours during the week.'

'Yes, needed a break was all, sir. Gets a bit lonely living on your own.'

They'd slackened their speed. The hill was quite steep, and though only approaching middle age, James Caborn continued to suffer from a debilitating leg wound received in Africa during the final campaign of the Zulu War. And so it was at a slow pace that they gradually came to within strides of their destination. As they did, Victor's hairline prickled at seeing the silhouette of a shape protruding from the foyer that fronted the shop's entrance.

James Caborn came to an abrupt halt, placing an arm across Victor's chest as if to stop him stepping nearer.

'What the hell's that in the doorway, Victor?!'

'Don't know, sir … better have a closer look.'

Cautiously, they moved forward, Victor's

short-lived hope of finding an empty sack quickly fading as they edged nearer to the shadowy form. When they came close, they saw the unresponsive shape was that of a human body, malformed by the nature of its arrangement. Victor fought to prevent himself from visibly shaking, a nauseous urgency intensifying in his throat – had the pair of villains gone too far? Had Davy and Boyd botched the robbery and killed some innocent soul in the heat of the moment?

When they bent over the body for closer examination, James Caborn gasped and threw his hand to his mouth in shock, immediately kneeling by the figure at his feet. Victor Thurgood rolled his eyes and inwardly groaned; it was worse than he could ever have feared. The prone figure stretched out before them was Ethan Critchlow: the senior partner himself.

Chapter 34
Nottingham 1891

The news was leaked on Wednesday morning, inevitably appearing in the Nottingham Journal by late afternoon. By that time, Victor was somewhat relieved, but at the same time, extremely anxious. He was relieved to hear the senior partner was alive and doing well, yet anxious the enquiry into the violent burglary was already in the capable hands of a celebrated investigator. Ethan Critchlow had sustained a broken arm and fractured jaw. Only later, after the bewildering effects of the anaesthetic had sufficiently cleared, was he able to mumble a few words of interest to Inspector Peter Leyton, and then only between alternating spasms of agony and persistent nausea.

James Caborn demanded to be updated at every juncture. He'd been quick to utilise his contacts at police headquarters – contacts occupying senior positions – the clubs and associations he shrewdly patronised proving extremely useful at times. In turn, Victor Thurgood anxiously awaited the updates relayed to him by his director.

As well as being concerned for his partner's wellbeing, Caborn was extremely angry. The amount stolen was not inconsiderable, and he chided himself for not banking the cash as he should have done. There were no worries concerning the legitimacy of the accumulated funds, as he had always made sure the amounts were legally accounted for. The tax office might nose about, if they ever bothered to get around to it. However, in that unlikely event, his legal advisors assured him such an inconvenience would be straightforwardly navigated. The overriding thought that continued to nag James Caborn was the fact that whosoever the perpetrators were, it seemed they'd found the money without too much bother. There was evidence of a convoluted search, but even so, the perpetrators' rummaging led a little too directly to the well-concealed safe under the stairs.

Apart from himself, there were a number of people who knew of the safe's existence – Ethan Critchlow and his wife, she having once been company secretary – Caborn's own wife, who occasionally assisted with office matters – and, of course, Victor Thurgood. Also privy were Mrs Body the cleaner and Percy the odd-job man, Percy being the one who originally constructed the housing that concealed the safe.

Caborn gave the names of those people to the inspector, who, in time-honoured fashion, assiduously recorded them in his little black book. Inspector Leyton had asked about the choice of safe, commenting that it looked second-rate and easily cracked. The derisive observation was not lost on James Caborn. He remembered dithering over which one to buy, settling for the cheapest, thinking it would be enough to resist the amateurish wiles of opportunist thieves. He still thought that submission to be plausible, even more so when the inspector said he thought the thieves knew what they were about: consummate professionals, in other words.

The day after the misdemeanour, Inspector Peter Leyton busily questioned those who knew of the safe's existence, somewhat fatuously inviting the wives of the partners to be interviewed. When James Caborn queried his reasoning, Leyton responded by saying the ladies might have innocently said something to someone at some time, those sort of misjudgements not being unheard of in such circumstances. By the time it came to Victor Thurgood's turn, he'd worked himself into a highly agitated state, utterly convinced he'd been found out already. Sweating profusely and recurrently scratching his head for no particular reason, Victor approached the small office made available to the inspector for his temporary use. Victor experienced a surge of fresh panic on observing the distorted image of the detective through the undulating glass of the office window. He took a deep breath before knocking, only walking in when prompted to do so.

'Mr Thurgood, isn't it?'

Leyton was slick, sleek and beaky, something like a hawk gliding on thermals, searching for potential prey.

'Yes indeed, that's me, sir.'

Victor thought to hang on to the jaunty sales style that had served him well over the years.

Leyton didn't so much as blink, his

sharp eyes penetrating Thurgood's own, searching for indications of deception.

'So you and Mr Caborn returned to the shop together last night, did you?'

The detective got straight to it: no introduction, no getting to know each other.

'Not exactly returning together, as you put it. I happened to be walking up Derby Road just as he was coming out of ... Shepperson, that's right, Shepperson Street.'

'Out for the night, were you?'

Yes, that's correct.'

'Come across anybody in town who might corroborate your presence, Mr Thurgood?'

'Corroborate? Blimey! Of course, yes. There were one or two in The Bell, and my lady friend, of course.'

'Name?'

Victor hesitated. He'd missed that one, all of a sudden realising he didn't want the police turning up at Ethel's place, especially if Billy happened to be about.

'Well, it's a bit delicate ... the lady in question being sort of married, you see.'

'I'm sorry about the delicate circumstances, Mr Thurgood, but we're investigating a serious crime here, one that might well have turned out even more sinister, so you can appreciate there's little time for niceties. The name if you please ... and the address where I can find the lady.'

'Ethel Bentley, if you must know. She lives at ...'

'Woolpack Lane, by any chance?'

Leyton's stare intensified even more, the slightest suspicion of a sneer developing at the corners of his paper-thin mouth.

'You know her? You know Ethel?'

'Oh, yes, Mr Thurgood. I think it's fair to say my uniformed colleagues have become quite familiar with her over time. I've met her myself, once or twice ... in the course of my duty, you understand. Nice lady. In fact, you might say she's a cut above others of her ...'

The detective let the words hang in the musty air, his sneer even more obvious. Victor blushed to his roots, cheeks burning like raging fires. His life was unravelling; in a short space of time, becoming the instigator of a most heinous crime and found to be consorting with a known prostitute.

'That's entirely your business, Mr Thurgood. Take my word for it, I'm not one to spread gossip of that nature. Perhaps you weren't aware of how long Miss Bentley's been involved in her profession. It peeves me to say, but she's what you might describe as an old hand.'

The deepening flush on Victor's face was not entirely the result of his embarrassment but also the product of his escalating anger. Despite everything else, the last thing he wanted was Ethel's name dragged in the dirt. He especially didn't like the way Leyton was talking about her. Victor thought a lot of Ethel Bentley and respected her for what she represented to him, no matter her so-called profession.

'Did you know about the contents of the

pilfered safe, Mr Thurgood?'

Leyton had smoothly moved on, totally unfazed by Victor's observable annoyance.

'Yes, of course I did. Why wouldn't I? I'd like to think my managerial status allows me to know what I'm responsible for when trusted with the sole charge of the building.'

Victor thought it was a good answer, perhaps one Leyton hadn't entirely expected.

'Are you aware of the amount stolen?'

'No, although I'd guess it's not insignificant.'

'You were never present when the safe was opened?'

'Never once, no. Mr Caborn rightfully demanded his privacy at such times.'

'I see ... d'you think the thieves had some assistance from within?'

'What?! Most unlikely, I would've said.'

'Unlikely? Hmm ... Did you say you were in The Bell when it happened?'

'No, I did not, sir. I simply said I was in The Bell that evening. I have no idea exactly what time the robbery happened. How could I possibly know that detail? And by the way, as you mentioned the word "corroboration", the landlord there can verify my presence! As can Ethel, of course ... not to mention the proprietor of the Oyster Rooms across the road – where we enjoyed a tasty snack together afterwards!'

'Calm down, Mr Thurgood, no one's doubting your word, though we may or may not need to verify your whereabouts ... if only for the record, of course.'

'Of course ... please forgive me. The thought of the incident distresses me. I respect and admire Mr Critchlow. What the poor man must have suffered is beyond the pale.'

'Indeed, it is unfortunate, Mr Thurgood – a robbery that went terribly wrong, and to Mr Critchlow's acute detriment. Still, even though he remains in a bad way, he did manage to pass on some very useful information.'

Victor wondered if it was simply his imagination, but he swore Leyton's eyes flared wider when he spoke those last words. And had Leyton also purposefully leaned towards him at the same time, as if to better observe his reaction?

'In fact, he was lucid enough to impart a few interesting details regarding the two men that assaulted him.'

'Really? Well, that's a good thing, isn't it?'

'Indeed it is, Mr Thurgood ... indeed it is.'

Victor Thurgood thought he could feel Leyton's eyes boring into his back as he turned to leave the office. There had been a lot implied during the brief exchange ... perhaps even more left unspoken. In his panic, he thought to advise Davy and Boyd to make themselves scarce for a while – after he'd received his share of the takings, of course. Victor desperately needed the money, so he'd simply have to take the risk of meeting with the villains, and quickly. Skipper Parry wouldn't wait much longer.

Chapter 35
Nottingham 1891

James Caborn's expression reflected his worsening mood. Not only had he lost the princely sum of ninety-four pounds – enough to purchase the small terraced house he'd thought about adding to his growing estate – it was beginning to look like one of his employees was complicit in the robbery.

Inspector Leyton had spoken to Caborn's partner, the unfortunate Ethan Critchlow, with some interesting facts emerging from their conversation. As fate would have it, Critchlow had inadvertently left some important documents on his desk when departing the office that afternoon. He was due to see the company's solicitors the following morning with view to adjusting the share levels he and Caborn had agreed upon. Ethan Critchlow was nearing retirement, and certain financial matters needed addressing prior to his leaving the company. The meeting had required an early start, and as their offices were situated on the opposite side of town, Critchlow decided to take a hansom cab ahead of schedule. Anxious to have the documents to hand before setting out the following morning, Critchlow resolved to return to his office to collect them that same night. Beginning his half-mile walk from home at just before a quarter to seven, he arrived at the shop almost exactly at quarter past the hour.

The startled Critchlow found that one of the

entrance doors had been forced open, the crudely splintered wood suggesting it had been jemmied. The damaged door itself was rattling gently in its frame, encouraged by the moderate wind blowing across Derby Road. With the benefit of hindsight, Critchlow realised he should have walked away and raised the alarm, but he hadn't. Instead he'd foolishly called out before vigilantly entering the darkened showroom. After taking a step or two inside, Critchlow discerned the glow of a candle flickering in the gloom. Then barely a moment later, he felt the appalling impact of something solid smashing into his chin, a multitude of stars consequently flashing before his eyes as he slumped helplessly to the floor. As if that were not sufficient to incapacitate the elderly man, whoever hit him proceeded to kick and stamp unmercifully at his fragile body. Gamely struggling to rise in order to escape his torment, Critchlow's supporting arm was then dealt an exceptionally savage blow, the arm immediately and horrifyingly broken. He remembered hearing himself scream through the absolute agony of it. Even so, he remained lucid enough to snatch a glance at the scuffed boots that hurriedly passed by him. And in that moment before he completely lost consciousness, he swore he heard a voice whispering hoarsely, 'Christ Almighty, George!'

***

The first light of suspicion fell on young Percy Winkley, the handyman who made and fixed things. Percy correspondingly helped sweep and mop, lift and carry, load and unload and put out the bins for collection. In fact, there was nothing much beyond Percy's original remit that he hadn't become involved in during his short career – apart from anything whatsoever to do with customers. Such was his manner and appearance, Percy was strictly prohibited from appearing on the shopfloor whenever customers were in sight. Strive as he might to improve his image, Percy remained a scruffy and unkempt individual with an annoying habit of saying the wrong things at the wrong time, and loudly to boot. He was also thought a bun short of a baker's dozen. Putting all those characteristics together, it didn't take long for Inspector Peter Leyton to dismiss the idea that Percy had sufficient intelligence to plan anything other than changing the brush on his broomstick. If anything, Percy was bewildered by it all, complaining bitterly that he'd be the one ordered to clear up the mess and mend the panelling around the offending safe. The inspector clearly had had his patience tested, Percy being prone to stuttering and blaspheming when becoming overly excited, which was inordinately often. With Percy Winkley and the cleaner out of the frame – Madge Body being in her late sixties, a devout Wesleyan and a particularly overactive member of the local temperance society – the remaining personnel, apart from a couple of part-timers who knew nothing of the safe, consisted of the two partners:

James Caborn and Ethan Critchlow, their respective wives, and the enigmatic manager, Victor Thurgood.

Discounting the partners and their spouses for every good and obvious reason, Inspector Leyton was then left with only one viable candidate, namely Victor Thurgood. That was assuming the robbery was not simply one of a speculative nature, a notion the inspector had by that time rejected out of hand. And so with his mind made up, Leyton hot-footed it back to the station, determined to put a plan into place without further delay.

***

Only one of the felons was propped against the bar in The Postern Gate Inn, looking like he hadn't a care in the world. Victor wondered how anyone could be so untroubled after what had been inflicted on Critchlow. Why had they needed to use that amount of violence? Especially against an old man like that.

Victor Thurgood was seething, hopelessly ensnared in an overwhelming mix of anger and trepidation. He'd convinced himself that Inspector Leyton had him down as a prime suspect, though clearly, the detective's instincts were not sufficient to charge him. The law demanded quantifiable proof, and Victor had alibis lined up like wooden fairground ducks. Even so, Leyton had hinted at being in possession of significant information, and that worried Victor greatly. In his agitated state, he'd become increasingly convinced the police were closing in on him, his precious freedom at impending risk.

Leyton was as sharp as a razor, and Victor was certain the detective would ferret out the truth sooner rather than later. That's why Victor hurriedly conceived an idea – distressing though it was. A desperate strategy had come to mind, one that meant abandoning everything he'd ever worked for, but needs must if the devil drives.

Because of the growing urgency, Victor Thurgood became all the more impatient for his share of the proceeds. The coach was leaving the very next morning, seat booked and paid for. If everything went as planned, he'd be away and gone, then the plague could take them all – except for Ethel, that is. He wished no harm on Ethel Bentley. He'd thought about her a lot of late, wondering if he'd ever see her again. He could only hope so. Absurd as it seemed in that moment, Victor was entirely certain fate would in some way bring them together again, and perhaps not just for one last time.

Chapter 36
Nottingham 1891

Detective Constable Grouper was gasping for breath. He'd imagined transferring to the provinces would make life easier for him. However, as the new boy – even though he was pushing thirty – he was attracting the lion's share of duties others fought shy of, the latest jaunt being a prime example. The excuse from the boss was that nobody would recognise a peeler who'd only recently arrived from London. That theory suggested Grouper was best placed to follow the suspect into whatever dubious haunts he might choose to patronise.

Inspector Leyton had taken Grouper with him to Derby Road. After discovering a place to conceal themselves, they waited for Renshaw's store to close for the day. Ten minutes after the due time, two figures appeared on the pavement outside its entrance. They seemed deep in conversation, and when they came to go their separate ways, Leyton and Grouper agreed the parting appeared to be somewhat acrimonious. The first to leave was James Caborn, who proceeded to cross the busy road, carefully evading the carts and carriages predominantly flowing up the hill and out of town. The other of the two, Victor Thurgood, subsequently walked towards the centre of town at a brisk pace, face grim and determined.

'That's him, Grouper, that's our suspect – make sure you don't lose the bugger. Note everywhere he goes and record a full description of anybody he talks to, and note any names you chance to overhear.'

'Yes, sir, no problem. Leave it to me.'

'Good man. Off you go, then, and don't get too close or make yourself obvious.'

Grouper was tempted to tell Leyton not to tell him how to suck eggs – that down in the Smoke, things were a deal more sophisticated than they were in the East Midlands. Grouper had barely been on the Nottingham force for a couple of weeks, and already he was regretting his decision to leave the capital. It had seemed a good idea to transfer north, promotion in the London boroughs having become difficult of late. He blamed the Ripper murders after somebody reckoned recruitment was running high because too many glory hunters and odd types were applying.

The suspect he was following was no youngster; all the same, Grouper was struggling to keep pace. The detective was seriously overweight – 'Too much puddin',' some of his so-called mates had said. He'd never had much of a colour. A lot of big-city folk were like that, what with all the smog and traffic. Nevertheless, right then, he imagined his cheeks were glowing with the effort it took to keep up with Victor Thurgood.

That the fellow he was tracking was heading for a specific destination was nigh on certain in Grouper's assessment. He reckoned by body language alone that the suspect had a definite purpose in mind. After hurrying across the near empty marketplace, Thurgood marched by The Exchange building before accelerating onto Bridlesmith Gate. Grouper increasingly sucked air as he struggled to keep up with the fitter man, his quarry almost sprinting towards his destination.

Victor Thurgood breathed deeply and braced himself as he approached The Postern Gate Inn. The corner door at the head of Drury Hill was just in the process of closing behind another customer when he pushed against it and entered the busy saloon bar. Peering through the vapours of swirling tobacco, he straightaway noticed George Boyd at the bar, contentedly swilling a tankard of ale.

'George ...'

'Ay-up, Vic, fancy a pint, me duck?'

'Bleddy hell, Boyd! How can you be so unconcerned after doing what you did? Why, you could've ...'

'Keep it down, Thurgood, for all our sakes ... specially yours!'

Boyd's words were low and bristly, the threat behind them immediately bringing Victor to heel.

'I hope to God you've got the money, George.'

Victor's tone was all of a sudden more respectful, if not a little oily. Boyd sneered and chuckled, noisily hawking the phlegm from his throat before discharging a gobbet into the copper spittoon that rested by his feet.

'Owd yer hosses, Vic, ah got yer share in me pocket. Not that yer contributed that much.'

Their voices were low, their words all but lost in the general chatter.

'What was the final count?'

'Can't tell yer, me duck ... it were George as tallied up. He took charge like he always does.'

Victor began to worry. Grabbing the tankard that had been set before him, he took a serious gulp of ale, breathing hard over his ensuing words.

'Go on then, how much is my share, and where the bleddy hell is it?'

'It's in me inside pocket, ter answer that last question. Ah don't how much there is because George decided who gets what, and I ain't looked.'

Victor Thurgood experienced a flush of exasperation – had he been well and truly shafted after all? Not for the first time, he wondered why he'd been foolish enough to get involved with Boyd and Davy, both men proving to be complete blackguards. But then, he'd been so terribly desperate.

'Don't worry yer sen, Vic. If ah'm any judge, ah reckon yo've gorra decent share. If not ... who yer gooin' ter complain to, hey?'

Boyd was chuckling and rapping his empty tankard on the bar. The landlord was turned away, though, busy at the barrel, and Boyd saw his opportunity. Leaning in to his accomplice, he eased a slim package from the folds of his jacket and deftly passed it to Victor, who quickly seized it without so much as a sideways glance. The deed was summarily completed, and Victor could only wait to see what reward his felonious activities had bestowed on him. However much or little it was, he'd no choice but to settle for it, now being no occasion to challenge a man like George Boyd. Not for the first time, he wondered why George Davy had chosen not to be there that evening.

Detective Constable Grouper was in a quandary; did he follow Thurgood out of the inn? Or did he stay and watch the rough-looking cove a few stools beyond him? The inn was warm and comforting, and Thurgood would be off down the road like a dog after a rabbit. Only breathlessness lay in that direction. Furthermore, they already knew where Thurgood lodged, so what would be the point in following him there? No, best stay and watch the other one, maybe shadow him when he left … although the man looked to be settled in … perhaps one more beer, then … and the flaky pies looked inviting …

Victor's hands were shaking when he came to unwrap the ominously thin parcel. By the light of the nearest street lamp, he pulled apart the brown paper and sighed with relief, the release of pent-up emotion bringing a tear to his eye; the three creased ten-pound notes being sufficient to expedite his plan. Victor nervously looked about him to see if he'd been observed. The street was empty, though. He counted the notes again and sighed with fresh contentment. Thirty pounds would do very nicely. Maybe George Davy hadn't taken him for a fool after all. Although it was likely the crafty villain wanted to keep Victor sweet, thinking perhaps that he might come in useful on another day.

It was then that he thought back to his angry exchange with James Caborn on leaving the shop earlier that evening. Caborn's tone had been sharp and unfriendly from the beginning, in no way approximating the customary fashion he employed when addressing Victor. Caborn had ordered Victor to attend his office the following morning at seven-thirty sharp and without fail. Victor had asked the reason and was told in no uncertain terms that he'd find that out on the morrow. That might have been an end to it, but James Caborn could not resist a parting shot.

'There's something fishy about this wretched business, Thurgood, and I have my suspicions, as does Inspector Leyton. Prepare yourself for a frank exchange in the morning, at which time I shall not tolerate any prevarication. Bear that in mind overnight, sir!'

Caborn's harsh words had shocked Victor to his boots. Obviously, he was already judged guilty as charged – no doubt Leyton's doing. It looked very much like the game was up. In which case, it was just as well he'd slipped out earlier and made his arrangements – nothing whatsoever to lose now.

'Seven-thirty sharp, hey? Well, we'll see about that, Caborn!'

It was the first time he'd ever spoken to his

employer in that tone of voice, and in that brief moment it felt exceptionally good.

Thinking to burn his boats behind him, Victor decided not to return to his lodgings above the shop. Come what may, he'd be on the first coach north in the morning and in the very clothes he stood up in. There'd be no going back for bags or belongings. He never had found that photo – what a pity – he'd been pleased with its likeness. His decision meant spending the night at a friend's house in Arkwright Street, hopefully with a decent breakfast to send him on his way. After that, he'd ruefully say goodbye to the town he loved, perhaps forever. Freedom often came at a cost. There was one thing he might risk though – a compulsion he was finding ever more difficult to resist.

Chapter 37
Nottingham 1891

George Boyd ordered his tankard filled for the fourth time that evening. The beer he drank was the landlord's strongest and Boyd was feeling the activation of its potency. Just another one on the way home and he'd call it a day. He was reasonably happy with how things had worked out, and genuinely grateful the old fellow hadn't died. Not that he cared much for the man's wellbeing. The real benefit was the fact that if he did happen to get nabbed for the robbery, at least he'd be facing another jail sentence and not the gallows. All the same, it had been a close call. George Davy had lost control that night, something he was inclined to do when a darker mood was on him.

A habitual villain, Boyd was not averse to a bit of physical aggravation himself. Thieving was his business, though, and he only resorted to violence when there was little choice in the matter, whereas George Davy positively welcomed aggressive confrontation. He thought Davy was the luckiest villain he'd ever met; thinking if he fell off Trent Bridge, he'd come up dry. George Davy had got away with some bad stuff in his time, and it wasn't all down to luck. Crafty as a street rat he was, and always one move in front of everybody else. Nevertheless, they'd made a few pounds together since Boyd had known him, their latest episode being no exception.

He didn't know exactly how much there'd

been in the safe, although he'd been happy to take twenty when Davy divvied it up – not bad for less than an hour's work. He knew Thurgood had done better than himself because Davy had been straight about it, saying they'd never have known about the stash without him. He also reckoned they needed to keep Thurgood happy, as they weren't to know what he might come up with next – there always being a next time with squanderers like Victor Thurgood.

George Boyd drained his tankard to the dregs and made his way to the privy in the yard. Detective Constable Grouper had already worked out where the privy was but hadn't dared leave the bar. Having consumed a quart of beer, he too was feeling the urge to relieve himself. But when Boyd reappeared, Grouper's thoughts returned to the job in hand, the detective watching and waiting while the ruffian gestured to the landlord before barging through a huddle of drinkers on his way to the door.

'Goodnight, George. Mind yer sen down them steps.'

George! Grouper's heart skipped a beat when he heard the all-important name – surely now he'd get some credit for his night's work.

***

He heard the approaching click of her heels, the thought of her sending shivers through his parts. It wasn't like him to obsess over a woman. He could usually take or leave them – take them mostly, if he'd a mind. This one was different, though, and he couldn't work out why that was. Maybe it was because she'd been feisty enough to stand up to him. Not many had dared talk back to him – men or women – but she had, right enough. Whatever the reason, the thought of having her was like a recurring itch he couldn't quite reach.

George Davy's head was woolly from the whisky he'd bought that afternoon. It had been expensive, and he'd drawn a look from the landlord when he passed the tenner over the bar. Davy had made sure to buy it from an inn he'd never frequented before: posh place, south of the river where folk weren't likely to know who he was. He'd spent a pleasant morning walking beside the Trent and away from his usual haunts. After arriving home that afternoon, damp from intermittent showers, he'd settled into his comfortable chair, enjoying the whisky as much as the cuttings that decorated the wall in his special room.

And so it was a while later when George Davy heard the familiar heels passing by his door. Looking at the clock on the wall, he saw the hand had moved past six. It was a working day, and Billy Watts, ever a creature of habit, would likely be found in The Postern Gate or somewhere similar at that hour. That meant Ethel Bentley would be alone in her lodgings. Billy and Ethel rented rooms on the ground floor of the tenement, and Davy was confident the boarders upstairs wouldn't interfere in matters that didn't concern them – as was ever the way in such residences. Davy took another slug of whisky. Who cared anyway ... she was just another tart on the game. He'd chuck her a few coppers if she started wailing. He had drunkenly reached the point of no return, desperately needing to scratch the itch that had irritated him for far too long.

***

Without one of Miss Polly's introductions, it wouldn't have been worth her while leaving the house that morning. Then there was that business at the hotel, the new manager getting snotty about gentlemen guests entertaining 'lady friends' in their suites. As it turned out, the fresh-faced manager was yet another one looking for a backhander. She'd have to increase her prices if matters got much worse. It had been a long and tiring day and, to top it off, hardly a moment had passed without her thinking of Victor and the unfamiliar manner he'd adopted the last time they met.

The unexpected knock at the door caused her to stop what she was doing, thinking it was a funny time for visitors to call. Her heart thumped in her chest, fearing it might be the police after her. But then, they usually caught her red-handed, the way the magistrates liked them to – no argument and a hefty fine. Whenever she was caught, Ethel paid up rather than risk a sentence. She wasn't a blatant offender like some were, and she'd always been discreet, not to mention choosy about whom she did business with.

The knock came again, more insistent this time. Ethel dried her hands on her apron and went to the window that overlooked the street. Gently drawing back the nets, she immediately saw who was knocking, wondering what the hell he might want. She shuddered and immediately released her grip on the curtain. He'd caught her looking and was grinning smarmily – *cheeky bogger!*

He was knocking harder still, calling out as he did so.

'Open up, Ethel, I've gorra a bit o' summat for yer.'

She could tell by his tone he wouldn't leave her alone. He'd know she was on her own, and he wasn't about to take no for an answer.

'Ah just wanted to apologise for last time. Come on, Eth, me duck ... I don't want no bad blood between us.'

Ethel Bentley took a deep breath. Maybe he really was trying to make amends. Words spoken in drink and temper often didn't mean very much. Nevertheless, she'd not fraternise with him. Nor would he cross her threshold – *the very idea!* After running her fingers through her hair and removing her apron, Ethel made ready to answer the door.

***

He stifled a cough and took a sip of his beer, vainly hoping to ease the insistent tickle. The smoky blackness of his drinking hand reminded him of home and a hot bath by the fire. Billy Watts looked forward to that routine. The end of a working day was a most agreeable time for him – couple of pints or three, a soak by the fire, a good rub down and one of Eth's tasty dinners to follow. There'd been a time when they'd play dominoes or cards before taking to their bed for a different kind of game. Those shenanigans were few and far between these days, what with his health and her worn out from business.

Watts hated to think of her with other men, though she'd never taunted him with tales of it, not even when they'd exchanged harsh words, which didn't happen often of late. In spite of that, the thought still rankled him, even though he'd rarely mentioned or shown contempt for what she did. The truth was, he loved her and everything about her, apart from that particular issue, of course. In every other respect she was nigh-on perfect, never wronging or speaking ill of him. And at the end of the day, Ethel was there to nurse him through the worst of his bouts. Yes, he'd look forward to getting home.

The door had barely closed behind one customer before it swung open again, this time somewhat more forcefully. William Watts wrinkled his top lip in distaste. He recognised the dapper ponce striding purposely over to where George Boyd was standing. He knew his name well enough – Thurgood, it was – Victor Thurgood.

Billy had made it his business to find out who he was, having seen him crossing the road by The Mechanics Institute, arm in arm with his Ethel. Watts had been trundling along Burton Street when he spotted them. It wasn't the first time he'd seen them together, causing him to think their relationship might mean something more than the usual business. A few days later, fate had Watts gently encouraging his horse up Derby Road, hauling a delivery to the convent on College Street. The convent's usual supplier was a mate who'd taken to his bed with something nasty, so Watts was doing him a favour and turning a bob for himself.

After spotting a fast-moving figure on the opposite pavement, Billy Watts couldn't believe who it was that was outpacing his horse, straightaway realising it was the cocky bogger he'd recently seen hobnobbing with Ethel. Resisting the impulse to shout after the man, he urged his horse in an attempt to follow. Then, seeing the man disappear into a shop across the road, Watts pulled into the gutter and brought his cart to a standstill. After climbing down, he tethered his horse and made his way over to what was a draper's store. Becoming hesitant, he risked a peek through the open door, bobbing and weaving his head to see between myriad bolts of coloured material, surprised to see his rival busily shearing a length of cloth.

Billy Watts overcame his temper and wisely retreated from the scene, knowing for certain nothing would come out of making a fuss in those circumstances, except for him making a complete fool of himself. For some reason, though, he thought he'd benefit from knowing the man's name.

And so a couple of days later, he pressed a shiny sixpence into the hand of a match seller he knew, asking her to enter the shop on the pretence of browsing. She was a pretty girl and sharp-witted enough to hoodwink the man Watts carefully described to her. Later she came back to him with his name and title: Victor Thurgood, Retail Manager.

Watts glanced at the misted clockface that dominated the rear of the bar, deciding that out of interest, he'd wait and observe a while longer. He thought the two men he was carefully watching to be an odd couple, consorting so close and privately as they were. In terms of social status, Thurgood looked a class or two above the inveterate villain he was currently engaging so earnestly with. Billy Watts knew George Boyd well enough to think that way, Boyd being a close associate of George Davy, though second to him in most things, by all accounts. As corrupt and vicious as Boyd was known to be, George Davy was generally deemed the worst of the two – as wicked and cunning as any man this side of hell, some said.

Only moments after Thurgood had blown through the door like a gale, he was smartly followed by another man. Watts knew most of the regulars who frequented the hostelry but had never clapped eyes on the stranger before – the poor chap sweating like he'd run a mile and blowing like a clapped-out steam engine. Returning his attention to Thurgood and Boyd, George Davy once again intruded on Watts's thoughts, in particular the conversation he'd had with the villain a week or so earlier. It had been a Friday night and a decent atmosphere in The Postern. Someone had struck up a tune with a banjo and folk were singing and humming along as they usually did. Davy had sidled over completely out of the blue and surprisingly bought him a drink.

'Here's to neighbours, hey, Billy … cheers and good 'ealth, me duck!'

'Ah, cheers, George … and thanks for the drink.'

'Bin wokin' hard, have yer, Billy?'

'Allus am, George, that's my lot in life.'

'Ah, hard wok an' all in't it, baggin' and hauling coal.'

'Ah, yo' right there.'

'Ah'd yer gerrall that muck off yer, then? It must tek ages.'

'Ah've a bath in front t'fire.'

'Oh, ah. 'Spect she scrubs yer back, then, hey, Billy?'

'Sometimes, she does, ah.'

'Ah, I'll bet she does an' all …'

William Watts remembered the awkward conversation continuing in similar fashion for quite a while. In fact, it was the lengthiest conversation they'd ever had. They'd exchanged the odd perfunctory greeting now and then – them living on the same street and drinking in the same taverns. It seemed there'd been something more to it on that occasion, though. Watts hadn't missed the fact that Davy managed to turn the conversation to Ethel at every given opportunity; did George Davy really think he was that daft?

Chapter 38
Nottingham 1891

When she finally opened the door, she wished she hadn't. The sight of George Davy was forever intimidating, never mind when stood on your own threshold. Ethel could smell the stink of whisky on him, straightaway realising he'd had a few measures already. Davy was leering in her direction like drunks often did, encouraged by the alcohol that fortified their self-esteem. The bulk of him never failed to menace her, that enormous grizzled head sitting on the thickest neck she'd ever seen. Ethel was reminded of the hideous gargoyles that gaped from the church walls, what with his glaring eyes and that ever-present sneer that deformed his mouth.

'What's to do, George?'

'Well, ah just thought to mek up fer that little squabble we had t'other day.'

'Fair enough, best forgotten then, George. Thanks for that, must get on.'

'Owd on, Eth, how about us having a little drink together to mek it right?'

'Nice on yer, George, but Billy'll not be long, and he'll be wanting his supper.'

Before she could close the door on him, George Davy wedged his enormous boot into the narrow space that remained, eyes flared and determined.

'Oh, ah can guess where Billy is, me duck – he'll be keeping the landlord company fer a bit yet. Yo know as well as ah do how long it'll be afore he turns up.'

Ethel felt a wave of panic when Davy pushed more firmly at the door. She was thinking about screaming but knew nobody would come, not when they realised who it was she was screaming at.

'Come on, Eth ... yer know yer don't want ter stop me ... me and you's destined, me duck.'

'Bogger off, George, yer stinkin' lousy ...!'

Her slight frame was no match for the raw muscularity of George Davy. Strain as she might, she tottered helplessly, retreating only when the door inevitably burst open. Davy's prodigious frame was momentarily silhouetted against the light of the street beyond, his widening grin only evident after he'd slammed the door behind him.

'Now we'll see about it, Eth ... yer little teaser. You and me, gal, now there's a thing.'

He'd removed the half-emptied bottle from his pocket – the gift he'd spoken of – thinking to tice her with it. Then when she ran to the temporary refuge of her kitchen, he shrugged off the grubby overcoat that was fundamental to his roughness and carelessly pitched it over a chair. The battered bowler followed it, its absence revealing the tonsure that interrupted his lank and thinning hair. His lust was like that of a rutting boar, his chosen quarry now within easy reach.

Throughout her life, Ethel Bentley had incessantly fought to preserve her fragile dignity, more latterly the remnants of it – forever struggling to hold her head above the cesspool of shameful activity that sustained her existence. Her rewards for overcoming the discomfiture of her profession were the true love and respect of a good and faithful man and the perfunctory love of another. And she'd be damned if she'd surrender to the hulking brute that threatened her only sanctuary.

George Davy crossed the divide and was on her with deceptive speed, his formidable bulk crushing her so close that she gagged from the rancid stink of his unwashed body. Kick and squirm as she might, it made not a spit of difference. With one hand easily holding her fast against the wall, he scrabbled to unleash his manhood with the other, grunting and snorting like the feral swine he was. All she could think of was time ticking on; how much would pass before Billy came to her aid? Would he find George Davy squirming and groaning on top of her? Or her alone in a wrecked and revealing state? However he found her, would he ever believe the truth of it?

George Davy was wildly staring at her, the look in his eyes outlandish and frighteningly distant as he hurriedly lifted her skirts and ripped at her nether garments; at least he was until the hollow resonance of knuckle on wood caused him to wake from whatever dreadful fantasy he was imagining, his eyes darting and swivelling in furious exasperation.

Chapter 39
Nottingham 1891

Victor Thurgood made up his mind and swiftly changed direction. There would be time to spare before bedding down at his friend's house. In any case, he'd only sit and stew until morning. He'd no real hope of sleeping, or even resting, not with the jumble of thoughts that filled his head. He was saying goodbye to the town of his birth, to the remnants of his childhood, to family and friends ... and then there was her.

Ethel had grown close to him in ways that transcended their recurrent arrangement. There had been times when he thought he might even love her, though he would never engage in so tenuous a relationship. Not when knowing her heart eternally belonged to another man. Thoughts of abandoning her painfully reminded him how badly he'd treated her on the night of the robbery, shamelessly manipulating her feelings to his own advantage. He'd been unnecessarily offhand when they came to saying their farewells that night, and he thought he might at least have afforded Ethel some kind of explanation. In the end, he hadn't even had the good grace to say goodbye in a proper manner. He imagined her then – that engaging smile, those cheeky eyes, the ringlets of her red hair.

To his own bewilderment, his eyes began to well with tears, only realising then that he'd miss her dearly. In that moment he experienced a sudden need to make things right before he left her behind forever. And then he thought of Billy Watts, remembering his face from when Ethel had pointed him out from across a crowded square, the two of them beating a hasty retreat. Absorbed as he'd been in more pressing matters, Victor only fleetingly discerned the presence of Watts whilst wrangling with Boyd in The Postern Gate Inn. He thought Billy must have noticed him in turn – God only knew what the man thought of him and Ethel together.

After exiting The Postern, Victor recognised Billy's blackened cart and dutiful horse tethered over the road, knowing that Watts, from habit, would drive his rig to the stables before trudging back home. Victor calculated Billy's customary routines would leave him more than enough time to say goodbye, and this time in appropriate fashion.

***

Victor Thurgood bolted out of The Postern like his backside was on fire, George Boyd eventually leaving after him, sloping away with barely a nod to anybody. The podgy stranger followed in Boyd's wake, smartly abandoning the best part of a mutton pie and what remained of his beer. William Watts exchanged glances with an equally bemused landlord and decided he would also call it a day. The sight of the half-eaten pie caused his belly to rumble, thoughts turning to a hot soak and the supper that would follow.

Pulling his collar up against the spitting rain, he looked over to see that his docile horse hadn't moved so much as an inch. Billy Watts scratched the nag's ear with some affection before adjusting the blanket that protected the poor beast's back from the drizzle. Coughing and spluttering, Billy then climbed aboard his cart, untethered the reins, and clicked his tongue, the horse obligingly pulling for home. How he looked forward to the warmth of the fire and the peace and quiet of the coming night.

***

Engrossed as he was in his raging lust, George Davy had neglected to lock the door behind him. And so it was with a scowl of annoyance that he reluctantly turned his attentions from the writhing figure he had imprisoned in his arms. He didn't mind when they struggled, in fact his blood surged all the more. Even so, she'd bitten awful deep into his finger, the sharp pain of it bringing him to a furious temper. He'd thumped her then – not too hard – just a tap to the point of her chin. It made no difference whatsoever to his impending pleasure; struggling or slumbering, he'd enjoy it all the same. The knocking ceased as suddenly as it had started, and so he slavered afresh at the thought of the woman helplessly sprawled at his feet. Never mind checking the door; he'd be finished and gone in a trice. Then there it was again, the knocking louder and more urgent this time. George Davy knew the neighbours would be chiking from behind the nets, most likely thinking it was the crafty rent collector who called at unexpected hours. When it stopped again, he waited a moment, listening intently before turning back to his debauchery, only to be frustrated afresh by the sound of the opening door.

He knew it wasn't likely to be Billy Watts ... surely not yet ... and why ever would he knock? Whoever it turned out to be, they'd be worse for finding him waiting. Unless it was the law, of course. Even then, they'd need one or two more to take him down.

***

Victor Thurgood thought long and hard about his intentions, wondering if it really was such a good idea after all. Then after weighing the odds for the umpteenth time, he thought to carry on and chance his arm. And so with a deep breath, he cautiously crossed Woolpack Lane and approached the house where she lived. It had started to rain, and the day was fading to twilight, a glimmer of flickering light coming from behind the curtains. There was obviously somebody in, and he knew it wouldn't be Billy Watts. After furtively checking the street, Victor braced himself and knocked at the door. A few moments later, head cocked to one side, he knocked again, this time with more intent. Victor thought the resultant lack of response to be somewhat strange, knowing it was unlikely anyone apart from Ethel might be in the house, so he thought to try the door. He still wasn't sure if he was doing the right thing. Nevertheless, it was too late for turning back. Heart in mouth, he gingerly peered into the dimness of the room, thinking at first glance that it was empty of human occupation – then he noticed a movement from somewhere deeper within.

***

Dave Robertson reckoned Billy's horse only had two paces: slow and stop. Billy smirked at the memory. His partner was full of quips like that. Dave was a good bloke and hardworking. They both were, come to that, neither of them frightened of getting stuck in. That was why their partnership worked well and prospered. All things considered, life wasn't too bad. He and Ethel had a lot to be thankful for, despite the nature of her other life. He had decent lodgings, enough earnings to pay his way and some left over for a beer or two of an evening. If it wasn't for his awful cough, living would be nigh on perfect.

Billy Watts hacked yet again, spitting out the phlegm as he turned his horse into Woolpack Lane. Only a few yards more to the stables, and his working day would be over. When the cart straightened, Billy automatically glanced over towards his lodgings, much as he always did, looking for the familiar glow at the window and thinking how autumn would soon turn to winter.

***

Ethel was coming round just as George Davy looked up to see the figure framed in the doorway. Davy thought the man looked familiar, big and rangy as he was ... Thurgood, of course! He'd been using Ethel's services for a while. Then again, maybe the two of them were closer than he thought. Victor Thurgood absently closed the door, squinting as he tried to make sense of the scene he'd intruded upon. Was that really George Davy with his trousers about his ankles, Ethel's skirts above her waist? Seeing them together like that shocked him to the core. Whoever would have imagined it?!

Then Victor noticed Ethel stirring, as though she'd been asleep, moaning with discomfort as her eyes flickered open. It was then he saw it for what it was, part of him relieved when he realised the situation was not what he'd thought it to be.

George Davy was furious at how the situation had frustratingly developed. Of all the times for it to go wrong! He'd so nearly had her and now she was slipping away. Furthermore, the whisky was catching up with him, muddling his brain and slowing his reactions. He fumbled to arrange his trousers, barely managing to find his balance before Thurgood crossed the floor towards him. There was nothing much Davy could do to avoid the first oncoming blow, achieving no more than dodging the worst of it. The red mist rapidly descended on Victor Thurgood. The man staggering before him had caused him to abandon everything he'd ever held dear; more than that, he'd caught George Davy brutally defiling the woman he'd risked his freedom to see just one more time.

Blood promptly spurted from Davy's bloated nose, causing him to stumble over Ethel's rising body. Victor thought to increase his advantage by swinging a right hander to the side of the villain's head. Davy, however, was a seasoned brawler, and although befuddled, he had the guile to drop to a crouch, at the same time instinctively raising his arms to protect his face. Thurgood consequently overreached and lost his footing, Davy taking his chance to jerk a knee into his assailant's belly, effectively taking the wind out of him.

Recovering her senses, Ethel emitted a fearful scream on seeing Davy following with a ferocious blow to Victor's jaw, causing him to stagger and shudder erratically before dropping to the floor. George Davy menacingly stood over his weakened opponent, arrogantly readying his leg, intending to inflict even worse damage. Ethel Bentley narrowed her eyes and instinctively grabbed a meat skewer that lay within her reach. Then raising her arm to strike, she let out an ear-piercing screech and promptly mounted George Davy's back before he'd chance to turn from his intended prey. The frenzied attack took Davy by surprise, even more so when the spiral of tapered steel slickly entered the side of his meaty neck. Such was the intensity of their bloody and confused predicament, neither of the two whirling antagonists noticed the sound of the doorlatch being lifted yet again.

***

He couldn't have been the only one to have heard the primordial scream. But then, those and similar sounds were unremarkable in that part of town. Dwelling so closely together often brought situations to a head, and at such times, it paid to close your ears and mind your business: say and do nothing rather than involve yourself without personal cause. Nevertheless, the intonation of that particular shriek appeared somewhat familiar to him. So much so, it caused him to bring the cart to a sudden halt, scrambling down with an urgency he rarely employed.

Blinking forcefully as if to clear a waking nightmare, an incredulous William Watts tilted his head and took in the stumbling form of George Davy, a twisted spike jutting from his bleeding neck. Sat astride him with gritted teeth, his beloved Ethel was frantically riding his back like a demented jockey, snarling whilst scratching and beating the loathsome villain about the head. At the same time, floundering in the slick of somebody's blood, a confounded Victor Thurgood was attempting to rise from the floor and failing miserably. In that moment, it was nigh on impossible for Watts to make sense of the diabolical circumstances, but on seeing his dear Ethel ostensibly fighting for her life, Watts unceremoniously stepped into the fray. Breathing attendant dust throughout numerous years of hauling coal was slowly choking him to death. However, the muscularity acquired from lifting and carrying the contemptable rock was at least of equal proportion. And so when Billy Watts came to strike the already weakened villain, teak-tough and sturdy as the man certainly was, George Davy slumped to his knees with no more than a groan of utter despondency, his erstwhile fervour assertively subdued.

Chapter 40
Nottingham 1891

Ethel and Billy sat together on the sofa, Victor facing them, looking dreadfully drawn and uncomfortable. His head throbbed incessantly and his stomach ached something awful. He had never been savagely beaten before and could only imagine how long it might take to get over the ghastly experience. Ethel was even now shaking from the violent encounter, more so when she thought how much trouble she'd caused by simply answering the door. It had been an extremely close call – George Davy on the threshold of her violation. Despite her profession, Ethel had never before been attacked in that way, had always been lucky in that respect. There were men who would treat her as they would a convenience, but never any that forced themselves on her with such unconcealed savagery.

Ethel gave Billy a sideways glance, noticing how he looked into the distance as though detaching himself from the current state of affairs. It was Billy's way of dealing with difficult predicaments. How terribly sorry she felt for him. The poor soul didn't deserve any of this. He'd already put up with more than his fair share of her tribulations and dilemmas during the time they'd been together. It was strange enough having the two men in the same room at the same time, never mind George Davy stretched out beside them. They shared more than a few spots of splattered blood between them, Victor more heavily dappled than she and Billy were. His once immaculate suit – the checked one she liked to see him in – was way beyond a wipe with a damp cloth. Still, that was the least of their troubles. In the end, after an extended and excruciatingly awkward silence, it was William Watts who thought to speak his mind.

'Well ... ah don't know exactly what's gone on, or how it's come ter this predicament, but summat needs sortin' and that's a fact. I know the pair on yer's bin carryin' on wi' each other, so there's no point denying it.'

'Billy, I just want ...'

'Leave it, Eth! Ah don't want ter know ote abart it. Ah just want these boggers out o' my house, and sooner rather than later! Ah want me bath and ah want me dinner. Some on us as got ter gerrup early in the mornin'.'

'Understood, Mr Watts, but in the meantime, what shall we do about him?'

Victor was nodding in the direction of the prone George Davy, unsure whether the man still lived or not. Victor thought he looked in a bad way; the darkening slick of congealing blood and the bruises to his head stood out in stark contrast to the deathly pallor of his skin. Although enough to cause concern, those particular injuries paled into insignificance when compared to the spread of blood that drenched Davy's shirt from shoulder to abdomen. Victor shuddered to think how much of it the villain had lost. He looked over to Billy Watts, waiting for an answer to his question.

'He can't stop 'ere, can he? The cart's hover the road and it stands empty. Ah'll bring it hover and we'll stick him in it afore we decide what ter do next.'

Victor and Ethel looked at each other with quizzical expressions. Billy's words focussed their minds on the consequences arising from the evening's events. Though George Davy had initiated the situation, he'd ended up the most seriously injured ... maybe worse. As if reading their minds, Billy Watts pushed himself out of his seat and went to kneel by the villain's body. After prodding Davy's cheek and offering him a slap or two, he felt the cleaner side of the man's neck, leaving two fingers pressed against a vein for a while.

'Heart's tickin', faint though it is. Best tek him to a doctor or summat ... after we've tossed him in the cart, o' course.'

Victor didn't like the sound of that, certainly not given his present circumstances. He felt duty bound to assist in the removal of Davy from the house, but afterwards he'd say his farewells and make himself scarce, thinking it best not to tell them of his plans beforehand.

'What's goin' ter happen if he wakes up? He'll be round 'ere like lightnin'!'

'One foot in front o' t'other, Eth. Let's get this first bit hover with.'

Ethel Bentley closed her eyes and sighed. She was calming down and coming to terms with the situation. However, the future from thereon in looked awful bleak. Surely they'd be best moving out altogether, even if it meant a moonlight flit. One thing was certain: if or when George Davy recovered, he'd come looking for revenge ... and he might not come alone!

***

Billy Watts watchfully peered round the door, looking this way and that to see if anyone was snooping. Satisfied the commotion hadn't drawn any lasting attention, he crossed the cobbles to where his horse awaited. Not wishing to risk any undue attention, Watts did his best to stifle his cough. The arrival of evening had brought ever-darkening clouds that preceded the heavy rain that had now begun to fall. After manoeuvring his wagon as close as he could, Watts returned to the house to catch them talking together, noticing both Ethel and Victor had tears in their eyes. Though close to saying something spiteful, he chose instead to ignore them as best he could. There was urgent work to be done, and the situation involved him as much as it did Ethel and her fancy man.

Watts and Thurgood were both strong men, but George Davy was a considerable and awkward weight. After labouring to bring him upright, they each took an arm, thereafter supporting him as they might a stumbling drunkard. Breathing hard with the effort, they awkwardly walked Davy outside, step by strenuous step, to the very edge of the cart, managing to heave the body over the previously dropped side panel and onto the flat deck. Clambering aboard, they dragged Davy deeper into the cart, both men thankful to be laying him down and done with.

For one heart-stopping moment, they thought they heard him muttering, but when kneeling to check, Watts confirmed there was no perceptible change in Davy's condition. Billy Watts then mounted the platform and grabbed the reins, Victor Thurgood shuffling to sit beside him. After Billy released the brake and clicked his tongue, the cart began to creak and clatter over the slickened cobbles of Woolpack Lane.

Ethel had told them of a man named Felton who lived on Dean Street. 'Doc' Felton, she called him. She reckoned he was a surgeon who valued his drink more than his licence. She'd heard tell that Felton wasn't too fussy about the hows and whys, just as long as his palm was suitably greased. With Victor insisting on paying the fee, their intention was to leave George Davy in Felton's care and escape as quickly as they could. They agreed it was the best they could do in the circumstances, there being nothing gained by dumping Davy in an alley to fend for himself. At least this way, the villain might be thankful for their ultimate concern and even earn his favour. Much like the others, though, Billy Watts suspected if George Davy recovered, he'd come looking for vengeance regardless of what they did, and so he thought it best to be prepared. He'd have a word with his partner in the morning. Dave was no slouch when it came to that sort of malarky, and apart from anything else, Dave knew people – dangerous people.

Dean Street was only a short drive away, somewhere off Bellar Gate, they agreed. When they arrived there, they found the residence they were seeking a few doors away from the end of a cul-de-sac. When approaching the doctor's house, they absently noticed the gated railings of a graveyard spanning the end of the road before them. Victor Thurgood pointlessly hitched up the collar of his suit jacket. In the short time the journey had taken, he'd become completely saturated and thoroughly miserable. Any second thoughts he might have had about leaving his home town had been literally washed away.

After they creaked to a standstill by a street lamp, Victor volunteered to knock at Felton's door and hopefully strike an acceptable deal. Then, as he made ready to climb from the cart, he became motionless as though turned to stone. Something had stirred behind him, the sound of shambling movement immediately followed by the weight of a hand on his shoulder. Billy Watts heard it too, turning in time to see a massive form emerging from the bed of the cart.

George Davy resembled a resurrected corpse, rain streaming from his head in rivulets, doing its best to erode the coagulated blood that stubbornly clung to his face and neck. His widened eyes glittered in the lamplight, the sneering slant of his mouth further disfigured by a hideous scowl. Immediately panicked, Watts and Thurgood were of single mind, both men scrambling from the cart with equal intent to put as much distance between themselves and the hulking monster as quickly as possible.

Although Davy's senses were returning, his injured body neglected to keep pace with his murderous determination. In attempting to rush after the two fleeing men, he stumbled backwards onto the pile of sacks that had been his impromptu sickbed. Nevertheless, with intensifying thoughts of retribution urging him onward, he scrambled and pulled himself upright, raw strength progressively returning to his quivering legs. After cautiously feeling his way to the edge of the cart, he shinned the timbers and dropped to the ground, narrowed eyes searching the stormy darkness for his terrified antagonists.

Quite why the two men automatically ran in the direction of the graveyard was a question they might have found somewhat difficult to answer at the time. Nevertheless, that was the course they took, an enraged George Davy belatedly staggering in their wake. The path they hurried along led to the centre of the graveyard, a point where two other paths merged from different directions. For some reason, they both stopped and turned when reaching the convergence, standing to stare at the approaching villain through squalls of relentless rain.

'He'll keep comin', matey ... whether now or later, it matters not a jot. He'll keep comin', yer can be sure o' that!'

'So what do we do, Billy? Run or deal with him, d'you think? The two of us together, hey?'

'And do what exactly, Thurgood?'

Victor thought the question a fair one and didn't have an answer worth anything much. George Davy was getting closer by the step, his meaty fists even now flexing with murderous resolve. They'd dressed and tidied him before they'd put him on the cart, though not well enough, it seemed: shirt hanging out and flies open, meaningless details they distractedly noted as the monstrous villain edged within six feet of where they stood.

'Well, look 'ere, now ... the rats have stopped runnin' at last! Why's that then? Found a decent set o' balls yer can share between yer?'

'It's you what's in the wrong, George Davy ... trying it on wi' my woman like that!'

'Your woman? Everybody's woman, more like! Includin' that toffee-nosed ponce who's pissin' his pants at side on yer!'

Victor reared at that remark. As indeed did Watts, though for differing reasons. Billy took a step forward, recklessly angered by Davy's offensive comments, Davy doing the same, if only to show how keen he was to get at them. Knowing no amount of appeasement would ever restrain a man like George Davy, Victor fleetingly thought about running and leaving them to it, confident of outpacing Davy long enough to hotfoot it to his friend's house. That way, he could wash away the filth and blood and hopefully borrow some clothes. Then, with a degree of good fortune, he'd be ready and gone at first light. He couldn't do it, though, not and leave Ethel thinking him a coward. And how would he ever live with leaving Billy Watts in the lurch like that? The poor man didn't deserve any of the mess he'd innocently become involved in.

Victor Thurgood took a deep breath and stepped up to stand with the man he'd selfishly deceived, drawing a look from Billy Watts that resembled a nod of grudging respect.

'Well, bogger me gently ... suckin' up ter each other all of a sudden, are yer? Why, yer'll both be on her at the same time at this rate – that's if yer can still manage it by the time ah'm done wi' the two on yer!'

Davy's fresh torrent of abuse tipped the balance and Billy Watts reacted first, throwing himself at George Davy with flailing fists and promptly walking into a right-hander that fortuitously glanced off his cheek. In almost the same moment, Victor followed on, taking his chances when Davy began to lay into Billy's stumbling body. Victor thought he'd show the arrogant bastard what a so-called ponce was capable of when provoked. Fired up by that thought, he stepped in and caught Davy with a haymaker, rupturing his nose yet again, the villain screaming and gasping with the pain and shock of it. Seeing Davy's blood spurting afresh, Billy Watts scrambled to his feet and launched a savage uppercut that forced Davy to take a backward step. The mistake they made was standing to admire their work, thinking too soon they'd won the day.

George Davy swayed on the spot where he stood, shoulders slouched as though beaten, head sagging to his chest. His arms were dangling loosely beside him, blood from his shattered nose leaking to nourish the sacred ground beneath his feet. It seemed for all the world the fight had consumed him, but then the instant his adversaries relaxed their posture, the big man narrowed his eyes and charged like a wounded bull, scattering them aside before turning back on them, even as they dropped to their knees.

Determined not to miss the opportunity, Davy smashed his hobnailed boot into the side of Victor Thurgood's body, grinning wildly at the awful resonance of cracking bone. With Thurgood squealing and writhing on the ground like a stuck pig, Davy turned to see Billy Watts despairingly rising to his feet. Too late, the wheezing Watts saw the blurring fist that hammered into his jaw, the subsequent darkness bestowing on him a blissful if all too brief unconsciousness. Then, when Billy blinked and opened his eyes, he came to observe a most appalling spectacle.

Wincing at the encumbering agony of his worsening condition, Victor Thurgood was ever more fearful of what was still to come. The thought of a further assault on his already brutalised body instinctively caused him to roll away, the movement producing renewed surges of the agonising pain that already tormented him. As he rolled to a rest, he glimpsed a flash of activity in his peripheral vision, quickly realising it wasn't him currently under attack. Reaching out to balance himself, Victor felt his hand brush against something rough-edged, only becoming aware of its heaviness once his fingers closed around it. Ignoring the pain as best he could, Victor forced himself to his knees, seeing Billy Watts kneeling on the ground barely a yard away – George Davy bending over him, blade in hand.

Fighting against his indescribable pain, Victor tremulously rose to his feet and desperately threw himself in the direction of George Davy. Sensing the oncoming assault, the villain swung to meet the challenge, a flash of steel coming with him ... even as the chunk of broken granite smashed deep into his skull.

Chapter 41
Nottingham 1891

Detective Constable Grouper sat across from Inspector Leyton, flipping through his notebook as he smugly delivered his report. Grouper had followed George Boyd out of The Postern, through the darkening streets and alleys to a tumbledown property on Bottle Lane. There he'd stood in the shadows, observing Boyd climbing a flight of steps that stood beside a linen shop. Assuming Boyd rented rooms above the premises, Grouper waited until he saw the glow of a gas lamp coming from the first floor window, afterwards making his way to the station to write his report. Early the following morning, Grouper found Leyton already at his desk, a smouldering pipe firmly clasped between his teeth.

'Morning, sir.'

'Morning, Constable. How did it go last night?'

Grouper laid it on as thick as jam, embroidering the report to his own advantage whilst carefully leaving out details of the beer and snacks he'd consumed that night. Though finding it difficult to contain himself, Grouper held back the best part for his grand finale.

'George, you say! George … and talking with Victor Thurgood if you don't mind! Well, I never did. That's damn good work, Grouper. George … from Bottle Lane, hey?'

'Yes, sir. I expect we ought to pay him a visit

as soon as we can. I thought about tackling him myself last night, but ...'

'No, no ... you did exactly the right thing, Grouper! You can never tell what might happen with thugs like George Boyd. Now then ... we'll need to take a couple of uniformed officers with us if it's the man I'm thinking of.'

'You know him, then, sir?'

'Oh, yes, unless I'm mistaken, that address strikes a dreadfully familiar chord. You might say George is one of our regulars ... and a most disagreeable fellow at that.'

Though it was much too early to find him awake, George Boyd grudgingly surfaced when he realised the resolute pounding was coming from the direction of his own front door. Even in his somnolent bewilderment, he knew with some certainty the visitation didn't herald a social call. He'd heard it too many times before and wasn't at all surprised to be hearing it again. After all, he was odds-on favourite for just about anything involving felony in those parts, first port of call usually being George Boyd. They'd have a job proving this one, though, there being no witnesses to Davy laying into the old fart who'd foolishly interrupted them. He'd gone way too far as usual, had Davy, and not for the first time, by any means. In fact, if anything, he was getting worse.

'Get yourself to the bleddy door, Boyd, or we'll break the bogger in!'

'Owd yer bleddy hosses ... I'm mekkin' me

sen decent.'

The square of space directly outside the door was barely big enough to accommodate the two uniformed officers, leaving Leyton and Grouper to perch on the steps below. Leyton sighed, thinking it might be a long morning – George Boyd forever being an entertaining bag of tricks. The old rogue would reckon he had an obligation to lead them a merry dance before finally getting down to business.

'Come on, Boyd, let's be 'avin' yer ... we ain't got all bleddy day.'

It was the officer with the enormous ginger moustache that disappeared into his sideburns, his chinstrap keeping perfect time with the movement of his jaw as he spoke. The man was something of a legend at the station and a frightening sight for any villain. Leyton had been relieved to see him on duty that morning. Boyd could be a considerable handful when the mood took him.

'I'm 'avin' a piss ... yer'll 'ave ter wait!'

Long moments later, the door opened and the four policemen piled in, leaving Boyd amused by how many had come to take him.

'Hello, George, thought it'd be you.'

'Ah ... an' I thought it'd be yo an' all!'

As expected, he told them nothing and denied everything. They held back on the fact that the victim had overheard the name George and that Boyd had been observed in deep conversation with Victor Thurgood not long after the robbery. Only when all else failed did they decide to bring those particular snippets into play – or at least they would have done, had the chief inspector not so rudely interrupted the interrogation. The senior officer had leaned into the room, gestured sharply at Peter Leyton, and nodded his head towards the corridor. Although somewhat disconcerted by the abrupt nature of the disruption, Leyton mumbled something and submissively followed his superior to his office.

'Sorry about that, Peter, but you really need to leave this robbery business to others for now. A body's been discovered, and from what's been reported so far, it looks very much like foul play.'

***

The cemetery was a comfortable walk from the station, and so Peter Leyton dispensed with the need for a cab. The night's torrential rain had eased off around dawn, an occasional dab of blue breaking the mournful grey of the lingering cloudbank. Leyton was annoyed at having the interrogation interrupted. They'd just been getting to the interesting part when the chief inspector hooked him out. Murder was a serious business, though, and Leyton understood the need to have a senior detective at the scene. In any case, before he left the station, Leyton had called Grouper out into the corridor and told him exactly how the rest of the interview with George Boyd should go. Grouper was reasonably satisfactory, but he was no sleuth, and Leyton didn't want the fish to escape the net whilst he was away on other business.

'Stick him in a cell, Grouper. Tell him some new evidence has surfaced that we've yet to analyse before you resume the interview ... and keep 'Ginger' with you when you tell him, in case Boyd thinks to get shirty. I'll be back as soon as I can.'

Inspector Leyton knew the area well enough to know there were three entrances to the old cemetery – Carter Gate being one, Olive Street another and the nearest being Dean Street. When he came to the cemetery gates, he noticed a couple of capes and helmets loafing about and kicking their heels. They were awaiting some direction from a senior officer, even though Sergeant Pinegar was with them: the grizzled Pinegar being one of only a few Leyton knew he could rely upon. Approaching the group of officers, he noticed the cemetery path was slick with moss and took care not to slip. How they'd enjoy that yarn back at the station.

'Morning, Joe, what have we got, then?'

Leyton had already noticed the grey tarpaulin amidst the gravestones, billowing slightly in the morning breeze. The two constables made a show of slowly circling the covering, as though to protect its secrets from meddlesome onlookers, of which there were presently none.

'Dead male, Inspector ... discovered about

an hour or so ago.'

Sergeant Joe Pinegar rarely said more than necessary. It was a trait Leyton respected, as some of the uniformed officers liked to show off in front of detectives.

'Who found him?'

'Elderly lady placing flowers on her late husband's headstone ... that one over there.'

Pinegar pointed to a pitted stone resting cockeyed a few yards away.

'I've got the lady's details, sir. She caught sight of the body and smartly cleared off home for a nip o' brandy. Then, after that, she walked to the station to report it. Only lives a couple o' streets away, so her shillyshallying didn't cause too much delay.'

'Let's have a look at him, then, Joe.'

With a nod from their sergeant, the two constables lifted one end of the tarpaulin and carefully drew it back. The exposure revealed the mutilated remains of an extremely large, rough-looking man, his arms and legs splayed at irregular angles. The corpse was thoroughly soaked from the night's rain, even the darker stains of thickened blood somewhat diluted by the force of the deluge. Leyton immediately noted the knife that lay by the dead man's right hand. He thought it most probably belonged to the corpse and not to the killer. In his experience, killers didn't generally leave murder weapons that close to their victims.

'I think somethings been at him in the night, sir.'

'Yes, usually happens when left exposed,

particularly overnight. Has the doctor been summoned?'

'Yes, sir.'

'Photographer?'

'Flashed his contraption and was gone in a jiffy, sir. So there's nothing to stop the body being moved once the doctor's finished, is there?'

'You're right, Joe. Very well, let's hope the doctor can make sense of the particular wounds we're interested in. I assume you've had men searching the area?'

'Yes, sir, and I'll make sure they have another look round after the body's gone, though nothing of significance has turned up as yet.'

Leyton surveyed the graveyard and thought of the years of interment – scores of processions arriving to stand, heads bowed, alongside austere holes in the ground.

'I'll take the knife back with me, Sergeant, along with any other personal possessions he has on him.

'Right you are, sir. Would you like us to remove and bag them, sir?'

'If you would. You do know who he is … or rather who he was, don't you, Joe?

'George Davy, sir.'

'Aye, two Georges to fathom out, and in one morning. Strange, that.'

Sergeant Pinegar looked quizzically at him but chose not to comment – detectives said peculiar things sometimes.

Chapter 42
Nottingham 1891

'Nah, yer sure yer know where Dave Robertson's house is, aren't yer?

The youth shrugged and nodded.

'Yeah, bin there a time or two afore, Mester Watts.'

'Course yer have, son ... I weren't thinking. Off yer goo, then.'

William Watts watched the boy scamper to the end of Woolpack Lane before disappearing into Count Street. He reckoned his partner Dave wouldn't be leaving the yard for at least another thirty minutes, so at the speed the lad was running, he'd be there with time to spare. Forking out a few pennies to let his partner know he'd be late that morning was a small price to pay for the extra time it allowed him. Watts had enjoyed very little sleep and felt much the worse for the lack of it. What a night it had been. He'd found it difficult to come to terms with the happenings that had occurred since his session in The Postern Gate earlier the previous evening.

The particulars of the calamity were still spinning around in his mind, each appalling image tormenting him afresh. Although Billy Watts kept assuring himself all would be well, he remained worried to the point of distraction. The many possibilities and consequences were impossible to disentangle, each individual element a source of constant apprehension. Then there was Ethel herself, most likely sitting exactly where he'd left her – staring into space with swollen eyes.

Watts had driven Victor Thurgood back to Woolpack Lane, the wounded man bleeding profusely from the appalling injuries George Davy had inflicted on him, even as the murderous bastard himself was on his way to Purgatory. Watts had Thurgood to thank for his survival, stunned as he was with Davy hovering over him, a whisker from slashing his gizzard. In that moment he thought would be his last, Watts had glimpsed Victor Thurgood impossibly rising from the debilitating onslaught he'd been submitted to.

He recalled George Davy intuitively sweeping the edge of a blade across Thurgood's belly, his ensuant yell of triumph immediately subdued when Thurgood brought down a chunk of fractured marble to shatter the villain's skull. Watts himself had laboured to regain his feet, taking in the dreadful consequences of the brief exchange as he did so. Ignoring the wide-eyed corpse that had been George Davy, Watts had stumbled instead to where Victor Thurgood lay gasping for breath – the man who was once a detested rival.

The desperate trudge to the cart had been unpleasantly problematic, Victor's leaking blood drenching them both as they struggled to coordinate their exertions. Brawny as he was, Billy Watts had been beyond exhaustion when finally he came to lay Victor Thurgood on the saturated sacks that decked his cart. Though he was literally soaked to the skin, Watts had blessed the foulness of the inclement weather if only for the cover it afforded them. There'd been not a soul on the streets that night, such was the deluge that fell from the sky.

When they had finally come to the deserted cobbles of Woolpack Lane, Watts had no intention of pulling alongside his lodgings. Instead he'd gently urged his horse towards the shelter of the nearby stables. In times to come, Billy Watts would ease his conscience by recalling the considerable efforts he'd made to preserve Victor Thurgood's life. Against his better judgement, before leaving the scene, he'd laboriously climbed from the boards yet again, fully intending to seek the aid of Doc Felton. Yet despite his frantic knocking, there'd been no response whatsoever; Felton, he'd thought, was most likely deep in his cups by that time and well on his way to befuddled oblivion.

Ethel Bentley stood fidgeting by the window, her nerves in pieces as she solemnly awaited their return. At first she'd passed the time by washing and drying the spills and splatters of blood that stained the floors and walls of the tiny kitchen. Once satisfied she'd done the best she could, she poured herself a stiff drink and simply waited.

And so it seemed an eternity before she observed the familiar profile of Billy rounding the corner on the crest of his cart, her heart in her mouth when she saw no sign of Victor

Thurgood. At first transfixed by the sight of Billy passing by, Ethel then rushed to the door, leaning out to observe the tail of the cart disappearing towards the stable at the end of the lane. Reaching for her shawl, she dashed from the house into the driving rain, running towards the stable yard as fast as her legs would carry her.

The scene that met Ethel Bentley would stay with her for the rest of her days: her darling Billy gently cradling the head of the only other man ever to mean anything to her, perhaps more than she'd ever realised. Without hesitation, she clambered aboard to join them on the cart, and when she came to crouch by Victor's side, she noticed him blink and bestow on her the shadow of a smile. William Watts gave Victor's hand a gentle squeeze, nodding deferentially before discreetly climbing from the boards to allow them to say their goodbyes.

Victor Thurgood died in that moment, Ethel Bentley holding his damaged body as close as she dared to, smoothing his hair as she watched him quietly pass away. Despite the awful pain he'd suffered, he died with dignity, his contented smile forever locked in place as one last breath left his mortal consciousness. Ethel suppressed the urge to weep, determined to preserve her grief for sober moments of solitude. Even so, a single tear escaped her, though without so much as an accompanying whimper.

Momentarily breaking from tending his horse,

William Watts assumed from Ethel's forlorn expression that the man she held in her arms was dead. After a moment of bemused reflection, his thoughts returned to the practicalities of their situation. Two men had died that night, leaving himself and Ethel deeply implicated in their violent demise. He could only hope he'd not been observed and that the earlier ruckus had not been interpreted for what it actually was.

The saving grace was the way of life they shared in the commune. Even had anyone seen or heard anything untoward, the very last person they'd tell would be a policeman. There'd be a deal of whispering and speculation, but that'd be as far as it went ... unless, of course, a reward was posted. But then, whoever would post a reward for the loss of a man like George Davy? Watts's stoic nature prevented him thinking too far ahead – everything in order, and a step at a time.

Chapter 43
Nottingham 1891

'Where does that leave us now then, sir? What I mean to say is, with George Boyd being a known associate of George Davy ... and the fact the robbery was allegedly carried out by two persons of similar stature.'

'Let's not get too far in front of ourselves, Grouper – no matter how intriguing that particular proposition may be, there's no definitive evidence to suggest Boyd and Davy were accomplices. There was no money of any great value found on Davy's body, and we didn't find anything relevant to the crime at his lodgings on Woolpack Lane ... apart from that jumble of peculiar clippings and pictures – very disturbing, very disturbing indeed.'

'Yes, sir, as you say, sir, very.'

'And in any case, Grouper, George Davy, as rough and evil-minded as he was, had very little on his record apart from minor misdemeanours: mostly relating to drunken brawling, for which he's received warnings on a number of occasions. He was prone to describing himself as a hawker, one of a number of similar types selling cheap tack down by The Exchange. More often than not, though, he was more likely to be elsewhere doing God knows what.'

'Didn't you say he was a cunning bastard, though, sir?'

'Oh, indeed, was he ever. Crafty as a cart load o' monkeys, he is ... or was. He smartly extricated himself from more than a few tight corners, did the late and scarcely lamented George Davy. Of course, we knew he was a proper villain, but catching him for anything worth a serious charge proved difficult in the extreme.'

'What about Victor Thurgood, sir, still no sign of him?'

'Neither whisper nor trace, Grouper. I reckon he skipped town with his share of the plunder. The word on the street reckons he was in big trouble with the market boys, owing money to one or the other. If that's the truth of it, then I wouldn't blame him for running. And you personally checked on his girlfriend after we searched Davy's house – her living on the same lane. Ethel Bentley isn't it? Well known for soliciting, she is. Of course, she backed up his whereabouts at the time of the robbery, and so we've got no real evidence to go on in that respect.'

'I'm sure Caborn thinks Thurgood had something to do with the robbery, sir, the way he was speaking about him when I saw him yesterday. Caborn's far from being a happy man: reckons we should've nailed somebody by now.'

'Well, we have nailed somebody by now. What's George Boyd if he's not guilty? Sounds like Caborn only wants it to be Victor Thurgood. Boyd had money on him into the bargain, not much by comparison to what went missing, mind, but more than enough to raise some awkward questions. There's no doubting

Thurgood was involved – you seeing him in conversation with Boyd only the night after the robbery. Unfortunately for us, though, facts are everything ... and we don't even know where Thurgood is, for a start! Nor can we unequivocally prove you witnessed money changing hands in The Postern.'

'I'm certain there was some sort of exchange, sir, I ...'

'Even so, we can't prove it was money, Grouper. That's my point!'

'No, sir, you're right, of course.'

'Bugger me, but we don't even have enough to charge Boyd, not yet at least.'

'Looks like it's all falling apart, then, sir.'

'Aye, much like George Davy's murder – not a sign of a weapon and no hope of anybody talking. The three wise monkeys are abroad in St Mary's parish: hear all, see all and say nowt! Not a word from anybody, despite the posters going up. Still ... time yet, I suppose. Like you say, though, Grouper, it's falling apart; both robbery and murder will quickly fade into memory once something else turns up ... which, inevitably, it will.'

***

George Boyd smirked mockingly as he snatched up the money, cheekily fanning the two crumpled notes in the direction of the desk sergeant's impassive expression.

'You'll turn up again like a bad penny, Boyd ... I'll be boggered if yer don't.'

'Oh ah, we'll see abart that, then, mester.'

Boyd said nothing more, choosing instead to swagger by the three constables that stood by the sergeant's desk, winking at the ginger bogger that'd thrown him against the wall of his own parlour before painfully handcuffing him.

Stepping into the sunshine of a bright new day, George Boyd grinned to himself, breaking wind with a grunt of satisfaction before making his way to The Postern Gate Inn. He'd later think of his departed companion and snigger to himself some more. For once, he'd come out on top. Not by much, it was true, but he was a damn sight better off than George Davy would ever be, and that was a fact.

They'd asked Boyd about Davy's secret obsession, wanting to see how he reacted. Of course, he'd said nothing, what with George Davy being a fellow villain and coppers being a villain's eternal enemy. If only they'd been interested enough to put two and two together, they might've solved a few tasty misdemeanours they'd never previously known about.

***

The horse had never looked better, what with its brand-new leathers and brasses. To the horse's obvious pleasure, Billy Watts had untangled its mane and brushed its coat till it shone like a barber's mirror. Watts had not felt as settled as he was for as long as he could remember. It seemed their once insurmountable predicaments had been blown into buggery by the sharpening winds of autumn. Now here he was, proudly driving his freshly painted cart to the door of his lodgings. Sunday morning had brought bright sunshine, and the covering of early frost was already thinning under its strengthening rays. They were off to the bridge and over the river to enjoy the colours of the season before winter inexorably arrived. Ethel stepped out and returned his wave, turning to grab the hamper before locking the door behind her. She was wrapped warm and snug in her new winter outfit, looking as smart and sprightly as he'd ever seen her.

It had taken a while for her melancholy to fade, much as he'd known it would. She'd tried awful hard not to show it, but Thurgood's passing had obviously cut her deeply. William Watts was not by nature a jealous man. He'd already known of her other life when he'd wooed her. And she'd never hidden or flaunted it either. She was a good woman at heart, was Ethel Bentley, and he knew an ailing man like him was more than lucky to have a woman like her.

Ethel had asked where he'd got the money for the all stuff he'd been splashing out on. He'd blatantly lied, of course, not having the heart to tell her the truth of it. Watts had guessed what was going on, knowing Boyd and Davy came as a pair. And he'd seen Thurgood associating with Boyd in The Postern soon after news of the robbery broke. When it made the pages of the Journal, he'd wondered if

Ethel might put two and two together as well, much like he had. After all, Thurgood was the manager at the drapery and well placed to know about the hidden safe. All the same, he'd never get round to asking Ethel her opinion, thinking he'd best let sleeping dogs lie.

Ethel wrapped the thick blanket round her shoulders and tucked herself under Billy's arm. He smiled with pleasure at that, then clicked his tongue and flapped the reins. Both of them were looking forward to a day in the country, cold as it had turned out to be. She'd made a picnic for them and included a bottle of ale to wash it down. They'd no intentions of returning home much before dark, such was their contentment. Why, even his cough was behaving itself.

The money was coming in handy, too, the bigger part of it extracted from George Davy's pocket, the remainder from Victor Thurgood's. Not once did he feel bad about taking it. All things considered, what else was there to be done? If he hadn't taken it, who else would have benefitted? And the police hadn't been able to find out who was responsible for the robbery. Then there was George Boyd and the rumours about him walking from the police station with a fold of cash they'd failed to prove stolen.

That caused Watts to once again recall the night in The Postern, noticing Victor Thurgood thrusting something into his pocket before dashing away; it didn't take much working out.

He glanced at Ethel, comfortable with her head on his shoulder. Watts remembered how difficult it had been at first, coming to terms with the burial. He shuddered when recalling that awful journey before the break of dawn – what seemed like hours digging the hole in the wooded wasteland, all the time fearful of being discovered. Worse by far was lowering the poor fellow into his makeshift grave, knowing for all the world he was dead but all the time wondering if he really was. He'd heard about trances that imitated death, unreasonable though he thought it to be. Yet cold as the body was, he'd worried on that premise for many a while afterwards. She'd pleaded to help bury his body, but Watts wouldn't hear of it. He thought her memories were bad enough – what with the manner of Thurgood's passing – never mind witnessing the man's rudimentary committal.

Then there had been the worrying and the waiting, and the knock at the door that all but froze the blood in his veins. Sure enough, it was the police, seeing them on the doorstep all but causing Ethel to faint on the spot, such was her fear of what they'd come for. As it turned out, they'd simply sought to verify Thurgood's alibi for the night of the robbery, much use as it might be to them.

The detective named Grouper noted her substantiation, further asking if she knew anything concerning Thurgood's current whereabouts. Ethel said she hadn't the foggiest where he was and that her relationship was strictly one of a transactional nature. That seemed to satisfy Detective Constable Grouper. However, like most bobbies, there was always one more question to be asked before he took his leave.

'By the way, just one more thing concerning your neighbour ... George Davy, I'm talking about.'

'Yeah ... heard summat about some funny business. Word travels fast round here, Constable, specially things like that.'

'Do you know anything that might assist us at all, Miss Bentley?'

'Me? I should think not, if yer don't mind! All respects ter the dead, an' that, truth be told, George weren't a popular man in these parts. Like most people round here, ah went out me way to avoid him whenever ah could, in any case.'

'Yes, well, thanks again, Miss Bentley. Most helpful, I'm sure. If you should happen to hear of anything of interest, you know where we are.'

And then that was it – nothing more, and seemingly forgotten.

Chapter 44
Nottingham 1891

The year was approaching its conclusion, a dusting of snow descending to briefly cloak the municipal degradation. Though it was nothing to match the blizzards of the earlier months of that year, the very sight of snow falling gently to the ground retrieved memories of those erstwhile storms.

The Postern Gate was one of a number of hostelries offering warming refuge on a winter's night, and a good night it was with the weekend to follow: the fire in the corner blazing merrily, the banjo player beside its glow, readying to strike up a tune. Not a seat or table remained to be had, not even the stools by the frosted windows. The gathering was one of familiar faces – of geniality and the aura of Christmas to come.

'Come on, Eth, get it down yer, there's a girl.'

'Nearly pissed, you are, Billy, me lad. Yo mind yer footin' on yer way to the bar.'

Billy Watts cleared his throat yet again, the clag of it unquestionably requiring a whisky chaser to ease its roughness.

Ethel fondly watched him persuading his way through the crowd, a word here, a joke there. Most folk knew Billy Watts for a good man and let him through without hinder. They were a decent enough lot and mostly regular faces: Bobby Carter, the cheeky bogger, blowing her kisses behind Billy's back – Renee and Lizzie resting their arses instead of their backs, spending their hard-earned on gin and tobacco – Johnny Fishlock taking a break from stuffing the birds he trapped in Colwick woods. Why folk wanted dead things displayed in their parlours, she'd never know.

Whenever Ethel glanced at Fishlock, a shudder ran up her spine. He lived in the same lodgings as George Davy did and never so much as looked sideways at her. She thought maybe he didn't like women: either that or he'd something else to hide. Ethel sighed and chewed her bottom lip when she heard Billy coughing at the bar. She thought it was getting worse and wouldn't ease until winter had run its course. Poor Billy, he didn't deserve the trouble she'd brought on him.

'How yer doin', Eth, all right are yer?'

She looked up at the burly figure that was easing by her table.

'Ah, I'm right enough, George, thanks all the same.'

It was difficult to conceal the coolness in her tone. George Boyd did that to people, much like the other one used to. There was something of the underworld in even the kindest words that came from their mouths.

'How's your Billy? Is he alright an' all?'

'He's hover there, standin' at the bar, if yer must know.'

Ah, so he is … likes chuckin' his money abart these days, don't he?'

She didn't need to be a genius to understand

the insinuation. George Boyd had said similar things before, ever since ...

'Yo not far behind him, though, are yer, George?'

Her words hit home and caused him to move on with no more than a sneer, seeing Billy Watts making his way back from the bar, squinting in his direction. Not that he was bothered by that, thinking Watts would hit the floor before he'd even chance to put his dukes up.

'What's that bogger after, then, hey, Eth?'

'Leave it alone, Billy ... best not start owt. He's not woth it.'

'Bad news, that's what he is ... lets on he knows summat but knows nowt in the end.'

'Like we've said before, Billy, he knows yer seen him with Victor that night ... and no doubt he knew George Davy were after me. But he'll say nowt because he were more than likely involved himself.'

'Yeah, I bet yo right an' all. He enjoys tormenting folks as much as his mate used to do.'

'George Davy did a sight more than torment folk if them bleddy stories turn out ter be true.'

'I keep tellin' yer, Eth, they must be true. Fishlock swears he saw some bobbies chuckin' that stuff all hover the place when they was searchin' his lodgings – newspaper clippings and pictures, he said.'

'Yeah, that's what one or two reckon. Just think, though, Billy ... if George Davy really was the Ripper ...'

'Who?'

'Jack the Ripper. Never did catch him, did they?'

'Don't talk bleddy daft, Eth! I doubt as George Davy ever travelled further south than Leicester Market, never mind bleddy London. I can't remember many days goin' by wi' out seein' him somewhere round here. More likely, it were what they call perversion.'

'Well, I don't know ... maybe he just liked to imagine them things, God help us!'

'I were only sayin', no need ter get bleddy shirty abart it.'

They finished their drinks and said their goodbyes, the closing door of The Postern Gate Inn gradually subduing the continuing rowdiness from within. They set off for home in the frozen silence of whitened streets, arm in arm, walking to Woolpack Lane, looking forward to a warming nightcap before taking to the comfort of their bed.

It was nearing the end of 1891, and the snow began falling again, the chill flakes lightly brushing their faces. Life had turned for the better of late, though much like the snow of winter that accumulated to smooth the uneven streets, sooner or later, in this life or that, something would come to disturb its pristine surface.

Chapter 45
Nottingham 1968

Dancing the night away, well some of it, down at The Palais where we first met. Things are going well, and not just on the dancefloor – new year, new life, new job, new me. And new evidence too … pieces fitting into place.

'68 is starting well, never mind February Fill-Dyke – that's what Grandad called it – something about melting snow and flooding fields – miserable weather, I call it. The dancefloor fills up – Love Affair's 'Everlasting Love' – number one in the charts and rightly so. The beat is seductive. Ann laughs as I let myself go to its pulsing rhythm, dancing like they do on Top of the Pops – letting go is becoming a bit of a habit. We jig, shake and sing, and in the heat of it, we find each other's eyes … those words mean a lot to us.

The wedding is set for the first day of August. We'd originally settled for sometime in spring, but fate arrived to intervene. At least the boss allowed me to enjoy the New Year festivities before breaking the news on my return. It wasn't completely unexpected. Nevertheless, it came as something of a shock. He'd casually taken me to one side, saying he knew I was getting married and was sorry for letting me go at such a time. He explained how things had gone from bad to worse, whining on about work drying up faster than anticipated. After assuring me the decision had no bearing on my character or my work, he said there was no reason not to provide me with an excellent reference. Finishing on that, he wished me good luck and told me I'd be leaving at the end of the week. He then spun on his heels and disappeared without a backward glance.

That following Friday, I left the same building I'd first entered as a callow boy of fifteen. Despite the daily tedium, the once forbidding edifice had over time become something of a second home to me. In the company of my peers, I became accepted for what I was – simply one of their kind. Only much later would I realise I was but one of many to fall to a widening demise: the inevitable collapse of bygone skills, ancient and honourable trades dismissed in favour of smarter technologies. Still, every cloud has a silver lining, they say, though sometimes it's difficult to see one. As it happened, I found mine barely two weeks afterwards, even if I didn't know then just how silvery that lining would turn out to be.

After I'd felt sorry for myself for a couple of days, Ann provided me with a copy of the evening paper, together with an admonishing kick up the backside. And so I followed the daily routine, pencil poised, scanning the vacancy columns, circling anything even vaguely looking like a possibility. In the mornings, readied with names and numbers, I proceeded to try my luck. Then, after three soul-destroying days of weakening endeavour, only two claimed to be even half-interested in my limited credentials. Even so, wonder of wonders, one of them invited me for an interview.

The advertisement revealed no company name. It simply stated that the agency required a versatile young person for manual and clerical duties. Apart from a telephone number, that was the entirety of it. The lady who answered the phone with a squawk put me through to someone called Alfred. My subsequent conversation with Alfred was reasonably brief, me fleetingly explaining my previous employment and him dictating what was expected of me.

The following day found me searching for a company called Alfred Buskin, Theatrical Agent. After traipsing up and down Pelham Street, I eventually discovered a tarnished plaque screwed to a door that stood above two stone steps. After knocking a couple of times, I tried the door, hearing it complain when it reluctantly opened. The interior didn't look very promising – a small hallway leading to a bare wooden staircase, the walls either side a sludgy brown, likely painted sometime during the previous century. I climbed the stairs to find another door, this one bearing the proprietor's name etched into a cloudy glass panel. As soon as I rapped on its surface, the same squawky voice shouted for me to come in.

'Hello, sweetheart ... bet you're Arthur.'

Daphne Rowbottom was extremely busty, a dyed blonde of indeterminate age with black encircled eyes. After shifting some fading magazines and leaflets from a pair of antiquated chairs, Daphne ordered me to sit down and wait for Alfred. Saying he wouldn't be long, she gave me a sly wink accompanied by hand motions inferring Alfred was having a drink somewhere. That caused me look at the clock on the wall ticking just past eleven – Alfred was obviously an early starter.

After fifteen minutes or thereabouts, I heard the downstairs door moaning, and then the subsequent thud of heavy feet on the creaking staircase. When the inner door burst open, the pungency of whisky preceded the enormous frame of an exceedingly hairy man. The modest amount of face I could actually perceive was as red as a farmer's backside – a politer version of an expression Grandma often employed – the rest of it literally covered with a shock of grey hair. Alfred Buskin was a huge man with a voice to complement his corpulence.

In twenty minutes I had secured a new job, Buskin sending me away with the promise of two quid a week more than I'd previously earned. My duties were as yet unclear: 'bit of this and that', the ambiguous description no doubt barely covering the number of responsibilities I would be expected to carry out. At least it was worth a try, I thought, if only for a week or two.

***

'Come on, then, Arthur, tell us all about it! Cup of tea or something stronger?'

Quite why I'd chosen to tell the Booths about my new job before anyone else – apart from Ann, of course – I couldn't really say. Perhaps I found it easier with them than I did my own family.

'It's a theatrical agency, but ...'

They were looking at me quizzically, maybe wondering what on earth I was about to reveal.

'It's not what you might think, though I've already noticed some seedy types popping in looking for work. Mr Buskin handles all sorts of performers: actors, dancers, comedians, ventriloquists, impressionists and – this'll really interest you both – mind-readers, hypnotists and ... wait for it ... mediums, no less.'

'Oh, what have you got yourself into, Arthur? All sounds a bit risqué if you don't mind me saying.'

Edgar Booth was looking down his nose, much to the amusement of his wife.

'Come on, Edgar, give him a chance. After all, he needs the job, what with the wedding and all. Tell us a bit more about what you're doing, Arthur.'

Kate was slurring her words again, not so much maybe, but enough to remind me of the night she'd really hit the bottle. Quite why I continued to think about that, I didn't know, but I knew there was something about it.

'I do what I'm told, to be honest: fetching and carrying and bit of general repair work, washing the boss's car – nice old Jag – cleaning and tidying, that sort of thing. There's another side to it – Buskin calls it "running". You see, the majority of what he likes to call his clients can't afford telephones, so I deliver the details of their bookings as, unlike the post, I'm guaranteed to arrive the same day, which is just as well, because some of the bookings might be for that particular night. Sometimes Buskin sends me to collect fees from the clubs and pubs as well, as he doesn't altogether trust the clients being paid direct. He knows the business inside out, does Buskin ... you name it, he'll provide the entertainment.'

'Do you like working there, then, Arthur?'

'Yeah, I think so, Kate. Money's okay as well.'

'Hmm, well, at least it'll tide you over until something else comes along. Buskin, hey ... rings a bell for some reason.'

'Don't tell me you know him, Edgar?'

'No, I simply said it rings a bell.'

Of course we had a drink or two as we talked it over. Then I thought to tell them my other news, even though Bob wasn't there to hear it. Apparently, he was inundated with work – 'winter blues' the main cause, he reckoned.

'I've got something else to tell you – the results of some new research, in fact.'

They looked up at that, clearly not expecting to hear anything about the project that evening.

'I really wanted Bob to be present, but I'm actually meeting someone tomorrow night, with Ann, as a matter of fact.'

'Ann?'

'Yes, unusual, I know. The thing is, Ann's opened a door that might lead to something really interesting. She did ask me before going ahead with it.'

'At what point did Ann become involved? I thought you'd decided not to share those sorts of things with her, for her sake if nothing else?'

'You already know I had to explain some of it to her, Edgar. How could we be a couple if I kept everything from her? I've never said anything about the grimmer aspects of our affairs – nothing more than a sketchy idea of what we're trying to achieve, in fact.'

'Arthur, it's your business what you tell Ann, not ours. She's your wife-to-be, and marriage is about sharing things, the good and not so good. I think we'd all do well to remember that, Edgar.'

As he always did, Edgar Booth submitted to his wife's authority, blushing slightly at the gentle reprimand. After a suitable pause, I continued, avoiding Edgar's eyes for a moment as I began to explain.

'As you know, Ann works in the offices at Player's. She started there at the same time as a girl called Jill. Ann and Jill became friendly and socialised a few times. Anyway, to cut it short, Jill left to work for a local paper, doing much the same as she had before. Ann met up with her a week or so ago for a drink and a catch-up. It turned out Jill sometimes does a bit of work in the archives involving the transfer of paper records onto some sort of microfilm. It's actually called something else, Ann did say what it was, but I've forgotten.'

'Microfiche.'

'Yeah, something like that, Kate. How d'you know about that?'

'Dunno, must have read it somewhere or seen it on the telly – *Tomorrow's World*, probably.'

'There you go, telly's good for something. Anyway, Ann thought about me and asked Jill if there was any chance she might be able to find some old records. Ann said Jill was only too pleased to ask her boss and that all she needed were details of the events we were interested in. So, you think it might be worth a search, Edgar?'

'Yes, Arthur, I certainly think it might.'

'What do you suggest that we ask Jill to look for? Bearing in mind she'd be doing us a big favour and we shouldn't be asking too much of her.'

'Why not simply ask for anything relating to George Davy in 1891? After all, he's our chief protagonist, or so we believe. If you want to push your luck, what about this Thurgood character as well? He looks to be a man about town, and from what you found out from that furniture shop, he was most likely involved in the robbery when it was a drapery.'

'Okay, then, Edgar, let's see what transpires. Leave it with me.'

***

We took Jill to a pub on Bridlesmith Gate. It wasn't one I frequented much, but I thought it might be quieter in the week and ideal for a chat. Jill turned out to be an extremely nice girl, and I saw straightaway why she and Ann got on so well. What Ann hadn't told me was just how sophisticated Jill was. The other surprise was the way Ann rose to her friend's social level when we were talking together. I thought no matter how well you think you know somebody, there's always another side to them. After we'd finished our meeting, the three of us decided to make a night of it, moving on to The Bodega for another drink before saying our goodbyes. It was only three days later when Ann arrived with the news I was waiting for. Jill had spoken to her boss, and with her approval, had done the business as promised. It turned out to be more than I could have hoped for.

Chapter 46
Nottingham 1968

At first I thought it a dream ... perhaps half-dream. But now I know it to be real. I'd had a sense of her before – that lightest touch that took my troubled mind to sleep, that lost item found as if led to its hiding place. That presence by my shoulder to warn me of something I'd yet to learn of.

I know she is near, even now, in the dark silence of the early hours. Her presence is undeniable. Though I do not see her, I have a sense of her. I am beginning to perceive what I have so far denied. There are sometimes others here – others that have awaited my awakening. I have no fear of their presence – only a sense of indescribable peace.

I think I am stepping into the void. Thank God she is with me.

'Why are you smiling at me in that way, Arthur?'

'I think you know exactly why, Edgar.'

'So I was right, after all?'

'Yes, you must have been.'

'Welcome to my world.'

'You sound like Jim Reeves.'

'Jim Reeves? Oh yes, of course ... that wonderful song.'

We sat warming ourselves in the parlour, waiting for Bob Langham while Kate occupied herself somewhere. The glow from the fire matched the one that had burned within me from the moment I'd left my bed that morning – as if by magic, my anxieties blown away, mysteriously replaced by an overwhelming sense of liberation.

'Will I see things in the same way as you and Kate see them, Edgar?'

'Probably not, and just for the record, Kate's experiences don't always take the same form as mine ... or Bertie's, or even Violet's, for that matter.'

'Violet? I tend not to think of her in the same light.'

'Oh, if anything, Violet is the most perceptive of us, Arthur. Trouble is, she's not a particularly safe pair of hands ... a little erratic, one could say.'

'What d'you mean by erratic?'

'Unpredictable might well be another word, although mischievous is possibly closer to the truth. That's why Bertie tends to keep her on a tight leash – out of harm's way, so to speak.'

'She's a strange girl and no mistake.'

'Yes, you're right in that assumption, Arthur, she certainly is.'

'What are you boys talking about, and where's Bob got to, for crying out loud?'

Kate appeared carrying an extremely large plate of sandwiches over which was an equally large cloche. She was never happier than when hosting guests, and it never ceased to amaze me how she made the transition into that other world she sometimes inhabited.

'We'll wait till he arrives before we tuck in ... so hands off if you don't mind!'

Was there a touch of unsteadiness in her posture? I glanced at Edgar to see if he'd noticed, only to find him staring into the fire as though mulling something over. Kate was slurring more often of late, causing me to wonder if her fondness for alcohol was turning into something more concerning. Then, as if proof were needed, she returned to the kitchen, predictably returning with a tray of tumblers and a bottle of something. After placing the bottle and glasses next to the sandwiches, she plonked herself on the sofa beside Edgar and smiled at me.

For some reason, I sensed the moment had come; I simply had to ask the question that burned within me. He had appeared some time before, since then becoming increasingly insistent. For a fleeting moment, my deep-rooted fears returned, surging as though to test my resolve. I had to wonder – was this the way things were going to be from now on?

'I think I know who it is.'

'Sorry, Arthur, I didn't quite catch that.'

'The boy who sits with you ... is his name ... Alfie?'

For a moment they sat transfixed, their eyes flaring as they unwaveringly stared in my direction. Then, without taking her eyes from me, Kate closed her trembling fingers over her husband's grasping palm, Edgar eventually fracturing the brief hiatus.

'Do you really see him, Arthur?'

Though intense, the words were whispered, Edgar's expression one of wide-eyed incredulity.

'Yes I do, Edgar. I'm really sorry if it upsets you both, but I'm experiencing a forceful need to say something.'

'Thank God you are, Arthur ... you don't know how long we've waited for this moment.'

'Can neither of you see him or even sense his presence?'

'Our failure to experience either of those things has ever been a source of particular distress.'

'Does he seem happy, Arthur, or ...?'

The heartrending sobs that followed Kate's brief words pierced my heart like an arrow.

'Whereabouts in the room is he, Arthur?'

'At your feet, Edgar ... equally between the both of you. You should know at this moment that he is smiling ... no, actually, he's positively beaming.'

'That's because you've made us aware of him; he must be considerably relieved ... as, indeed, are we.'

Together they looked to where they thought he sat, each pathetically searching for the boy that, for all their shared endowments, they could not in any sense, earthly or otherwise, distinguish. I realised then that the gift released from my inner being was not entirely for my own benefit: more so, it seemed to be for souls that sought my assistance. Would my life never be the same as it had been?

***

When I looked again, he was no longer there. It seemed he'd faded in synchronisation with the knocking that came at the door. The spell suspending the three of us in a moment of missing time was immediately and unintentionally broken. The sobbing cry that subsequently came from the depths of Kate Booth's soul when I confirmed his absence was enough to break my heart. Bob Langham had unwittingly intruded upon something infinitely deep and personal, and the pall of its essence continued to linger, Bob's cheery greeting consumed in the mournful miasma.

It was Edgar who rallied sufficiently to relieve Bob's immediate state of bewilderment. The poor man must have thought he'd done something terribly wrong, such was the apparent frostiness of our reception.

'Bob, you must think us extremely rude. Please make yourself at home.'

Kate stood up, eyes darting from left to right, as though unsure of what to do next.

'Erm ... shall we have a drink and something to eat now Bob's arrived?'

Kate Booth had a way of snapping out of difficult situations by resorting to matters of domesticity, although this time, she was finding it more difficult to escape her current mood. After pouring the drinks, she passed the plate of sandwiches round, each of us robotically filling our plates out of a sense of duty.

'Bob, my dear chap, you need to understand that you walked into a complicated and very personal state of affairs. There are a couple of things we should explain.'

Edgar was struggling to inject some normality

into a tense and bizarre set of circumstances.

'I should have thought before I opened my mouth. It's not for me to speak on your behalf, Arthur, so perhaps you wouldn't mind taking over? Your earlier disclosure was interesting, and I for one would like to hear what generated your acceptance. Perhaps after that we ought to discuss the ... other matter ... if that's okay with you, Kate?'

Kate Booth smiled weakly and inclined her head, Bob gawping at each of us in turn, obviously confounded by our peculiar behaviour. Knowing where to start was a bit of a challenge. It was funny how a new job could play such an important part in changing someone's life.

'You might remember a little while ago, Edgar saying he thought I had the gift ... or whatever you may choose to call it. And you know how really upset and confused I was at the time: frightened more than anything else, I think. Well, a few days ago, my new boss asked me to spy on one of his clients ...'

***

'It's not really spying, Arthur, just a matter of checking up on him. Latimer's a wily old fox and not shy of a deception or two. For all I know, he might be making some good money at the end of his performances, passing the cap round and keeping the proceeds to himself. His contract stipulates I get a percentage of any extras over and above a percentage of the fee he earns from the venue. And it'll only take you an hour or so, old chap ...'

Buskin was glancing at Daphne for support, wasting his time as she was busy trowelling on her face paint. It was near to knocking-off time and I wasn't keen on doing an evening shift.

'I'd go myself, but I'd stand out like a sore thumb, and of course he'd give me a share if I was there in person, if only to get me off his bloody back! It's the times when I'm not there that bother me.'

Buskin chased every single penny, reckoning it was the only way to survive in business. He claimed the cheating bastards would just as gleefully shaft him senseless as pass the time of day. In the end, I gave in, but only after negotiating a small bonus. The increasingly irritable Buskin also issued a veiled threat, advising me how scarce decent jobs were becoming and how I should bloody well know when I was on to a good thing. Daphne later said he'd noticed how much I enjoyed the work, and I really couldn't argue with that: plus the fact that I was making more money than I ever thought I would.

Seven-thirty therefore found me outside a workingmen's club near Bulwell. The bleached pegboard by the entrance touted a one-night special – LAURIE LATIMER, RENOWNED SPIRITUALIST, SUPPORTED BY RESIDENT DUO, SID & IVOR.

I inwardly groaned and headed for the dated entrance, only to be met by a pug-nosed giant wearing an ill-fitting suit and badly knotted tie.

'Member?'

'No, do I have to be?'

'No ... yer can enter as a guest, me duck. But yer'll need an affiliated member ter sign yer in, all the same.'

I was about to turn away and call it a night when a loud voice behind me piped up.

'I'll sign him in, Hector, just gee him a bleddy ticket!'

'Know him, da yer, Daisy?'

'Should do ... he's me nephew ... aren't yer, me duck?'

The woman was on her own and looked a bit like Grandma, only younger. She was winking and grinning at me, things Grandma would never dream of doing. Hector shook his head and scribbled on a pink ticket before ripping it off a wad of the same. After half-heartedly passing it over, he asked me to pay what he referred to as a nominal fee.

'Remember yo responsible forrim all the time he's in there, Daisy. Don't goo forgerrin that, me duck!'

'Oh shurrup, Hector, and gerrof off yer high hoss!'

And that was it – Daisy smirking and tripping off in one direction, me sloping off in another.

'Thanks for that, Daisy.'

'Yer all right, me duck. Come an' see me if yer want a good time later on.'

Daisy was cackling at her own wit, making her way towards the front where three women of similar type sat waving to her. Meanwhile, I made my way to the bar and ordered a pint of Mansfield. The great thing about workingmen's clubs was that you usually got a good pint at a decent price. Knocking the head off the bitter, I went in search of a table at the rear of the room, one with a decent view of the audience. The club was filling quickly, the latecomers bustling in just as the curtains erratically opened to reveal Ivor on the organ and Sid on the drums. I knew which was which as the word SID was crudely daubed on the skin of the bass drum. Following a few odd slaps of applause, they immediately got into their stride, playing up-to-the minute melodies, as they claimed – up to the minute a few years previously, maybe.

Sid worked himself to a sweat in no time, Ivor gurning and miming his way through 'Hoots Mon' and 'Mambo Italiano'. Continuing in similar fashion for ten or fifteen minutes, they were interrupted only once: one of the bar staff bringing them a pint each, the two musicians nodding to a flat cap in the audience affectedly raising a thumb to acknowledge their thanks. I imagined the routine barely changed from decade to decade. And why would it? A lot of folk sought comfort in such familiarities. Sid ended the session with a couple of booms on the bass drum, the duo then ambling off the stage to a ripple of indifferent applause.

After ten or so minutes of queuing for drinks and urgent trips to the toilets, the audience began to settle again, the dimming lights creating an air of inactive expectancy. In the subsequent semi-darkness, a searching spotlight eventually caught up with Hector and his ill-fitting suit, the dour giant striding purposefully across the stage towards a cockeyed microphone.

'Good evenin' ladies and gentlemen ... norra bad crowd in tonight. Before we get crackin' though, ah'd like ter remind yer it's bingo next Thursday ... and the accumulated jackpot is ... wait forrit ... owd yer watter ... seven pound three shillin' an' six!'

Hector held up his hand, waggishly quelling the exclamations of feigned excitement before recovering the audience's attention.

'Now then ... without further adieu ... and back by popular demand ... it's my personal pleasure to once again introduce the amazin' ... the mysterious ... Laur-ieee Latimer!'

Entering stage left, a hunchbacked wisp of a man attired in dated frock coat and top hat prowled towards the microphone, expanded eyes darting hither and thither as though seeking a singular individual within the craning crowd. Throughout the entrance, Hector remained on stage, arms extended to welcome the oncoming performer. Then, clapping loudly into the microphone, he exited backwards, nodding knowingly at the crowd as he did so. When Latimer leaned forward to scan the sea of attentive faces, suspenseful stillness pervaded the room, the audience absorbed in a moment of anticipation.

'A name comes to mind ... not entirely

clear... what's that? You say your name is ... Wilf? Will ... William, perhaps?'

'Willy ... it's my Willy!'

The voice had come from deep within the tittering audience, its high-pitched resonance charged with hopeful obsession.

'Yes, of course it is ... We have Willy in our midst!'

A few guffaws came to interrupt the titters, causing Latimer to reassert himself. He clearly hadn't intended or anticipated the comic interlude.

'You've given him confidence, madam; his presence is much clearer now. Tell me, was Willy a bashful sort of a fellow, by any chance?'

The woman rose from her seat, a rush of whispers chasing round the room when her hand flew to her mouth.

'Yeah ... ah were only saying ter somebody earlier on, it'd be a miracle if my Willy turned up tonight. He never did like the limelight.'

After that I slumped into my chair, lit another cigarette and swallowed my beer, fully expecting to be bored out of my mind for the rest of what was laughingly called a performance. Before I left the office, Buskin had revealed Laurie Latimer's chicanery, saying how he secretly let his wife and two grown daughters into the venues. He added that venue staff were often in on the deception, depending on potential takings. Latimer's wife and daughters would mingle with the crowd, keeping their eyes and ears open for valuable clues. Then once the show started, they'd sit in the audience, listening and watching for each other's coded signals. I drew on my cigarette and mused on Latimer's blatant fraudulence, wondering what Edgar Booth might make of it all. It was only shortly after that when the moment arrived. Later that night I would more intensely reflect on the quirks of my destiny, realising then that my life had turned again – this time taking me into another realm entirely.

The more I considered them, the more the sound of Latimer's voice diminished, as did my awareness of the crowd – except, that was, for the three individuals that were looking directly at me. The two men and the one woman were not in any sense together, each standing motionless by the person I could only assume they were bound to. There was no mistaking the fact that they were staring only at me, soundlessly imploring my assistance. Though my skin prickled and my heart thumped against my chest, everything suddenly made sense. The dogged fog of confusion was suddenly clearing, Edgar Booth's sagacious words reverberating in my ears.

He'd casually claimed I had inherent ability to see beyond the living world, and I had been too quick to deny his assertion. Now, in the meagre light of a smoke-filled suburban club, his conviction seemed highly plausible. In truth, I knew he'd been right in what he alleged, yet in spite of this, I had stubbornly refused to accept what should have been obvious to me all along.

Anxiously aware of their increasing desperation, I became mindful of my powerlessness. I instinctively knew they were pleading for help, but I failed to understand what I could accomplish in so public a place. It seemed even the netherworld was subject to the physical constraints of conventional life. It was the sudden clamour of enthusiastic applause that served to disturb the enchantment, creating within me a sense of lost time. Meanwhile, Latimer was taking his bows. He'd been walking amongst the audience before returning to the stage, there to further milk their plaudits.

I looked back to where I thought they were, straightaway realising they'd faded with the burst of applause and the brightening of the house lights. For a moment, I bowed my head, the memory of their despondency leaving me with feelings of remorse and inadequacy.

For all of Buskin's misgivings and to the best of my knowledge, no extra monies were collected that evening. Latimer had finally left the stage, the herd subsequently stampeding in the direction of the exits, to their televisions and to their comfortable chairs by the fire. Somewhere amongst them were three disheartened people, each of them totally unaware of how incredibly close they'd been to the desolate souls of their dear departed.

Chapter 47
Nottingham 1968

The family is gathered, the faces are long. We sit at the table, its top extended as in times of celebration and mourning – this time neither, though more the latter than the former.

The note sits crumpled amidst empty mugs and overflowing ashtrays, its simple testament ingrained in our minds – simple yet crushing.

Some of us are not surprised, though we keep our council – not a time for knowing words. Mam's eyes are red and we hear a sob. Grandma sighs and reaches out.

He is gone and the family is broken. We wonder why – why has he gone? The question is not yet spoken, but I think I'd long sensed the answer.

Edgar Booth was clearly not paying attention to our conversation. I imagined he was struggling to balance his feelings. If we'd only been chatting about my psychic abilities, I'm sure he would have eagerly contributed. However, the appearance of Alfie had clearly staggered the Booths to the point of bewilderment. Once he'd been made aware, Bob typically followed up the matter of Alfie's manifestation with a raft of penetrating questions, moderating his manner when observing the devastating effect it was having on the Booths' demeanour.

'I am sorry, I do understand how upsetting it must be. Maybe it would help if one of you explained the circumstances of Alfie's ...'

He'd put the question sympathetically, the undertone of compassion causing Kate's head to drop as if to hide her emotion. Edgar moved in and hugged her to his chest, reminding me of that summer's evening at the church hall – the same shared sadness they'd left unexplained.

'I think it falls to me to relate the reasons for what must appear to be our despondency.'

Edgar Booth awaited his wife's nod of approval before continuing, his words faltering with barely contained sentiment.

'We rarely speak of it ... even between ourselves. Such is the freshness of the pain that remains with us to this day.'

For a moment, I thought he was about to break, but then with a breath of determination, he managed to hold himself together. Looking at us from over his reading glasses, he continued to explain.

'We had waited so long that when he arrived we were overjoyed. We were not able to have our own children, you see, but it was as if Alfie was ours the very moment he entered our lives. He was barely ...'

Edgar's mouth creased into a wan smile, his words catching in his throat in his effort to relate the circumstances.

'He was only ten years old when it happened. He'd been an absolute joy and brought nothing but light into our world ...'

'We loved him so much!'

Kate's emphatic interruption caught us off-guard, such was the passion she conveyed. The couple took a moment then, hugging each other as though they were alone in the room.

'At some point, Alfie began to insist on going to school under his own steam. He was growing up far too quickly ... soon to be leaving the juniors behind and embarrassed to be seen anywhere near the school gates with either or both of his parents. How we wish we ...'

'Try to go on, Edgar ... it might help both of you if you let it out.'

Bob's suggestion radiated his depth of feeling, his tone one of genuine concern. He clearly wanted it said and done with, if only for their sakes.

'Very well, thank you, Bob. He was walking to school with some pals of his, something he normally did. Witnesses say they were larking about, pushing and shoving each other as lads often do. Of all people, it had to be one of the teachers driving the car that morning. There was nothing much the poor chap could have done; even so, he was never the same again. Neither was the boy who pushed him ... a little too forcefully perhaps ... though of course without hint of malicious intent. Alfie died in hospital the following morning. We were with him at the end ... if only to hold his hand.'

We left it there for the night, struggling to find appropriate words to alleviate the outpouring of renewed grief that came with the telling of Alfie's demise. We stayed only long enough to mutter our inadequate condolences before taking our leave. Once outside, I turned to wave at the couple, who were standing with their backs to the light of the hall. It was then I saw he'd returned – Alfie with them once more, smiling his thanks in my direction.

Chapter 48
Nottingham 1968

Stepping inside for the very first time – walking amidst clocks and ornaments, glass and pottery, tables and chairs, baths and sinks and – there he is, late Saturday afternoon. Outside the sky has darkened; it is fitting.

A look of surprised embarrassment and I am ushered away to a quiet corner. Then it's, 'Sorry, son, but it had to happen ... this girl I met ... we're going away ... leaving town for another place ... me and your mother, it was never right ... a new life for me and something better ...'

'Okay, Dad, I sort of knew ... see you sometime ... really must go. Oh, by the way, here's an invitation – August the first if you want to come, but please ... come alone. New life for me as well. One you'd never believe in a million years! Bye, Dad ... wish you well.'

Two weeks had passed since Bob and me had left the Booths' house, and we'd not heard from them since. Bob said he'd tried phoning but to no avail. For my part, I had been to their house on two occasions, knocking on the door, and finding nobody home. At the time, I thought it was a good job I had Ann for company, as people were disappearing out of my life at quite a worrying rate. Then, thankfully, a letter arrived from Edgar, saying sorry they hadn't been in touch, but they'd decided to go to Filey at the last minute to blow the cobwebs away.

The letter went on to say they'd like to meet Bob and me the following Saturday if we could possibly make it.

When I phoned Bob later that day, he said he'd already spoken to Edgar and thought he sounded more like his old self. I was pleased to hear things were getting back to normal and said I'd see him Saturday, noticing the pause before he answered.

'Best not to mention Alfie again, Arthur ... even if you imagine seeing him.'

'I didn't imagine seeing him, Bob; he was there, I can assure you of that. All the same, whether you continue to deny these happenings or not is your prerogative.'

The exchange was meaningful but amiable enough. I recognised that I was becoming hardened to the world around me, choosing my own pathways and beginning to recognise myself for what I was. Perhaps it was time for those around me to accept that too.

***

'I think it's only right to apologise on behalf of Kate and myself for our behaviour when we last met, though I'm sure you understand the emotion of the moment.'

'I don't think it's necessary for you to apologise, Edgar. I think I speak for both of us in saying we fully understand such terrible circumstances would seriously test anyone.'

We were, ironically, sitting in the loungc of the George Hotel – neutral territory, so to speak. Maybe the Booths were reluctant to have me at their house for a while, thinking perhaps that Alfie might put in an appearance again, thereby resurrecting their grief – much as they treasured his memory.

It was left to me to steer the conversation to other matters, and so I reached into my satchel for the report I'd put together some weeks previously.

'I bet I know what you've got in there, Arthur!'

'Yes, Edgar. Jill's provided some interesting cuttings.'

Bob looked confused. He'd missed out on the conversations we'd had about Ann's friend's offer to do some research on our behalf. We'd not had the opportunity to speak of it since the last meeting took a decidedly different turn. Once Bob was on board with the preamble, I began to share the information Jill had obtained, taking great satisfaction in seeing the emergent interest it generated. Reading from the cuttings, I told them of the robbery, detailing the names of those involved, more particularly the parts involving Victor Thurgood's assumed guilt and subsequent disappearance. That in itself raised a few eyebrows, as did the copy of the statement made by the senior partner of the drapery business, one Ethan Critchlow: the injured party who stated that one of his assailants had called the other by the name of George!

With some animation, we spent time deliberating on which of the two Georges we thought might have done the deed, or even if both of them had been involved. Moving on to the demise of George Davy as recounted in a separate report, to their utter amazement, I told them of his death by violent means, most likely murdered by an assailant or assailants unknown – the cause being a significant blow to the skull by an undisclosed heavy object. However, it was noted that small fragments of embedded stone had been found in the wound during the post-mortem process.

We could only guess at the implications and correlations of the other parties: of William Watts there was no mention, nor of Ethel Bentley. It seemed any further evidence relating to associations involving the four long-departed souls was limited to disclosures arising from our regressions and séances.

The ultimate question, therefore, remained unanswered – were we once the characters whose names were written on the pages before us? Or had we simply deluded ourselves into believing the corresponding manifestations were authentic?

'You won't like what I'm going to suggest to you but I'll chance my arm just the same, then you can come at me as you will.'

The Edgar Booth of old had returned to us, the light of his erstwhile enthusiasm shining from his mischievous eyes. That Kate by this time approved of whatever he was about to propose was in little doubt, her own excitement being equally evident.

'Before I go any further, please forgive me,

but I must say something you might not like, Bob. You, of all of us, remain the least convinced about all this. Despite the evidence in front of you, you continue to deny the presence of any existence other than that of this present world. For some reason, you stubbornly resist even the most credible results arising from the regressions you paradoxically conduct. Please tell me … why is that?'

It was a straightforward challenge, and Bob was clearly uncomfortable with the question. He was shifting in his seat, just one of the habits he adopted when becoming overly anxious. I was interested to see how he'd deal with the confrontation. There had been times when I thought the same as Edgar, remembering Bob's relief when Albert Keates claimed he'd cleared his house of the malignant spirit that allegedly haunted his bedroom. How could he possibly deny the existence of the paranormal after going through what he himself said he'd experienced?

'Oh, come on, Edgar, it's not as if I categorically disbelieve there's nothing more to life and death than what we traditionally accept. And I do agree that some of the evidence we've uncovered is compelling, much like what I thought happened in my own house. Nonetheless, I have to balance those occurrences with the logic of my profession. Having treated people suffering from severe self-delusion, I know that to ignore the power of an emotionally charged imagination is dangerously incompetent. The strength of its persuasion is often extraordinary. Dare I say there are many people much like me, people who really don't want to believe in the unexplainable, regardless of how convincing the evidence may be. I think part of me has been wanting to say that for some time, Edgar.'

It was Edgar's turn to fidget. Perhaps he was realising just what he'd created and how much it affected us all in our different ways. Bob was not finished, though. Maybe he was taking the chance to release his bottled-up feelings.

'Please understand my dilemma. Despite everything I've said, I'm extremely worried at the prospect of what we've unearthed. Even so, I find it difficult to resist my natural inquisitiveness; that's why I'm still here, truth be told. Much like you, Edgar, and Kate and Arthur too, I imagine, I simply cannot bring myself to walk away without knowing the truth, whatever it may turn out to be.'

It was a profound statement that underscored the confusion of a brilliant mind – a man in some ways overthinking life. Bob Langham was better at asking questions than answering them, though in this instance, it appeared Edgar Booth was satisfied with his explanation.

'A lot of what you say makes sense, Bob. I asked you that question because what I'm about to propose might cause you in particular to become even more anxious. If that proves to be the case, then it might be a good time to consider if your inquisitiveness alone is enough to make you want to continue the journey.'

Kate Booth chose her moment, purposely interrupting Bob before he had chance to respond.

'If you think about it, Bob, you're the only one here who doesn't claim to have any psychic talent ... or maybe you do. After all, what was lurking in your bedroom if it wasn't a dead person?'

'To be fair, Kate, that's slightly different. Lots of people claim to see ghosts, though not all of them communicate their intent.'

'You're entitled to your opinion, Edgar. But sometimes I think the lines are more blurred than even you believe they are.'

'Touché, madam.'

Even given the seriousness of the moment, I enjoyed seeing them back to their old selves. It made me even more determined not to mention Alfie. It looked like the boy only sought his mother and father when it suited him, like living children do when bored with the drone of adult conversation. Though I'd never actually conversed with him, I supposed the abstract thoughts that entered my mind whenever he appeared might be the beginnings of my own spiritual development. This left me thinking that I needed to improve my skills before actually talking to the dead. The more I opened my mind, the greater my control seemed to be, and I believed that, with practice, I might purposely ignore a presence to the point where I forgot it was there. Kate Booth had been right about that: 'You don't have to see them if you don't want to, Arthur.'

Bob was clearly frustrated. He'd been outed, and found himself in an even greater state of confusion.

'You mean you don't want me to be part of the project anymore, Edgar?'

'You know perfectly well that's not what I meant, Bob. You're as much a part of our group as you always have been. We've been here before, though, haven't we? Only this time, we're approaching the endgame. In principle, your commitment has never been in question, but your belief in the paranormal definitely is. You must decide where you stand, Bob, but before we go any further, please hear me out.'

Edgar was not currently questioning my own resolve, thinking my decision to willingly step into the world of spirituality was sufficient for him to acknowledge my commitment. Even though I was at the beginning of my journey, at least I was now of his kind. Edgar looked at Kate, whose smile of approval was more than enough to confirm her awareness of what he was about to say.

'Spending time in Filey was a spur of the moment decision; we so desperately needed to get away. What happened with Alfie was very trying for both of us, inevitably bringing back bad memories as well as good. In the long run, though, it was the release we'd hungered for, so thank you, Arthur; we both think your purpose in our lives was defined that night.

You have a fundamental goodness within you, and that's why I struggle to come to terms with the premise that you're the living incarnation of George Davy. All the more reason why we should make one final attempt to solve the conundrum.'

He was nearly there. I hadn't missed the telling word he'd uttered only moments before when questioning Bob's commitment – endgame. For some reason, I sensed whatever came soon would represent the final time we worked on the project together before going our separate ways.

'Many years ago, we stood on a hill near Filey in Yorkshire, contemplating the leaden panorama of the sombre North Sea. It was the very week before Alfie came into our lives – a few days away to dream dreams of the family life we'd prayed for. Then, just days ago, we stood on that very spot again, thinking of him much as we do each day. This time, though, thanks to Arthur, it was a different experience – for although we still felt his earthly loss, we knew at last he was happy and at peace.'

Alfie appeared from nowhere then, and I thought they sensed my observation. If they did, I could only hope they were better for knowing.

'We found our peace in Filey, and for the first time in years, we considered ourselves able to plan ahead. In the wake of that, we decided to sell our house and move away, somewhere rural, perhaps. It was something we'd been reticent to do before, believing the house somehow detained Alfie's spirit within its confines. We also questioned what else was holding us back, coming to the conclusion that it was the project itself. At first, it had been nothing more than a passing distraction – a diversion to help us deal with Alfie's crippling loss. Somewhat unsurprisingly, however, it became a preoccupation: a provocative mystery absorbing more and more of our time. Then, in what now seems the blink of the eye, we're near to unravelling the secrets of our past relationships ... and to a degree, we feel there's little more we can materially achieve.'

'Oh, do get to the point, Edgar, for goodness sake!'

'Yes, right, Kate, thank you!'

Edgar Booth was a natural thespian and could be extremely long-winded, though what he had to say was invariably of interest.

'Given our history together, I hardly dare speak the words but ... I think we should conduct one last séance – one last effort to come even closer to the truth.'

I saw Bob's head drop, his chest swelling as he sucked in a deep breath before speaking.

'Seriously, Edgar, do you really think that's advisable? You must consider what happened before. God only knows what your impulsiveness might invoke.'

'So, you're a believer after all then, hey, Bob?'

'Oh, for goodness sake, Edgar!'

'Go on, Edgar, finish off what you were

saying, for crying out loud. We shouldn't be arguing the pros and cons until we've heard you out.'

'Thank you, Arthur, I will. I propose we travel to Newark again. I've already spoken to Bertie and he's okay with that ... providing he and Violet are invited to participate on this occasion.'

'Violet! Didn't you say she was unstable, Edgar?'

'Yes, yes, Arthur, I most likely did. I appreciate she's bloody unpredictable, pardon my French. Nevertheless, truth be told, she's probably the most talented out of all of us. Bertie promised to keep her on a tight rein, so I tentatively agreed, thinking she might just invoke the breakthrough we're looking for.'

'Five psychics might be enough, I suppose ... and then there's Bob, of course; that's if he decides to join us.'

Bob grimaced at my audacity: true to form, shifting in his seat and gnawing at his lip.

'Edgar, wearing my professional hat, I must say I think your proposal is unwarrantable if not downright hazardous. Poor Kate's suffered more than enough. How on earth could you possibly subject her to any further ...'

'You need to understand it was my suggestion, Bob. As I've said before, I'm prepared to take the risk if there's a chance of settling things. If nothing comes of it, at least we'll have tried our best before finally calling it a day.'

Edgar Booth raised his eyebrows at that,

throwing up his arms to demonstrate his growing impatience.

'What do you think, Arthur? Are you for or against?'

'I have to agree with Kate. After all, what've we got to lose? We've come this far together, so I think we should see it through and be done with it once and for all. Anyway, if we're honest, I reckon we're naturally coming to the end of our endeavours.'

There he was again, only this time he wasn't acknowledging me – instead he was staring lovingly at his parents, an iridescent radiance about his form. Then, little by little, he became less and less distinct, languidly melding into a glow of light until he was completely gone. I sensed Alfie was beginning his journey into a better place, leaving his loved ones to complete their earthly lives, waiting in the transcendent hinterlands for them to follow.

Chapter 49
Nottingham 1968

I'm sure they were there before I closed my eyes – four shapes in the darkness – us or them? Had they come to reveal the truth, or had they come to seek it?

When I woke to the early light, there were no such shapes, only the usual shadows. Once upon a time, I used to wonder if anything was there ... now I know there is. The reckoning is near. What will I do when this is gone? Will I nurture the gift that grows within me? Or will I resist its demands? Whatever is to become of my being?

It was difficult for me to comprehend the empty feeling and sense of loss that saddened me. These people were intimates I had grown close to and learned from. Could this really be our final venture together?

The four of us were in Bob's car again, this time our company devoid of quips and banal conversation. Even the weather suited our common mood: spring rain thudding at metal and glass, squeaking wipers fighting against the drumming squalls. Without much comment, we passed the minster and the apple garden before passing through the eagled portal, crunching gravel as we came to a rest.

'Nice weather you've brought with you, I must say!'

Albert Keates was lively and looking spruce,

a sharp haircut accentuating the angular jut of his jaw.

'It's been like this all the way here, absolutely pouring down.'

Kate Booth was attempting to overcome the atmosphere that lingered from our sullen journey, the ambience of the house doing little to lift our mood. The furniture was arranged differently this time – the same chairs, but placed around a smaller table, its top already bearing the obligatory candle. There was no sign of Violet and no reference to her absence. I wondered if Keates had thought better of the idea. Then, as if to answer my question, I detected the sound of her snapping heels on the bare floorboards.

We turned as one to see Violet Manners framed in the doorway. Ever the attention seeker, Violet milked her moment in the spotlight. Then, after pausing to treat us to her customary wave, she commenced to promenade in our direction.

''Lo, everyone, lousy weather, in't it?'

Violet did love a miniskirt, jet black this one, complimented with matching heels and heavy mascara.

'No need for introductions. We all know each other and why we're here ... so, shall we?'

Albert Keates ushered us to our respective seats, nodding imperiously at Violet, who obligingly clicked her way to the sideboard, returning to the table with glasses and a large carafe of water.

'I thought we'd get down to business

straightaway, maybe have a drink and socialise once we're finished ... if that's okay with everybody?

We nodded and muttered our approvals, Edgar Booth then tapping the table with the edge of his glass to attract our attention.

'Before we begin, I'd first like to voice our gratitude to Bertie for playing host yet again. Extremely generous of you, Bertie, I must say. Thank you kindly.'

'My pleasure. Thanks for inviting us to participate – Violet and I are looking forward to it. I've briefly explained things to Violet, by the way: the regressions and the history you've uncovered. Rightly or wrongly, I also thought to mention that monkey business at your place, Bob. Everything still okay, is it?'

The question obviously took Bob by surprise and he seemed discomfited by it. He'd been reluctant to attend at first, but in the end, he claimed he couldn't resist the possibility of finding the truth.

'Yeah, everything's fine, Bertie ... thanks again for what you did.'

Bob's tone suggested he wished he'd never mentioned his problem in the first place, such was his obvious embarrassment.

'I'm pleased to hear it, Bob. Always glad to be of help.'

I looked to see Violet's reaction and straightaway wished I hadn't. She responded with a flirtatious smile and blatantly winked at me. It looked like being an interesting evening. The extra participants had already brought a distinctively different edge to the gathering. Who knew what Albert Keates and Violet Manners would get up to as the evening continued?

'If we're all ready to begin ... Edgar, if you'd be so kind.'

'Thanks a lot, Bertie. Well, then, it was agreed between the four of us that we'd have one last shot at getting to the truth by holding a group séance, hoping we might contact one or more of the spirits I and others believe were our spiritual predecessors. Understandably, there's conjecture as to whether or not the four of us, singularly or collectively, actually knew one another during the Victorian era. I realise of late that my original proposition might be something of a longshot. Nevertheless, interesting evidence remains to support my claim. We shall see.'

Edgar turned to his wife as if to prompt her, Kate smiling in return before quite deliberately glancing from Bob to myself before preparing herself to speak.

'I know exactly how much this business means to Edgar and the effort he's put into it. Lord knows, simply finding Arthur was difficult enough, let alone persuading him and Bob to believe in what must have sounded like a ridiculous theory. Since then, however, we've shared some interesting experiences. For my part, I was nervous to start with, worrying that our late son might be negatively affected by the spiritual nature of the undertaking. Nevertheless, Edgar can be very persuasive, so in the end, I agreed to become involved. Anyway, what I really wanted to say at this point is that whether or not we find any more proof, I want to say how much both of us think of Bob and Arthur. You've become like family, and we've shared an awful lot together, so ... we'd like to say thanks to you both for joining us on this extraordinary journey.'

Kate couldn't bring herself to say much more, and she really didn't need to. I recognised the sincerity of her feelings and I'm sure Bob did too – you didn't have to be psychic to sense that. When we responded in kind, I thought our words seemed inadequate, yet they were heartfelt all the same. Bertie and Violet had the good grace to respect the moment, neither of them saying a word or showing any signs of impatience. I had a feeling that we'd prematurely said our formal goodbyes, that what remained of the parting of ways would follow more naturally. For now, though, it was time for business to commence.

***

The curtains were drawn, and a million motes haphazardly descended into the uncertain light of the candle, the faces round the table shimmering in the radiance of its faltering flame. Awkwardly, we entwined our hands – Kate's to my left, warm and dry, Violet's to my right, soft and clammy.

'Let's take a moment to concentrate our

thoughts ... reflect on the reasons we're gathered here.'

The patter of rain and the relaxed resonance of Edgar Booth's voice fittingly prepared us for what we were about to engage ourselves in: attempting to contact long-dead people whose names had become familiar, our only related and quantifiable image being that of a man named Victor Thurgood. Although Edgar Booth had once claimed to have perceived the ghost of George Davy, I had to question his assertion, thinking at the time it was more likely an innocuous ploy designed to intensify our interest.

An awkward silence followed Edgar's pronouncement, and looking round the table, I couldn't help noticing the air of sombreness, some of the expressions wary and constrained. Yet when glancing at Violet Manners, I found her smiling somewhat immaturely. Maybe it was little more than a game to her – or was she aware of something we had not yet distinguished?

I don't think mine was the only mind wandering when the candle flame flickered wildly for no explainable reason. Only seconds after that, an indeterminate breeze came to cool my face. Sensing something of indefinite nature had arrived, I anxiously looked about me for corroboration, noticing Violet had turned to look directly at me, the smile on her face more hesitant than it had been. I thought Edgar must also have noticed something anomalous, his eyes darting from one to the other as though seeking confirmation of his intuition.

'If a spirit has joined us … please make yourself known.'

It might have been coincidental, but Edgar's timely words caused me to shudder, even more so when Kate's hand squeezed mine in what I first thought was an act of reassurance. Edgar noticed our activity, his eyes narrowing when they found mine. Though he said nothing, I thought the subsequent look he gave Violet Manners was more than a passing glance.

'I repeat … please … make yourself known. I sense someone is here with us.'

With those words, my left hand began to shake, yet not by my own volition. Kate's grip on me was intensifying, sharp fingernails drawing blood from my ruptured skin. In that moment, I thought to break the circle, convinced she was under attack in some way. Before I could, though, Kate Booth stilled her writhing and slouched forward, her head twitching fitfully before slumping to her chest. There was no movement round the table. More remarkably, Edgar Booth remained in his seat, staring at his wife as if in expectation. Turning to Kate, I watched her mouth open, her lips quivering as though making ready to speak, the resonance from within her only too familiar.

Ah'm 'ere, right enough … no need to call fer me again.

Kate Booth raises her head slightly and to one side, her sneering lips strangely out of sync with the words she speaks in another's voice.

Edgar straightens his back and bluntly imposes himself.

Is that you that speaks, George Davy?

Ah, in the bleddy graveyard afore ah were even dead ... yer bastards!

I remember the headline – 'Local Man Found Dead in Cemetery' – shivering at the verification, thinking surely it cannot be anybody but George Davy.

Who are you calling bastards, George?

Edgar is bravely confrontational, though his underlying anxiety is obvious. More so when he sharply glances at Kate, a disturbing cackle emanating from deep within her. Then there is only the irregular swell of her laboured breathing, until ...

She knows me, alright ... especially now ah'm inside her ... at long last.

There is more cackling, only this time cruder and more strident. Kate's body begins to tremble, her grip on my hand tightening accordingly. Despite the pain of her nails digging ever deeper into my flesh, I tolerate it, sensing that in some way, I am part of her salvation.

'There's more than one of 'em, oh my goodness!'

It is Violet's voice. She's staring at Kate through widening eyes, skewing her mouth in a manner of disbelief. I turn to Edgar, desperate for him to take control, find him squinting in Kate's direction.

The circle of hands is broken. Albert Keates rises decisively from his chair, fierce determination in his expression. Violet's hand immediately relinquishes mine, as, thankfully, does Kate's – she has lost control of herself and is rising to her feet as though manipulated, robotically clawing at something only she can see. Albert Keates has come to stand beside her, without further ado uttering a rapid stream of incomprehensible words.

I become aware of the lightest of touches on my shoulder ... unspoken words impelling me to leave that place. Though I take comfort from her protective advice, I fear I must stay until this matter is resolved.

I must be missing time ... drifting to awareness from a soporific malaise. When I blink my eyes, Albert Keates is near to where I last saw him, spitting words at something unseen. Edgar is with him, visibly exasperated at his failure to calm his wife's worsening condition. Despite their combined competence, both men are being tested to their limits. Bob Langham arrives to grapple with the woman, who seems uncontrollable.

'Ooh, that's a mistake, in't it?'

I swing towards Violet; the untimely nonchalance of her words upsets me, the resentment in my response transparently obvious.

'What did you just say, Violet?'

She stares past me, eyes like saucers. I turn back to see Bob Langham straining to disengage from Kate's desperate attentions, shocked when he realises he's the sole focus of her fury. Edgar Booth and Bertie Keates move in as one to intervene, only to be hurled aside like children, though their interference allows Bob to break away. Kate Booth follows, close on his heels, clawing the air in his wake.

Crouching like a stalking predator, Albert Keates hurries after them, his invocations heavy with exasperation. Breathlessly scrambling to his feet, Edgar pursues the curious procession until they come to a place where the candlelight barely penetrates the shadows. It makes me think of the light switch by the door, reasoning that an infusion of bright light might regenerate a degree of normality. Then I remember my feet are like lead ... that time is distorted and moves without me.

'Rouse yourself, Arthur ... Arthur ... do something! Like that other time!'

Again, it's like I've woken from the deepest of sleeps, and without the slightest idea of what she's talking about.

'Violet, I don't know what you mean ... my feet won't move ... switch the damn lights on, please!'

After grinning and shaking her head, Violet nods to somewhere behind me. When I turn my head, I discover a frightful pastiche: Kate

Booth, slumped and splayed, lies with an equally comatose Albert Keates, the pair oblivious to the engagement being enacted beside them. Bob Langham, his bloodied features contorted with rage, is physically assaulting Edgar Booth, who curls into a ball against his superior physicality.

That something is manipulating me is beyond any doubt, and if proof were needed, my feet are released from their indiscernible shackles. I simply cannot stand to witness an elderly man being beaten into submission. Hurling myself at Bob Langham, the momentum of my advance smashes him into the wall, the blundering collision forcing the breath from his lungs. Then, as I awkwardly gather myself to restrain his weakened body, I am forcefully brushed aside. Having woken from his unsolicited slumbers, Bertie Keates has come to my aid, rapidly immobilising Bob Langham in a most professional and effective manner.

Only when it was over did I come to assess the quagmire of confusion that had enveloped me throughout the outbreak of unmitigated violence. Though I had some recollection of certain phases, the lapses continued to elude me. Kate Booth had recovered her senses. Edgar, bruised and dishevelled, was more slowly becoming his customary self. Despite his bloodcurdling transition, we worried for Bob Langham the most. Albert Keates assured us Bob was simply knocked out and would recover without lasting damage. Having witnessed Bob's controlled disablement at Keates's hands, not one of us thought to question his prognosis.

After cleaning and tidying ourselves as best we could, we took advantage of Albert Keates's drink's cabinet, a few generous measures assisting our return to relative normality. It was then that Violet, for reasons known only to herself, took me to one side, clearly impatient to update me on what I had missed. Positioning herself a little too closely, she revealed that Bob Langham had retreated, with Kate after him: that much I did remember, and the fact that Albert Keates and Edgar Booth followed them in that order. I had a vision of that ghastly procession in my head, thinking it was after that when I blanked.

According to Violet, during my time away, as she called it, whatever was possessing Kate began to attack Bob Langham in a frenzy. And when Albert Keates intervened, he received an accidental elbow of sufficient force to send him down, his head hitting the floor, putting him out like a light.

Violet went on to say that it was about the same time as Bob Langham began his transformation. The normally mild academic had apparently morphed into a savage beast, his intent being to violently assault Kate Booth and anyone else within touching distance. I think it must have been around that point when I returned from wherever I'd been, although Violet rather derogatorily proclaimed that I'd most probably fainted.

Violet had returned to take her seat at the table, whilst the rest of us stood and watched Albert Keates helping Bob to his feet. Keates had volunteered himself, saying it might be best because nobody really knew how Bob would react when he surfaced from his stupor. As it turned out, Bob was simply in a state of bewilderment. Kate Booth, regardless of the violent confrontation, went to comfort him, there being no hint of consequent animosity between them. After all, what had passed was not of their doing; the unquestionable culprit had returned to wherever he abided when not intruding on our earthly lives.

Aware that the room was yet in a state of semi-darkness, I thought to turn on the light by the door. However, when I came within touching distance, her voice sharply carried across the room.

'Not yet, Arthur. We need to continue; the opportunity's too good to ignore.'

The thought of arguing the point with Violet Manners in such circumstances was not an attractive one, and I think I was not alone in thinking that. Almost as one, we turned towards her, as if in thrall to her compelling superiority. Light from the guttering candle was playing on her face, her hands provocatively splayed on the table in anticipation.

'Looks like I'm the only one here that can

sense them! They'll be breaking down the doors before the rest of yer notice! Who'd a' thought that, then, hey? Room full o' so-called psychics ...'

Violet was enjoying her newfound ascendency, her posturing clearly irritating some more than others – not least Edgar Booth and Albert Keates.

Though discernibly suffering from his injuries, it was something like the Bob Langham we knew who spoke for the first time since stirring from his unconsciousness.

'For God's sake, will somebody please explain what the bloody hell's going on?'

In truth, most of what he demanded to hear rather negatively involved himself. With that foremost in our minds, what could we say? It simply wasn't the moment to conduct an inquiry. Furthermore, Violet was demanding our attention, and, unfathomably, nobody seemed inclined to question her authority. We must have resembled a gathering of shuffling zombies as we grudgingly made our way back to the table. Violet scrutinised us with narrowed eyes as we came to take our seats. Though weary and disenchanted, we settled ourselves with a consensus of grim acceptance.

Seated for only a few seconds, I felt a breath of air once again brush by my cheek. I thought I must be getting used to her arrivals, instinctively knowing when she was there, if only at those times she wanted me to. Then I had to wonder if she was always there, only choosing to make herself known on particular

occasions. I looked to catch Edgar's attention, wondering if he could see her too. After all, that was how this crazy undertaking had begun – meeting him in The Horse and Groom that fateful day – the strange old man who stepped in from the rain.
Violet was commanding the table. Evidently, the séance was about to resume, and unreservedly under her influence. It appeared even Albert Keates was ceding to his niece's authority, though his acceptance was clearly not without its humiliation. I remembered Edgar saying he suspected a spiritual potency in Violet that exceeded that of anyone else currently in the room. Then I thought that maybe Albert Keates had known that all along. Furthermore, it crossed my mind that Violet might in some respect have been associated with the four of us in those faraway days. The winding pathways of fate had led us to Albert Keates and then in turn to Violet Manners: the very medium we now, somewhat grudgingly, looked to for enlightenment. Was the mischievous Violet the keeper of the elusive door? Was she about to turn the key?

During the short time I had known her, I thought Violet Manners' demeanour to be infantile and annoyingly facetious. Whether that had been a façade or not was debatable. However, at that moment, there was no mistaking her character, her words unemotional and without embellishment. It was an unlikely style that she adopted but impossibly hypnotic.

Whoever's there ... speak up and tell me who you are.

To our consternation, Kate slumps forward as though to order. This time she is smiling contentedly, though, to all intents, serenely departing her earthly consciousness. It seems that on this occasion, whoever is about to borrow her body enters with good intent.

Come on then, I know yer there ... get on with it and tell us yer name.

Violet's unsophisticated approach is remorseless, her staring eyes shimmering in the candlelight.

When at last it comes, the responding voice is inordinately calm.

Why it's me, sweetheart ... Billy ...

I know full well who Billy is. Even so, his voice awakens a swarm of dormant butterflies. And when I look around, I notice Edgar has paled – though there is a degree of relief in his expression. Then, when turning my attention to Bob Langham, I get no sense of reassurance from his anxious look.

Billy, you say? Billy who?

Them as matters already know.

The voice is clear. There is no wheezing or coughing to break its resonance. That notwithstanding, there is no doubting that William Watts is with us. The question remains: are the others with him? Kate Booth wakes from her stupor sooner than expected. If that means Billy has departed, then his visitation has been disappointingly brief. Kate looks mystified by the attention she's receiving and looks to her husband questioningly. He nods and smiles and cannot help breaking the ensuing silence.

'It was him, Kate – William Watts himself. At least we got that much right.'

We are distracted by a mewling sound that cuts into Edgar's pronouncement and look to see Violet's head rolling from side to side, her mouth languorously opening and closing, the whitened bulbs of her eyes almost lost under her mascaraed lids. Remarkably, the voice that comes from her is not unworldly in its nature; it is still her own.

There's too many talkin' at once ... settle down, will yer!

'Ask about George Davy, Violet ... ask them!'

Bob Langham has rudely interrupted Violet's interaction. His lips are drawn back and his face burns red with anger – am I alone in thinking he's turning again? There is no response from Violet Manners. Then, when her head turns to the ceiling and her mouth opens vacuously, I can only believe she has disengaged herself from our presence.

I hear yer well enough, yer bastards ... I hear yer.

It's not Violet but Bob who's snarling menacingly at us. Albert Keates jumps to his feet, clenching and unclenching his fists meaningfully, all the while watching Bob Langham like a hawk. Edgar and Kate Booth exchange anxious glances, emphasising the concern that grows amongst us. Although the circle is broken for the second time that evening, the otherworldly exchange continues on regardless of their activity.

Awful dark and misty, but he's there right enough ... he's harmless now ...

I am confused, thinking, *why are those words coming from Violet?* I am slipping into the darkness again ...

I know it's she that soars with me. I can discern her imprecise form in my peripheral vision. She keeps perfect pace by my shoulder. Then, when I turn to observe her the better, she swiftly twists away. It would seem I am never to wholly observe her, at least not in this life. I have a perception of this place, of something not yet attained. There are others here, much like me, who drift and hover, aimlessly searching. Some glide towards me with enquiring eyes, then with fresh purpose, they fly to another. They are fleetingly familiar ... yet they are not of my existence.

There it is again, that distant yet familiar voice ... calling ... demanding ...

Tell us yer name.

I am confused ... does the voice call to me?

Who is there? Who has come to us?

There is a light at the end of the interlacing spiral. Her voice beckons me towards it, drawing me into its encirclement.

Will yer please tell us yer name!

My name is Victor.

The smooth hand that gently squeezes mine belongs to Kate Booth.

'You went away somewhere again, Arthur. Seems you're making a habit of doing that. Only this time was different – on this occasion, someone else's voice came out of you! Do you remember anything about that?'

It wasn't too different from waking from a regression, the predominant variation being that when I opened my eyes, there was an audience staring with bemusement in my direction. When I finally recovered my faculties, the first thing I noticed was Edgar Booth absent-mindedly shaking his head, although he did have a smile on his face. Violet Manners was smiling too, only in a more self-satisfied sort of way. When I looked at Albert Keates, however, I sensed an unmistakeable air of irritation.

Nevertheless, in the end it was Bob Langham who took my attention the most. He sat with his head to one side as though intellectually solving a conundrum. I couldn't help thinking there was an element of resentment accompanying his expression when he eventually caught me looking at him.

'It's really difficult, Kate. The thing that immediately comes to mind is wherever I went to, it had a familiarity about it. And I know I wasn't alone. That's really all I can be certain of.'

'Well, I can tell you that when that voice came out of you, Arthur, it was extremely informative.'

I looked round in astonishment, understanding then why I had become the sole focus of attention, Edgar Booth in particular looking at me like the cat that got the cream.

'I dread to think what I might have been saying. Do I really want to hear what it was?'

'In the beginning, you were mumbling away about nothing much that made any proper sense. Violet really had to work hard to get anything coherent out of you, but then when she did, it was well worth waiting for.'

Everything was closing in on me, the evening developing beyond anything we might have reasonably expected. From a personal viewpoint, I was finding it difficult to come to terms with the chaotic memories of violence, and friendships broken and mended in mere moments of time. The regressions had been an acceptable diversion. Although occasionally disturbing, they were an absorbing part of a greater mystery. Being informed that I'd been an unwitting intermediary in a spiritual séance, however, was an entirely different kettle of fish.

'It was Victor Thurgood whose voice came out of you, Arthur. That's three out of the four lives we've unearthed, young man! George Davy's presence earlier this evening was prolific, even though it came at a higher cost than any of his previous visitations. However, this time, under psychic conditions, we've heard from both William Watts and Victor Thurgood for the very first time. Somewhat annoyingly, though, that leaves Ethel Bentley out on a limb - the only one yet to come through in this particular séance.'

'She was with them, though, Edgar! She might not have spoken to us, but she was definitely with them ... Arthur said as much ... or as Victor, he did, if you want to look at it that way.'

I swung in my seat and stared at her in astonishment. Kate Booth made a face like a naughty schoolgirl caught with her fingers in the pastry bowl.

'Oh, I did, did I? And exactly what did I have to say?'

'Why don't we listen to the tape, Arthur? I think that might be best in the circumstances.'

'Tape? What tape?'

'The tape Bertie switched on at the beginning of the evening. It's been running all the time, until just now, apparently: everything that's gone on since we first sat down.'

I glanced at Keates. He was holding his palms out in mock defence.

'Folk don't always act naturally when they know they're being recorded, Arthur, and Edgar did agree beforehand.'

When Albert Keates walked to the sideboard and flicked the play switch, the by now familiar butterflies stirred within my stomach, though more than they ever had before.

There is a note of exasperation in Violet Manner's voice.

Will yer please tell us yer name!

Victor.

There yer go. Well, thanks a lot, Victor. You took yer time, though, din't yer?

It is a fascinating style that Violet adopts.

Are yer still there, Victor?

Here, yes ... yes.

The voice fades in and out – the tape, maybe. I keep reminding myself it's me the voice is coming from, and I've never sounded more expressive.

Where are you, then, Victor?

There is a sharp intake of breath. When it arrives, the answer conveys a sense of desolation.

Woods ... earth ...

What woods yer talkin' about, then, Victor? Tell me whereabouts the woods are.

For a while there is nothing but laboured breathing.

How would I know where they are?

What's yer full name, Victor?

Thurgood ... it's Victor Thurgood ... oh ...

There is a faint sobbing from him. Kate squeezes my hand and I wince at the memory of her flaying nails.

What happened to yer, Victor?

It is a seminal moment and we are close to an answer. He has drawn close to me, so much so, I imagine our spirits mingling.

Dead in the ground ... own fault ... should have gone, should have let things be ... too late now.

What things, Victor? Tell us what yer mean.

No matter ... must take my place ... there's a path where they wait for me ... oh, dear Eth.

Eth's waiting for yer, is she?
Must go ... too late now.

It is the last we hear from him. I can only hope that Victor Thurgood is to finally escape the perdition that ensnared him.

'Let that be an end to it, Violet. Surely we've had enough for one day!'

Rather surprisingly, Albert Keates's terseness had an unwelcome effect when it brought us down to earth.

'If I'd known it was going to turn out like this, Edgar, I might have made my apologies!'

'Yes, indeed. Sorry for the pandemonium, Bertie, although you know as well as I do, you can never tell what's going to happen with these kinds of sessions.'

'Even so, Edgar, you must admit this evening threw up a few more unexpected ...'

'Quiet! Another's coming through... and of her own free will.'

'A woman! Goodness me, restore the circle immediately!'

Edgar Booth reached out his hands and encouraged everyone to do the same. Muttering under his breath, Albert Keates grudgingly returned to his seat, thereby reunifying the broken circle. The stub of the candle was all but spent, the stink of its pending demise heavy and noxious. There looked to be only minutes remaining of its diminishing light before darkness came to envelop us.

You are welcome at the table ... what's yer

name?

We look around in expectation, nervously wondering who has been chosen to deliver the words on this occasion. Against the odds, strangely, it is Violet herself, eyes closing, head swaying to a rhythm only she can perceive. Then ...

It's me, sweetheart ... must hurry, no time ...

The voice is strongly accented and coarse, much like that of the one she speaks through.

Why such a hurry? What yer rushin' for?

It is more natural – a reciprocal conversation. I look to Edgar and furrow my brow. He reads my question, shrugs, and tightens his mouth as if to say so what?

The game's hover, me duck ... as bin fer a while, since ...

Tell us yer name, then ... me duck!

Violet's abrasiveness equals that of the spirit's candid tones.

There's folk there who already know, sweetheart.

All the same ... tell me!

Ooh ... yo a grouchy tart, ain't yer?

Oh, alright then ... please ... tell me yer name.

We hear a chuckle, and then another of quite different tone; someone is with her.

Eth, they call me.

You're Ethel Bentley?

Ah, I am.

Who's there with yer, Eth?

All on em ... even George.

Kate Booth is agitated, interrupting the exchange in her unrestrained impatience.

'Ask if Billy's with her ... and Victor.'

At first, only Violet's head is twitching, the convulsions then running to her arms and shoulders. It is hard not to notice the unmistakeable look of concern that crosses Albert Keates's face. At the same time as I worry for others, I also worry for myself. That feeling is taking me again – it becomes overpowering, the feeling of time passing ...

They tremble at Violet's shoulder like gossamer webs in a puff of air. And standing apart from them is another such form, this one alone, as if confined in a restraining mist. I am of no physical form, yet I struggle to penetrate the fluctuating vapours, wishing them still enough for me to discern their features.

Drifting closer, perhaps on the very current that causes the wraiths to quiver, I see they observe those that imagine the presence of their souls – save for the one who stands apart with hate in his eyes ... the only one to be staring at me. At last I recognise the bond between us, the transcendent unison of lives lived through the course of time.

Frustratingly, they begin to fade, turning as one to tread the requisite path – following the one that guides them to their destination ... he is so young ... so small.

As they turn to look back in farewell, I think I see him smile at last and nod his little head towards me.

Peace comes to me in that moment ... and to

him too, I hope.

Once it was over, we returned to ourselves and to the vestiges of normality – a few drinks and occasional titters of nervous laughter. Edgar Booth and Albert Keates took themselves to a corner, their conversation decidedly animated. By design or happenstance, Violet Manners had chosen to sit with Bob. I think like me, the others had discovered an entirely different aspect of Violet's character that evening, further exhibited by the compassion she was currently awarding Bob Langham, a man whose quantifiable world had been turned on its head.

'It's starting to feel a bit like our last waltz, Arthur.'

'Yeah, I must admit, it looks a bit that way, Kate.'

'Tell me what you really saw when you were ... away.'

'Like I said, Kate ... ghosts ...just ghosts, and maybe only in my mind.'

'Don't give me that old nonsense, Arthur. You know what you saw, and it wasn't your imagination.'

'I don't really know why you're so desperate to confirm what you already know, Kate.'

'I need to be absolutely certain they were all there, Arthur. It means a lot to me ... you mean a lot to me. You always have.'

'Of course they were all there, the four of them together. Though the one I thought was definitely George Davy stood apart from the others. It was very much three and one.'

'It looks like George has finally been put to rest, then, regardless of his history. We can only hope he finds some peace; after all, he was once a human being like the rest of us.'

'Yeah, I get the feeling you're not alone in wishing for that.'

'We'll never know the entire truth, will we, Arthur?'

'Probably not, but I know I won't be looking for it anymore.'

'Just between the two of us, Arthur, I know deep down that me and Edgar were once Ethel and Billy. And I'm just as sure there was something or other going on between Ethel and Victor.'

'Whatever are you suggesting, Kate Booth?!'

'What did I just say, Arthur? We'll never really know the truth for sure, will we?'

There was a glint in her eye when she squeezed my hand, and I couldn't help but give her a cuddle. There was certainly a tear in my eye, and I wasn't surprised to see Kate welling up when we came to pull apart.

'What about Bob, though, Arthur? He must be feeling terrible right now – that dreadful beast possessing him like that, and on top of everything that went on at his house. Who'd have believed what happened to him? The poor chap took quite a beating, one way or another.'

'Yeah, you can't help feeling sorry for him. At the same time, I can't help feeling a sense of relief, if I'm honest.'

‘Yes, I can understand that, Arthur. After all… who’d want to be the living incarnation …?’

We parted at that, a sigh coming from me, not for myself, but for her. It had been a difficult decision, but in the end, on balance, I think it was the correct and compassionate one. What good could come from me telling her Alfie had passed forever? Or even that he’d been with those four at the end, guiding them into the light. I will remember his mischievous smile to my own dying day, forever wondering why it reminded me of Violet Manners.

Chapter 50
Nottingham 1968

So many well-wishers wishing us well. Gifts and well-meant platitudes. We meet and greet and pass the time, waiting for the bells to toll ... and for the belle to arrive. And when she does, in all her beauty, my heart soars skyward, those infernal butterflies now dancing a jollier tune in my churning belly.

Edgar leads her to the altar. How generous of him, how generous of her.

Standing on the brink of our mutual life, we must wonder at our future – at the good days to come and at the bad that must accompany them. Then the vows, the ring and the kiss that seals it all – such are the moments of that happy day.

The speeches were history and the food had been cleared. And as the sun lowered to ease the baking heat of late afternoon, the music began to take us deep into the night. Taking the lead, as was the custom, we nervously stepped through the primitive movements of our dance, our clumsy efforts duly earning a round of obligatory applause.

Once the reception had gathered pace of its own accord, Ann and me, as man and wife, tapped our toes and observed our guests. The modest dancefloor, crowded with gyrating figures, was surrounded by tables abandoned by eager dancers or attended by smatterings of family and friends. It seemed all the phases of our lives were represented there that evening – our families, of course, and friends from work, past and present.

Buskin and Daphne turned up with genuine smiles and generous presents – the Booths likewise. I had only half expected Bob Langham to attend, given our lack of recent contact. But there he was, smiling wanly, arm in arm with Julie Sommers. The escalating guest list precluded a number of people we simply couldn't accommodate – Albert Keates and Violet Manners being amongst those whose absences were not desperately regretted. I couldn't begin to imagine what Violet might have resorted to when under the influence of alcohol.

We thought we ought to circulate and thank people for joining us in our celebration, and for the gifts they'd so generously donated. Once we'd done the rounds, we separated, each to spend special time with close friends and family. My lot were huddled around one of the larger tables, only Grandad missing, Grandma snorting that he was off his face somewhere and me thinking she wasn't too far behind in that respect. Mam had knocked a few back too, by the looks of her. She embraced me tightly and shed a few demonstrative tears – some for me and some for her own abandoned self. My sisters were similarly emotional, hugging and kissing me in front of their smirking boyfriends. Then Grandma stood and pulled me to her, slurring that I had matured at last and wasn't such a prat anymore. Alcohol does that to people sometimes.

Searching for Grandad, I found him sitting at a table with Dad, himself the cause of much negative emotion. After fetching a pint, I made my way to where they sat, unceremoniously plonking myself between them.

'Bit like old times, don't you think?'

They each gave me a look and burst out laughing, the fact we'd had a drink or two making things a little more comfortable between us. Then Dad passed the fags round and told us once more how sorry he was and how badly he'd let everyone down – particularly Mam, me and my sisters – then telling us yet again how he'd needed to get away, all the same. Always two sides to every story, he reckoned.

After he'd rambled on in similar vein for a while, Grandad intervened with one of his hackneyed jokes, purposely lightening the mood, if only momentarily. And so after a few awkward silences, we agreed to call it a day, me warmly embracing Grandad Fred before turning awkwardly to Dad. He squeezed my hand for a while before letting go, leaving me there with a jaded smile and a lasting comment.

'Good to see you settled and happy, Arthur. Ann's a lovely girl. Be sure to keep in touch.'

Barely withstanding the emotion of the moment, I simply nodded and turned away to where the Booths and Bob Langham were seated. Julie Sommers was standing to one side, deep in conversation with Buskin and the busty Daphne, an incongruous encounter if ever there was one.

The last knockings of a memorable day found the four of us together again, perchance for the very last time. After going through the necessary motions and thanking them for their gifts, I thought to say how interesting it had been working with them on the project, and how much I would miss seeing them. We chatted in similar manner for a few minutes before Bob broached the inevitable question I had expected but didn't want to answer.

'Before we go our separate ways, Arthur, I really need you to answer me something, if you would.'

He'd unthinkingly lapsed into professional mode, which I didn't think appropriate in the circumstances. Intending to remind him of the occasion, I immediately relented when I saw the desperation edging from behind his impersonal façade.

'And what question would that be, then, Bob?'

It came out harsher than I'd meant it to, and although he appeared discomfited, he nevertheless carried on.

'I realise I've been a difficult beggar at times, often airing contradictory views, but despite our individual differences, I want to say that I genuinely think a lot of you all. Even so, Arthur, I really do need to hear the truth about …'

'About who you were in another time –

which one of those four lives you were?'

'Precisely that, Arthur. I think it boils down to the two of us, doesn't it? You or me. You claim to have experienced them all, so it seems you're best placed to answer that particular question.'

'And it's a difficult one to answer, Bob – but here's a suggestion – I'll tell you what I think, okay, but first I need to know what you think the answer is?'

He blew out of the corner of his mouth, obviously nervous about revealing his hand before I exposed mine. It wasn't what he was expecting, and it gave him pause for thought.

'It's just as difficult for me as it is for you, Arthur. What occurred at Bertie's house was nothing short of horrific. Since I learned about my behaviour that night, you can appreciate how much it's played on my mind. If it weren't for Julie supporting me, I think I might have had myself committed, although in actuality, I remember little of it – something I think common to most of us at times. All the same, I've a nagging feeling I couldn't have been anyone other than George Davy ... and that's the infernal truth of it!'

He gritted his teeth and screwed his eyes against the pain of his admittance. I felt for him then, much as I think we all did. He was literally spoiling the party, but I could see how close he was to breaking down completely.

'I wouldn't be so sure if I were you, Bob. I know I'm certainly not.'

The three of them regarded me with varying

degrees of curiosity, and perhaps for differing reasons.

'Remember the early days, everybody? I reckon all of you were pretty certain who George was at that point – why, even I was thinking along those lines. In fact, the only glimmer of hope I had was when Albert Keates said something about spirits not always being connected to the obvious person – that the one thought to Davy therefore, might be attributed to any of us, even someone not of our circle. Even so, I remained convinced it was me, and much like yourself, Bob, I detested the thought of inheriting George Davy's soul.'

He looked at me long and hard before responding, studying my body language much as he might a client.

'I understand what you're saying, Arthur, but at the end of the day, you admitted to seeing them – more importantly claiming you thought one of them acknowledged you more directly than the others ... as if you shared something, perhaps. The crunch comes with Victor Thurgood. You know what he looked like from his photograph. Therefore, the question gets simpler – was it him who singled you out? Were you Victor Thurgood all those years ago ... or was it me?'

If anyone doubted that eyes alone have the capacity to radiate a heartfelt plea, then they would only need to have looked into Bob Langham's own eyes to find the incontrovertible answer.

'We're never going to know for sure, Bob.

Truth is, I really can't be certain either way. You need to appreciate that wherever I was at the time, the figures I saw were indistinct. Be that as it may, I admit that for one fleeting moment I imagined it to be George Davy that sought to catch my eye.'

The trace of an approving smile fractured Edgar Booth's tight-lipped mouth only a moment before he intervened.

'There you have it, Bob – as much as we ponder, we can never be sure of the exactitude of our lives, past or present, so maybe it's best we leave it there. We are what we are at this time and not what we were before. We must literally put the past behind us and get on with our contemporary existences. George Davy, Victor Thurgood: it's not really of any consequence now. They're gone, yet we are here. And we must do our utmost to enjoy the lives we have now ... whilst we can.'

'Yes, I totally agree with that sentiment, and let's not forget why we're here, Bob; it is Arthur's wedding day!'

Bob looked suitably uncomfortable, colouring slightly at Kate's well-meant admonishment.

'Of course, Kate. Sincere apologies, Arthur. That was really selfish and inconsiderate of me. And you're quite right, Edgar, what point is there in bothering with those things any longer?'

Rather fittingly at that juncture, they raised their glasses to me. We were saying our very last goodbyes.

And so, with mixed feelings, I finally walked away, though not before feeling a restraining touch on my arm after taking a few short steps.

'You forgot your drink, Arthur. Your glass remains half full – better than half-empty, I suppose.'

'Thanks, Edgar. Never miss a trick, do you?'

It was much like the day we first met, the day I began my journey into another time – if not another world entirely.

'You might like to know you weren't the only one to see them, Arthur. Believe me or not, I saw them too, most likely around the same time as you did, though by slightly different channels, of course. You already know that I had previously observed the one I thought to be George Davy, but this was the first time I had seen any of the others – Ethel, Victor and Billy. You know very well what you observed, and who each one of us represented in that faraway time – so thank you for bringing it about, Arthur.'

'Me!'

'Yes, Arthur, you more than any of us – the youngest member of our circle, though I think in spiritual terms, you're older than any of us: a man already of many lives. By the way, I should also thank you for what you said to Bob. It was a valuable lifeline you threw him, indeed, at your own expense. God bless you for that, Arthur Campion. Goodbye again, old friend. Live life as you wish it to be.'

I meet Ann in the middle of the dancefloor, one last twirl before we leave for home. We sway and smooch to the haunting melody of Procol Harum's Whiter Shade of Pale, a song that will fondly linger in our memories. And as we dance, I sense she too is with us, at my shoulder once again. I picture her floating there, arms raised above us, enjoying our happiness as much as we are.

I will come to see those four again, those spirits of life gone by ... though perhaps only in my deepest dreams. For they are gone forever now, leaving only the distillate of their departed souls in our precarious safekeeping. Soon we will join them, all of us ... each in our own time.

The End

Note from the Author

Although *Disturbing Time* is entirely a work of fiction, I have made reference to actual buildings, establishments, businesses, hostelries, places and things in general that were in existence during the 1890s and/or the 1960s, some sadly long gone, others surviving and thriving. Any persons and incidents depicted in such places, however, are purely figments of my imagination, and in no way adversely reflect on the people or establishments mentioned.

Although Nottingham's Victorian and 20th century thoroughfares, locations and events have been faithfully researched, in some instances artistic licence has been sympathetically applied, for example Always Yard did not actually exist, but Alveys Yard did, and in the same area – the latter name easily misconstrued from the handwritten census.

If the results of hypnotic regression are open to argument, the existence of its practice is not. Indeed, I refer to two authentic 20th century examples in Chapter 4: the works of Arnell & Dulcie Bloxham and those of Morey Bernstein. Such references are merely intended to set the scene, and any mentions, suggestive or otherwise, are taken from those widely reported both at the time and thereafter.

I was born in Nottingham, went to school

there, and worked within the city and its suburbs for many years before retiring. For those reasons, I thought to include examples of the local accent. I concede that my interpretation is subjective and only one of a number, so apologies to anyone who construes the accent differently. Please also bear in mind that the book may appeal to a wider readership, including those who might not easily appreciate or even remotely comprehend a lengthy interlinked sequence of typical Nottingham dialect.

The idea for *Disturbing Time* arose from my interest in local history, limited though it is, and from my own family's Nottinghamshire roots, which trace back to the early 17th century. As in the book, a lot of that history involves the Lace Market and the wider parish of St. Mary. Any observations of those areas, Nottinghamshire in general and its populace only apply to the story and are not meant to offer factual or accurate comment or detail.

There is another reason for putting pen to paper, though it is of a more ethereal nature. The incident described at the beginning of the book is one of a few, each experience perhaps suggestive of something beyond this life. How comforting.

Michael Christopher

About The Author

Michael Christopher is a retired company director, currently living by the coast in South Devon with his wife and soulmate of many years. They have two daughters, both of whom share the family's fondness for art and literature.

Michael's own love of storytelling began with Jonathan Swift's, *Gulliver's Travels*, thereafter, the likes of H.G. Wells, Dickens and Jules Verne – writers who stirred a young man to believe in the unbelievable.

Though a work of fiction, DISTURBING TIME was inspired by experiences and memories from Michael's formative years.

www.blossomspringpublishing.com